The
Kingdom
of
Childhood

The
Kingdom
of
Childhood

A Novel

REBECCA COLEMAN

MIRA®

Recycling programs for this product may not exist in your area.

ISBN-13: 978-0-7783-1278-9

THE KINGDOM OF CHILDHOOD

Copyright © 2011 by Rebecca Coleman

For questions and comments about the quality of this book please contact us at Customer_eCare@Harlequin.ca.

www.MIRABooks.com

Printed in U.S.A.

First Printing: October 2011
10 9 8 7 6 5 4 3 2 1

To Catherine

"The wiser being in us leads us to this person because of a relationship in a previous life… We are led to this person as though by magic. We now reach a manifold and intricate realm…our youthful energies begin to decline. We move past a climax, and from there we move downward."

"You have no idea how unimportant is all that the teacher says or does not say on the surface, and how important what he himself is as teacher."

—Rudolf Steiner

In Bavaria the snow is always very deep. Once the first flakes fall it quickly buries everything that rests on the country earth: hedgehog nests, lost underpants, drawings of a crucified Jesus clumsily wrought in colored pencil, worn bars of Fels-Naptha laundry soap good for removing most stains. I have seen all of these things vanish beneath that snow that rots everything, and if ever there was anything colder or more beautiful than a German winter I have yet to experience it.

But when I was a girl of only ten, stumbling through my first months in that country where I was more alone than I have ever been before or since, where even my teachers babbled nonsensical words at me and my mother's mind grew knottier by the day, I could hardly understand that I should appreciate such loveliness with my whole heart, because, rest assured, things would get worse for me. That year I felt homesick for Baltimore, where the winter sky teased for months and then, perhaps late in February, would shake loose its clouds in an orgy of the stuff that snapped power lines, threw cars into a whirl, and brought our modest, industrious little city to its knees. I preferred a good crisis to a dependable case of cabin fever. But in any case I spent much of that winter outdoors, with my mother gone, my father putting the house to other uses.

Every day I had to stomp through the drifts to catch the school bus. Back then we all wore dresses like Caroline Kennedy, our skirts swirly and pert and often impractical, and what a cross that was to bear. The icy water would seep through my tights and then I'd be bone-cold until lunchtime.

One morning, it must have been a Saturday I suppose, I went out to play in that snow. It was a fresh snowfall and still looked magical. We had learned a song in school, in German of course, about a walk through the snow, and I sang it as I marched through the field across from my house, turning around to look at my boot prints. I didn't understand all the words, but the song had a very sweet tune, ethereal, you would say. And amid snow everything seems so very silent, you know, I imagine I must have enjoyed how clear and alone my voice sounded.

Down the road lived my classmate Daniela and her brother Rudi, who was older and went to the high school. I often spent time in the barn with him in the afternoons, biding the last of the daylight in the quiet and the peace of nature, away from our rented home. Well, I suppose he must have heard me while he was working in the barn, because next thing I knew he was waving his big hand from across the field, and then he bounded over to me in those thick rubber boots, calling, *Judy, Judy*. He asked me if I liked to sled. I told him I did, even though my mother always forbade it because she said it was too dangerous. But I thought it sounded exciting,

because when I was small she had often read to me from a
book of children's poetry, and I remembered the poem that
began—

> *Come fly with me, said the little red sled*
> *I'll give you the wings of a bird, it said*

—and beside it there was a drawing of a little Flexible Flyer
with a smiling face. He told me his sister Daniela had a cold
and couldn't go, but that he would take me if I liked. And so
I ignored my mother's warnings, and I went with him.

He fetched a sled from the barn—it was a toboggan,
really—and we walked through the field to the churchyard.
First we passed the shrine to the Virgin Mary, and then there
was an old graveyard, and downhill from it, an empty lawn
covered by a smooth snowdrift. The hill was quite steep in
some places, and in others, not so steep but very long. I was
afraid to go down by myself, so Rudi climbed on behind
me—goodness knows how, because he was so big and I remember the toboggan was shorter than I was—and down we
went. What a thrill it was, the way the cold air rushed across
my face and filled my lungs as we flew past everything at
once. I thought, *this is the way the astronauts must feel,* because
that was during the Space Race, and adults were always telling
children what an amazing time we lived in because of it.

In a short while I could go down the slower hills alone,
but the steeper ones I only dared if Rudi sat behind me. I felt
like I could do anything if he was there. It sounds silly to say
it, but sometimes, when it was time to go home after visiting
him in the barn, I felt like clinging to his leg like a toddler
and burying my face in his waist, and begging him, *please
don't make me go back there.* I tell you, he must have thought

I was the peskiest child. Lord knows why he tolerated me. I suppose it was his weight that made the sled feel so much safer with him on it. And he could brace his legs along mine, which must have made me feel as though I couldn't fall out.

In my memory we went up and down the hill for hours, although it couldn't have been nearly that long. A few times the toboggan overturned, tumbling both of us into the snow, and I remember his laugh when that happened. Jolly, as if he were really having fun. I don't recall the trip back to the house, only that it was warm when we got there.

I mean his house, not mine. I had never been inside past the mudroom, but this time he brought me into the kitchen and sat me down at the little table. It was a modern kitchen but on the wall there hung those carved wooden molds for spice cookies—*lebkuchen,* they called them. One was carved with Struwwelpeter, a horrible character from a book they made us study in school. A boy, but with yellow hair in a frizz like a monster's fur, and sad, vacant eyes. His fingernails twisted like claws and he wore a prim schoolboy outfit on his deformed little body. I remember I asked Rudi, *who would want to eat a cookie shaped like Struwwelpeter?* And he laughed.

He said, *Your tights are wet, take them off.* And so I did. He helped me pull them off when they twisted around my ankles, then sat on the floor before me and rubbed my feet and toes to warm them. *Your feet are like ice cream,* he said. He meant that they were like ice, but the word for both is the same in German. Then he took my tights and hung them by the woodstove, and gave me a cookie to eat while we waited for them to dry.

The cookies were *lebkuchen,* although the round type, not made in molds like the ones on the walls. They tasted of cinnamon and cloves and the dark, syrupy flavor of the honey the bees made in the deep pine woods nearby. I remembered such cookies from Christmas, and Rudi said they were left over; but this kind had a smooth, white, starchy disk on the underside, and I asked him what it was. He said the disks were called *oblaten,* that sometimes people spooned the cookie dough onto them before baking and sometimes they didn't. He liked them either way. Then he said, do you know, they are the same type of wafer used by the priest during Mass. Exactly the same, only not blessed. So if you put a blessing on it, it becomes the Body of Christ. And if you do not, you can use it to make a cookie.

I thought that was interesting, that my cookie could have been something sacred. But instead, here I sat beside the woodstove with my tights dangling from the back of a chair, with my classmate's older brother beside me, eating a honey cookie. And there was nothing holy about it at all.

Well, that's all I remember. After my tights dried I put them on and went home, I suppose. In the spring, when Easter came and I happened upon the shrine again, I realized that lawn beyond the old graveyard was actually the new graveyard, where the markers were metal plaques that lay flush against the ground. So that day Rudi and I had gone sledding, we had all the while been sledding across the graves of the dead. I don't know if he realized that, although I imagine he did, having lived in that town all his life. Maybe it didn't matter to him. Or maybe he thought the dead would not begrudge the living a bit of joy.

I thought about this story many years later, as I stood at the grave of my best friend, Bobbie, surrounded by all of our teaching colleagues and a few of our friends from college. I had never mentioned Rudi to her, and I wondered if now, with her beautiful spirit freed from the confines of its dim human senses, she somehow knew even the few secrets I had kept from her. *Let me explain,* I wanted to say, but of course it was much too late for that now.

At the graveside service, the minister offered what he must have believed were words of comfort. *Do not despair,* he said, *that the dead are lost to us forever. We will meet them again in eternity, for that is the hope we have in Christ Jesus.* I folded my arms over my chest and knew I agreed with him that the spirit lives on, but I would never sentimentalize it so. It is a painful thing to have unresolved business with the dead. But the dead have unresolved business with us, too.

PART I

THE QUEEN OF FASCHING

I

1998
Sylvania, Maryland

I suppose in the beginning it was a love story. The school into which I had wandered, following my midwife's directions to sign up for a natural-childbirth class held there in the evenings, was a fairy-tale cottage of apricot walls and cabinetry built from knotty pine. In the kindergarten room, knitted dolls waited in a line beneath a large bright window; wooden fish, painted in pale washes of color, leaped from a swirl of blue silk arranged on a shelf. At the center of it all sat a lantern, nestled among the seashells and pine cones strewn on a small table. Its blue overlay was decorated with the silhouette of a young girl with her skirt held out, catching in it the stars that fell like coins from the sky. I knew it was a scene from a fairy tale, one I had heard many years before on the other side of the ocean. I remembered many stories from that place and that time, but this one was notable in that it ended in happiness and not horror.

The teacher who found me standing loose-jawed in her room, one hand on my burgeoning belly and the other on my hip, did not need to ask me if I had ever been in a Waldorf school before. The answer was obvious enough from my gaze of uninhibited wonder, and as I was soon to learn, every aspect of the Waldorf life is meant to inspire that feeling which rose in me very naturally, as though I were a tired pioneer stumbling into a lush valley and suddenly declaring, "This is the place." I didn't question why that room pulled at me so intensely, because as soon as I walked in, I knew: it reminded me of the school I had attended as a child in Germany, with shiny leaves of ivy hanging like garlands above the windows, a guitar beside the teacher's desk, and the tables outfitted with wooden boxes of beeswax crayons in colors so hard and bright that they carried an elemental cheer. The boxes contained many colors, but not black. Black was not allowed. I received this information like a coded phrase: here we have your German childhood, and we have removed the black crayon.

Now, nineteen years later, I had shepherded hundreds of kindergartners through their introduction to our brand of wonder, watercolors and the occasional case of ringworm. The baby traveling upside-down in my womb that day, blissfully ignorant of her mother's budding fanaticism—my daughter Maggie—had attended Waldorf clear through to college. Scott, my son, was in his final year of high school, and he was finishing up not a moment too soon. The school year had only just begun, and already my boss, Dan Beckett, had opened our Monday-morning staff meeting with an announcement that Sylvania Waldorf School was financially insolvent and might go under at any moment. This was a regular weekly feature during the previous year, and so that morning I sat at a student desk listening to him in respectful silence, toying with my earring and musing idly on the erotic dream I'd had about him the night before. My love affair with Waldorf was still alive in my soul, but until the new boss arrived it had never occurred to me that it might be consummated.

If I was distracted that day, a reasonable person could hardly blame me. By lunchtime I had dealt with two potty accidents and one black eye on a scrappy student who, quite honestly, had it coming. In the afternoon I sent home a child showing symptoms of measles to two panicky parents suddenly reconsidering their commitment to holistic medicine. Now, at long last, my mug of coffee and I made our way down the covered walkway that connected the Upper and Lower Schools. My son Scott's choir practice was almost over, and with that I would finally be able to go home and crawl into bed under a pile of duvets. Hopefully the oxygen deprivation would knock me out quickly.

Rounding the corner to the multipurpose room, I felt a bit more relaxed just to hear the beatific voices of my son and his choirmates. The madrigal choir was by invitation only, and sang, for the most part, medieval and Renaissance songs a capella. Scott, a senior, had a fine voice but no particular love of music. He stayed in Madrigals because the school required an extracurricular and he found the other options, in a word, "lame."

As I slipped in the back door I spotted the small group clustered on the risers at one side of the stage. Drawing closer, I could pick out Scott's voice in the baritone section. They sang *The Holly and the Ivy* in preparation, I assumed, for the Advent Spiral ceremony around the holidays. They were certainly getting an early start.

I sat in a folding chair and sipped my coffee. As their teacher issued a few parting instructions and the group dispersed, Scott meandered toward me with two other young men in tow: Temple, the quiet boy with whom he had been friends since first grade, and another one I did not recognize. Hitch-hikers, I predicted.

"Hey, Mom," Scott said. "Do you mind giving a couple people a ride home?"

The trio lagged behind me on the way out to the parking lot, with one of them—the extra one, from his voice—singing a potty-mouthed parody of *The Holly and the Ivy* to the de-light of his friends. By the time they piled into the back of the Volvo, the conversation had reverted to the two-syllable monotone of teenage boys.

"Who lives closest?" I asked, turning out of the parking lot.

"I do," said the crude one. "Left on Crescent, right on Lakeside, follow it down."

I turned up the radio and tried to think ahead to my eve-ning, rather than backward to the terrible day, without much success. Three of my students, now, were out with the mea-sles, with a fourth case likely in the works. At any other school this would be a cause for alarm, but many of the parents in our school community had reservations about immunizing their children, and as a result we had periodic outbreaks of arcane diseases. Although the teachings of Rudolf Steiner, the originator of our school's philosophy, supported some of these ideas, I did not share their view. I had thought myself a rebel to society at large when I joined the Waldorf School movement, yet once inside the community I chafed just as often, but kept my dissents secret. I vaccinated my children, circumcised my son. I owned not one but two televisions. I ate plastic-wrapped American cheese.

The voice of the new boy rose from the backseat. "Monica Lewinsky walks into a dry cleaner who's a little hard of hear-ing."

Scott's enthusiasm was immediate. "Ooh, Temple, have you heard this one?"

"Uh-uh."

"Monica says, 'I've got another dress for you to clean.' The dry cleaner says, 'Come again?' and Monica says, 'No, it's mustard.'"

Scott and Temple dissolved into laughter. I glanced into the rearview mirror and caught the gaze of the boy, his broad grin conveying pride at his own joke. Black hair, razor-cut at the edges, mostly hid one of his eyes, but the other sparkled with mischief. I raised my eyebrows at him in the mirror.

"Not a good joke for mixed company," I said.

"Sorry, Mrs. McFarland," he replied with great insincerity.

"Yeah, Zach," Scott added, clearly gleeful at the chance to gang up on his friend. "Don't talk to my mom like that. What's your problem?"

Muted thuds ensued, the sound of punches being thrown. When I came to a stop at a traffic light I turned around and barked, "Knock it off!"

Temple, in the middle seat between the two, looked relieved as Scott and his friend quickly straightened up. After years of being a double authority over Scott's buddies—both parent and teacher—I was not shy about correcting them. I looked the black-haired one in the eye again and demanded, "How old are you?"

"Sixteen."

"Then please act like it. I don't mind giving you a ride home, but I will if you all act like a bunch of wild animals."

"Green light," said Scott. As I turned around he mumbled, "Zach, you wild animal, you."

"That's what your mom said," Zach retorted, sotto voce. As they convulsed with suppressed giggles, I propped my elbow against the window ledge, rested my head in my hand,

and sighed deeply. In addition to the pile of duvets, a glass of wine might be nice. Or two.

My erotic dreams about my boss began not long after he arrived on the job from a large, flourishing Waldorf school in the Bay Area. With an overgrown mop of thick dishwater-blond hair and icicle-blue eyes like a husky's, he was reasonably good-looking, if young, and not a bad candidate for a subconscious fantasy. But Dan Beckett was only one of many. Since my husband had exchanged his libido for entrance into his Ph.D program three years before—or so it seemed—I'd begun dreaming about random men in bizarre situations, as though my mind, in its deprived state, grabbed whatever scattered ideas were available and smashed them together. This was comical when it involved my neighbor's landscaping guy or my former physics professor, but problematic when my coworkers or a kindergartner's father stepped in—or both, as in the case of Dan, whose son Aidan was in my class. Facing these men afterward, I couldn't help feeling as though we were all conspiring to keep the affair under wraps. Dreams had this effect on me: I knew where they ended and reality began, but they tended to bring ideas into an area where the circles overlapped, making the absurd seem more feasible.

And so after a glass of red wine and a chin-deep hot bath foaming with Weleda's lavender bathing milk, I had drifted off into a slumber that ended in an awkward, boss-induced dream hangover. At least this time I had managed a full night's sleep. Sometimes the incubus awoke me, memorably but inconveniently, at 3:00 a.m.

As I went off to work the next morning, I made a mental note to avoid the front office. With luck, I would make it all the way until dismissal time without encountering Dan.

"Oh ho ho, what do I see?" I sang to the small people clustered at my sides. "Has a gnome come looking for me?"

The children peered at the classroom before them. A moment ago they had been outdoors, digging in the sand and playing on the cooperative swing, racing along a line of tree stumps. Now they had returned to find an amber playsilk square strewn on the floor and a piece of driftwood from the nature table upset beside it. Disorder was always the work of gnomes.

"Oh ho ho, they come and go," the children sang back, "quickly as the wind does blow."

I smiled and sank to my haunches to speak to the children at eye level. "In a few moments our mothers and fathers will be here. Let's clean up the mess this naughty gnome has made and then have our puppet play."

The children got to work. I felt anxious to draw the workday to a close, for it was Friday and the weekend held great promise. My husband and I would be celebrating our anniversary at Fallon, a bed-and-breakfast in the Blue Ridge Mountains which we'd first visited long ago, before even Maggie had been born. Given that I'd barely seen the man since he began his doctoral dissertation on sustainable aquaculture, and despite the fact he'd been hopelessly surly since then, I anticipated the trip as if it were a first date. I needed this weekend with Russ, if only to refocus my mind from the ever-growing list of men my subconscious was plundering.

But until then, I had work to do. I led the puppet play and the afternoon verse, rang the small brass bell three times, and sent the children off one by one with their parents. Each time the classroom door opened, I caught a glimpse of an unfamiliar black-haired woman, unquestionably pregnant, standing in the hallway chatting with the headmaster. Most likely she was the mother of a prospective student, and my romantic weekend would need to be put on hold for a few more minutes while I schmoozed her.

After all the children but Aidan were gone, I shook her hand in the hallway and invited her into my classroom. She wore a scarf stylishly tied in her long hair and the sort of kid-leather Mary Janes popular with the yoga crowd. I guessed her age to be in the middle thirties, possibly younger, but her muted Asian features threw off my guesswork. Dan sidled up beside her, his face plastered with his beatific pastor smile. I blinked away a snapshot memory of him sneering and dripping with sweat, stark naked.

"Judy, this is Vivienne Heath," he said, and I imitated his smile. "She's volunteered her son to help you with the Christmas bazaar. He needs to earn some service hours, so I thought, why not give Judy a hand?"

Indeed. The last thing I needed was a Boy Scout to supervise while I attended to my annual frenzy of unappreciated volunteer work for my employer. In an exulting voice I said, "Wonderful."

"We just moved here from New Hampshire," she explained. "He's building a playhouse to auction as a project for his woodworking class, but he'll need more hours than that. He's very creative. I'm sure he'll work hard for you, although he might need a little refresher about some of the crafts."

I nodded and tried to mask my surprise. Woodworking was an eleventh-grade subject. I realized she must be considerably older than I had guessed. Yet here she was, about to have another baby. *Better her than me,* I thought. I was ready for a second shot at a lot of things in life, but mothering a newborn was not one of them.

"If you want to talk crafts, Judy's your woman," Dan told her, and patted me on the shoulder. I stiffened. "She can probably spin straw into gold."

Vivienne grinned. "Is that a course at the Steiner teachers' college?"

I twitched my shoulder out from his grasp. "If it was, he'd have me locked in the workshop right about now."

He laughed, and I watched Vivienne Heath's gaze shift from me to my boss and back again. Dan always upped his show of goodwill and camaraderie around me to compensate for the fact that we hated each other. Upon his arrival the previous year, it had quickly become clear that he thought I was a dinosaur excavated from Woodstock; I disdained him for being a bourgeois bohemian. The ideological tension ran deep even before I began having vivid dreams of coupling with him. Whatever uptight vibe Vivienne was observing could have come from either source.

"Speaking of the workshop," said Dan, "he's in there working right now. Perhaps you can drop in and say hello before you leave."

"Of course." I shouldered my purse and gave my classroom a final glance. "I'll head over right now."

"Thanks so much. I'm sure this will be a wonderful experience for him." Vivienne turned her head and smiled at me. "Have you met my son? Zach Patterson?"

It dawned on me suddenly. The black hair and eyes. The faded, peachy tan. Barring the pregnant belly, the slender and neatly toned frame. I suppressed a groan.

"I have, as a matter of fact," I said, impressed by my own composure. "He and my son are in the madrigal choir together. I brought him home the other day."

She narrowed her eyes slightly. "He didn't tell one of his Lewinsky jokes, did he?"

"He did."

A sigh of disgust escaped her lips. "I apologize for that. If it's the joke I think it is, he's been telling it to his father's employees, his uncles and even his grandfather. Quite the comedian, that one. He's probably getting revenge on us for listening to too much NPR."

"Maybe he finds it upsetting," I suggested. "Losing faith in one's leaders and all that. Maybe it's his way of relieving the stress."

She smirked and responded with a snorting little laugh. "You don't know my son. He doesn't have stress. He just wants to use dirty words in front of adults. It gives him a thrill."

Beside me Dan shifted uncomfortably. "Yes, well," I quickly added, "I'm pretty experienced with teenagers. I'm sure I'll be able to keep him in line."

I said goodbye to Dan and Vivienne and headed out in the direction of the workshop, taking the long route to avoid walking past Bobbie's history classroom, now occupied by a young teacher who bore no resemblance to Bobbie in either looks or spirit. On the first day of school I had made the foolish decision to drop by and peek in. The sight of all those teenagers chatting and working and laughing, going on as though she had never been there, sent me into a spiral of depression so confounding that I spent all afternoon empty-ing dropperfuls of Bach's homeopathic Rescue Remedy into my coffee. Since then I employed the methods of avoidance and repression to deal with my grief, and while I knew the conventional wisdom declared that this was a poor idea, it had always worked fine for me.

The bedraggled workshop building sat behind the school, an oversize shed in need of some serious love and exterior latex paint. Amish craftsmen had been contracted to build it ten years before; it had been trimmed and painted by the school's juniors and seniors, and left unheated except for a woodstove they fed with scraps from student projects. That much I knew, because the underwriters had canceled the insurance on that building three years before unless we agreed to put in a heating system that complied with building code. The funds didn't exist, and so the building survived on vigilance and hope.

I heard Zach Patterson before I saw him, crouched on the floor of the workshop beside a very loud saw. With safety glasses over his eyes and his shaggy black hair shielding his face, I would not have been certain it was him were it not for the backpack lying on the table, the initials ZXP drawn in big bold letters on the front pocket with a black marker. I wondered what the X stood for.

"Hi, Zach," I yelled over the din of the saw, trying to start the partnership on a friendly note.

He looked up at me through a haze of sawdust and shut off the power. When he stood, he pushed the glasses onto his forehead, offering me a first good look beneath that mop of hair: unruly skin and inexpertly tended facial hair, rounded out by eyes a bit too large in proportion to the lean angles of his cheeks and jaw. What mothers call "the awkward stage" was slow in letting go of Zachary Patterson.

He extended his hand. "Thanks for the ride the other day, Mrs. McFarland."

"You're welcome. Your mother just dropped by to tell me I'll be working with you on the bazaar. I didn't make the connection between the two of you until our conversation was almost over."

"That's because she looks more Chinese than I do," he said bluntly. "It throws everybody off."

"I think it was the last name that threw me. I've seen your name on the Madrigals roster, so when she said she was a Heath, I didn't put together that you were hers."

He nodded. "It gets more confusing when you meet my

dad. He's blond and really tall, so nobody ever thinks I'm his kid, even though I've got his last name. Then they expect my mom to have a Chinese-sounding name and think my dad must be the Heath. It happens all the time."

I smiled politely. "That's the modern family for you, I guess."

He returned my smile with a grin of his own. "Yep. The obscuring of ancient wisdom."

"What do you mean?"

I had taken the bait. "Steiner said the mixing of the races obscures the ancient wisdom. You can blame my parents for that."

I closed my eyes for a long moment. "Steiner never said that."

"He did, but it's okay. He was a product of his time. And so am I." Pulling his glasses back down, he rearranged the plank of wood in his hands and asked, "Did you need me for something?"

"I just wanted to discuss the expectations for your service hour credits. I'm not sure if you'll fill all thirty hours, but I can find as much work for the bazaar as you're willing to do. Painting, assembling booths, pricing crafts, you name it."

"Got it," he said. He sank back to his haunches and aligned the board in front of the sawblade. "Whore myself out until the school says I'm done. I can handle it."

I glowered at his back. He was like a mouthier, less easily punished version of Scott. I hitched my purse onto my shoulder and said, "Well, I'll be away for the weekend, but let me know if you need any assistance."

"Where are you going?"

The personal question took me aback. "To the Blue Ridge Mountains with my husband for our anniversary."

"That's cool," he said. "I like the mountains. It's weird to live in a place that doesn't have them. When you look outside it's like your eyes don't know where to rest. There's no anchor. It's just emptiness. It sucks."

He was right. Maybe that explained why I felt the way I did. Lately the sense nagged at me that a nascent dark thing was coming, and that, as my midwife had once said, there was no way out of this thing but through it. But perhaps it was simpler than all that. A matter of finding an easy place to rest one's eyes, and with them, one's thoughts.

I smiled at him, and, in an abashed, close-lipped way, he smiled back.

2

In his earliest memory, Zach is nestled snug in bed with his
mother, back to breast, skin to skin. His father is there as well,
his back broad and winter-pale, his spine curled in sleep. It
must have been February, because Zach is secretly sucking a
pink strawberry candy of the type sent by Grandma Moo, his
Chinese grandmother, every Chinese New Year. Most likely,
this being New Hampshire, there would have been snow on
the ground as tall as himself. And yet there he is, warm beneath the featherbed and his parents' indigo batik quilt, nurs-
ing his hoarded candy. Sucking slowly, so she won't notice.
This is what he remembers—the drowsy heat, the angled
sunlight, the solid sweetness in the middle of his tongue; and
the way his heart palpitated when his mother suddenly asked,
"Zach, is that candy I smell?"

That was all. Some of the details, in retrospect, stood to
reason: for example, his mother had slept shirtless for years,
having slipped into the habit during the several years in which
she nursed him. And Grandma Moo—so called because she
was his mother's mother, her *mu*—had sent those pink candies

in their crinkly strawberry wrappers every year of his life. *Gung hey fat choi,* the red greeting card always read; and his mother often murmured "emphasis on the fat" as she unpacked the small boxes of white chocolate pretzels, spongecake petits fours, popcorn balls and sugared almonds. Forbidden like poison, they were the sorts of foods she tolerated only once a year and only for a taste, before dumping the boxes into the trash and force-feeding Zach a quart of vanilla kefir as an antidote.

Yet stripped of reason, the memory is purely sensual. There is nothing before it, but much after; the quiet room, the cavelike warmth forming the Big Bang from which his consciousness unfurled. It occurred to him that he would have no recollection of that pleasure, had he not been caught in the act of disobedience.

But Zach knew that this consciousness, as he understood it, was nothing more than an island in the great stirring sea of his mind, that formless dark which informed everything. In it were his dreams, some remembered, most not; there lingered all the moments of pain and fear and pleasure his childmind had failed to process. But also there lived the ancient shapes his teachers called, altogether, the collective subconscious: the witch, the white knight, the princess in the tower, the devil. A body of archetypes, a language of symbols passed down through time, birth by birth, like the code for the shape of an eye, the blueprint of the human heart. A racial memory.

The room was different now—painted sky-blue rather than mint-green, and relocated to Maryland—but the bed was the same, a Colonial four-poster built by his dad, and the quilt was the same, although faded by wash after wash. And the child curled at his mother's belly was not him but his sister, the not-yet-born. She carried a Christmas due date, and as the months wore on Zach found himself anticipating the birth with surprising eagerness. His friends, for the most part, expressed a sort of repulsion on his behalf, centering around the evidence that his parents were still having sex. Without exception Zach found these remarks amusing. Were their parents just really good at keeping it quiet and sneaking around? Wasn't that the point of being an adult, that you could screw with impunity?

On this day, after his mother finished volunteering him to work with Scott's bitchy mother on the holiday bazaar, she received a visit from the midwife, which redeemed the day somewhat. Zach liked the midwife. Her name was Rhianne, she was somewhere between his age and his mother's, and every time she arrived at the Pattersons' she appeared dressed for gardening. Faded blue jeans, rubber-toed boots from L.L. Bean, a flannel shirt with the sleeves folded up. Zach sat in a chair near the far wall of his parents' bedroom while she examined his mother with a stethoscope, listening for the baby's heartbeat. His mother's belly, golden-pale above the indigo bedspread, looked like the moon.

"Do you want to listen, Zach?" Rhianne asked him.

He shook his head. "I heard it last time."

"I can feel an elbow," she said. His mother laughed, and Rhianne waved Zach over. "Feel it."

He moved to the edge of the bed beside his mother's legs and allowed Rhianne to position his hands on the giant expanse of belly. "Elbow," she said, and then with her right hand over Zach's, "spine, and her little tuckus."

"That's cool," he said. His mother beamed at him.

"Have you started buying things yet?" asked Rhianne of his mother. "Sling, diapers, bassinet?"

"Here and there," she replied. "We won't be needing a bassinet. She'll just sleep with us, like Zach did. Although hopefully not until she's seven." She shot him a look of loving reprimand.

"Wasn't my idea," said Zach.

"Every time we tried to put you in your own bed, you snuck back into ours."

"So, you should have beaten my ass."

The women both laughed. "Listen to the child," said his mother.

"He's hardly a child," said Rhianne. "You've got one almost-newborn and one almost-man."

"He's still a child yet," insisted his mother. "Take a look at his bedroom and you'll see what I mean."

After Rhianne packed up her instruments, Zach walked her to the door. He knew what was coming, because Rhianne pulled him aside after every visit. She considered it part of her job.

"Your mother is very invested in believing you're still a little boy," said Rhianne, "but we both know that's not true."

Zach shrugged. "She knows me pretty well. She's just thinking like a mom."

"I'm sure she's concerned about displacing you with the new baby."

"I don't feel displaced."

"Do you have any concerns you'd like to talk about?"

He shook his head. "I miss my old friends and stuff. But my new school's okay."

She nodded. "Do you feel healthy?"

He knew this was her way of asking the whole range of unaskables—whether he was using drugs, harboring suicidal thoughts, or living in terror that he would wake up one morning blind, with hair on his palms. But he had no such concerns. He said, "Yeah, I feel great."

She reached into her bag and took out a purple drawstring

pouch. With a tug, she pulled it open and held it toward him. He gave her a bashful smile and took out two condoms.

"Sure that's all you need?" she asked.

"I'm sure I don't even need these," he replied, "but they're fun to have around."

"Someday you'll find them useful."

He smirked. "So people keep telling me."

"You're only sixteen," she reminded him. "There's no hurry. But when the time comes, make sure you have 'em handy. Because love comes and goes, but herpes is forever."

Zach grimaced. "Gotcha."

"And if you ever want to talk—" here she patted his shoulder "—you know where to find me."

"I know."

He let her out the door and retreated to his bedroom, where he dropped them in his underwear drawer with the others she had given him. They *were* useful, if only for experimenting with how long he could coast on the wave before losing control. He called it "Tantric Sex for One."

In the beginning with Russ, when he was a bespectacled undergraduate with a simmering anger I mistook for understated masculinity, I had the soaring feeling that together we were really something special. He was the pet of the college's top marine biology professor, the student president of the fledgling Greenpeace group, a member of the rowing team. Lanky and tall and argumentative, he had a talent for the verbal dogfight and took pride in reducing others to silence. In our dorm building I had grown accustomed to hearing his voice, clipped and strident, as a fixture of late-night conversations in the lounge. When, during those debates, he began to defend the views I quietly voiced—including me as the second member of his Russ-against-the-world faction—I felt exalted.

When we began dating, I felt chosen. In the exhilaration of falling in love, either with him or with the idea of being worthwhile, it was easy to overlook the hulking shadows of what his untethered youthful traits would become. I was, one might say, otherwise occupied.

This is what I did see: visions of the two of us walking like overeducated angels into the urban squalor of New York City, him to clean up the Hudson River, me to educate the impoverished youth. With a baby on my hip, we would fly overseas and join the expatriate community in France while Russ devoted his expertise to cleaning up the Seine. After a few years we would move home to a nice brick Colonial and be the toast of our cadre of hip academic friends. There would be parties. There would be wine, and framed photos from a ski trip to Vermont, and a chocolate Lab with a red bandanna around his neck.

Well, I had the house.

But just as Russ had proven himself less brilliant than his professor suspected and downscaled his plans, my own vision of the Perfect Life had shifted. The passion I felt for the stories, the methods, the esoteric philosophies of Rudolf Steiner was all-enveloping; I threw myself into it with all the devotion a new convert has to offer. The Kingdom of Childhood, as Steiner called it, was like a magical forest we guarded with a human chain, in which young spirits unfolded like cabbage roses and children could explore with absolutely no fear. We draped their bassinets with pink silk so they would see the world, literally, through a rose-colored lens. We sliced their apples asymmetrically, so the idea of mass-produced form would not even enter their consciousness. What my friends found trivial, I embraced. God, or his philosophical equivalent, was in the details.

Lately, though, I had moved from a touch of malaise to the

brink of a full-fledged burnout. I blamed it on a contagious case of Scott's senioritis. With my youngest child about to complete his thirteenth year of schooling, I accepted that my personal investment in a philosophy so intense and consuming had just about run its course. But at forty-three I had more experience and commanded more respect than any other teacher at Sylvania, with twenty years of my working life still ahead of me. In the beginning I had fallen profoundly in love with the idea that if I could go back to a past that predated my own, touch the things that had existed since the dawn of time—wood, wool, stone—I could wipe clean the grime that had gathered on me in this corrupted world. And even now, every once in a while when I sat in the rocking chair and took in the cathedral silence of my empty classroom, with the afternoon sun slanting just so on the baskets of knitted elves and folded silk squares and lengths of gnarled wood, from the depths of my heart I thought: *I believe.*

Driving home from a long day in that classroom, I let my hands rest lightly on the steering wheel and my thoughts drift to the Blue Ridge Mountains. It was perceptive of Scott's friend to note the relaxing effect their silhouette has on the mind. A calming vista was something my mind yearned for, and, truthfully, it yearned for many things. I had always been a small person—"an elf of a girl," my father used to say—but lately I had begun to feel like a collapsing star, as though packed into my little frame was the weight of a full universe of unmet goals, unreconciled mistakes, and all the raw-boned loves of my girlhood. Some days I suspected nothing but a broad spectrum of psychiatric drugs and a skilled and compassionate therapist would help me. Other days, I figured a good orgasm would suffice.

A dinging noise jarred me from my thoughts. The gas-indicator light had been red since morning, but this happened

often, and from the odometer I had judged the car had enough
gas to run a few nearby errands. I pulled into the right lane
warily and kept driving, but soon the car began to sputter
and I made a quick right turn into the parking lot of a bank,
coasting into a parking space just as the Volvo exhausted the
last few drops of gasoline. For a moment I sat, staring at the
steering wheel as though the car might take pity on me and
change its mind. But it did not and, gathering my purse and
handwork bag, I climbed out with a heavy sigh. This was not
the first time I had abandoned the car for this reason. Russ
would not be pleased.

My mother is a basket case, Scott sometimes said aloud to an
invisible audience.

But teenagers always do. What child has not, at some point,
decided his or her mother is crazy? It's a staple of American
youth, sure as cotton candy and fireworks and that first jin-
gling set of car keys.

I walked on the shoulder in the uneven wind of the passing
cars and mentally reassured myself I was not a basket case.

I am adaptable.

Not the type to make a crisis out of a small matter.

And the house was not far, not so very far, in the scheme
of the universe.

It was nearly six before I made it home. My husband, miracle of miracles, was already there. As I walked in the door
I caught the stinging smell of burnt toast. In the kitchen he
stood before the skillet in a tense posture, spatula poised over
a grilled cheese sandwich with its topside nearly black.

"I have a roast going in the Crock-Pot," I said.

"I don't have time for all that. I've got a class in thirty
minutes and I had no idea where you were or when you'd be
home."

I pulled out a chair from the kitchen table and sat. My husband, Russell, who had once been attractive in an edgy and intellectual way, had the look of a man who was moments away from giving himself an aneurysm. This was nothing new. It had developed shortly after he began his Ph.D program three years before, and had gotten steadily worse ever since. For a while I worried that he was sitting on either a serious medical problem or an affair with a grad student. But no evidence ever turned up, and I found myself faced with the idea that his hair-trigger temper and contempt for me had nothing to do with complaints either physical or sexual. He had his good days and his bad, but overall, I was gradually resigning myself to the fact that my husband was becoming a cranky old asshole.

"I'm sorry," I said. "I meant to be home earlier."

"It's just as well." He slapped the sandwich onto a plate, turned off the burner, and glanced out the window. "All right. Where the hell is your car?"

"It's in the Citizens Bank parking lot."

He slammed his plate down on the table. "Oh, for Christ's *sake,* Judy."

"I'll send Scott to fill it up later."

He glared at me. Behind his glasses his eyes were a blazing blue. "Explain to me again why you can't take your car to the gas station like a normal human being."

"Because I'm not a normal human being. You know that."

"What are you going to do when Scott is in college? What are you going to do then?"

I sat in silence. Realizing no answer would be forthcoming, he picked up his sandwich and stuffed it in his mouth. A bite of bread and cheese filled out his cheek like a sudden growth.

"I'll have him do it tonight," I repeated, after the silence had derailed a bit of Russ's momentum. "I assume we're tak-ing my car up to Fallon tomorrow."

"It doesn't matter. I can't go with you."

"What?" I felt my face crack from careful steadiness into a scowl of disbelief. "What do you mean you can't go with me? It's our anniversary trip. It's been planned for weeks."

"Our department chair went into the hospital with chest pains. I need to take his place at the conference this weekend."

"What conference?"

"The one where he was supposed to be giving the presenta-tion that I'll be giving instead."

"Russ. Can't one of the full professors take it?"

"Sure, if I'd like to flush my career down the toilet."

I stood and brushed by him, then snapped off the Crock-Pot. "There you go exaggerating. It can't just be a good move or a bad move. It has to be a gigantic crisis."

"This is what you don't understand about careers," he be-gan, "due to all those years you've been sitting in a rocking chair singing 'Kumbaya' and handing out the fingerpaints. Other people's jobs have this thing called *advancement*. And the way it works is, when something crops up, you don't say, 'oh, jeez, I have to go to the mountains with my wife this weekend.' Because if you do, you get to be the Dean of Remedial Dumb-Shit Classes at the community college."

I took a deep breath through my nose and closed my eyes for a moment. "All right, then. I'll cancel the reservations and we'll just go out next weekend. Maybe Saturday. We can get Chinese." Chinese food was Russ's weakness. We had eaten many a paper-boxed meal, back in college, on a bed with a raincoat spread between us for a picnic blanket. It had become something of a tradition that carried on into our marriage, for a few years at least.

He sat down across from me and shook a pile of chips

directly onto the table. "No can do. I need to work on my dissertation all weekend."

I sighed. "Russ."

"Judy," he fired back, matching my tone in a nasal pitch.

I met his eyes and tried not to let it turn into a glare. "Maybe one night during the week, then. I just thought Chinese would be nice."

"Getting my damn Ph.D would be nice, too. And it's hard to do that when you try to take over my schedule with your demands for entertainment."

He shoveled a pile of chips into his mouth with his fingers. Behind him, Scott lifted the lid on the Crock-Pot, glanced at its contents, and set to work making himself a cheese sandwich. I rose from my chair and leaned toward Russ, resting my knuckles on the table. Scott, sensing danger in the quiet, turned just enough to cast a nervous gaze on me. In a hissing whisper I told Russ, "I HATE your Ph.D."

"I don't *have* a Ph.D," he hissed back.

"And I hope they never give you one," I spat. Voice rising, I added, "I hope you're stuck in committee hell, talking about goddamned Iceland and its goddamned fisheries for the rest of your life. I hope you *die* revising the fucking thing."

"Jesus, Mom," said Scott.

Russ raised his eyebrows high and nodded adamantly. "That's *nice*, Judy. Wow, I feel like celebrating our marriage all of a sudden. How about some *mu shu* pork?"

In the months that followed I felt bad about what I said. But you see, I only meant I hoped he would be revising his dissertation for the rest of his life, unrewarded. I didn't mean it literally, that I hoped he would die.

3

The history teacher was hot. At five foot four or so, she was short enough to make Zach feel tall standing beside her, and she had a lot of loosely-curled hair the color of black coffee that bounced against her back as she moved across the classroom. When she turned to write on the board, her butt jiggled beneath her pencil skirt in such a way that Zach wasn't gaining a great deal of knowledge about the Roman Empire.

"When Tacitus visited Germania," she told them, her voice bearing just a hint of a Spanish accent, "he called it 'hideous and rude, dismal to behold.' He found the people warlike, with a violent system for justice. Traitors were hung from trees. Adulterous wives had their hair cut off and were driven through the streets naked, by their husbands, with a whip. Cowards and those of loose morals were buried in bogs under mud and held down with willow branches. Tacitus wrote that this was because glaring offenses must be displayed as a warning, but pollution must be concealed. He said, 'No pardon is ever granted, for no one turns vices to mirth here.'"

The girls around Zach sat with their pens poised, their expressions serious and a little offended. The guys grinned.

"I thought you guys would like that part," their teacher said. A low titter made its way across the classroom. "Remember this as you write up your group reports. A written history doesn't have to be boring."

There was a squeal of chair legs against flooring as the students turned their seats around to break into small groups. Zach had partnered up with two other Madrigals: Temple, whose SAT score was somewhere around the hundred-and-fiftieth percentile, and Fairen, who was also bright but appealed to Zach because the sort of friendship he hoped to develop with her, in another era, might have gotten one of them buried in a bog. She was lovely in a fine-boned, slightly asymmetrical way, with a long white throat and multi-pierced ears that stuck out past her hair when it fell, white-blond, on both sides of her face. Zach found her pale, bejeweled ears fascinating. Scott called her "Dumbo."

"A history of Maryland written in the style of Tacitus," Temple read from the sheet in front of them. "We could hammer this out in a weekend. And it's not due until right before Christmas break."

Fairen rolled her eyes. "This is what happens when the real teacher dies in July and they have a month to fill the spot."

Zach looked over the sheet and scowled. "We're supposed to do a section on the 'legends of Maryland.' How does Maryland have any 'legends'? It's a frigging *state*."

Temple patted the desk noisily with his palms and let his gaze drift toward the ceiling. "We could look up old Indian stories, I guess. Or urban legends. Crybaby Bridge, the Chesapeake sea monster, that sort of thing. The Bunny Man."

"What's the Bunny Man?"

"A guy in a rabbit suit who runs around with an axe,

chopping up people who get onto his property. People claim he hangs out at the old hospital complex off Pine Road. It's abandoned now, but it used to be a tuberculosis hospital."

"I know that place," said Fairen. "I've driven past it a bunch of times. Scott said it was a mental hospital."

"Scott's a moron. But it doesn't matter. We can put that part in as a legend, too, since everyone believes it even though it's bullshit."

She folded her hands like a model student and looked down at the list of requirements. "It says we need to have five illustrations. Maybe we can go down there and take some photos. It'd be really cool if we wait until the project is almost due and the trees are all bare and wintery looking."

Temple shook his head. "It's a five-hundred-dollar trespassing fine if you get caught. Plus there's all kinds of druggies and skinheads and runaways who hide out there."

Fairen smiled. "Zach here's a black belt in judo. He can take 'em on. Or we can ask Scott to come with us. He's pretty scrappy."

Temple groaned. "*Don't* ask Scott. He'll be dragging us down there every weekend just because he knows his folks would flip out if they knew he was doing it. I don't care that he's like that, but he's not going to pull me down with him."

Zach looked at Fairen to see what she would say. He had known these people for only a couple of months, since he had moved to town and started participating in the summer Madrigals concerts at senior centers and music camps. He felt comfortable with Temple and Fairen and her fairly obnoxious friend Kaitlyn, but Scott remained something of a mystery to him. He carried himself like the silverback gorilla of the pack, and perhaps his mother being a teacher was the reason why; on the first day of school, it had taken only minutes for Zach to infer that Scott's ass was the one to kiss if he had any intention of fitting in. Scott was a senior, and had been at this school all his life; yet in his Abercrombie khakis and rugby shirts, he looked more like he had been airlifted in from a prep school than raised on brown rice and folk tales. Even so, Zach liked the guy well enough. Not that disliking him seemed to be an option.

"Listen," she said, "I just want to take a few photos. If you don't want to go, fine. Zach and I will go, and I'm sure Scott will be happy to come along."

Temple looked to Zach for help.

"I think it'd be pretty cool," said Zach. "It's supposed to be based on *Germania,* after all. It says in there that they offered human sacrifice. Maybe if we make it real creepy, she'll think it's genius."

Temple folded his arms against the desk and dropped his head onto them in resignation. Above it, Fairen smiled at Zach. It wasn't that Zach believed Fairen's idea was better. On the contrary, he thought it was risky and dangerous, and not in a fun way. But he felt compelled to support her anyway, based on a bit of wisdom taught to him by his dad: never side against a strong woman, because it never ends well.

4

1964
Mainbach, West Germany

They lived in a tidy half-timbered home at the end of a country road, there in the rural reaches of Bavaria. Five days a week, sometimes six, Judy's father climbed into his navy-blue Mercedes sedan and drove to Augsburg Air Base, twenty minutes away by Autobahn. Although he was a civilian, he could have elected for his family to live on base, to have Judy attend the fifth grade at the American school, but John Chandler spurned these things. His daughter was no military brat. He was an expert on the cultures of the Soviet republics, and no expert on culture would wall up his family in cinder-block Americana for two years while the heart of West Germany beat just outside the guard towers.

The rented house came fully furnished and appointed, with a lovingly tended garden out back and views of farmlands and a distant steeple. Sonic booms from American aircraft thundered frequently overhead. At John's urging, the family cultivated the habits of the Bavarian people. Every morning at half past eight Judy's mother hung the featherbeds out the windows to air. On weekends they ate their largest meal at noon, often after a brisk hike at Jägerkamp or Miesing. Around the supper table John frequently enthused about the fine healthy practices of the Germans, such as playing sports well into adulthood and not being nosy about their neighbors.

When they first moved into the home, the garden was in full bloom: bright red poppies, the purple globes of thistle, delicate and poisonous cups of foxglove, bleeding heart blossoms hanging on a stalk like a string of predictions. Blueberries burst ripe on the bushes, and Judy liked to eat them as she played, imagining herself to be a caveman's child traveling through a wild land never before seen by human beings. Her own Eden, a child's Eden with no lurking specter of defilement, no serpent watching her; she slipped the slender cups of foxglove over her fingers, licked the backs of poppy and nasturtium petals to make designs on her bare legs. Her sandals slouched in the dirt beside the hens-and-chicks that lined the rock garden, the plants swollen with rain and primeval as her fantasies.

At breakfast her mother served her a hard roll from the market and a soft-boiled egg in a leaf-green eggcup. She hung out the featherbeds and lined the birdcage with page four of the *Stars and Stripes*. She tapped the cat's bowl five times on the back porch and then walked Judy to the bus stop one mile away.

At the new school nothing was familiar. Judy could not write in the impeccably tidy rounded hand with its looping *G*'s and calligraphic *H*'s. She spoke no German, could not read music, knew no prayers. At reading time the class read moral tales from *Der Struwwelpeter*, a large flat book on whose cover a pigeon-chested boy stared outward with a hollow

expression, his fingernails grown to hideous claws, his yellow
hair like steel wool. A billowing red shirt and green tights clad
his stumpy body. She could not understand the poem about
him, and was glad.

As cooler weather crept in, the blueberry bushes turned a
flaming red. The bleeding hearts shriveled, and the remaining
plants revealed their skeletons: the dry rattling husks of the
poppies, the fragile mother-of-pearl leaves of the bony beige
Silbertaschen. Only the chrysanthemums remained, their slim
white petals bursting like fireworks from a tight little button of a head, the last flower before winter. Judy was largely
bored, and so often her mother sent her to play at the home
of a German girl, Daniela, their nearest neighbor a few lots
away.

They didn't speak the same language. That was part of
the problem, although Judy doubted she and Daniela would
have been friends in any tongue. The girl was overbearing
and precociously athletic, while Judy frequently missed any
ball rolled to her in kickball and felt her bladder seize at the
very thought of climbing a rope. Daniela's idea of fun was
to demonstrate a gymnastic trick and encourage Judy to try
it, and then, when she failed, to jeer at her in the universal
language of mockery. She was the baby of her family, with an
older sister and brother who rolled their eyes at her outbursts
in a way Judy could not. By October Judy had given up on
Daniela and, when forced to play at her house, walked straight
around back to the barn and hung out with the girl's older
brother, Rudi, who spoke serviceable English. Sometimes she
did her homework in the barn, and as she worked he helped
her untangle the incomprehensible words before her.

"Der Struwwelpeter!" Rudi exclaimed one day, when she
pulled out the text and her copybook. "A terrible book!"

Judy smiled broadly with relief. So she wasn't alone in detesting the thing. "Did you have to read it?"

"Of course. It's to frighten children. To make you behave and have bad dreams at night." He sat beside her on the bale of straw and flipped it open to a story about a girl who played with matches. He read with enthusiasm:

"Doch Minz und Maunz, die Katzen,
Erheben ihre Tatzen.
Sie drohen mit den Pfoten:
'Die Mutter hat's verboten!'"

Judy said, "I don't know what any of that means."

Rudi rolled his hand in the air, suggesting a broad translation. "It means that when Pauline lit her match, the cats Minz and Maunz put out their claws, and cried, and said, 'Your mother has forbidden it!'"

Judy nodded. "And then she burns to death and turns into a pile of ashes."

"Yes," affirmed Rudi. The humorous creases at the corners of his eyes belied his serious tone. Quoting from the book, he said, "'It's very, very wrong, you know. You will be burnt if you do so.'"

"You made it rhyme in English."

"I did not even realize. You should not read these things. Look at *der Struwwelpeter* on the front. Your hair is not like this. Your nails are short and neat." He lifted her hand in his own rough one and examined her fingernails, then briskly rubbed her fingers with a clasp of his thumb. "You see? No reason to read this. You are a good little girl, not a bad one. You should read a happy book."

"My teacher says I have to read this one."

The bale shifted beneath his weight as he leaned toward her. His smiling face came close enough that she could see the blond shadow on his jaw, the midnight-blue ring around his cornflower irises. In his low, conspiratorial voice he said, "Sometimes teachers are wrong."

The blasphemy was so absolute that she laughed. His eyelashes batted once at her laughing breath. He sat up, his grin still fixed in place, and rubbed her back in broad, firm circles, the way he stroked the cow before he milked her.

By December even the dead garden was gone. Night fell quickly and left her no time to be bullied by Daniela or watch Rudi care for the sheep and muck out the barn. There was only her home, where her mother had taken to daily plucking imperfect leaves from the houseplants and arranging the kitchen tools in order by shade of black. And there was school.

On the first day of Advent her class made windows of colored tissue and Popsicle sticks, covered in squares of black construction paper split down the middle. The teacher hung their creations on the long wall of glass windows, regimentally neat as Judy's mother's spatula drawer. But each day a child would fold back the construction paper to reveal the bold fractured rainbow inside. They practiced songs for the *Weihnachtskonzert* to be held just before Christmas and rolled salt dough into kings and shepherds for nativity scenes. Every Friday their teacher laid an evergreen wreath, set with candles, on a desk, then took out her guitar and dimmed the lights. Together as a class, in the dark and accompanied by the plaintive guitar, they sang a quiet and meditative Advent hymn. Then the teacher struck a match and lit one candle, then two, then three, as Christmas drew closer and closer.

It was like undressing together, this frankness about spirituality. To John Chandler, Christianity was a tourist attraction that came in the form of holiday street festivals and medieval churches. He took his family along as though on safari, looking upon the holiday goods as though these were relics of a primitive tribe which viewed volcanic eruption as evidence of the Sun God's anger. Judy guessed he didn't know about the overt Catholicism of the Bavarian public schools, and that if he had, he would have assumed her intelligent enough to pay it no mind. But in the snowy darkness of the German winter, singing in unison in the candlelight, Judy was starting to suspect she might love Jesus.

> *Alle Jahre wieder*
> *Kommt das Christuskind*
> *Auf die Erde nieder,*
> *Wo wir Menschen sind.*

She made a salt dough shepherd and named it Rudi. She opened her tissue window and counted eight remaining. She sang the rough German hymns that sounded to her ears like the original language of humanity, like cavechildren gathered on a solstice dawn waiting for a razor of light to appear between two tall stones. Because who could say there wasn't a Sun God? Who could call it primitive to believe, long ago, one man might have brought light into a dark world?

The effect of it all—the numbered translucent windows, the nativities with empty cradles prepared, the three lit candles and a fourth awaiting—was a feeling that time was welling beneath her feet, about to burst forth into light and fate and fury, shedding the darkness—for better or for worse—like a husk. It was the feeling that *something was about to happen*.

And it did.

5

It was a boiling-hot day for mid-September and, as a cost-cutting measure, the school's air-conditioning had already been shut off for the season. At the end of the school day I steeled myself for a visit to Bobbie's old classroom and stepped in with a commuter mug full of iced tea and my hair piled up in a clip, trailing strands that curled with sweat. The iced tea I had purchased at McDonald's on my lunch hour and, to hide my patronage of such a corporation, guiltily dumped into my rinsed coffee mug before returning to work. In my car I covered the plastic cup with an insulated reusable bag from Whole Foods and slipped out to the parking lot for re-fills when nobody was looking. If there wasn't a clause in my contract that required this behavior, there may as well have been. But I didn't mind. If a veteran like me didn't respect the folkways of the Steiner school, then why would anyone?

Sandy Valera stood at the front of the room erasing the blackboard with quick, efficient strokes. High above, inked onto a long banner bright with a rainbow of watercolors, scrolled the quote, "Man is both a fallen God and a God in the becoming." Rudolf Steiner's name was written beneath it in small but reverent capitals. It was hard to get used to seeing Bobbie's handiwork hanging above the head of the woman who had replaced her. So many years I had known Bobbie, never imagining the absurd idea that she might die. Even after her cancer diagnosis, we all thought she was getting better until all of a sudden she wasn't anymore—she had taken a turn, and then it went so fast. We had been a proud band marching behind our standard-bearer, and then suddenly the street ended in a jagged line and down she slipped into the black nowhere, leaving the rest of us stumbling backward, cacophonous and disoriented.

"You ready for the staff meeting?" Sandy called out to me.

"I hope so."

"I think Dan's got something up his sleeve," she said. "The grand plan to bring us all wealth and happiness."

"Why is it always about *money*." I sighed. "All the things we need to address with these kids and it always boils down to the issue of *money*. I can't think of a subject that bores me more."

"You're happy with what you make, then?"

"Of course not."

She laughed. From a hook on the wall she retrieved her purse and looped it onto her shoulder. The hanger was brass and bore the image of three monkeys, each above its own hook: see no evil, hear no evil, speak no evil. Bobbie, who had carried no purse, always hung her jacket from the third hook. Sandy hung her purse from the first.

"Maybe he'll give you a raise," she teased.

"My husband would like that."

"How was your anniversary weekend, by the way?"

"It didn't happen. He had to work. I spent it making new dolls for the Hansel and Gretel puppet play. Exciting stuff."

She straightened her skirt and frowned sympathetically. If she had been Bobbie, I would have expanded on that with my pent-up frustrations: how much it dragged me down that every time I walked into a room, contempt oozed out of Russ like snot out of a kid's nose. How my children were almost grown and now I yearned to embark on all my long-deferred adventures: to see Stockholm and Amsterdam, to try absinthe and get puking drunk in the tradition of the great poets, to have wild sex in sketchy locations—with Russ would be just fine, if he was willing—and to grow myself a garden as paradisiacal as the one I remembered from my childhood. I would tell her how I felt as though Russ and I were two captives tied back-to-back to a pole, and while I was willing to whistle at the sky and look helpless until Scott left for college, I felt ready to start chewing through the restraints when nobody was looking.

But she wasn't Bobbie. I liked Sandy, but she was only the woman I had been assigned to help get oriented on short notice; and though we might be real friends one day, we weren't now. She was youngish and pretty and unmarried and still winked at life to suggest it come and get her. If she and I had anything in common beyond our place of employment, I did not have the ego to presume it.

And so I followed her brisk walk to the multipurpose room, hurrying on my shorter legs to keep up. Partway there she reached over and patted me on the back, as if to say she understood, or, perhaps, that she pitied me.

"We had an auditor from the Department of Health in our office this morning," our headmaster told us teachers as we settled in for our meeting. "She is concerned about the number of religious affidavits we have on file in lieu of vaccination records. Also, it seems we have a number of families who have turned in neither a vaccination record nor an affidavit. Clearly our record-keeping leaves much to be desired."

We stared uncomfortably at our shoes.

"We will be following up with those families in the coming weeks," he continued. "The longer this continues, the more it makes the pro-vax and anti-vax families feel at odds with each other. We cannot afford to give anyone the impression that the atmosphere at this school is contentious. And when I say we can't afford it, I mean that very literally. Which brings me to our next item."

I looked up from the floor, glad to move on.

"In light of the current situation," Dan began in an artificially cheerful voice, "we have decided to hold our first annual class ring sale for the Upper School, beginning Monday."

The murmur was immediate, but I looked left and right despite it, calculating from my colleagues' expressions whether they felt as shocked as I did. Surprise, but not disapproval, was apparent on the faces around me. I lifted my hand and spoke without being acknowledged.

"I disapprove," I said.

Dan met this with a thin smile, clearly prepared for my reaction. "I understand, Judy, but the board of trustees has decided it."

"Then the board of trustees needs to reconsider," I countered. "Those rings can cost hundreds of dollars. They represent exactly the sort of consumerist culture we oppose here. The parents are not going to like that one bit."

"We receive eighteen percent of each ring sold."

I shook my head. "I don't care if we make a hundred percent. It's a complete contradiction of the values of the school. I understand we need to raise funds, but that is the wrong way."

Andrea Riss, the first-grade teacher, spoke up. "Judy…with

respect, our other options haven't been realistic. The recorder and lunch basket sales netted us very little. I don't know how it is in the kindergarten, but my classroom is suffering. Most of my chairs have threadbare seats and I only have two knights left in my castle. And my harp hasn't had strings for a year now."

A clamor of complaints went up. I looked at Dan, expecting him to call for order, but he remained silent in his chair, tapping a pen against his notebook and gazing in my general direction. Finally I spoke above the din.

"I do understand," I said, and waited for the noise to die down. "But tight budget or not, this is a Waldorf school. For almost twenty years I've been explaining to parents why their five-year-olds can't wear their Spider-Man and Little Mermaid shirts to school. I've led more seminars than I can count about the kiddie industrial complex. I will break out in *hives* if we send these kids home with glossy brochures for some artificial trophy they can buy on an installment plan. The idea is—" I considered my adjective for a moment. "Repugnant."

"Well, the trustees have approved it." Dan met my glare with a look of false good humor. "Let's move on."

"Let's discuss it further."

His gaze turned icy. "Let's move on."

At the end of the meeting, I gathered up my bags a bit too slowly and got caught behind the cluster of teachers filing out of the room. His hand fell heavily on my shoulder. "Judy, can I speak to you in private?"

He closed the door behind the last teacher and turned to me with an apologetic frown. "I knew you weren't going to be happy about that. I felt it coming as soon as the trustees gave me their recommendation."

"I'm astonished that you signed off on it. How could

you? *Class rings,* of all things. How about a Duke Nukem video-game tournament? We could charge admission."

"You're overreacting."

I widened my eyes in indignation, but he held up one hand. "Don't start with your list of the principles this school was founded on. I've been working in Steiner schools for as long as you have. *Your* board recruited me here based on that. Because this school was failing."

"It's never been *failing.* It's been poorly managed."

"You're damn right it has been. I'd never seen a College of Teachers so dysfunctional, and *you* served on it. We wouldn't need to make these concessions if the school had gotten its act together five years ago, or ten. How white is your classroom?"

Confusion took the edge off my anger. "What?"

"How white is it in there? Because we can't bring in kids from the neighborhood without financial aid, and we can't provide financial aid if we can't even cover our utility bills. We have to take whichever families can pay, and you know what that means. The school gets whiter and richer and richer and whiter, and if you ask me, that's selling out the principles more than the rings ever could."

I glared at him without replying.

"You need to face facts, Judy," he said, his voice lower than before. "This is about survival. I didn't pack up my family and move across the country so I could bring down your school. That should be obvious enough to you. My son is in your class, for God's sake. I came here because I believe in this. But my first priority is to keep our heads above water. It has to be."

"'Life is the unknown and the unknowable,'" I quoted, "'except that we are put into this world to eat, to stay alive as long as we possibly can.'"

"*Yes,*" he said with passion. "Kahlil Gibran, right?"

"Jonathan Livingston Seagull," I corrected, and met his ice-blue gaze. And there, for a single unnerving moment, I felt my reproach stumble over the electrified wire of my dream of him: a memory that had never happened.

In the hallway, the other teachers left me alone. Even Sandy hurried ahead. They walked to the parking lot in pairs or trios, chatting amongst themselves. It was a little like high school: nobody likes a know-it-all. In a few days I would return to their good graces.

Stepping out into the parking lot, I heard the squeal of a saw from the workshop and turned toward the sound curiously. So far as I knew, I was the last to leave; could a student still be working at this late hour? I sidetracked up the path and pushed open the heavy door. There stood Zach, working on the same saw with which he had been occupied the previous day, now hoisted onto the worktable. Sawdust twinkled like glitter in the sharp, low sunlight.

I called, "Are you allowed to work in here unsupervised?"

He blew the dust from a board. "Technically, no."

I stepped inside and let the door close behind me. "Well, at least you've got your safety glasses on."

"I wear contacts. The sawdust would scratch my eyes up if I didn't." He pulled the glasses off and added, "You look wiped."

His observation surprised me. My experience with teenagers had taught me they possessed an almost aggressive skill for ignoring the emotional states of adults. It was the same way they handled pet messes or dirty dishes: you can't be held responsible for what you fail to observe.

"Dr. Beckett and I had a difference of opinion at a faculty meeting," I explained, probably unwisely.

His interest was immediate. "Oh, yeah? Over what?"

I infused my weary voice with a bit of sardonic enthusiasm. "We're going to have our very first class ring sale."

He snickered. "That's lame."

"Do you think so?" Again I was surprised. Normally Waldorf students leaped at the opportunity to take part in the forbidden rituals of the ordinary public high school.

"Of course. Steiner would not approve."

"I thought you and Steiner were butting heads."

He offered his abashed grin again, turning a piece of wood over in his hand. "Over me being a crime against nature, yes. Not over anything else."

"*Nothing* else?"

He shrugged. "I've liked my schools and all that. I'm happy. I've got no complaints."

I walked around to look at the playhouse. The pile of boards that had been laid out on the floor the day before were now assembled, the corners dovetailed together with smooth, perfect notches. I ran my fingers over the edges and admired the scalloped gingerbread trim laid out on the worktable. The project had all the marks of competence, which was far more than I had expected out of a high school junior. It was certainly better than anything Scott had done in his arts classes the year before.

"It looks like the project's coming along well," I said. "When do you expect to have it done?"

"A couple weeks. It needs to be finished by the end of the term so I can get a grade. I wanted to do a thatched roof, but Mr. Zigler said it would be a fire hazard."

"He has a good point."

"I suppose. I like fire, so for me that's a selling point."

I chuckled. "Not if someone's inside it, though."

"I guess not, yeah. But it would make a cool prop for a pillage scene in a play. I bet it would burn like a mother."

I indulged him with a wry smile. "So what *are* you going to do for the roof?"

"Cover it with acorns. The kindergarten at my old school had one like that. It'll look cool."

"Where are you going to find enough acorns to cover the whole roof?"

He pointed to a box against the wall. *Greg's All Natural Potato Chips,* read the '60s-style bubble script printed on its side. Acorns filled it to the brim. I asked, "Where did you find all those?"

"The woods. My mom actually let me take the car for once, so I could collect them. In the service of the higher good."

"You'll have to show me. I could use some of those for a craft project, myself." I peeked into the playhouse and examined its tight corners, giving it a slight shake to see how well it held. It hardly budged. "The joinery is beautiful. You're very good with your hands."

His grin was lascivious. "That's what they tell me."

Pointedly I ignored his remark. I asked, "How are you getting home?"

"I told my mom I'd call her when I'm done."

"Do you have a cell phone?"

"No, I'll call from the front office."

I gestured to the windows that looked out on the empty parking lot. "Everybody's gone."

He grimaced. "Well, that could be a problem."

"Come on, I'll give you a ride."

"I guess I'd better take you up on that."

I helped him tidy up the room, stacking the playhouse pieces on a shelf and sweeping up the considerable pile of dust. If he could devote this much time and care to a school project, then perhaps the bazaar tasks would be more painless than I had come to anticipate. The immaturity I had witnessed in our earlier meetings appeared to be mostly for show. About some things, at least, he seemed more focused and thoughtful than Scott, who would be eighteen in short order. Not that Scott was a good stick to measure by.

As Zach climbed into the passenger seat of my car, I picked bits of cat hair from his shirts—a T-shirt featuring a photo of the Earth behind the legend "Love Your Mother," worn over a thermal undershirt that appeared to attract pet hair like a lint roller. "How many cats do you have?" I asked.

"One. Is it that big a deal?"

"I don't want it to get all over the car. My husband's allergic."

He sat still, tolerating my grooming. "That's a sign of evil."

I laughed. "Why do you say that?"

"Cats are the servants of the moon goddess. Only evil people can't tolerate them. It's like garlic and vampires."

I grinned and examined his expression to see if he was serious. "The moon goddess, huh?"

He smiled. "It's just something my mom says. It's a joke."

"I don't know about that. You haven't met my husband. She might be onto something."

His laugh was embarrassed. "I didn't ask."

I fell silent, a bit chagrined to have crossed some invisible line in complaining about Russ. The sound of the radio filled the car, traffic and weather. Once the discussion of the news resumed, it took me several moments too long to pick up on the deejay chatter: the Starr Report, in gory detail. My fingers flew to the preset buttons.

"Don't worry about it," Zach said, not fooled by my sudden interest in Top 40 music. "You can't get away from it. They'll be talking about it on this station in about ten seconds."

"I can try."

He chuckled. "You sound like my mom. She's super

laid-back, and even she freaks out every time they talk about it on the news. Which is every minute of the day, in case you've missed it. Personally, I think it's hilarious to hear a news anchor say 'oral sex.' It's like the best prank ever."

"Except it's not a prank. At all."

"No, but it's still funny. The stuff the Starr Report says Bill Clinton did—have you heard it all? He's the president of the United States, and I'm sixteen, and *I* think some of it is really juvenile. Like the stuff with the cigar? Come *on.*"

"It's quite a letdown. I was a big Clinton supporter. Now I don't know what to think."

"My folks were, too." He fidgeted with the air vents. "Were. Are. Whichever. I think it's dumb to go after him over something that stupid. When you think about it, you *have* to laugh."

I slowed for a stop sign. "At the absurdity, perhaps. At the jokes, no."

"Why not? They're funny."

"They're inappropriate."

"Bill Clinton and Al Gore go to a diner for lunch," he began.

"Zach, *no.*"

"They read the menu and the waitress comes over and asks the president if he's ready to order. Clinton tells her, 'Yeah, I'd like a quickie.'"

"Zach," I warned.

"The waitress says, 'A quickie?! Sir, given the problems you have had lately with your personal life, I don't think that's a good idea at all. I'll come back when you're ready to order from the menu.' As she walks away, Gore leans over and says, 'Bill, it's pronounced *Quiche.*'"

The smile I had been forcing myself to restrain won out. I giggled.

"That's a good one," I admitted.

He drummed his index fingers against the dashboard. "Thank you. Want to hear another one?"

"No. Please, spare me."

He gestured toward the window as I approached his house. "You can pull into the driveway."

I parked behind a little convertible with its canvas top up. LIVE FREE OR DIE, read its license plate above the number. He hitched his backpack onto his shoulder and I watched him meander up the sidewalk, the hems of his jeans raveled where they brushed the ground. He was so lanky they barely stayed on his hips. When he unlocked his front door and the light from the foyer glowed suddenly in the gray dusk, he turned toward me and waved goodbye. I held up a hand in acknowledgment and watched as he slipped inside, shoulders hunched, hair hanging in his eyes.

ZXP, his backpack said.

I did wonder what that X stood for.

Vivienne Heath called me on Friday night to inform me that Zach wanted to use the workshop over the weekend. Could I come in to unlock it for him and to supervise?

"For a few hours," I conceded, already resentful of giving up even that much of my Saturday. "In the morning, because I have plans later. Can he be there at eight?"

To my surprise he was. When I arrived he was already sitting on the workshop steps, backpack slung over his shoulders, headphones on his ears. He said nothing when I let him in and got right to work, moving around the shop with a familiarity that made him look like a very young professional. I sat on a stool with my newspaper and coffee, and read.

As he worked, he sang to himself. It seemed almost unconscious, and when I stole a glance at him, I saw him briskly measuring and marking as he sang. Apart from the rest of the madrigal choir, I was struck by the beauty of his individual voice. It had the pure, clear-spring quality of a child in a boys' choir, partnered with the faintly raspy undertone of a voice only recently changed. It wasn't the voice of a rock star, even if rock was what he was singing—a sad song, bittersweet and mournful.

"That's a very depressing song you were singing," I said when he pulled the headphones down, letting them rest around his neck. He sat down at the adjacent side of the table from me and hoisted up his backpack.

He smiled. "It's Ben Folds Five. I didn't realize you were listening."

"Is that the name of the song, or the band?"

"The band. 'Brick' is the name of the song." He unzipped his backpack and pulled out a notebook, a bottle of green tea and an organic granola bar. Flipping the notebook to a schematic drawing of the playhouse, he examined it while swigging from the tea bottle. He unwrapped the bar and took a bite. It was no wonder he was in such good shape. When Scott was younger I had fed him exclusively out of natural-foods stores, but since adolescence he would only eat like that if the pantry offered him no alternative. Maybe Zach was in the same boat.

I pointed to the initials on the front pocket of his backpack. "What's the X for?"

He grinned and took a drink of his tea. "I'm not telling you that."

"Why not?"

He shrugged. "Why should I?"

"It's probably for Xavier."

"It's not Xavier."

"That's the only boy's name that starts with X."

He bit into the granola bar. With his voice muffled by granola he replied, "No, it's not."

"Well, what is it, then?"

I waited until he swallowed for my answer. Then with a sly expression he asked, "If you're so curious, why don't you just look it up in my file? You're a teacher, aren't you?"

"Because I don't want to go nosing around in your business."

"Nose around all you want. I'm an open book."

I sipped my coffee. "I don't know any teenager that's true for."

"You do now."

"Come on, just tell me."

"What's in it for me?"

I considered the question. In his eyes and at the corners of his smile I could see a hint of the mischievousness that, for him, had always preceded an off-color remark. Before he could crack a joke in that vein I replied, "Coffee."

"What kind of coffee?"

"Whatever you want. Starbucks."

He wrinkled his nose in distaste. "Starbucks is corporate."

"Well, it's what we've got around here. This is the 'burbs, not New Hampshire."

"Tell me about it," he said. "What about with a black-and-white cookie? I love their black-and-white cookies."

"I don't know about that." I took a drink of my own corporate latte. "Steiner might not approve."

He laughed. "Seriously, are you buying me off?"

I nodded. He gauged my seriousness and replied, "It stands for Xiang."

"That starts with a *C*."

"No. In Chinese, the *X* can make a *ch* sound. It means 'arising.' Or 'spreading his wings to fly.'"

I gave him an admiring look. "Does it really?"

He nodded. He looked a little proud. "Zachary Xiang Patterson," I said, carefully pronouncing each crisp word.

"I have the coolest initials on the planet."

I gazed at the black-markered initials again, a code I could suddenly read. Then I admitted, "I probably wouldn't have guessed you were part Chinese if I hadn't met your mother."

"I am, though," he insisted. "Feel my hair."

With a short laugh, I declined the offer. "That's okay."

"Seriously, feel it." He bent his head toward me. Reluctantly I stroked it, as if he were a puppy. The choppy edges of his haircut belied the texture, which was silky, slippery. "It's the same as my mother's," he said.

"Softer than it looks."

"Yeah. I have Asian earwax, too."

I grinned. "What's the difference?"

"It's flaky instead of goopy. And I don't stink when I sweat."

Bemused, I considered whether I could remember evidence to the contrary. "Is that supposed to be an Asian characteristic? That sounds like a myth."

"It's not true for everyone, but it is for me. And it's a good thing, too, because you ought to smell my dad sometime, when he gets working. He's like an NFL locker room after a game."

I raised my eyebrows. "Thanks for the warning."

"So when do I get my coffee?"

"I'll take you and Scott out after Madrigals on Monday."

"What about tomorrow? My mom told you I'm working here all weekend, right?"

I sighed. "No, she didn't tell me that. Does that mean I'm babysitting you tomorrow, too?"

He shrugged with unconcern. "I thought you were."

"Then I guess I am," I told him ruefully. "But the coffee will still be Monday."

"I can live with that." He hiked his headphones back onto his ears and hopped off the stool, heading back toward the playhouse with the bottle of tea in his hand. Today he wore a black T-shirt, almost outgrown, with no thermal beneath it. When he reached for the trim pieces on an upper shelf he revealed a stomach that was smooth and faintly muscular, divided, below his navel, by a narrow line of black hair.

I looked away.

Even the Style section of the newspaper was crammed with items about the repercussions of the Starr Report. Zach was right—it was unavoidable. I turned the offending sections over so he would not be inspired to perform another comedy routine. Instead, I picked up the Travel section.

Escape from D.C., it said.

I rolled my eyes and glanced at Zach. He squatted by the jigsaw and twirled the smallest plywood pieces past its blade, his fingers hovering just at the edge of the plastic guard. The neat muscles of his biceps leaped and danced.

I turned my attention back to the escape from D.C.

That night I had a dream.

In it I was a child, walking out to the garden to pick blueberries. The trees on either side of the path were green and full; straight ahead, the fallow field unfurled like a moonscape of brown earth. At the blueberry bush I squatted and began plucking berries from the bottom branches, where they ripened first, eating greedily. The juice left purple splotches on my fingertips and the hem of my dress.

Suddenly I heard a voice, a man's voice speaking German in a friendly way. I looked up and there stood Zach Patterson on the other side of the bush, smiling and talking to me. I understood him perfectly, and even as I dreamed some small part of my mind marveled at my understanding. Instead of answering I kept eating, gorging myself on berries, letting the overripe ones fall onto the toes of my sandals.

You're getting very messy, Judy, he said, a teasing reproof, still speaking in German.

I glanced at him carelessly and said nothing.

He came around the bush and crouched beside me. He wore the clothes of a farm boy—boots and stonewashed jeans, a ratty green T-shirt. When I felt his fingers beneath my chin, I swallowed. He brought his face to mine and kissed me on the mouth, soft-lipped, sensuously. But I was only a child.

I squatted still, let him kiss me like a man kisses a woman, and felt the doom of knowing I would be in trouble. Beside him I felt so small.

He parted my lips with his tongue. I understood English and, miraculously, German, but I had no word for this feeling in my belly, the hidden warmth in hidden cells awakening, this current coming to life along a skipping path. And yet, fused with the warmth was a pattering fear. Fear that crammed down into my stomach just above where the current swirled and roiled. Fear that trembled my mouth but did not close it, welcoming the surety and heat that his brought, the way his hard jaw steadied mine.

To taste another's mouth is to enter their body.

And so into my belly he went, where the blueberries lay hidden away: the cavechild fruit, made by nature, devoured by fantasy.

6

On Sunday I brought a stack of my students' old watercolor paintings and worked alone for an hour, cutting them down to greeting-card size and folding them in two, before Zach turned up. Annoyed, I was prepared to offer him a few choice words for wasting my time, but one look at his face silenced me. His headphones were already on, aggressive music buzzing through, and he wore the same jeans and T-shirt from the previous day, now much worse for wear. He nodded an acknowledgment and got to work fitting the trim onto the structure, wielding the screw gun as though he might also use it on the first person who dared get in his personal space.

I felt safer at the table, cutting out cards. It was just as well; I found it difficult to look at him without superimposing dream-Zach onto real-Zach, and standing face-to-face with the kid would surely be stranger still. When he squatted down to drill a piece of trim into place, I was struck by how accurate my mind's calculation of his body had been. The proportions of his shoulders and arms, the tapering of back to waist, even the almost springlike ease with which he fell to his haunches and rose again: the dream seemed to rest over him like a transparency, and as he moved, his body fell perfectly into place behind the memory. I remembered my sudden, irrational unease at Dan Beckett's imploring gaze, and wondered at my mind's penchant for collecting the hidden beauty of obnoxious men.

I reached into my canvas school bag for twine and scissors just as the screw gun let out a high-pitched whine that indicated it had slipped. I looked up in alarm to see Zach throw it out the window of the structure, then roll onto his back and clutch his face with both hands.

"Mother fucking fucker," he said, loudly but in a level voice.

I ventured toward the house. "Is everything all right?"

"No. I just spent an hour putting this shit on backwards." He slid out of the house and ripped off his headphones. They hung around his neck as he sat up, his knees against his chest, and rubbed his eyes. "And I got sawdust in my contacts."

"You didn't have your safety glasses on?"

"No," he snapped. "I was too occupied with messing shit up to remember them."

I sat cross-legged on the floor beside him. "What's the matter with you?"

"I'm just tired of this. I didn't get enough sleep, and then I overslept, and my mom came in like the Wrath of Khan to get me up. I didn't have breakfast." He wrapped his arms around his knees and rested his forehead against them. I rubbed his back in a firm, comforting way, and he leaned his whole huddled form against me. His skin was drum-tight over those lanky bones of his, with not an ounce of fat for padding. "I'm *starving,*" he repeated. "I'm never going to make it 'til one. My mom'll be picking up my corpse."

As if on cue, his stomach rumbled audibly. "Okay," I said. I patted his shoulder. "Come on. I'll get you fed."

He lifted his head and looked inordinately happy. "Seriously?"

"Yeah, we'll run out to 7-Eleven. But then I'm off the hook for Starbucks. Come on."

At the store he trailed me silently inside, branching off to the Slurpee machine, where he took the largest cup they sold and filled it with layer upon layer of frozen slush in lurid colors. His snack selections were more conservative: two sticks of cheddar cheese, an apple, and a tube of chocolate-covered sunflower seeds. Like most of my students, he probably considered those a decadent junk food. He had likely been trained from birth to consider the other items on offer, like gummy candies and Nestlé-brand chocolate bars, tantamount to ingesting drain cleaner.

"That looks vile," I informed him once we were back in the car, nodding to his Slurpee. "What would your mother say?"

"Whatever. I've seen what's in *your* fridge."

I strapped my seat belt and shot him a wry look. "I beg your pardon."

"Beg all you want. Anyway, it's good." He tipped the cup toward me. "Try it."

I gave a short laugh. "That's okay."

"Go on. I don't have cooties."

The purple straw practically touched my nose. I met his eyes, then took a drink. It felt like a quick slip through a rabbit hole of time, sharing a straw with a friend of sorts, as though I were a high-schooler myself. "It's not bad," I conceded.

The cup retreated, and he offered a mild, satisfied grin. The straw went back into his own mouth, his knee wedged against the dash as if he owned the place. As I backed out of the parking space I asked, "What's wrong with my fridge?"

"You've got all sorts of crap food in there. Hot dogs and pepperoni and that cheese dip that comes in jars. You *never* run out of Coke."

"*You* drink it."

"Yeah, but not at home. My mom won't buy that stuff, and the main reason is because you teachers tell her not to."

"*Steiner* said not to," I corrected. "Nourishing foods and nourishing fluids. It's our job to implement that within the school. We don't have to practice all of it at home."

He shook his head and grinned around the straw. "Lie."

I glanced at him with some offense. "No, it isn't."

"Yes, it is. You're supposed to do it all and you know it." Tipping his head to face me, he added, "Can I ask you something?"

"Not if it'll get me fired."

"Is it true that you kindergarten teachers really believe in gnomes?"

I snickered. "That's a trade secret. Officially, we do."

"My grade-school teacher always swore up and down that she did. And I know Steiner said they really existed. But I always wondered if the teachers actually buy it."

I twisted my mouth to one side and considered how to answer. "I don't believe in very much," I explained, "and I certainly don't believe in little fat men in pointed hats running around with rakes and spades. But I do believe in spirits in general, mischievous ones included. What Steiner said was that if you don't make spiritual progress during your physical incarnations, you come back as a gnome. So maybe we all have a little bit of that gnome in us, that aspect that carries grudges or won't forgive." I shrugged. "It's not an original idea, that the lesser spirits get banished to the wild. The ancient Irish believed spirits lived in bogs, you know. In Denmark they seem to find mummies in the peat all the time, sometimes with ropes around their necks. It usually seems to be connected with water, for some reason. Don't ask me why."

"Ms. Valera talked about that type of thing. This Roman guy, Tacitus, he wrote that in Germany they used to put the prostitutes in the bogs. Then they wedged them in there with stakes. It was supposed to be so their souls couldn't get up and wander around."

I chuckled. "Sounds very German, indeed."

"Yeah, we have to write a group report based on it. Except ours has to be on Maryland, and I'm in charge of the crime and punishment section, and it's nowhere near as interesting."

"Maybe you should talk about our laws against interracial marriage," I suggested, edging my tone with humor. I slowed for a red light and added, "It was still illegal here when I was a girl. I hear it obscures the ancient wisdom, or something like that."

"That's me," he joked. "I like to complicate things for you white people. If it wasn't for me, you *would* believe in gnomes. But I sit down in your car, and *wham*." He spread his arms wide, whacking me in the arm with his Slurpee cup. "You're off the path. No longer drinking the Kool-Aid."

"My coworkers will find out, and I'll lose my job."

"Oh, I won't tell on you. I'll just use the information for blackmail."

"Is that the worst you can find on me?"

He shrugged. "I don't know, is it?"

I smiled privately.

"Ooh," he said. "Maybe it's not. I'll have to find out all the dirt on you."

"Dig away, kiddo."

He jabbed me in the arm again, then in the waist, again

and again until I laughed out loud. And for a moment, for the first time in perhaps my entire life, the things I guarded made me feel mysterious instead of dreadful.

With Zach's belly full of apple, cheese and various food dyes, he seemed to be in much better spirits. Hours of work stretched ahead. With a glance toward the parking lot that was empty except for my car, I told Zach I would be back later that afternoon, then crossed my fingers and hoped no injuries or fires would occur in the meantime.

"I can handle it," he said, his voice edged with glee.

I ran my errands, stopping by Russ's college to pick up stacks of brochures for Sylvania School's College Fair the following week, then took myself to the dining hall and picked up a sandwich that came with a handful of brittle, inedible potato chips. On my way around the circuit I paused at the bakery counter and ordered two cookies: one chocolate chunk, one black-and-white.

The weather was lovely, crisp but not yet cold, and so I carried my foam container up the hill to the benches that surrounded the reflecting pool. As I ate I watched the skateboarders coast up and down the concrete terracing, grinding on the giant sundial, all bold energy and stumbling grace. A few looked old enough to be college students, but most did not. They all wore close-fitting T-shirts and baggy jeans hitched even lower on their hips than Zach's. Their bodies looked solid as stones. Nothing moved but muscle and sinew; and they seemed so careless about it, as if it were nothing to move through life in a package so neat and dense and perfect. I ate my cookie and smiled forgivingly when a skateboard ran up against my ankle, and one of them, a young man with a headful of wavy golden hair, jogged over and said, "Sorry, ma'am."

After a while I collected my trash and left. Something inside my chest felt pinched, bunched up and tied with a tight string. I think it was the place in my heart where the joy of youth had once been: a phantom pain.

Zach met me at the entrance to the workshop. His thumbs were hooked in the pockets of his jeans, and he was smiling. Before I had even fully crossed the parking lot, he called, "It's done."

"You finished it?"

He grinned and nodded. "I did. Finally."

I held out the paper sack. "And here I thought you'd need sustenance to get through the last stretch."

"Hey, I don't mind." He took out the cookie and ate a quarter of it in a single bite. "Black-and-white," he said approvingly, spitting crumbs. "You came through after all."

"So let's see what you've got."

I followed him through the door, past the tables scattered with tools and the hulking shapes of metal saws. The air smelled of clean, fresh wood, and motes of sawdust danced in beams of light near the windows. In the very back it sat, at the very midpoint of the back wall, Lilliputian but still so large it amazed me that Zach had built it on his own. Gingerbread trim scalloped the roof's edges and the flowerbox below the front window. All around its base was fiberglass stone, rolling so naturally that it appeared stacked by hand. The artificial tree that he had attached to its back, arching above the acorn-covered roof to shade it with leafy branches, made it look even more impressive. I flipped open the topmost Dutch door and peeked inside at the tightly joined corners, the fairy-sized wooden box attached beneath a window to hold secret treasures.

"It looks perfect, Zach," I told him. "You did a top-notch job."

"Thanks."

"The school should get a lot of money for it. You ought to be proud." I walked around the sides, admiring his work. "It's actually worth all the grief and misery I put up with."

He shot me a cheesy, achingly innocent grin. In a singsong voice he said, "Thank you, Mrs. McFarland."

"Yeah, yeah."

"Aren't you going to look inside?"

I regarded the small space with amusement. "I'm a little big for it, don't you think?"

"Naw. You're pretty little for an adult. And it's bigger on the inside. You'll see." He crouched down and crawled inside. Squatting on one side, he stuck his head out the door and said, "See, I fit. And I'm about a foot taller than you."

"Not even close, shorty."

"Whatever. Come on in."

I got onto my hands and knees and squeezed into the doorway. He was right—once inside, the height of the roof afforded a bit more room, and I could kneel comfortably. Still, it was sized for five-year-olds. I felt a bit claustrophobic.

"Fee fi fo fum," said Zach.

"This must be what Snow White felt like among the dwarves," I said.

"Are you calling me short?"

"Not in here. In here, you're huge."

"Why, thank you. My reputation precedes me."

I giggled. He grinned at his own joke. I shifted my weight forward, accommodating my aching knees, and suddenly Zach's hands were on my upper arms, and his face was moving very close to mine, his lips parted, eyes half-closed.

I did not resist. What I felt was not surprise, not

repugnance, but a sense of déjà vu: conjured to life was the image of him in my dream, kissing my child-self as if I were a woman. Even the first touch of his lips felt familiar; but then the kiss deepened, and his tongue touched mine, and everything changed. The warmth in my hips was liquid and instant and I welcomed it like an old friend. I twisted my fingers in his belt loops and pulled him to me. His groan of approval set my mind afire with a singular thought: *follow this through, as far as it takes you.* What I had mistaken for idle attraction now revealed its face: I wanted all of him, and monstrously so.

His mouth moved down my neck, and as I tipped my face upward to allow him, he slid his hands under my shirt and lowered his face to my breasts. Sawdust speckled his black hair, dusting my hands as they meandered to his shoulders and arms. When he rose to meet my mouth again his eyes were hazy and unfocused. The taste of his mouth, the smoothness of his taut wiry body beneath my hands, the scent of his skin—all thrilled me with their unfamiliarity, their sudden intimacy. I circled my thumbs into the waistband of his jeans and cursed the playhouse for being too small to afford space to lie down.

And then the door rattled. A woman's voice called, "Zach?"

He tore away from me and in an instant was standing beside the worktable, hands folded over his face, rubbing as if to force himself awake. I followed more slowly, my shaking hands and legs providing unsteady support. The high and open space around me seemed foggy at the corners, surreal. I asked, "Who's that?"

"My mom." Turning toward the door, he called, "Hold on a sec, I'll be right there." He sank onto a stool and, setting his elbows against the table, dropped his head into his hands and groaned.

"What's she doing here?"

"Picking me up. She's right on time." With a deep sigh, he rummaged in his backpack, pulled out his thermal shirt, and tied it around his waist. Then he clawed his hand back through his hair and uttered a grunt of disgust.

I stood a good distance away, out of sight from the door's rectangular window. My arms, crossed tightly over my chest, shook steadily. I felt sick with gratitude that I had not bothered to unlock the door from the inside. Gratitude to whom, I had no idea.

For the first time since the noise at the door, Zach looked at me. Inwardly I winced at the frankness of his large eyes, his gaze still a little uneven. He gave a short laugh and said, "Seeya."

"'Bye."

He shouldered his backpack and hopped down off the stool, his posture a bit bent under the weight. He pulled open the door and, with a muttered greeting to his mother, was gone.

I forced my quivering knees to guide me over to the stool where he had been, and, teeth chattering, carefully sat in the imaginary haze of his warmth. I looked at the tools still strewn around, then at the playhouse, where the sawdust on the floor swirled into whorls where our knees had been.

With an awful darkness clouding my mind, I thought: *What have I done?*

7

1965
Mainbach, West Germany

The line of evergreens lay beneath a cold blue sky, cloudless despite the snow-covered earth below it. At the top of the hill Judy exhaled hard, her breath blurring the scene before her, the flocked fabric of her scarf moist with condensation.

"Go on," said Rudi. "All by yourself. Exciting!"

She shook her head.

"Just one time."

She shook it again. "Not without you."

He sighed and laid down the toboggan. She climbed on and grabbed the string, and he nestled himself in behind her, his legs in his butternut canvas trousers firm along hers. He wrapped his gloved hands over her mittens and, chest thumping against her back, surged the sled forward. Cold wind shocked her face, and she screamed with pleasure.

Toward the bottom he hit an icy spot, banked right, and again they tumbled out into the snow. His weight against her was brief but reassuring as a thick wool blanket. As he staggered to his feet he laughed and reached for her hand, and despite all her obstructing layers of coats and wraps she felt weightless, no less so with his arm around her shoulders than when he pulled her up from the ground.

"Let's go home," he suggested. "Get warm."

They trudged back to the farmhouse, through the cold silence of winter. Her legs felt numb where the snow had melted through her tights. With sidelong looks she studied Rudi's face: the pink flush of his cheeks, the nubbled sheared wool that lined the earflaps of his cap, the way his hard steady breathing revealed his crooked canine teeth. When they passed beneath a tree beside the barn, a scurrying squirrel knocked a branch's worth of snow onto their heads, and she laughed.

"Hang your coat on the nail," said Rudi. Inside the house it was so warm her bones ached with the sudden contrast. Nevertheless she approached the woodstove with outstretched hands, exhaling a slow breath of relief at the draw of the fire.

"Your tights are wet," he observed. "Take them off, or you will get sick."

"I'll be cold walking home."

"We will let them dry by the fire. Your boots as well."

She sat in a chair and looked around the kitchen as she tugged off her boots. The walls were lined with wooden cookie molds, carved with designs she recognized. A heart encircled with flowers. Adam and Eve beside a tree. The Musicians of Bremen, stacked like a pyramid. Even Struwwelpeter, his blank eyes less haunting without color.

"Who would want to eat a cookie shaped like Struwwelpeter?" she asked.

Rudi grinned. "In my grandmother's time they made them. A treat and a punishment all together." He watched her struggle with her tights, then sat on the floor before her and helped pull them off. Wrapping his toasty hands around her toes, he grimaced. "Like ice cream. So cold."

"They sting. Maybe I have frostbite."

He rubbed them between his hands and cocked his head. "What is frostbite?"

"When your toes turn black and fall off from the cold."

"Ah. *Erfrierung.* No, I don't think." He stood and washed his hands at the sink, then poured himself a cup of coffee. "Would you like Ovaltine? Or a cookie?"

She accepted the cookie from him and sat swinging her legs, stretching her toes. As the milk warmed he shrugged out of his suspenders, pulled off his shirts, and hung them on chairs by the woodstove: a button-down, a thermal, and finally a cotton undershirt. His suspenders lay in a tangle at his hips.

Slowly she ate her cookie and watched Rudi prepare her Ovaltine. Experience had taught her Germans were immodest by her American standards, but Rudi half-naked still came as a shock to her. He was a man like her father: hairy around his navel and under his arms, smooth across his chest and unashamed to be shirtless. When he turned to face her she looked down, embarrassed, and paid attention to her spice cookie.

"Why is the bottom white?" she asked, turning it over so he could see it.

"So it won't stick to the pan," he explained. "We call it in German *oblate.* They are the same as at church."

"I don't go to church."

He looked mildly surprised. "It is the same as the Body of Christ blessed by the priest. But of course these are not blessed, or it would be a sin. So you can eat it for a cookie, and there is no sin."

She considered this idea and felt a mild thrill. Many times her family had visited historic churches, admiring the architecture and the artwork, but stopped short of participating in the religious rites that amused her father so. Now she was getting a taste of the mysterious white wafer the Germans approached with such veneration, slipped into her afternoon snack like a comic into a schoolbook. It seemed starchy and plain, but the dark spice of the cookie made it quite palatable. She accepted her cup of hot Ovaltine from Rudi and drank deeply.

He retreated to his place beside the counter and sipped his coffee. The scene struck her as being almost like that of a husband and wife, silent in their kitchen together. She imagined her Ovaltine might be coffee, and the limp crocheted dishtowel her own handiwork, and the bare-chested man beside the stove her husband, warming up after a day of work on the farm. Because if she could choose any husband in the world, of course it would be Rudi.

"The animals must be getting very cold," she said, in tentative German, like a concerned housewife.

He offered her an indulgent grin. In German he replied, "They'll be fine. They stay warm by their own body heat."

"Even when they sleep so far apart?"

"Yeah. There's not much warmer than a barn in the winter, especially if you've got as many animals as we do. And in the summer it's hotter than Hell." He pursed his lips, gazing at her as if to evaluate her level of understanding. Then he added, "You're getting very messy, Judy. Come here."

She stood and heard a shower of crumbs hit the floor. Suddenly she felt the stickiness of Ovaltine above her lip and crumbs at the corner of her mouth. Some grown-up housewife *she* had been, covered in food like a toddler. She felt a wave of shame.

From the distant airfield a sonic boom rumbled like thunder, shivering the measuring spoons on their nail. Rudi turned on the tap and ran his hand beneath the hot water, then rubbed it against her mouth, the fingers of his other hand gently cupping the back of her head. "There," he said in English. "All clean now."

She knew what was next: he would tell her that her tights were dry and it was time to go home, and then she would be alone again, with only her mother growing fragile as a drying flower, ready to crumple to dust at the lightest touch. Impulsively she threw her arms around Rudi's waist and buried her face in the soft spot below his ribs, with the warmth and the smell of him to blind and to smother her.

"There, there, now," he said, his voice ever so uneasy. "You can always come back tomorrow."

At the beginning of March the Chandler family piled into the navy-blue Mercedes and drove to Munich to see the Fasching parade. The jubilant crowds gathered along the streets and waved cardboard noisemakers in a rainbow of colors. Men wore masks with spindly noses and twisted smiles, their eyes vanishing into shadowed holes. Grown women dressed like babies, in pacifiers and bonnets, while clowns towered high above on stilts. It was as though Judy had entered a nightmare world in which all of the adults had gone awry. Her father bought her a rabbit-ear headband and a donut filled with orange marmalade, which she ate slowly as the floats and revelers passed by. Everywhere it smelled like beer.

They walked to a churchyard set up with booths for a children's carnival, with face-painting and games. Balloons attached to the tables batted in the March wind, their tethering ribbons twisting together. A lady brought out a sheet cake divided into squares and asked each child to choose one.

Judy bit into her square and found a lima bean inside. The lady clapped and told her that meant she was the Queen of Fasching. Another lady painted her face with a bunny nose and whiskers to match her headband. Then they got back into the Mercedes and drove home.

"It's what they used to do in the old pagan days," explained her father as they accelerated onto the Autobahn. "They baked a cake with a nut hidden in it, and whoever chose that piece got to be the tribal king for a year."

"That's pretty lucky."

"Not as lucky as you'd think. After a year they sacrificed him to their gods and sprinkled his blood onto the earth."

Judy turned the lima bean over in her hand. "Oh."

"Maybe we'll skip the Fasching parade next year," her father added. "Just in case."

She smiled. She loved these Saturdays: the hikes in the mountains, the visits to elegant castles, the meandering tours of medieval streets during which she could hang on her father's hand. His breezy humor made her feel light and safe, after the everyday dread of her mother's rigid order. She accompanied them on these trips but stayed very quiet, almost as if she had left her mind at home. Home, where a pencil carelessly left in a side table drawer provoked a fit of shaking, impotent hysteria, as though Judy had accidentally punched through a thin membrane and left her mother hemorrhaging sanity onto the living room floor.

"Moo cow," said her father. "Look out your window, Judy. There's a calf. First I've seen all season."

She glanced at the baby cow with mild interest and thought of the one in Rudi's barn. Now that the days were growing longer again, she had returned to visiting him in the afternoons before supper. She changed from her Mary Janes to her green rubber rain boots, filled her backpack with her homework books and thick beeswax crayons and a fountain pen, and clomped down the road to the barn. She kept an eye out for his sisters: Daniela, who would shout at her in bell-voiced, barely comprehensible German, and Kirsten, older than Rudi and recently graduated from school, who tended to bustle around collecting eggs and sweeping the walk. Judy preferred her time with Rudi to be private. If she came at the right time she would find him sitting on the milking stool with his head halfway under the cow, legs sprawled wide in a careless display of male confidence.

Sometimes he grinned and squirted her with milk straight from the udder. Sometimes he gave her corn to scatter for the chickens, or the balls of wool collected from bits caught in the wood of the sheep pens. High above on the barn wall hung a crucifix, which he paid no mind, as though living beneath the twisted body of Christ were the most natural thing in the world. Rudi was right: even when deep snowdrifts lay outside, the barn was as warm as a bedroom. Before milking, Rudi grabbed a shovel and energetically mucked out each stall. Judy sat on a makeshift bench of straw bales, her knees pulled up beneath her skirt, and allowed her clear mind to absorb the image: a crucifix, Rudi and cow shit.

It was all so plain and bare, the life in the barn. The wool was greasy because it was made that way, the corn she threw to the chickens dusty by its nature. The animals ate, then shat where they stood, because that was what animals did. There was no hidden reason for anything at all, nothing inscrutable or perplexing. It was the opposite of her own life, over which she was trying hard to pull a curtain of normalcy. Her mother had begun flicking every light switch three times. If a crust of food remained on a plate, she threw all the dishes back in the sink and started over. When she opened her weekly package from the butcher and it contained an extra chicken leg, she fell

into a chair, mute and sweating, breathing through her flared
nostrils like a fish tossed to the bottom of a boat. Toward the
end of March, Judy's father sent her to the psychiatrist.

Three days a week she had to go to Augsburg Air Base for
treatment. Because her husband was important, they sent a car
for her. For the first week they left Judy alone in the house,
but the laundry stacked up and gave her mother panic attacks.
At that point her father walked down to the house beside the
barn and inquired, in his German that was quite clear and
good, about hiring Rudi's sister, Kirsten, as a domestic. Judy
watched through the window as the two fathers discussed
the specifics. She eyed the young woman who stood beside
them with her hands folded behind her back: a tall girl, thin
but wide-hipped in her flared knee-length skirt, with blond
hair in two braids that crossed at the center of her crown. A
deal was struck, and she shook John Chandler's hand with a
solid wag of her arm that struck Judy, trained by a father who
cared about such things, as a bit unrefined.

The young woman, Judy soon discovered, was very capable. She managed things just as Judy's mother did, airing
the duvets and keeping the birdcage clean, folding her father's
shirts like a shelf display at J.C. Penney. She visited on the days
Judy's mother had treatment, and on those days she always set
some dish to simmer in the Dutch oven for their supper—
pork chops with syrupy apples, beef stew flecked with little
golden *spätzle*. She tutored Judy in German as she went about
her work, and as she cooked she played American hit music
on the radio. For the first time in Judy's memory, her home
was filled with delicious scents and cheerful melodies, and
on Kirsten's workdays she looked forward to coming home
after school. Each day stood in contrast to the next, because
in between the afternoons of the Beatles and veal cutlets with
lemon slices, there were those in which the silence echoed

in her ears, the tension gathered in each room as though the air had not stirred for hours, and her mother sat at the table alone eating leftovers from the refrigerator. Gone was the old mother, slim and lovely with her Jackie Kennedy bouffant, and in her place was a new one whose teased hair looked like an accident and whose backside filled the entire chair. It was because of the lithium, her father told her, privately. Judy wasn't sure what it was, but the word sounded like something very light. She pictured a pink helium balloon floating into the sky, its string trailing. It sounded like something that would be good for her mother, to feel effortlessly lighter, skipping through her chores with her feet barely touching the ground. But instead, her mother only grew heavier. She sat in the orange-print armchair covered with clear plastic, sipped from a cup of coffee, and watched television shows in German. Her hands shook slightly, and sometimes the coffee sloshed onto the chair cover.

But then the next day arrived again, and with it Kirsten. She brought them brown eggs from her chickens, and the apple strudel Judy's father loved. She smiled at Judy often, and called her *Mausi,* which meant "little mouse," with the affection usually reserved for a sibling. In the kitchen she scrubbed their dirty laundry with the Fels-Naptha bar before loading it into the machine, sprinkling it with water and working in the lather with the kind of force her father called *elbow grease.* As she worked she swayed her hips to the radio music, and in the living room Judy danced, too, waving her arms up and down in front of her as she had seen on *The Ed Sullivan Show.* On one afternoon, partway through such a performance, her father came home. He laughed at Judy's antics, grinning as he walked through the living room, into the heart of the gaiety, to greet Kirsten. She stepped out of the kitchen, her hands still bubbly with lather, her heart-shaped face shining as though freshly scrubbed. She held up her palms in a jazz-hands pose and, dancing, sang along in her approximate English to "I'm Happy Just To Dance With You." Judy laughed, and so did her father; and then he held his fingertips up against Kirsten's and danced along with her. Kirsten did not look surprised. She only smiled and followed his steps as though now *they* were the act from *The Ed Sullivan Show,* and they both knew this routine, having practiced it a hundred times before.

Judy had stopped dancing. She stood and watched them, her mashed-potato fists hanging at her sides, her slice of strudel heavy in her stomach. When she fell asleep that night, and the next, and the next, it was not the dancing that lingered in her mind, nor the smiles they exchanged. It was the image of her father's hands touching Kirsten's lathery ones, the way his fingertips lit against hers like a bee landing on a foxglove petal. She had made his favorite strudel. She had worn her best dress.

Only gradually did the understanding unfold in her: that it was not the shaking, the counting, and the lithium that were conspiring to ruin her family. It was the girl.

The psychiatrist decided what Judy's mother needed was an in-patient stay, and so not long before Easter she packed two suitcases and went away until some future date when the doctors would decide she was better. Judy was told she might visit on Sundays, and her father hired Kirsten to work five days a week. Rudi's presence in the barn had become less reliable, but despite this, Judy often slipped in with her rucksack full of schoolwork and sat on a bale that faced the crucifix and tried to feel, if not peace, then the possibility of comfort. How this tortured man had supposedly redeemed her soul was a mystery to her, but she hungered for any morsel that might ease her pangs of anxiety.

"Why so sad?" Rudi asked her one day, on an occasion when he strode into the barn and found her already there, sitting and watching the cow, her paper and colored pencils discarded beside her. She had been using the *Struwwelpeter* book as a lap desk. The miserable boy stared up at them from the cover, bowlegged and sallow-cheeked, his clawlike hands spread uselessly. He appeared to be shrugging.

"I want my mother to come back."

"She will. The doctors will make her better, and then there will be no more *flick-flick-flick* with the light, *bop-bop* with the cat bowl. You will see."

Judy shook her head. "Every time they try to make it right, it goes wrong in a different way. She wasn't like this back home. She was just neat, and liked things to be in order. Now she falls to pieces if they're not. And she's fat."

Rudi laughed. "Fat?"

"Like somebody filled her full of air. She had to get all new clothes. My father says it's from the medicine."

The door creaked open, and Kirsten stepped in. "*Hallo,* Judy," she said, and gathered up the white enamel milk pans that sat in a row near the window. Their clatter broke the somber mood, but when she left, Judy pulled her legs up to her chest and wrapped her arms around them, pressing her forehead against her knees.

Rudi squatted down beside her and smiled. "Come with me," he said.

She followed Rudi to a shed at the far corner of the property. When he opened the padlock, she looked back over her shoulder with an edge of nervousness. From the barn she could see her house, but from this shed she could see only the barn and Rudi's house and that of his neighbors, an elderly couple whose names Judy did not know. Rudi swung open the door on its crumbling hinges and stepped inside. With hesitating steps Judy followed him past the threshold. The shed smelled of muddy soil and a haze of gasoline, stored in a dark red tin beside the old tractor. The air within the shed was cold, with only the narrowest slivers of light knifing off the rusted ends of garden tools. Rudi waved her inside and stepped into a corner.

"What is it?" she whispered.

The door thudded shut behind her. Rudi made a shushing noise and, with a crooked finger, gestured her toward him. She followed and sank to her knees beside him, hiking her skirt to keep it from the moist ground. A movement caught her eye; she pulled in her breath. And then Rudi carefully lifted from the quivering pile a tiny animal no larger than a chipmunk. He held it toward her in both palms.

"Go on, hold it," he said in a quiet voice.

"Is it a mouse?"

"No. *Igel.*"

"Eagle?"

His hands pushed toward her again. "Go on."

She curled her fists against her stomach, afraid. It didn't look like a bird, but in the small light it was difficult to see. Rudi extended his hands almost to her stomach and by reflex she reached out, not wanting this strange creature to crawl into her dress. At that moment he eased the animal into her hands and, sliding his hand beneath hers to support them, crouched behind her. With an arm on each of her sides, and both of his hands now beneath hers, her fears eased. The little creature snuffled, lifted its face, and she realized it was a hedgehog.

"Oh!" she cried. "Oh! Will it bite me?"

"No, no." His breath was warm against her ear. "Very gentle. Very soft."

She supposed he was giving her instructions. The animal itself was not very soft. Its tiny spines tickled her palm, and its squirming body seemed on the verge of sliding from her hands. But Rudy anticipated its small wiggles and kicks, tipping his hands beneath hers to ease it back to safety. Despite the need for quiet, she laughed aloud.

"Shhhhh," he reminded her.

She looked up at his face and saw the peace that farmwork always laid over his features. When speaking of family or school, he was always animated, comical even; but the work of nature seemed to pull him back to the peace of the center, the windless sea that did not move.

She cupped the hedgehog in her hands and nestled back into Rudi's chest. She felt the quiver of his ankles finding their balance, and smelled the hardworking scent of him, of the earth around roots and the bristled fur of animals, the copper tang of the tools he held, the rugged sweat of a grown man.

Easter passed and the daffodils bloomed, sending up green shoots suddenly to displace the crocuses that had endured the last snows. Judy was glad for the warmth that allowed her to leave her itchy tights at home, and walked home from the bus stop with her rucksack tight against her back, her skirt swinging gently against her knees. The broad fallow fields sprawled in all directions, their rugged brown soil glazed with rain; in the distance rose the smoky blue silhouette of the eastern Alps, Jagerkamp and Miesing, where her family had hiked the summer before. Through the vivid sky flew American fighter jets on practice exercises, engines whistling, leaving slim contrails in their wake. When she turned onto her own street she saw her father's car in the driveway. Kirsten would be there, too, but Judy needed to change clothes before hurrying off to the barn, so the discomfort would have to be endured.

As she walked up the path toward the back door she ran her hand over the heads of the bright yellow daffodils that lined the walk; they bobbed and waved alongside her. She pushed open the door and stepped into the tidy living room with its maize carpet freshly vacuumed, brightened here and there by shards of sunlight from the spotless windows. The Supremes belted out a song on the radio, their voices as smooth and flawless as the ribbon of cream Kirsten poured from the pitcher onto her father's strudel, and the whole house smelled cheerfully of pork and spiced apples, laced with a note of butter. Yet nobody seemed to be home. In the kitchen the laundry floated in the sink, unattended; next to the Dutch oven, the box of strike-anywhere matches had been left out. Judy was not allowed to touch them, but the story of Pauline had made her curious, and no one was around to see. She slid open the box and held one by its rough wooden stem, examining it closely. She struck it against the counter, the side of the stove, the metal cabinet, but it did not work. Finally she struck it against the wall and like magic it engulfed in flame. Judy smiled. *It crackled so, it burned so clear,* said the poem; and it was true. But Pauline had been a foolish girl who had not put it out in time, and so Judy puffed a breath of air against it. The fire vanished, and the kitchen filled with the smell of birthday wishes.

It was strange, but not unpleasant, to find the house so empty. She wandered down the hall, peering into each room: the spare bedroom her father used as an office, the bathroom, her own bedroom with its duvet fluffed high as a cloud. Standing in her doorway, she heard a muffled noise from the next room, a steady squeak like a window loose on its hinge. She turned the knob to her parents' bedroom door, just as a fighter jet flew by overhead and drowned the creaking noise in its resonating sonic boom.

Later she would remember seeing nothing. Nothing at all: that she had turned the knob and seen nothing but the black vacuous space of blindness. Past the door the world ended. Past the door lay the incomprehensible dark.

The blackness had swallowed her father, and when he returned she recognized an impostor.

8

I dressed for College Fair night with a sense of dread. Scott had no desire to go, having already settled on the likely prospect of attending a school near Baltimore known more for its kegger parties than its academics. Yet we had no choice; it would look bad if either he or I skipped it, since I knew parents looked to our family for evidence that Waldorf kids could compete on a university level, and I needed to show up armed with enthusiastic stories about how well Maggie was doing at college. Three days had passed since the afternoon in the workshop, and in that time I saw Zach only through my classroom windows, coming and going from the parking lot. At times my mind grew nearly hysterical with questions I could not possibly answer. I feared his resentment and anger, his morning-after remorse, but most of all I was terrified he would run his mouth; even if he harbored no ill feelings, teenage boys were not legendary for their discretion. Surely he would tell *somebody,* and if one kid at Sylvania found out, they'd all know by lunchtime. Every time a colleague glanced at me, every time I heard my name called, my heart squeezed with fear. I *had* to talk to Zach, if only to emphasize to him that I was sorry, it had been a terrible mistake and it would never happen again as long as I lived.

The parking lot was crammed with cars. As Scott and I made our way down the hall, I felt a lump form in my throat as I saw the playhouse situated right in front of the main office. Parents surrounded it, making approving cooing noises. Zach stood nearby, leaning against the wall between the house and a table filled with information about the holiday bazaar. When he saw me his gaze sharpened with recognition but his expression did not change.

Vivienne, however, lit up with a smile and came toward me, a welcoming hand extended. "Judy! Have you seen it? Hasn't he done an amazing job? I'm so impressed I can hardly stand it!"

I nodded. "He's been hard at work."

The shadow of a grin played at Zach's mouth. I took that as a positive sign. When a teenager wanted to be dour, nothing could stop him.

Vivienne grasped my hand. "Thank you so much for taking so much time out of your schedule to make the workshop available. Zach can do great things when he makes an effort."

Zach rolled his eyes, absorbing the verbal stress his mother had placed on the last few words. Scott, standing impatiently beside me, said, "I'll see you in the multipurpose room."

A crush of parents awaited me along the way, peppering me with questions. I worked my way around the room until I caught sight of Scott near the far corner, roughhousing with his friends. Medieval Judo—that was their name for it. The game consisted of stagecraft martial arts combined with trash-talk in imitation of *Monty Python and the Holy Grail*. Zach was with them, having slipped through the crowd much faster than I could. As I approached I saw Temple had Zach in some sort of a kung-fu grip. Zach twisted around to release himself, then crouched into a low spin-kick, which sent Temple flying theatrically backward. Scott rushed to Temple's aid by grabbing Zach from behind under both arms and flailing him from side to side.

"Stop, knave!" shouted Zach. "Or I will unleash my Singaporean Fart Attack!"

Scott was unmoved. "My faith will protect me, good knight!"

"Scott," I said loudly. I tipped my head pointedly toward the semicircle of college information booths.

"In a minute," he called, none too friendly. He locked his hands at the front of Zach's chest and hauled him backward. Then, as if it were nothing at all, Zach got his feet under him, twisted at the waist, and threw Scott off his balance, flipping him forward and sending him skidding across the floor on his side. My eyes widened, but Scott didn't seem hurt. He uttered a surprised laugh and got to his feet.

"Seen anything that looks interesting to you?" I asked, more or less rhetorically.

He answered with a you-must-be-kidding-me look and brushed past me to the booths, randomly swiping brochures.

I sidled up near Zach, who lagged behind as the girls wandered off with Temple. Once alone, we both looked over the noisy room, full of excited upperclassmen chatting up perky college reps. A dozen urgent questions fought for precedence in my mind. After a silence I asked, "Did you tell anyone?"

He shook his head, not breaking his focus on the milling crowd. A shock of hair mostly covered one eye, and his mouth looked brooding, serious. He hesitated, then asked, "Did you?"

I chuckled. "Of course not. Do you think I'm insane?"

A hard sigh escaped his nose, like a noiseless laugh.

"I'm sorry for what happened," I said quietly. "Do you want to talk about it?"

His nod was slight. "We can go someplace. I've still got stuff in the workshop."

"I can meet you there in a few minutes if you like."

"All right." He turned and disappeared out the side door. I checked on Scott, who had regrouped with his remaining friends on the opposite side of the room, and made my way toward the workshop via a door off the main hallway.

The enormous room was dark when I stepped inside, except for a single fluorescent fixture in the far corner where the playhouse had been. Zach crouched on the balls of his feet beneath the yellow light, brushing sawdust out of a power sander. He did not look up when I came in.

"I'm sorry," I repeated.

His shoulders twitched with a laugh that held no humor. "*You're* sorry. I've been waiting all week to get called down to Beckett's office. I knew I was in deep shit."

I frowned and came closer, stopping at the edge of the square of light. "Why would you be in deep shit?"

He looked up and grinned—at my bad language, I assumed. "Over what happened. You looked *pissed*. I didn't mean for that to happen."

"I wasn't pissed. I was terrified. All week *I've* been waiting to get called down to Beckett's office. So I could get fired."

He dismissed days of mortal fear with a shake of his head. "I'm not telling anybody."

"Well, I didn't know that."

He stood up and laid the sander on the shelf, then jammed his hands into his back pockets. "Trust me, getting Scott's mom fired wouldn't do me a whole lot of good here. All my friends are his friends."

"I appreciate that," I told him. "But it was my fault, and I promise you it won't ever happen again. If you don't want to work with me on the bazaar anymore, I completely understand. I'll tell your mom there's a senior who needs hours. It won't be a problem."

"Nah, I'm not worried about it. I'll just keep away from confined spaces."

My laugh held an edge of mortification. "I don't know what I was thinking, Zach. I'm so sorry. I swear to you I've never done anything like that before. My husband has been a jerk lately, and I've been lonely, and—" I stopped, realizing Zach had never asked for an explanation. "I must have been in a mood. There's no way to justify it."

"It's all right. I thought you were cool with it at first. But then the look on your face after—I figured you thought I took it too far."

Right away I shook my head. "Oh, no. I didn't think that at all."

At first his eyes registered confusion. Then he looked to the side and grinned.

I winced at his interpretation. "Okay, let's wrap up this conversation," I suggested, to his laughter. "Crazy mistake. It'll never happen again. Done."

"Done," he agreed, and in my earnest need to wish it away, I chose, with a bold enthusiasm, to believe it was true. I had, after all, made a career out of fairy tales.

"So, anyway," he said in a louder, lighter voice, "the playhouse is done. Great, huh?"

I replied with a quick nod. "Beautiful. I'll sign off on all thirty of your service hours. Wonderful job."

"Jeez, Teach," he said, and the sarcasm in his smile was infectious. "You're paying me off? I don't think that's legal."

My laughter bubbled over, but even as I laughed I felt a shadow at its edge, the giddy feeling brought on by a sense of hopelessness. The danger loomed much larger than I had feared.

Not because he might report me.

But because he would not.

When my students ran out our classroom door to the playground, they did not spread out like bees, as they usually did, but gravitated toward a single point. It didn't take long for me to realize why. Zach's playhouse had been moved to the sidewalk between the playground and workshop, left behind, evidently, on its way to storage. Around the side of the workshop I spotted two teenagers wrestling a metal trolley past the concrete parking barriers.

"Let's move to the play area, boys and girls," I said. "This is for the Christmas auction. It needs to be tucked away safe and sound."

Max popped his head out of one of the shuttered windows and grinned at me. "Out, Max," I urged. I pointed toward the little wooden bridge in the sand pit. "Look, your friends are playing Three Billy Goats Gruff."

"They're playing Grenade Bandits," he corrected.

"Well, why don't you go play with them."

As he scurried out, I shut the Dutch doors in relief. I felt thankful the playhouse was not destined for my classroom. Watching the children run around in it was unnerving. In the days since my encounter with Zach, even—perhaps especially—after I knew my job and life would be safe, I found myself mired in uneasy guilt and gloomy self-reflection. *What could have possessed me to do such a thing?* I wondered. I had spent my entire adult life in the service of a single master: pure childhood. Not God. Not a messiah or a prophet. Only childhood at its most undefiled, a walled garden as big as a child's imagination could stretch, into which no evil thing could enter. I had obsessed over the minutiae of the color of a silk square, the finish of a toy horse. With a religious devotion, I worked to ensure that the unformed mind would experience only what was natural, what was pure. Now, in my failure to control a most natural impulse, I had revealed the wildly impure.

A lapse of reason, I thought. It wasn't his youth that intoxicated me, but the way he had of bringing my own youth to the surface; with each passing hour with him another year seemed to fall away, until the woman in the mirror would have appeared to me a stranger. When he kissed me, he recognized the girl radiating out from within me. But I was not that girl anymore. Any jury of my peers would be happy to remind me of that fact. And because of that, I had to find a way to stay oriented in time, not to succumb to the pull of his camaraderie. If I needed affection so badly, then I needed to find a lover my own age.

I clutched at the knot beneath my head scarf and turned my thoughts toward the choir trip coming up at the end of the week. Sylvania's madrigal choir had won a spot in a regional competition in Ohio, and so for four days I would be away from home, supervising teenagers but also free, off and on, to do as I wanted. In a year or so that might mean the chance to find a replacement for Russ, but at the moment I lacked enough nerve. Instead I would try to *think* like a free woman rather than a confined one. In my mind I would be nineteen again, attuned to the undercurrent of hunger in the way men greet women. Rather than shrug it off, I would welcome it.

"Teacher's base! Teacher's base!"

The sound of my children's voices brought me back into the moment, and I worked to decipher their meaning as I watched them chase each other across the dampened sand that flew out behind their sneakers like brown sugar. All at once I spotted

Aidan racing toward me at full speed, his small arms pumping hard, fine blond hair flying; his face bore an ecstatic smile. I grinned at the sight of it and braced for impact, knowing what Aidan knew: I was the safe zone. Small, but rock-solid.

I still had no reason to doubt it, then.

My goal for Ohio was to have a fun, enriching, self-actualized time pursuing grown-up things. Antiquing, learning about Amish life, tasting wine. In less than a year Scott would be off at college and it would be my turn to enjoy the pursuits denied to me during the thick of mothering. And if ever I needed a pep talk about the scintillating fun of adulthood, it was now.

Now, as I watched my teenage charges touch and jostle each other as they filled their buffet plates with the building blocks of heart disease, laughing and joking, stacking on a third or fourth brownie. Now, as they bought magazines and bubblegum and showed up twenty minutes late with perfectly flat-ironed hair. Removed from the fairy-tale paradise of Waldorf school, they dove into American consumer culture as if it were a deep-water quarry on a hundred-degree day. Had I been more naïve, I would have found it disheartening. But, as I reminded myself while I examined quilts in a farmhouse shop, even the Amish allow their teens to go a little crazy with the confidence they'll return to the fold. *Rumspringa,* they call it; and if the Plain People can tolerate smoking and drag racing, then I could overlook tabloids and corn syrup.

Overlooking the way Zach shadowed Fairen's every move, however—that was not so easy. Touching her shoulder, her ear, her waist. Adjusting himself covertly in his jeans. His desire for her was throwing itself against the walls of his body. I felt determined not to care.

During my few free hours I drove down the tourist strip in

search of crafts to bring home—pottery, wood carvings, tex-
tiles. Always, I was searching for new things for my classroom,
a glazed bowl for the nature table or a toy sheep for a tableau.
In the quilt shop I came upon a handsomely carved sleigh
bed, mahogany like my own. Draped with hand-stitched merchandise, it looked cozy and darling. I ran my hand across the
smooth wood and recalled the day Russ and I bought ours
on a trip to Vermont. We were engaged then, weekending at
a bed-and-breakfast, and found ourselves booked to a room
that held one treasure after another—an apothecary cabinet,
a pewter Revere bowl, a gorgeous bed. Russ laughed when
he turned over the bowl and found a price tag. We soon discovered the whole room was for sale, a clever sales technique
for romantic young couples. We wrote a check that accounted
for both our bank accounts and my next paycheck, and had
the bed shipped to his apartment.

I hadn't cared about the expense; in fact, I'd embraced it.
My own parents, for their entire marriage, had slept in twin
beds. Things hadn't gone well for them. I loved the fact that
when Russ and I climbed into the same bed together, we
all but ate each other alive. Even Bobbie, whose disdain for
Russ had been thinly concealed, envied us in that respect. *I
need to find myself a man who looks at me the way he looks at you,*
she told me more than once. The only wedding gift I wanted
was a bed big enough for all he and I wanted to do in it, one
magnificent enough to suggest the importance of its function.

But now Russ was a stranger. Half the time he seemed
wound up tight as a spring; the other half, disinterested in
anything but setting his feet up in front of the TV, or sleeping. The week before, I had come home to four messages
on the answering machine from his boss and his teaching
assistant trying to find him for the class he taught. When I
pushed open the door to his home office I found him sprawled

facedown on his ragged old sofa, his arm dangling loosely, like a napping baby's. The condensed glare of the desk light, hard and dense as a star's, caught in the dull shine of his wedding band. For a moment I'd thought he was dead, and in those otherworldly seconds before his foot and fingers twitched in sleep, what I had felt was a rising wave of relief. I felt shamed by it, but weary, too. I couldn't make sense of him anymore, this man who slept beside me, when he slept at all.

I looked over the quilts, a dozen of them, artfully arranged on the mattress, but didn't have the heart to buy one. Beautiful as they were, to spread one over my bed would feel like draping a sheet over a dead body. I bought a doll blanket for my housekeeping corner, and drove back to the hotel.

At ten o'clock I left my room and parked myself at the midpoint of the hallway, sitting on the floor where I had a view of every door in both directions. Almost immediately, one door cracked open, then quickly pulled shut. I felt a cosmic irony at being appointed the Sex Police. When my generation had once declared all people over thirty to be hypocrites, we had been right.

As I sat guard, I worked a needle in and out of a square of velveteen, making a small dream pillow for one of my kindergartner's birthdays. I was forever making these velveteen pillows, yet even after sewing hundreds I still enjoyed the process: focusing on a particular student, on who he or she might grow up to be, on the things that make the child an individual. Inevitably I loved the child a little more after making his or her birthday pillow. Today's was for a little girl named Josephine, a curious little blonde who desperately wanted to learn to read. She often tied a blue playsilk around her shoulders, and liked most to play with the wooden fish and dolphins. She had one loose tooth, a sign she was on the brink of a jump in maturity, both physical and mental.

It was not difficult to work up fond feelings for Josephine. As I sewed, I became aware of a man coming out of the next room down and sitting on the floor as I did. Now and then I felt his gaze on me, surreptitious. Finally he asked, "What are you working on?"

"A pillow for one of my students."

"Pretty small pillow."

"It's a dream pillow. I'll fill it with lavender and barley. It's to put under their sleeping pillow. A birthday gift."

"Oh." He looked up and down the hallway. I stole a glance at him: fortyish, solidly built but not fat, a hairline not yet in retreat. He wore khakis and loafers, and, seated on the floor with his knees up, long stretches of his white socks were visible.

I asked, "Are you a chaperone?"

"Yeah. My daughter's here for a choir competition."

"I figured. So is my son."

"Oh, yeah?" He turned to look me full in the face. "So are you the lookout for sinful behavior?"

I chuckled. "Apparently so. I guess they assigned our kids to the same hallway."

He twisted to stretch his right hand toward me. As he re-balanced his weight against his left hand, I caught a glimpse of his gold wedding ring. He said, "I'm Ted."

I shook it. "Judy."

"Nice to meet you, Judy. We're from St. Scholastica."

"Is that a Catholic school?"

"Yes. In Michigan."

I nodded, but didn't volunteer the details about my school. People always asked question after question, and it was an interview I didn't feel like engaging. I went back to my pillow.

After a while Ted said, "Well, I don't see a lot of action going on. I think they'll stay put."

"Clearly you don't know teenagers."

He smiled. "Let 'em learn. They say virtue untested was never virtue at all."

I knotted the thread and bit it off between my teeth. "That doesn't sound like the Catholic-school approach to me."

"Well, I'm not Catholic."

"Is your wife?"

He paused, his tongue half in his cheek. "No. It's a good school, is why we send her. But the academics are what we appreciate, not the conservative teachings."

I tried to hide a smile, smoothing the velveteen against my thigh. "I'm not particularly conservative, myself."

He nodded. After a moment's hesitation he said, "So if I asked you if you'd join me for a drink, you might not feel too bad about abandoning your post."

I considered that. "I don't know," I said. "It wouldn't look good for another chaperone to see me downstairs when they know I'm supposed to be on duty."

"I said 'a drink,'" he pointed out. He waved his thumb toward the wall behind him. "They gave me a really good minifridge."

"Did they really," I mused. "Here in Amish country, of all places."

He smiled in an earnest way. "Yeah, well, I'm not Amish, either."

His mouth on my neck, my breasts, my belly; his hands beneath my thighs, hoisting my legs around his waist; all were eager, hungry, as though the long drive from Michigan had been a patient journey toward adultery that was finally, blessedly, over. His mouth tasted, beneath the fresh sting of Jack Daniel's, of cigarette smoke. Beside his ear, his skin was minty with aftershave. He stepped on the toes of his socks to peel them off before undoing his pants, a subtle stab at vanity that struck me as disarming.

Not that I had much time to be disarmed. Once he lifted my chin and found me willing, he moved quickly. I might have wondered if he made a practice of this, prowling for easy sex as the sideshow to his daughter's choir travel, except that he seemed so grateful, so conventional. He said my name over and over, *oh Judy,* or *Judy Judy Judy,* as though we had an intimate history together. But somehow from his lips my name managed to sound isolated, alien—one he had just heard over a handshake and was repeating so as not to forget.

And so I was half old flame, half stranger. He screwed like any husband in his forties, well and skillfully, without any shadow of kink. So clean and plain he might have been my own.

But in the thick of it, after the initial shock of his mouth and hands but before his weight and breadth were over me, I forgot about him. When he grazed his lips down my stomach and—good Ted, experienced Ted—lifted my thighs over his shoulders, I closed my eyes and saw, like a broken and grainy filmstrip, someone else. All motion: dark hair swinging, the twitch of a cheek muscle, the shivery tensing of biceps. Zach. Zach above a faceless woman, all of him in dreamlike grays, traveling along a sensory arc in parallel with me. And it was not until Ted came up laughing, murmuring *shhhh, shhhh,* did I realize he was still here, and Zach elsewhere, someplace where the waves of my cries were tumbling to right now, like a sonic boom.

On their last day in Ohio, Zach and his friends got up early to sing in the final competition, taking second place, which pleased Zach tremendously. The grown-ups took them out to dinner at a Pennsylvania Dutch buffet in celebration, and by eight they were back at the hotel. He watched TV with Temple for a while, then slipped out with a handful of change to get them each a soda from the vending machine at the end of the hallway.

As Temple's root beer clunked down to the retrieval slot, Zach heard a whisper coming from the corridor. It was Kaitlyn, peeking out from the doorway around the corner. "Hey," she said, low-voiced. "Is Temple asleep?"

"Nope. We're watching TV."

"I'm bored."

Zach shrugged. "You can join us if you like. If you can dodge the chaperones."

She smiled, signaled him with a double thumbs-up, and tiptoed down the hall in her frog-print pajama pants. He grinned and pushed the button to dispense his own soda, then stuck his head into the room, the door of which was still ajar. Fairen lay on her stomach on the far bed, reading. She looked up and said, "Come on in."

"You want to come watch TV with us? Kaitlyn's on her way."

She wrinkled her nose. "I don't watch TV."

"Oh, come on. Don't tell me they've brainwashed you *that* bad."

"I'm not brainwashed. I just don't care for it."

He stepped inside and shut the door behind him. She closed her book and rolled onto her side as he approached, and he sat on the bed beside her. "You're reading *The Little Prince* in French?"

"I like *The Little Prince*."

"I did, too, when I was seven."

She poked him in the abs. "Where's your shirt?"

"I just took a shower. Gonna go to bed in a little bit."

"You don't wear pajamas?"

He snickered. "No. I sleep in my underwear, unless it's frickin' freezing."

"Boxers or briefs?"

"What do you think?"

She smirked and ran her finger under his waistband, behind the elastic. The touch excited him instantly. She tugged his boxers high enough that she could see them, then said, "That's what I thought."

"Are you sure?" he joked. "You want to double-check?"

To his surprise she popped open the snap of his jeans and tugged his zipper halfway down. Then she looked into his eyes and grinned. "I see you like this game. I'm flattered."

"Yeah, feel free to ignore that."

With her finger she drew two dots above his navel, poked him in its center, and drew a semicircle beneath it. "Happy face," she said. Beside it she drew a downward arrow. "Right there."

"Not very. Can you draw a 'frustrated as hell' face?"

"You and me both."

"Oh, please. I don't get why girls say that. Walk up to any guy on this trip and tap him on the shoulder and he'd be glad to help you out with that."

She reached up and tapped him on the shoulder.

"Don't tease," he said. "It isn't nice."

She curled her whole hand around his waistband and tumbled him onto her. In the pure shock of it he pushed himself up on his arms, then looked into her face and kissed her without hesitation. As things escalated she began pressing his shoulders downward, then his head, and he wondered what strange wormhole the universe had opened up for him in which Fairen Ambrose was coaxing him to go down on her. But he was happy to roll with it. Ten minutes ago he had been getting a root beer for Temple; now the can sat on the night table, gradually moving toward room temperature while Zach cast off most of what remained of his naïveté. As he worked he felt her body wind tighter, tighter, unbearably so; and then, just as he thought she might push him away, she collapsed in a fury of obvious and wild pleasure. He rose to his knees in awe of what he had just made happen. It felt like a superpower.

"Get back up here," she said.

He crawled back up the bed and stretched his body over hers. She wrapped her legs around his, shrugging his loosened jeans even lower. As she tightened her grip he grew aware that the only thing stopping this from being sex was the presence of a single layer of cloth. He pressed his face into her neck and growled in frustration.

"Too bad we don't have a condom," she said.

"Oh, I've got one," he replied. His voice was muffled by his lips against her throat.

"Seriously?"

He reached into his pocket to produce the one he always carried under strict orders from Rhianne, and held it up between two fingers.

"Oh, goody," she said. "Put it on."

He gladly obeyed. As he made the necessary preparations she turned onto her stomach and looked back over her shoulder at him kneeling behind her, and when he met her eye he felt himself seized by the sense that they were nothing but two animals rutting in the woods, driven to mate—without any higher purpose, without any sense of propriety or time. He started out as gently as he could, but he had been on edge before they even started, and as his control slipped away he grabbed her hair roughly into a ponytail and, teeth gritted, let his instincts overtake him.

The image that lingered—behind his closed lids and, later on, in his dreaming mind—was the look on her face when he twisted his fist in her hair: nose wrinkled, canines bared. It was *sex*. She had looked that way for only him, because of him. No matter what else happened, that was his to keep.

9

Zach found it intoxicating, this discovery of what his body could do to a girl. He thought of nothing else during the first three-hour stretch of the drive back to Maryland. He had hoped to wrangle a seat in the car in which Fairen was riding, but after his disappointment ebbed, he decided it had been fortunate. It would be difficult to sit next to her, maintain an appearance of propriety, and not go insane. He had not seen her since he left her room the night before, and he knew this was in his best interest. If she could see the depth of his lust or the magnitude of his desire to be with her again—and again and again—she might feel put off. He knew little about the nature of girls, but one thing he did know was that nothing derailed a relationship faster than an imbalance of love—or any of its close relatives.

And so he stared out the window at the stubbled cornfields and called up, over and over, the shape of her body. The flare of her shoulders above her shoulder blades, shapely as wings; her small round navel between angular hipbones; the scooping shadows between her belly and thighs. He thought of her face, the fine twin points of her top lip above the curvaceous lower one, her knowing eyes and fine brown lashes, the way her silver earrings climbed the edges of her pale ears like filigree.

He was in no mood for conversation, but it didn't seem to matter. Scott gazed out the other window, headphones in place, probably wading around in similar thoughts about his own girlfriend, Tally. Exhausted from the night before, he fell asleep against the window and dreamed of her. Then the car's purring motor unexpectedly fell silent and he awoke with a start, disoriented and blinking at the sudden light.

They were at a rest station along the highway. Judy slammed her door, followed by Temple, who had been in the passenger seat beside her. Scott rested his head against the window, eyes closed, music in a fog around him. Zach smacked his arm lightly, and Scott opened his eyes.

"Rest stop," Zach said.

Scott shrugged. "I'll stay here. Get me a Coke, will you?"

Zach unfolded his stiff muscles and headed into the building. He made his way to the bathroom, then washed his hands and caught up with the rest of the group. The whole caravan of Madrigals kids was gathered by the pizza shop in the food-court area. When he saw Fairen looking at the menu above the cash registers, he approached her from behind and poked her in the waist with both index fingers.

"How're you doing?" he asked.

She shrugged. "Okay. Tired."

"You and me both." He glanced around to be sure no one was paying attention to their conversation, then said in a low voice, "I keep thinking about last night."

She smiled, but her smile seemed thin. "Yeah, pretty crazy."

"Yep. Not in a bad way."

Abruptly, she turned and began to walk away. He pursued her and, catching up, grabbed her wrist to get her attention.

She jerked it from his grasp and when she turned her hard eyes on him he gazed back full of dismay.

"Give me some space, will you?" she snapped. "It wasn't very nice, what you did."

"What did I do?"

"Pulling on my hair like that. I wasn't going anywhere, you know. There was no need to treat me like a freakin' farm animal."

The crowds of people moving all around them seemed to exist in a different world. Zach was alone, with only Fairen standing across from him with her strange stony stare, barking words at him that made no sense. After the silence in which he struggled to gather his thoughts he asked, "Well, why didn't you say anything then? Or after?"

"Because I'm bigger than that. I'm not going to bitch you out and make it awkward. But it's done now, all right? So give me *space*."

"I'm sorry." He stuffed his hands in his pockets and squinted at her, his head tipping, entreating her to forgive him. "Really, I'm sorry."

The sidelong look she offered failed to absolve him. She disappeared into the crowd of Madrigals gathered in front of the pizza stand. He stayed in place, his feet unwilling to move, his rumbling stomach unexpectedly silent. With pizza in hand she walked past him, back to the car she had been traveling in, without even acknowledging him. By the time he slammed the car door and handed Scott his soda, he felt bewildered almost to tears.

Back on the highway, Judy turned on some crap '70s music. He fished his CD player out of his backpack and put on the headphones, turning up the Goo Goo Dolls loud enough to drown out her purple hippie haze. By the time it reached the eleventh track, he had himself so worked up that the despondent lyrics of "Iris" were intolerable. He shut off the player, tore the headphones from his ears, and chucked the whole setup into his backpack.

"You okay back there?" asked Judy.

Temple was asleep, his head lolling against the window. Scott was still gazing out at the landscape through half-closed eyes, portable CD player spinning. In a grudging voice Zach replied, "Yeah."

"You've been very quiet."

"I'm tired."

"I think you ought to stay home tomorrow and sleep in. You can tell your teachers I told you to cut class."

He indulged her with a half smile. Keeping her eyes on the road, she reached back and patted him on the thigh. It was enough to remind him that he wasn't repugnant to every woman on earth, only to one, and that lifted his spirits very slightly. He looked at Judy's mild expression, her hands back at ten and two on the wheel, and considered how crazy it was that inside that Suzy Homemaker exterior was a woman who'd grab his ass while tongue-kissing him in a room where they could easily have been caught. Suddenly he laughed. He said, "Turn up the radio."

She twisted the dial. "Do you like this song?"

"Like it? I love it. I love the Lemonheads." Sometimes the radio seemed to be possessed. It could read his mind.

She grinned. "It's not the Lemonheads, it's Simon and Gar-funkel."

"It's 'Mrs. Robinson,'" he insisted. "It's a Lemonheads song. I'm sure of it."

"Then they must have covered it, because this is Simon and Garfunkel. They're not going to play the Lemonheads on an oldies rock station. And I remember this song from when I was your age."

He gave up the argument. She was probably right; what he had mistaken for an unfamiliar version of the CD track was starting to sound more folksy than live. Still, the coincidence was uncanny. He glanced at Temple and at Scott, and then, satisfied that they were too brain-dead to be listening, asked, "Do you know what it's about?"

"Sure I do. Do you?"

He worked up his nerve and said, "It's about an older woman who's into younger guys."

She laughed. "Everyone thinks that, just because they played it in *The Graduate*. But that's not it at all. That's got nothing to do with it."

"What do you think it's about, then?"

Her fingers flexed on the steering wheel. She glanced at him in the rearview mirror and said, "It's about a woman who's going crazy. She's trapped in the suburbs and in her crappy marriage and she's losing it."

He nodded. Her interpretation wasn't as interesting as his. He said, "Ah."

"Or rather, she's lost it."

He looked at her, at the funny smile she had on her face, her eyes properly focused on the road. She laughed again and said, "Depressing, isn't it?"

"Yeah. I like my version better."

She rolled her window partially down. The sound of the wind crashed through the car, drowning out the music. She rested her elbow against the ledge and held her fingers up to the outside air, moving them as if to better feel the wind. "Maybe it's both," she said. "Would you blame her?"

On Monday afternoon Dan lingered in my classroom when he came to pick up Aidan. As the other children left, one by one, with their parents and caregivers, I regarded him with a combination of curiosity and dread.

"How was the choir trip?" he asked.

"Very nice. The kids took second place."

"Didn't destroy any hotel rooms, did they?"

I acknowledged this with a quick laugh. "Of course not. Model citizens, every one of them."

"I expect you had a better weekend than I did, then." He glanced toward the hallway, then at his son, placidly playing with toy animals on the carpet. "The auditor from the Department of Health called me on Friday. She wants us to voluntarily close the school for a week until the measles infections subside. I told her no."

"Tell her yes," I said immediately. "Whatever it takes to appease them."

"We can't do that, Judy." His tone disparaged my solution, making him sound, for the moment, much like Russ. "I'll have fifty parents in here asking for prorated refunds of their tuition dollars. The kids who've had their shots aren't at risk, and the others have probably been exposed already. A closure won't make any difference at all."

I shrugged. "I think it's a ridiculous situation, any way you look at it. The school has no control over whether parents vaccinate their children. All we can do is get our paperwork in order, and beyond that, no one can hold us accountable for the decisions of the parents."

"That doesn't mean we won't turn into the piñata for it anyway. And if our enrollment numbers are down next fall, we're pretty screwed."

"We're always pretty screwed. We get by."

The skin around his eyes creased with irritation. "Maybe your definition of screwed is different from mine. I mean the kind where we *don't* get by."

I laughed. "How are those class ring sales going, by the way?"

"Don't take a dig at me. I'm doing all I can. But I need your help. We have two events coming up."

"The Martinmas lantern walk and the bazaar."

"Yes. I understand Bobbie Garrison was usually the one to handle the lantern walk, and that you sometimes assisted—"

"*Always* assisted. She and I have worked together on projects since college. *Had* worked. Whichever." I waved a hand to dismiss my jumbling of tenses. It was a common problem in speaking of Bobbie, the way I shuffled and crunched through words like leaves in various stages of decay.

"Yes, well, obviously we need extra hands to take care of it this year, since she's not around to do it."

"She's not, indeed," I said coolly. "She's unavailable."

He held my gaze with an expression of superhuman patience. "And I know the faculty feels her loss very deeply. If you can take over the planning, that would be a huge help. Make it a tribute to her. I think everybody would appreciate that."

"I'd like that."

"And this year it's very important that we put the event out to the community. Call the local newspapers and see if they'll send photographers. Advertise the bazaar everyplace that makes sense. And for the lantern walk, we need to try to get as many kids to show up as humanly possible. I'm worried that the school is starting to look undesirable. That will be death for us next year unless we turn it around."

I nodded. "I'll do everything I can."

His words were slow, carefully chosen. "I recognize...that your kindergarten is what compels most of our parents to enroll their kids in Sylvania Waldorf. It comes recommended, then exceeds their expectations. I don't always agree with you about the direction of the school—"

"You don't *often* agree with me," I corrected.

He laughed uneasily. "True. But I do recognize that the strength of a Waldorf kindergarten will make or break the school. And so I...*honor* what you offer us."

"Thank you." Behind him, the door opened and Zach sauntered in, wearing a black Led Zeppelin T-shirt printed with an image of Icarus arching toward the sky. He hooked his thumbs in his jeans pockets and approached me, smiling.

"Howdy, Teach," he greeted me.

"Mr. Patterson," replied Dan with enthusiasm. "How goes school?"

"Fine. Good."

"Are you getting a lot done on the bazaar?"

Zach nodded. His hair slipped into his eyes. "It's going better than usual this year," I interjected. "We have quite a few donations from the community. Massage certificates, doll-making, things like that. And the crafts are starting to come in. The third grade made some beautiful beeswax candles."

Dan smiled. "And we have that playhouse you built for us, Zach. That'll bring in some excellent bids. It's a wonderful job you did."

"Thanks. My dad's a carpenter. I've been doing that stuff, like, forever."

Dan nodded and clapped him on the shoulder. "Very good. Keep up the good work."

He departed, leaving my classroom door ajar. As soon as he was out of earshot I turned to Zach and asked, "What do you think you're doing?"

He widened his eyes and grimaced, shoulders twitching uneasily, the body language teenagers always use to let an adult know she's crazy. "Asking you for my next job," he told me.

"I told you I was going to sign off on all your service hours."

"Yeah, but I didn't think you *meant* it. You can't give me a free pass on a graduation requirement just because you made out with me."

I closed my eyes and tried to gather my flagging patience. "Zachary, I thought we agreed we were going to forget all about that."

He shrugged. "That's fine. But, like, if I expected you to sign off on me when I didn't do all the work, then I wouldn't be forgetting about it, right? I really would be whoring myself out."

"Zach."

"I'm just saying." He caught my pleading gaze and shrugged again. "I'm showing character and integrity."

I sighed. "Don't come to my classroom, all right? I'll give you the work, but you can come by my house to talk to me about it. When you come waltzing in here when Dr. Beckett's speaking with me, it looks suspicious."

His laughter mocked me. "And me coming over to your house wouldn't? C'mon. He knows I'm working with you. He's the one who set the whole thing up. Don't be paranoid."

I considered his reasoning for only a second, then shook my head. "Sorry. I don't feel very reassured."

"That's because you're paranoid."

He looked at me from under those shaggy bangs, and the impishness in his gaze was the same as the first time I'd looked at him in my rearview mirror, chastising him for his dirty joke. Now I took in the irreverence in his eyes, the mild humor in his smile, and considered the curious nature of his draw to me. In Ohio, secure at the end of Fairen's invisible

leash, he had seemed so young that I wondered at my sanity
for ever having engaged with him. But there would come the
moments, as now, when his eyes would snap sharply, know-
ingly, or he would stretch his lean body with that peculiar
confident grace, that *conscious* grace—and I could feel the
rumbling thunder of the man he would become, and the urge
to reach for it like a soap bubble I knew would be destroyed
in the grabbing. It was something I needed to resolve.

"I don't think this is the right place to discuss this," I told
him. "Do you mind if we finish this conversation somewhere
else?"

"Depends," he parried. "Are you going to buy me coffee?"

In Judy's car he slid the seat back, ostensibly to make more
legroom, but really so he could watch her in a covert way.
Thinking about Fairen, about Ohio, brought on a gloomy,
cloudy feeling, yet a quick segue to the memory of his return-
trip conversation with Judy lightened his mind. In the days
that followed he had spent a fair amount of time teasing out
the subtext of their "Mrs. Robinson" conversation, weighing it against his memories of her response in the playhouse,
and concluding that, for all her uptight frowning and prissy
apologies, she didn't regret it at all and would eagerly do it
again given the opportunity. The concept was, at once, both
dangerous and delectable. It was a rush.

At Starbucks he leaned against the rounded counter of the
service area, watching Judy as she paid, and tried to gain
some measure of how his theories might find root in reality. Not for the first time, he felt doubtful. Her face—wide
at the cheekbones, tapering to a small childlike chin—had a
youthful quality to its shape, but around her eyes and forehead
she was unmistakably forty-something, unimpressed with the
world and a little tired. Her long dark hair was interspersed

with coarser gray strands. She was not the sort of middle-aged woman with bleached hair and a push-up bra, staking out the pool boy in a loose towel. And yet there was something about her—in her slim body, perhaps, or the tight mouselike way she moved—that spoke of a keyed-up part of her, a hair trigger that, by chance, hadn't been knocked in a while.

He wondered, in an idle way, how many lovers she had had. How long it had been for her, or, for that matter, how recently.

All the tables were crammed with teens recently released from the public high school; Zach knew there was no chance they could sit and talk, as Judy had planned. The barista handed him his coffee, and Judy, in her efficient way, took hers as she walked past and moved straight out the door.

As they climbed back into her car she shook her hair back and said, "Do I need to just take you home, then? That took longer than I expected."

"Nah. It's better if I drink this first. My mom doesn't like it when I drink coffee. She says the caffeine is bad for my bone development."

She smiled. "That doesn't surprise me, after what you said about my fridge."

"Yeah. My parents are really big on that stuff. I was a vegetarian until I was fourteen. My folks still are. But once I hit puberty I started craving meat, even though I'd never had it. So I took that as a sign." He sipped his coffee. "I'll probably go back to it once I stop growing, though. It's, like, ingrained."

"The nutrition part, or the cruelty-to-animals part?"

"Both." They were parked perpendicular to the storefront, and he watched the people walking in and out, focused only on caffeine. "My parents are major pacifists. They had a hard time with it when I was five and I desperately wanted to take karate. We compromised on judo because the principle is to use your opponent's force against them. They were okay with that." He set his knee against the dashboard. "My mom tried to get me into yoga instead, but it didn't really take. She's a yoga teacher, you know."

"No, I didn't know."

"Yeah. She's been taking me with her to her classes since I was born. I'm good at it, it's just not my thing. But even she's not doing it right now, since the midwife put her on bed rest."

Judy nodded. "How's she feeling these days, your mom?"

"Tired of being pregnant. She's going stir-crazy. The midwife warned her if she doesn't settle down she'll hurt herself and won't be able to have the baby at home, and that kind of freaked her out. She doesn't want to go to a hospital."

"I can understand that. Maggie and Scott were both born at home."

"I was, too. So she wants that, but she also believes in wellness over illness and she says being in bed all day is terrible for her circulation. She's always talking my dad into giving her foot rubs to get her *chi* moving."

Judy sighed and leaned back, both hands around her coffee. "I wish someone would do that for me. The only time I sit down all day is for storytelling. It's like being a waitress."

"I can rub them," he offered.

She laughed. "I don't think so. The point of this coffee run is to lay out some professional boundaries, not to get my feet massaged by you."

"Don't make a big deal out of it. I give them to my mom all the time. I know reflexology. My dad taught me."

She gave him a doubtful look.

"Nobody's watching," he said. "C'mon."

He turned in the seat to face her and held out his hands. With a sigh, she slipped her foot out of its shoe and set it on his knee. He pulled it onto his lap and began with his thumbs beneath the first and second toes.

"The different areas correspond to different parts of the body," he explained. He moved his thumbs around, demonstrating. "Lungs. Liver. Stomach. Massaging removes obstacles that block your *chi*."

"There's definitely something blocking my *chi* these days."

"Maybe it's your kidneys." He rubbed a spot at the center of her foot. "The Chinese believe the kidneys hold massive amounts of *chi*. Do you feel anything?"

"I don't know about my kidneys. It feels good, though."

He worked his way down to her heel, then back up, rubbing between each toe. She relaxed against the door and closed her eyes, shoulders easing backward, and he grinned.

"See, it's working," he said. "You're starting to melt."

She laughed. "It must be my kidneys."

Her foot arched in his hand; feeling the response of her body aroused him. He moved his fingers lightly up her Achilles tendon to her ankle, massaging around the small bones. She did not twitch or pull away; instead, she stretched her calf to give him more room to work.

"You know you can give a woman an orgasm if you rub a certain way?" he asked, and her eyes opened, following her rising brows. He walked his fingers around her foot in the pattern he had read about. "It's like, ankle, stretch, thumbnail up the arch. Repeat."

"Have you ever done it?"

He grinned and rubbed the back of her calf. Still, she didn't flinch. "No. Do you want me to try?"

"Let's not," she said, but left her foot where it was.

He ran his nail up the midline of her foot, and her toes curled. "Come on," he pressed. "I won't tell anyone if it works."

Her gaze drifted to the customers outside the Starbucks. He realized, with an electric thrill, that she was considering it. Teasingly he added, "I bet that's what's blocking your *chi*."

One of her eyebrows went up. "If it was, would it be any of your business?"

"I don't know. Do you want it to be?"

She smiled, but it looked thin, even bitter. "You don't pay much attention to the news, my friend," she informed him, and the familiar phrase caught him by surprise. Quietly she continued, "And this is what I wanted to talk to you about. People go to jail for things like this, Zach. Women do. Teachers do. Somebody always finds out."

"They go to jail for getting their feet rubbed?"

"No. They go to jail for getting involved with students. And only one party ever gets blamed, no matter who instigates it. Do you know which party that would be?"

"You're not involved with me, though."

Her cheeks lifted in the slightest hint of amusement. "You just propositioned my feet."

"They're just feet."

"But that's not the kind of foot rub you give your mother, now is it?"

"No, but my mother doesn't stick her tongue down my throat, either."

Her smile grew weary and she tugged her leg from his grasp. "I need to take you home. I don't think your mother would want to have any role in this conversation."

"You might be surprised. She's not as uptight as you think."

Judy slid her foot back into her shoe. "Well, I know a little more about mothers than you do."

The condescension in her tone made him feel small. He knew a thing or two about adults and their secrets, and he was tired of them—his own parents in particular—acting like he was too naïve to make even the most obvious connections. "You don't know much about *my* mother," he countered. "She's not uptight at all. She cheated on my dad with one of her yoga students."

She narrowed her eyes. "What?"

"She did. A guy who was in her Dynamics class." Zach knew the man's name, but couldn't bring himself to say it. Ponytailed, with thin, hairy legs, he often came to class in a shirt printed with John Lennon's face and the caption, "Long Live Dr. Winston O'Boogie." Over time Zach came to think of him by a private nickname: Booger.

"He wasn't a kid or anything," Zach continued. "He was probably like 28 or 29. I think that's one of the reasons why she was so gung-ho about moving away from New Hampshire. He was still at her studio and I think she felt weird about being pregnant around him."

Judy nodded as though none of this surprised her, and her unimpressed reaction both disappointed and soothed him. Perhaps the act he had seen as a gross betrayal, a secret calamity, was normal enough in the world of adults; perhaps he had overreacted. She asked, "Is he the father of the baby?"

"I don't think so. I'm pretty sure they broke it off awhile before that. I think." He hoped. "We moved in June, and I hadn't seen him at the studio since the fall. But I was doing judo after school most days, so I don't know. I didn't want to see anything I'd feel obligated to tell my dad about, so I kind of avoided the studio once I figured out what was going on."

Her laugh was full of grim understanding. "I did the same thing when I was young and realized my father was having an affair with our housekeeper. Oh, I was so angry. And I blamed *her,* really, not him. He could do no wrong, because he was my father. But *her*—oh, watch your back, sweetheart."

He chuckled. "Yeah, same here. Hey. Give me your other foot."

She plunked it onto his lap. "How did you figure it out?"

He shrugged and began to massage her sole. "I just knew. There wasn't any one blazing moment where I caught them in the act or anything. It's just that there's a certain amount of touching that goes on between yoga teachers and their students. You get familiar with it, so you can tell when it goes beyond what's normal. And it was definitely beyond normal."

"Maybe you did see it, and you blocked it out."

He worked his fingers down the middle of her foot, and frowned. "What do you mean?"

"I mean maybe you *did* catch them in the act, and you just don't remember. I think that happened to me. I remember coming home and finding the house empty, and turning the doorknob to my father's room, and then running down the path, crying. After that I knew to stay out of the house when she was there. But I didn't see a thing, not that I recall." She drew an oval in the air in front of her forehead. "It's as though, in the filmstrip of that sequence of events, that part of the film was exposed. Not that I'm complaining. If it was that traumatic, I'm sure it's better if I don't recall it. I've got enough odds and ends knocking around in there."

He shook his head. "I don't think that happened to me. I'd be pretty messed up if it did, and I don't think I'm too messed up."

"I don't know about that," she said, and he grinned. "I've never had to pull a student aside before to ask him to mind his manners with me. Can we come to an agreement about that, please? Because I'd rather shake hands on it now than have to do my Mussolini impression down the road."

"Maybe I'd like your Mussolini impression."

"Oh, stop it. Come on now."

It was like a judo match: find your opponent's point of weakness, and exploit it. Judy's was easy to identify: the words marching dutifully out of her mouth didn't match the supple way her muscles responded to his touch. She had rested against his thigh a small model of what the rest of her body would do, were it not for the little problem of propriety.

Her gaze was firm, and he met it easily, still smiling. He moved his hand slowly over her foot: *ankle. Stretch. Thumbnail up the arch.*

She stretched her toes in a fan, and smirked.

Repeat.

Repeat.

She lifted her foot from its resting place on his leg. Slowly, she ran it along his inner thigh. It came to rest at the front of his jeans, and only when she nestled it against him did he pull his breath in through his teeth. His hand flew to caress the part that caressed him. He tried, and failed, to control the urge to arch against the counterpressure. In the moment of blinding arousal his head tipped back against the closed window and, faintly, hurt.

"Stop screwing with me, Zach," she said, her voice low but infused with a wavering note that was almost like fear. "I mean it. It's not cute and it's not funny. It's my fucking *job*. It's my reputation. I'm not going to throw it all away so you can play seduce-the-teacher. Because you wouldn't know what to do with me even if it worked."

Her foot retreated, and she pushed it down into its shoe. He shifted back into his seat and combed his hair over his eyes. As the engine turned over, he said, "Sorry."

"No problem," she said, and crazily, her voice was light and pleasant. "So. There's a box of woolen sheep in my closet that need price stickers. You can come by and get them tomorrow afternoon."

"Come by your classroom, you mean?"

"Sure." She turned her face toward him and smiled, as though nothing had transpired. "I don't see why not."

IO

During our second year of college, long before either Bobbie or I had heard about a thing called Waldorf school or realized we would make a little life together teaching in one, we shared a dormitory room decorated with my *Last Tango in Paris* poster and her collection of monkeys of all kinds—plush, balsa wood, jade, coconut shell, cartoon. Her late mother had sewed her two matching twin-sized quilts covered in tiny rosettes of calico, and these we spread on our beds on opposite sides of the little room. The year before, our schedules had been nearly identical—we were both elementary education majors. Sophomore year we had no classes together, but shared two of the same professors, one of whom had something of a reputation.

"He's a lech," Bobbie warned me early in the spring. "One of my friends had him last year. He'll try to make you buy your A."

"With what?"

"Blankets and beads. What do you think? If you go to talk to him, keep a good distance." She gestured a wide arc around her body. "Room for the Holy Ghost, as the nuns used to say. Or else he tries to do that trick on you like your mother probably did with the cantaloupe."

My mother had never done that trick with the cantaloupe, but I had an idea of what she meant. "What if he scoots in and does it anyway?" I asked. "He's the professor," I added, because at that point in my life I had not yet attended enough Women's Lib rallies to understand I was a little behind the times.

"Kick him in the balls," she suggested.

I laughed rather hysterically. "I could *never* do that," I told her. It was not that I didn't understand revenge. I did, and quite well; perhaps *too* well. The type that came easily to me was that which was quiet, which comes from the side, which might seem, through squinted eyes, like an act of God. What I could not imagine was the sort of violence where one looks another person in the eye and watches him suffer. It seemed barbaric, and more importantly, not my style.

I had thought about that when Zach stroked my foot as it rested on his thigh, massaging its inside arch between his thumb and index finger like my breast in that professor's hand. I hadn't kicked that man as Bobbie instructed. But I was older now, and I knew there existed more interesting varieties of pain than a knee planted in the groin. There was the kind that shut down all pleasure, and the kind that came folded in with it.

By the time I returned home from our Starbucks trip I felt confident and a little victorious. With Scott out with his girlfriend and Russ still at the office, I ascended the stairs to my room, dragging behind me the suitcase from Ohio that had been sitting in the dining room since my return. In a month or so Russ would be flying to Iceland for a research trip, and as much as I avoided his office at all costs, I would

be considerate enough to finally reunite it with the others in
the set so he wouldn't have to hunt for the right size. The door
creaked on its hinges and I shied back, as if he were home to
hear me. Straight back was the old sofa, sagging in the center
of each cushion; beside it sat a pile of professional journals
marked with yellow sticky notes. Against the windowless wall
stood a battered desk the color of milky coffee, his computer
in the center like a one-eyed heathen god perched on its
shrine. While his office at the university offered a bit of décor
that suggested a higher purpose for the work therein—photos
of rugged crab fishermen earning a living, the beauty of nature along the fragile Arctic coast—his home office dispensed
with such fripperies. I crossed the dingy carpet to the closet
and tugged the largest black suitcase from its spot beneath a
copy-paper box and a pile of sweaters.

As I dropped it on its side, it hit the floor with a noisy
rattle like a child's toy instrument. Strange. Unzipping it, I
found a plastic grocery bag with the handles all tied together;
inside were a jumble of white medication bottles. I tried to
remember where they could have come from. Russ's root
canal earlier this year? Or perhaps they had belonged to my
mother before her death several years ago, and someone had
stuffed them in here after we cleaned out her house? It seemed
odd that they were not amber prescription bottles, but the
type which sit on a pharmacist's shelf, large and labeled only
with the drug information.

Valium. Xanax. Dexedrine. Nembutal.

I looked up at Russ's computer, then at the Xanax bottle in
my hand. For a moment I just stood there, reading the labels
in confusion. Then it slowly dawned on me that these bottles
had not been set aside and forgotten. They had been hidden.

I zipped the smaller suitcase inside the larger one and put
them properly away. Then I lifted the grocery bag and took

the whole mess downstairs, feeling nothing more than a bit of curiosity and a small, germinating seed of anger.

Russ came home just past nine-thirty. He looked surprised to find me seated in the rocking chair by the fireplace, watching the door. Tiny rectangles of light glinted off his glasses as he tipped his head to peer at me over them—progressive lenses were just around the corner for him—but then he dropped his black shoulder bag onto the floor and headed toward the kitchen.

"Russ," I said, and the dark, syrupy note to my voice caused him to stop and turn.

"I was putting a suitcase away in your office today," I began, "and I found some things in the closet I think might be yours."

His reply was hostile. "What were you doing in my office?"

"Putting away a suitcase. I just said that."

"It's *my* office. You shouldn't be in there."

"I pay the mortgage, too, dear."

"Not much of it."

I hefted the bag from the floor beside me and set it on the coffee table. It had occurred to me that the medications might, in fact, be Scott's. He was a clever enough kid to hide things in plain sight, and enterprising enough to try it as a business venture. But it could have been either of them, for what did I know of this type of drug use? When I was Scott's age, drugs didn't come from a lab. They grew on farms, or in my case, in a series of buckets under Gro-Lites in the root cellar of a house around the corner from the deli.

"That's not yours," he said.

"I realize that."

"*God,* Judy," he said, explosive all of a sudden, his face wrenched, arms flying out at his sides. "I get home from a long day at work and you *dump* this shit on me. Get a fucking *hobby,* why don't you. I work like a dog all day. I don't need this."

"So they're yours, then? Not Scott's?"

He half turned toward the hallway again and curled his lip at me. "As if you'd be in a position to judge Scott or anybody else. The Queen Stoner herself. Our Lady of Recreational Pharmaceuticals."

I regarded him with an indifferent glare, and he snatched the bag from the table. "Stay out of my office," he ordered.

"Better hope you don't get caught driving on that stuff," I warned. "I won't be bailing you out. You can sit and rot for all I care."

"I wouldn't call you. Why would I? You haven't given two shits about me in years. I'd call my lawyer."

He hustled up the stairs with his stash, and I rocked my chair gently. A year ago this conversation would have gone very differently—screaming, begging, tears. But my eyes felt utterly dry. Something inside me felt ready for war.

Eight months, I thought. Only that long until Scott graduated from Sylvania. A year from now I could be anywhere in the world. I would be free.

I feared I wouldn't even know where to begin.

Monday wasn't going well for Zach. At the top of his chemistry test was a red-penned note: *See me.* Fairen was ignoring him, flirting with a guy from the swim team. He couldn't even go straight home that afternoon, obligated as he was to stop by Judy's classroom to pick up some bazaar-related advertising sign he was supposed to repaint. And although he had grown to like *Parzival,* the previous English unit, *Dante's Inferno* was doing nothing for him. He didn't get it.

The concept of Hell bored him. He didn't care if Dante's

view was progressive for its time or deeply personal or raised questions about society. He just didn't give a shit. Also, he didn't like having to examine Francesca's adultery and how her lust for Paolo showed a "weakness of will." He preferred to think about lust on the following terms: you wanted someone, and they said yes or no. Francesca's miserable sham of a marriage made it even less explicable why she and her lover ended up in anyone's version of Hell. Zach believed to his core that the world was ultimately fair. With the obvious exception of his father, he believed if some other guy was balling your wife, odds were on some level you deserved it.

He endured the afternoon. He endured Dante. As soon as class was dismissed he chucked his backpack onto his shoulder and brushed past his classmates. He pushed through the door of the Lower School and made his way to Judy's classroom, where she was bidding farewell to a little kid whose nanny had to be at least twenty minutes late.

He leaned against the wall and waited for the nanny to quit arguing with Judy and leave. Russian accent, long unfashionable braid, chunky ass in shorts with legs cut too wide to look normal on a woman in her twenties: she didn't pay the tuition bill, and Judy's curt reminders about the schedule betrayed that she was aware of this. He controlled a smile and bounced his heel against the floor impatiently. Finally the woman left.

"And you," Judy sighed, turning to face him. "Zachary Xiang. What can I do for you?"

"I'm supposed to pick up a sign."

She blinked and shook her head in irritated confusion. "Sign. What sign?"

"Some wooden sign that goes by the side of the road to tell people when the bazaar is. That lady in charge told me I have to repaint it."

"Am I supposed to have this item in my possession?"

He shrugged loosely. "She said you had it in a closet or something."

"Oh, God." She turned and walked toward the back of the classroom, where a closet door stood ajar. Her hair, dark brown and trailing all the way to her waist, looked ratty at the ends and in need of brushing. She stepped into the shallow closet, moved a couple of baskets, pushed aside the faded spare dress-up robes that hung on hooks on the wall, and said, "I have no idea where it is. Check back tomorrow and maybe I'll have found it. Maybe. If I get around to it."

"What's the matter with *you?*"

"The matter with *me?* I've had the weekend from hell. Would you like to hear about it?"

"Not really. I'm reading *Dante's* fucking *Inferno.* I doubt you can top that."

"Dante's Fucking Inferno," she repeated. "Sounds like they've updated it since I was a girl."

In spite of himself, he broke into a grin. "Bad teacher. Some example you're setting. First the gnomes and now this."

She raised her eyebrows high and, with a comical wide-eyed glare, latched the closet door. "Fuck the gnomes," she replied.

"Listen to you," he marveled. "Your *chi* is *messed up.*"

"So," she said crisply. "Tell me where this happy hunting ground is that you've found for acorns. Because I need to get this craft project underway, and I'd like to drive out there this afternoon while I have time."

"These woods behind a town house development. It's not far."

"Where is it?"

"Off Pine Road. By the abandoned hospital."

"What abandoned hospital?"

He sighed and glanced out the window at the sun still

relatively high in the sky. "I can't explain it exactly. I guess I can ride along and show you if you want. If you count it toward my hours."

She hoisted her purse onto her shoulder and hooked a sweater over her arm. "I count everything toward your hours. You know that."

He snorted a laugh. "You told me to stop making jokes about that."

"Well, I'm in a mood." Her thin slippers slapped the floor as she made her brisk walk out the door. "Follow me. I'm parked around the side."

The air was still summer-warm, at least what would qualify as summer-warm in New Hampshire. As she drove, she hummed along with Joan Baez on the radio; he popped a piece of gum in his mouth and endured the music. When the roads grew smaller he offered directions, guiding her through the subdivision. They parked at the edge of the lot, not far from the metal gate that stood between the end of the road and the woodland path. He slid the books out of his backpack and shouldered it so they would have a means to collect whatever they found.

"Up this way," he told her. He hiked up a steep embankment into the woods and heard her footsteps behind him. As they wound their way between the trees, he added, "They say there's a guy in a rabbit suit who haunts all around here. They call him the Bunny Man."

"The things people come up with," she said. "It sounds like a German children's book character. When I was a girl they would have put him in a story to warn us about the perils of sleeping with stuffed animals for too long, or eating too much Easter candy, or something."

Zach laughed. "It's definitely not for kids. He's supposed to carry around an axe."

"All the better. The one we had in the book I read as a child was a boy with claws and ghoul eyes. '*Der Struwwelpeter,* here he stands, with his dirty hair and hands.'" She wrinkled her nose at him in a jesting sneer and raised her tensed hands. "Don't forget to cut your fingernails, boys and girls. If you don't, you'll turn into a monster."

"That's messed up."

"You don't know the half of it," she said, but her voice was light. "I think it scarred me for life."

Zach replied with a broad grin. They had crested the hill and had to brace themselves for a descent toward a creek in the distance. The trees became farther apart, the brush thinning to almost nothing. When the land leveled off, Zach slowed and indicated the ground with a wave of his hand. "Here you go. All over the place."

She made a sound of delight and set to work scooping acorns into her palms. He set his backpack against a tree and crouched to help her. Before long the pack was half-filled, and Judy, now on her knees, still avidly swept acorns into her hands. He asked, "How many do we need, anyway?"

She peered at what she had collected. "Oh, that should be plenty. I'm so used to finding none that I didn't realize we'd gathered so many. And you still have leftovers from the play-house roof, don't you?"

"Some, yeah."

"Well, this should certainly do it." She set her hands on her hips and surveyed the ground with a look of satisfaction. He took the last few acorns in his hand and, rapid-fire, chucked them at her back.

"Hey, now," she said. She picked up a few and threw them back at him. He retaliated with several more, and then, dodging hers, slipped a handful down the back of her jumper. When she chased after him he took off, diving behind a tree just a moment too late to avoid catching one on the forehead; and then, with mock indignation, grabbed her around the waist and hauled her, squealing, back in the direction of the car. She was so *small,* barely more than five feet tall it seemed, and a hundred pounds at most. But she could kick like a girl gangbanger in a street fight, and got him in the shin so hard he winced.

"Damn," he said, setting her down. "You're strong for a midget."

She turned to face him and laughed. Her fingers were hooked in his belt loops—perhaps for balance, perhaps for the excuse to touch him, but either way, they were there. The sun, piercingly low in the sky, threw rays of light against her cheek. When he tipped his head and kissed her, he could not be sure who had instigated it. He knew only that her mouth felt as ardent beneath his as it had the first time, and his touch met with no resistance just as before, and when her hands slid down the back of his jeans he knew there was no one around who would knock at the door this time and put at end to it. The end rested wherever Judy determined it to be, because *he* certainly wasn't going to stop her.

Not a chance. Not when her mouth moved so quickly to his neck, his nipple, down the belly to—*she wouldn't, would she?*—release him from his boxers into the liquid heat of her mouth. The sound that escaped his throat was somewhere between a groan and a whimper, and she raised her gaze to meet his. At the dark hunger in her eyes the pleasure zigzagged wildly through his nerves, and in deference to his wavering knees he leaned back against the tree behind him.

"Lie down," she whispered.

He swallowed his gum and did as she asked. Leaves crackled beneath his head and heels. The aggressive sunlight needled through the trees. He laid his arm across his eyes, expecting her mouth again. But instead her palms plunked down beside each of his ears—one, two—and when he opened his eyes her hazel gaze locked with his, intent, calculating almost. Her dark hair blocked the sun like a tattered curtain.

She said, "If you want to say no, now's a good time."

He quickly recalibrated his expectations, wondering if his eyes betrayed his surprise. "I need to get a condom on," he warned her, uncertain still of her intent.

"Do you have one?"

"Yeah."

She smiled. "That answers my other question."

He wedged his fingers into his pocket. "What was it?"

"Whether you're a virgin."

"Nope."

"I can't tell you how happy I am to hear that," she told him dryly.

He felt his face break into a grin. Her nose wrinkled with pleasure, eyes squeezing shut, as she eased herself onto him, and he let the back of his head relax into his palms so he could watch her. The submissiveness alone was exquisitely relaxing; her inwardly drawn face changed endlessly above him, and its small movements mesmerized him, offering a blessed distraction. The weight of her body pressing him against the earth felt snug and comforting. Only when her back arched in the way he knew, tension shuddering, did he reach for her hips and allow his thoughts to narrow down to the sea-warm inner space of her, everywhere rounded, everywhere rose, into a guiltless and freely offered climax he couldn't have stopped if he tried. At the end of it he let his hands fall exhausted to his sides, *savasana,* and he laughed, looking up at her grinning face in sheer elation. He felt ready to conquer the whole fucking world.

II

1965
Mainbach, West Germany

Judy's father was skilled at many things. He was fluent in Russian, German and French, and conversant in several languages of the smaller Soviet republics. He knew everything about college basketball, played an excellent game of tennis, and could fold a square of paper into a little balloon that one could inflate with a puff of air. When they visited famous buildings he could point out the features of the architecture—*dentil, fret, triglyph*—and, when Judy grew tired of sightseeing, he could hoist her onto his back and carry her for seemingly infinite lengths of time, looping her knees over his arms that rested on each side of his trim waist. He could do anything, Judy was certain, that was of any importance.

It was not conceivable that he might do something which was terribly wrong. Kirsten, however, was a human like any other, and so onto her Judy projected a double helping of mute rage. The girl had always been kind to her, but now grew openly solicitous, asking in simple German whether Judy preferred ham or salami *butterbrot* for lunch with a look of rabbit-eyed fear. Her father never addressed what she had seen, and the events of that afternoon—the empty kitchen, the muffled squeaking, the violent shattering of her vision like a flashbulb in reverse—never repeated themselves; Judy might have finally shrugged it away as a bad dream had it not been for that look. The fear acknowledged the crime, and the crime made Judy writhe inwardly with her own unspeakable terrors: that her father would choose to return to the U.S. and abandon her mother, nodding and inert, to her small room at the military hospital. That he was not the father she knew at all, but a seething mess of primitive urges leaking out around the seams of his tennis whites. That Rudi's family would discover what their girl was up to and send the men over in a rage to match Judy's, pitting against each other the men she loved most.

Not that she had seen a great deal of Rudi that season. When she caught up with him in the barn he was as friendly as ever, but he did his chores expediently now. Not anymore did he linger to stroke the cow's nose or to show Judy how to fashion a few pieces of straw and a length of wool into a small star, telling her, as he turned it in his hands, the fairy tale about the generous girl who was showered with stars from heaven that turned into coins as they fell. She missed him awfully. One day when the air was warm and breezy she took the long way home from school, following the gray and winding road to the church behind which she and Rudi had gone sledding the winter before. Her two French braids, plaited by Kirsten that morning, still pulled tight against the skin of her temples; her folded socks were the whitest they had ever been. As she approached the church she could see, jutting from the ground at odd angles behind it, the tombstones of the old cemetery: lozenge and cross-shaped, decaying at the edges, flecked with moss. Between these she and Rudi had dragged their toboggan, moving among the dead as if through a crowd at the market. She remembered the weight of his body when they took a curve too tightly and tumbled into the snow. His gloved hand, grasping hers to pull her to her feet, was so strong. In her belly the ache set in. There would be no second winter with Rudi. By then Judy's family would be long gone.

For the first time, looking out over the cemetery, she noticed the grave markers at the base of the hill that lay flat against the ground. During the winter they had been covered in snow. The realization alarmed her for a moment before she shoved it aside in her mind. Human beings, after all—for this was the lesson she had gained from months of taking dictation from *Struwwelpeter*—got what was coming to them. One's fate was the consequence of one's actions, and the poorer the choices, the poorer the results. The dead had ended up there for a reason. And she was not to feel guilty if she and Rudi had treated their resting place as a playground, for it was the task of the living to look with a cool eye over the cautionary tales they represented, and shrug, and remember to eat one's soup and not play with matches or go out in rainstorms.

At the side of the church was a little stone chapel dedicated to the Virgin Mary. Judy leaned against the entryway and looked around inside. The little room was cool and quiet. On one side stood a black iron stand filled with flickering candles; straight ahead, two short pews offered visitors a place to sit or kneel. At the very back stood the statue of the Virgin, its stone pure white and soft-looking, like chalk. Beneath one of her feet was a crescent moon; beneath the other, a serpent. A crown of dull metal stars circled her head. Several times since the early spring Judy had made this journey, never crossing

the threshold but simply looking in—not quite with the de-
tachment her father showed toward such things, but not quite
with the belief of her classmates, either. Like an infant she had
begun to form the most primitive impressions of these human
icons, based formlessly on blind need. In the barn there was
Christ, under whom thrived warmth and friendliness and
raw gentle life. In this low stone building there stood Mary,
who commanded peace and quiet, who was a mother but
never trembled or stumbled or violated or *was* violated. The
human tribe owed its people one or two who were beyond
reprimand. One or two—and that was all—not subject to the
vagaries of the body or the mind, through whom the light
could slip as it does between immovable stones. Such people,
if they could be relied upon, would be the beginning and end
of everything. They would look down from heaven upon a
selfless girl, one who stood nearly naked beneath the stars,
and shower her with blessings. For the world was fair.

From the doorway, she whispered the *Ave Maria* her teacher
had taught her.

Then she hiked her rucksack higher on her shoulders and
walked home.

A *rat-a-tat* sound emerged from her house, faint at a distance, while Judy was still as far away as Rudi's place. The
noise ceased as she started up the walk that wound to the back
door. She pushed it open, and there on her mother's coffee
table stood a young woman of about Kirsten's age, gathering
her skirt while Kirsten knelt on the floor beside her with a
mouthful of pins. Kirsten barely looked up. "*Guten Tag,* Judy,"
she murmured through her closed lips, and continued pinning
up the hem.

"So that's his daughter," said the other girl, in German.
"She's small."

"She can understand you," Kirsten replied in a warning tone. To Judy she said, "This is Eva. She's a friend of mine."

Judy offered no greeting, letting her rucksack slip from her shoulders and thump to the floor beside the radiator. She had lately taken to leaving messes for Kirsten to clean up—harmless disorder for the most part, with occasional minor catastrophes for which Kirsten would be blamed. On the dining table sat a sewing machine, the one from the storage room, which Judy's mother had never used. Large scraps of cloth, eggshell white and sprigged with tiny pastel flowers, lay in heaps on the table. A pair of pinking shears sprawled open, like the gaping mouth of a wolf in a fairy tale. The rounds of its handles looked to Judy like cartoon eyes. She ran a finger across the line of triangles along the blade.

"Don't touch that, *Mausi,*" said Kirsten, using the nickname Judy had lately come to hate. Where once it had seemed so fond, it now seemed calculated to emphasize her insignificance.

She looked up at the girl who stood on her coffee table, bare-shouldered in the half-finished sundress. The girl's dark hair was neatly rolled and arranged. Her features were strong, with a shapely jaw and brows that made her eyes look daunting, but her bow-shaped mouth was almost petulant. She looked down at Kirsten's pinning and said, "I think you should make it shorter."

Kirsten gave a scandalized little cry. "*Eva.* Wouldn't be ladylike."

"Rudi would like it."

She laughed. "Oh, Rudi." With a few smacks at the base of the skirt to shake out the wrinkles, she added, "There. All straight now. Take it off."

Eva shrugged out of the dress, which Kirsten caught as it fell. Judy watched the young woman, clad only in her bra and

girdle, as she stepped down off the table and lit a cigarette.
She shook out the match and raised an eyebrow at Judy.

The sewing machine clattered on. Judy turned and walked
into the kitchen, which smelled, in a way that tingled in the
back of her throat, like sauerbraten. Very quietly she turned
off the burner beneath the Dutch oven, watching the small
blue flame diminish and then disappear. But that was too obvious. Kirsten would know she had turned it off to be spiteful.
It would be better if she turned the gas back on but left the
burner unlit, so it would look like a problem with the stove.
Kirsten would know better, but have no proof.

She turned the dial back to its previous setting, hearing the
very quiet hiss grow ever so faintly louder.

"Mausi."

She looked at Kirsten, whose gaze was locked on the rattling machine.

"Bring me the basket from the storage room. The one that
has the thread in it."

Judy stared at her impassively. *"Ich verstehe nicht."*

Kirsten looked up. "Yes, you do. You know what thread
is." She tapped the spool at the top of the machine.

With a reluctant shift of her shoulders through the doorway,
Judy headed down the hall to the storage room. The basket,
frilled at the top in calico, sat on the shelf directly ahead. She
passed it and turned the corner of the small, L-shaped room.
She kicked at an old typewriter sitting on the floor, then ran
her hand along the winter coats hanging from the rod: her
father's khaki trench coat, her mother's camel's-hair coat that
fell to her ankles and was now certainly too small, and her
own green wool coat with the deep cuffs. She pressed her face
into it and hoped to smell winter.

"Judy!" called Kirsten.

There was a murmuring of conversation. The other girl's

voice rose, and Judy heard the creak of footsteps moving across the floor. A moment later she heard a shriek.

Kirsten sounded alarmed. "What is it?"

"The gas is on, but the burner isn't lit. My God."

Judy stepped between the coats and, although hers hung mostly above her head, wrapped herself in its bottom. A moth fluttered out. She ducked against its gray, flapping wings, and then thought, *of course.* Her mother had not been in a state to put it in mothballs. By next winter it would be full of holes.

"Judy!" shouted Kirsten, this time with far greater urgency.

She spun around in the coat as if it were a cocoon, pulling until it came down from its hanger and wrapped around her torso. Below it her summer skirt lifted from her spinning, floating in a circle, like a dancer's.

On the last day of school, as soon as the bus dropped her off, Judy took off at a run down the country road toward her home. Her rucksack, empty but for a single book, thumped against the small of her back with each footfall. The trials of home were, for a few precious moments, forgotten. She carried two parting gifts from her teacher, who knew she would not be back for the following school year: the *Struwwelpeter* book, which she carried in her pack, and a large gingerbread heart with *Viel Glück* written on its face in jaunty pink icing. *A good-luck wish for our newest friend,* her teacher had declared, smiling upon Judy fondly. The heart, wrapped neatly in wax paper, she cradled against her body as she ran. She wanted to share it with Rudi, because she knew he liked gingerbread, and also because it was a heart. It smelled mouthwateringly of cinnamon and confectioner's sugar. When the barn came into view she picked up her flagging pace, crunching gravel beneath her saddle shoes as she cut across the driveway, then criss-crossed the perfectly manicured front lawn.

She shrugged off her rucksack by the gate and let herself into the barnyard. The barn door was ajar, buoying her hopes that he would be there. The white hens ignored her, scratching in the dust for hidden bugs. From an open window she heard Daniela's strident voice, an argument with her mother or father in vehement German that carried on the gusty breeze. The wind sucked the edges of the curtains outward, twisting them wildly like waving hands.

A metal rake stood propped beside the partly-opened barn door. Judy was thin enough to slide in without moving it, which was fortunate, because the hinges were old and tired and the heavy door usually stuck in a rut of mud. She gripped the gingerbread against her chest and stepped inside, pulling in her breath to call for Rudi; but before she could speak his name, she saw him right before her.

He was there, seated on a straw bale with his back to her, his shirt in a heap on the ground; straddling his lap was the girl who was Kirsten's friend, wearing the flower-sprigged dress Kirsten had sewn for her, its white crinoline flaring out on each side of Rudi's waist like two chrysanthemums. She was facing him, and Judy could see now that Rudi's disregard for the crucifix that hung above them was absolute: he kissed her with his hand behind her head and his mouth pressed hard against hers, so ardently that all the gentleness Judy knew of him was gone. The girl's hands traveled across the creamy skin of his back, her pace languorous, and when they circled around to the front of his pants he dropped his head back and disturbed the silence with a noisy, quivering sigh.

Judy took a large step back. One shoulder at a time, she retreated out the barn door. She let herself out through the wooden gate and threw the gingerbread heart into the mud. At home, Kirsten stood at a living room window, cleaning it with ammonia sprinkled onto a crumpled page from the

Stars & Stripes. The bow of her apron bobbed at her hip, and her feet were bare.

"*Guten Tag, Mausi,*" she greeted Judy.

"*Guten Tag,*" Judy replied. She looked into Kirsten's eyes and wondered how it is that a soldier fights and a savior suffers, but a woman, in lying down, rules everything.

12

Zach was a Pisces. I discovered this while rooting through his school file, not long after. It should have come as no surprise—I had already suspected as much by his nature, and his March birthdate only confirmed it—but I felt chagrined nonetheless. Sixteen and a half, and solidly so. I had hoped he was nearly seventeen, as if it made a difference.

Say no, I remembered imploring him. Because I knew the wrong was in my intention, and his was powerful enough to stop it. But he hadn't wanted to, and so there was nothing left to hold it back. The frenzied desire I felt for him surprised even me. I had thought I wasn't capable of it, all the way up until I crawled over him on all fours and knew I would have him or be consumed by what burned in me for him.

It took me no time at all to make an appointment with my midwives' practice, once I could no longer pretend I wasn't going to do what I had just done. I knew enough to understand I was out of my depth when it came to the contemporary rituals of birth control. Prior to the moment Ted produced a small foil packet from the night table, I had never seen an unwrapped condom that wasn't on a safe-sex poster. Russ had no use for the things, and my only other serious boyfriend, Marty, hadn't either. Back in the 1970s, the solution was simple: the woman went on the Pill, and that was that. Clearly Ted had caught up with the times, and now Zach had proven to be a devotee as well. But anything that could break or slip off provided too great a margin of error, by my accounting, especially when the stakes were as high as these.

As I signed my name on the clipboard at the front desk of the midwives' practice, I asked, "Is Lynnette here today?"

The heavy woman in the pastel-print scrubs didn't take her eyes off her computer screen. "No, she doesn't work here anymore."

I blinked. "She doesn't? Really? But she delivered both my kids."

The typist looked at me with a smile at the corner of her mouth, and I imagined she was gauging my age and thinking I was lucky if my midwife was still alive. "We have several excellent practitioners," she said dryly. "When were you last here?"

"About three years ago," I told her, chagrined. So much for my annual well-woman visit. I hadn't given it the slightest thought before last week.

"You'll be seeing Rhianne Volker today. She's new to our practice but has a lot of experience. I'm sure you'll like her." Her smile was not a reassurance so much as a period at the end of her sentence.

I sighed and took a seat. Once back in an examining room, I glanced around at the sterile surroundings and ruminated on how much more *medical* midwifery looked now than it did when I was having babies. Back then it all seemed touch-and-go in someone's converted spare bedroom, quilts and blood pressure cuffs competing for shelf space. I relished feeling comfortable with it, affirming to myself the naturalness of the birth experience. Now, I could hardly see the difference between this office and an obstetrician's.

The door opened and a short-haired woman came in, wearing a lab coat over a band T-shirt and jeans. "Hello, Judy," she said with a glance at my chart. "I don't think we've met. I'm Rhianne."

"I haven't been here in a while."

"Several years. Have you been anywhere else for your care?"

I grimaced. "No. I used to come every year like clockwork to get my birth control prescription renewed, mainly. But I haven't needed it in a while."

She sat in a molded chair and smiled. "And now you do."

"Yes. People do still use the Pill, right?"

She laughed. "Yes. Things haven't changed *that* much. There are other options available, though, if you'd like me to discuss them with you."

I shrugged. "I'd rather just go with what I know."

"That's fine. So how are—" she glanced at my chart again "—Scott and Maggie?"

"Oh, they're doing well. Both busy with school." I shifted my weight on the sterile paper of the exam bench. "Do you have children?"

"Not yet. Someday." She smiled again and stood to wash her hands at the sink. "I'm glad yours are well. You should send in pictures. We always love to put up photos of the babies we've delivered, all grown up."

I chuckled. "Now, if *that* doesn't make me feel old."

"I'm sorry." She pulled on a pair of gloves and turned to face me. "Now, shall we get started with our exam?"

As the noodles boiled, Zach mixed up a batch of cheese sauce from a bag of yellowish powder, smashing butter down with the side of a fork. He felt a little guilty cooking up such a lame meal for his mother's lunch, but with her regular trips to the grocery store cancelled because of bed rest, he and his father had let the pantry get way too bare. Rhianne would be over shortly, leaving him no time to indulge any sort of vegetarian creativity with whatever remained. The important thing was to get her fed.

He took the glass bottle of milk from the fridge and eye-balled three tablespoons, then took a swig from the bottle. It was good, he considered, that she was having this baby in the Maryland 'burbs. In New Hampshire she had an arrangement with a local farmer to provide unpasteurized, straight-from-the-cow milk for their family's use—officially, due to what the law required, for the use of the cat. The farmer never questioned Luna's three-gallons-per-week requirement, and it was not until Zach was in high school that he realized the practice was unusual even among the most hardcore health enthusiasts in his community. Here in Maryland, the best his mother could do was organic glass-bottle milk, pasteurized but not homogenized, home delivered twice a week. He had never gotten sick from the raw stuff, but the pregnancy made him feel protective; it was probably better for her to drink the thin watery version everybody else was used to.

He drained the macaroni and ladled the concoction into a bowl. She sat up in bed and smiled at him when he entered the room, her black hair in its clip slightly askew.

"It's the best I could do," he said, apologizing in advance. "It's the organic version, though. It's not Kraft or anything."

"It's fine, Zach." He handed her the bowl and pulled over the chair from the corner of the room, turning it around before sitting to rest his arms and chin against its back.

"How's school going?"

"All right. We're reading Dante."

She made a murmuring noise of approval. "How do you like it?"

"I don't. I hate it, as a matter of fact."

She restrained her laugh, chewing macaroni, but her shoulders flexed with amusement. He continued, "But Spanish is fun, and choir's all right. Ohio was really fun."

"That's good." Knitting her brow in mild concern, she added, "You seem to be making new friends here. Aren't you?"

"Yeah. Temple's pretty cool."

"And Fairen? You seem to like her."

Again he shrugged, this time looking away. His mother took the hint. "We'll make a trip back to New Hampshire next summer," she promised him. "The baby will be six months old by then, sitting up and everything. Can you imagine? And you'll be able to see your old friends then. Jacob and Arne and Sam, all of them. You can call them anytime you want, you know. We're not worried about the long-distance bills."

"They have their own lives," he said. "I'm out of the loop now. And guys don't talk on the phone like girls do. You know that."

"I do know that." She put her hand over his. "I never intended to uproot you in the middle of high school, sweetie. I'm sorry we had to do that. But your dad's business is doing much better here. He's got so much work now, he needs to hire three more full-timers."

"Yeah," said Zach, and his voice sounded abrupt even to him. This was not the subject he wanted to talk about. The more his parents took the time to explain why they were in Maryland, the more it all felt like a ruse. For all he knew, it might have been the truth; maybe it all came down not to paternity, but to carpentry. Yet trying to believe that forced him to consider the possibilities more than he already did. He just wanted to accept his circumstances and get on with his new life. That new life, after all, offered enough dramas of its own without him dragging in theoretical ones from New Hampshire.

The doorbell rescued him from further musing. "Rhianne's here," he said. "I'll let her in."

The visit was perfunctory. She listened to the baby's heartbeat, dipped the little test strips into her urine, and told Zach's mother to get a glucose tolerance test, which caused Vivienne to balk.

"You know I'd rather not have any of those sort of interventions," Vivienne told her.

"This isn't an intervention, this is a diagnostic," Rhianne explained. "Your sugars are a little high. It's a good idea to get it done, in case you've got gestational diabetes."

"It's probably just carbs from the macaroni and cheese I just ate."

"Maybe, maybe not. We'll find out. It's not the first time you've tested high."

Vivienne held her open hands on both sides of her waist—or where her waist *used* to be, in any case—and asked, "Do I *look* like someone who's prone to gestational diabetes?"

"You're forty-one years old," said Rhianne, "and your sugars are higher than normal. It's up to you, if you're not concerned about delivering an eleven-pounder."

Vivienne grimaced. Rhianne patted her knee and said, "I'll see you in a couple of weeks. I'll leave the paperwork on the dining table." Then she beckoned Zach to follow her to the door.

"Is my mom going to be okay?" he asked in the foyer.

"She'll be fine. It's a routine test. She probably had it done with you."

"She probably didn't."

Rhianne smirked and offered him the drawstring bag. He reached in and pulled out a whole handful.

"Whoa," she said. "Fun to have them around, huh?"

He responded with the broad bashful grin of a guy caught being most impressive, and crammed the freebies into his jeans pockets.

"Is this a new development in your life?" she asked.

"Sort of."

"Want to talk about it?"

He shook his head. "It's safe and all. I'm covering up. And she's on the Pill."

"Good, but there are other things that matter, too. Mutual respect, emotional maturity, things like that."

"Yeah, I got that stuff, too."

Rhianne laughed. "Are your parents aware?"

He felt his expression go instantly serious. "No. And don't say anything to them, all right? They've got enough going on. They might freak out."

"Not a problem. You can trust me to keep your confidence." Her smile was tight-lipped but warm. "And whenever you want to talk, I'm here."

The chances he would ever discuss Judy with Rhianne were exactly zero, but nevertheless, her kindness touched him. "Thanks," he said, and opened the door to hurry the conversation to a close. "Well, seeya."

On Friday I took a half day to visit Maggie at college, now that she was all settled in. The drive up to St. Mary's took two hours each way. Past Baltimore the roadside landscape of metal poles broke to real trees, the hills grew higher and higher, and my thoughts began a tug-of-war between Maggie and Zach.

In her most recent phone call—which had been a while

ago, come to think of it—Maggie had told me she had decided
for sure on a major in biology. *High time,* I thought, given that
this was her second year of college. But Maggie had always
been a bit perplexing to me, a bit apart from what I had anticipated. She had been an even-tempered child, quiet and
cooperative and easy to please—yet as far as I could discern,
she had no passion. Nothing set her off, worked her up, put
her in a state to argue. This bewildered me, for how could
Russ and I—two people who could be not just enthusiastic,
but *fanatical* about our few interests—have produced such an
indifferent daughter? As she grew older it had been a struggle
to find ways to relate to her. I had thought she would come to
confide in me more when boys entered her life, but Maggie
moved through her preteen years still scornful of the opposite
sex, settling into indifference as high school wore on. Once
again I considered myself, and Russ, and wondered: where
on earth had *that* gene come from?

Still, it was none of my business, a fact of which I constantly
reminded myself. Maggie was old enough to do, or not do,
as she chose. And I was, after all, carrying on enough for the
both of us. Given how negligible my judgment could become where sex was involved, perhaps it was for the best that
Maggie cared little about it. At her age I had fallen for Marty,
gone to bed with him, and all too quickly watched him become jealous and controlling, his teasing sense of humor turning manipulative and mean. But as young as I was, and as
naïve, it had been difficult to know how to end it. If Maggie
could be spared the heartache of that, I would be glad of it.

I turned off the exit ramp, rolling up the window against
the thundering wind. Maggie would be waiting for me at the
front door of her building, and was probably already there. I
turned up the collar of my jacket, and tried to focus on her
alone.

★ ★ ★

"You missed Parents' Weekend," she said.

I tucked my hands into my jacket pockets and frowned. "What?"

"It was two weeks ago. I thought you were going to be here." Her bottom lip looked petulant and her thick brown ponytail fanned across her shoulder like some sort of Roman helmet decoration gone askew. She had gained some weight around her chin. One doesn't become immune to the Freshman 15 just because one hits the thirty-credit mark.

"You never said anything about it," I informed her.

"The school sent a flyer."

"*Maggie*. The school sends us a lot of things, most of them asking if we want season football tickets or if we'll pay up five hundred dollars for a memorial plaque at the alumni center. You're a sophomore now. I thought we were past those orientation events."

She tightened her fleece jacket around her waist. "Well, I was just lonely, is all."

I offered a tight smile. "How's the dating scene?"

"Oh, *Mom*."

I took her out to a pizza place just off campus, coercing her into filling up the tank while we were on the main drag. As soon as we were seated I understood why she had chosen the restaurant. The noise level was ungodly, and the tables were so close together that the constant jostling distracted from any focused conversation. This was a punishment for my asking the dating question, I was sure of it.

"So how are your biology classes going?" I shouted over the din.

She gave a bouncing nod, indicating things were as well as could be expected. "Good," she replied. "The science courses

are always good. I learned something really important over
the past year."

"What's that?"

"That the stuff they taught us in science at Sylvania is utter
bullshit."

I peered harder at her. "What?"

"Utter bullshit," she said, more loudly this time.

I pondered this—both the supposition and the fact that
it was the first time I'd ever heard Maggie say anything so
aggressive or profane. Finally I said, "That's a pretty broad
statement to make."

"It's true, though," she replied stridently.

I nodded. After a moment of silence, I said, "Well, I've always thought Waldorf was most ideal for the younger grades."

She gave a benign smile, her hands folded between her
knees. The waiter plunked a pizza down between us. Then
Maggie added, "Also, I've started going to church."

"What?"

"You keep saying *what,*" she pointed out. "Is your hearing
okay?"

"What church?"

"The Baptist church on campus."

"The *Baptist* church?"

"That's the one."

She had taken a slice of pizza and bitten off the end, but
I couldn't even think about eating. All around me was the
clanging of silverware, the hum of conversation loud as road
construction. In the kitchen, someone dropped a glass. Yellow
light glared down, the sort that makes bugs die.

"Why?" I asked.

"It's a nice group of people," she said, her voice already
growing hoarse from the strain of speaking. "Really uplifting.
We go out on Sundays, tracting."

"*Tracting?*"

"See, you *can* hear," she observed, nodding. "You keep repeating back everything I say."

"It's because you're speaking English," I told her, "but not any English that makes any sense to me."

"That's because you're narrow-minded."

I reeled back against my chair. "Well, that's the first time anyone's ever lobbed *that* one at me."

"Probably because the only people you associate with are the same as you," she noted helpfully.

I took a slice of pizza and removed the greasy pepperoni before biting into it, to prevent myself from replying.

"The thing is," Maggie continued, "I've realized I spent eighteen years sheltered under all this nonsense, learning all this stuff that doesn't matter, from people who are generally hypocrites…and then out in the real world, once I stopped fighting it, I realized the world doesn't explode if you admit fairies don't exist and you can't dance your way to a higher consciousness. It's a matter of being logical."

"I suppose that's where the Baptist Church comes in."

She raised her eyebrows slightly and strung a long piece of mozzarella into the air. "Redemption is logical," she said. "Compared to a lot of that crap I digested, it's practically Newton's Law."

I nodded. "So this is what rebellion looks like in one of my kids."

"I'm not rebelling. This is who I've been all my life. I just didn't have the language to talk about it, since all they speak at Sylvania is New Age gobbledygook. I never fit in at that stupid school and you know it. All I ever wanted was to be a regular person in a normal American family. One where I can go to a barbecue on the Fourth of July that isn't full of people telling their stories about how they got out of the Vietnam draft." She smiled and leaned in. "But you asked about the dating scene."

"I did," I said, overjoyed at the change of subject. "Anything new to report?"

"Just one small thing," she told me. "I've taken a Purity Pledge."

It was absurd, the degree to which Maggie was rebelling against her upbringing, but even as part of me laughed at it, part of me also mourned. I remembered looking down at her as she nursed at my breast, a tiny squashed creature clad in a white onesie and the pink hat Bobbie had crocheted for her, and gravely resolving in my heart that things would be different with her than they had been with my own mother. All through my childhood my mother had struggled for her sanity, and some years I observed she wasn't struggling nearly hard enough. I picked at a thread tangled in the wool near the center of the hat and thought about what I had been in my mother's life—a lumpy little defect in the middle of a regimentally ordered pattern—and that my children would never be made to feel that way. They *were* the center. They *were* the pattern. And despite it all, Maggie had grown to believe that I had placed the schema for childhood above the child herself. That I had strangled her with the safety net.

That night I went to bed in a melancholy mood, tucking the hotel pillow beneath my head and musing on my thoughts of my daughter. *Quit being so emo,* Zach would say, using a slang term that had stumped me before he explained it meant overly emotional. Most likely he was at my house tonight, visiting with his friends, drinking my Coke. If I were there I would be offering him a ride home, taking a quick detour to the lake as we had two nights before, when he had clutched a hand in my hair and laughed when it was over and said, *oh my god, that felt amazing.* I had beamed beneath the praise as though a professor had declared me his very best pupil. As we doubled back toward his house, the radio station briefed us on the latest news of the impeachment proceedings. *I wonder if he regrets what he did with her,* I said to Zach, and he replied, *are you kidding, it's the sport of kings.*

I fell easily to sleep on the memory. My mind was glad to return to the midnight-dark interior of my car, the haste of unbuckling, the luxurious ease of his body submitting to my attention. He groaned, then laughed, then spoke, but his voice had changed; and so I looked up at him, his face pale amid the shadows, his short hair dirty blond, eyes a faceted blue. Even through the haze of dreaming I felt the shock of seeing his face, so unlike Zach's, but it did nothing to deter me. When he reached for me he smelled of copper and soil, touching me with rough hands that did not spoil the pleasure that shivered through my belly, oblivious to the shame.

13

Zach stood in Judy's kitchen, up to his elbows in sudsy water, felting balls of wool. The pastel spheres bobbed in the water: pink, blue and a minty green, all sized for a toddler's hands. Assembly-line Waldorf crafts: his primary-school teacher would have groaned. But the bazaar was approaching. The toys had to be finished, to sell.

Zach squeezed water from the green ball, agitated it between his hands, soaked it again. Across from him Judy plunked a yellow ball onto a tray lined with a towel: her fifth.

"You're way faster than me," he said admiringly.

"I do this all the time," she replied, a rueful undertone to her voice. She squeezed the water from a lavender one, coaxed it into a spherical shape, and dunked it back into her basin. "I enjoy it. When I was young and we lived in Germany, after school I used to go to our neighbor's barn and watch their son take care of the animals. He would hand me bits of wool from the sheep and I'd knead them into balls like this. I didn't know a thing about felting, of course. It was just something to do." Lifting the lavender ball from the water, she added,

"The texture of it always takes me back to that place and time. And that boy. His name was Rudi."

"Rudi," Zach repeated, rolling the *r* and drawing out the *u* in a mocking accent.

Judy clicked her tongue. "He was very nice to me. It was so isolating living there. Having no friends. My father screwing the help." At this Zach snickered. "That boy's kindness meant the world to me then. You look like him, a little. Not in the coloring. He was very Aryan that way. But around the mouth, and something about your eyes every now and then. And your body."

He laughed openly. "My body. How old did you say you were, again?"

She smiled. "I just mean how wiry you are. I suppose he was about your age, and that's typical. Yet Scott, for example, is built solid, like Russ. Temple just looks skinny through and through. But Rudi—he looked like skin stretched over muscle. I had never seen anything like that before I knew him. And you're that way, too."

The soapy water was beginning to saturate his skin. For a moment he set down his work and wiped his hands with the bottom of his shirt. When she smiled at the gesture, he said, "Sounds like you were doing a lot of checking him out, for a six-year-old."

"Oh, no. I was about ten, but there was never anything like that. I always saw him as a—a safe harbor, I suppose. Never as a sex object. Not at all." Another felted ball emerged from the water and into her hand, perfectly formed, as if by magic. Her smile shifted secretly. "Although, you know—I did have a dream about him the other night."

"About *R-R-R-Rudi?*"

This time she laughed. "Yes. The night I visited Maggie. It was quite graphic. When I woke up, I found the whole thing very shocking. I didn't like thinking of him that way. In my mind he's almost a saint. Or a savior."

"Was it a bad dream, then?"

She smiled again, tight-lipped. When she met his gaze, her eyes twinkled. "No."

He laughed. Blood surged in a sudden rush through his veins. He kept expecting her to discard the whole idea of having him as a lover, and coming up astonished when it persisted. And it persisted all over the place: in her classroom, the workshop, her Volvo parked by the lake, and, of course, the woods. When he balked at the timing or setting, she sank to her knees and unzipped him and from there he could hardly argue. On those occasions she seemed perfectly content, and while it made no sense to him he simply accepted his good fortune and admired her efficiency. Thus far the crafting session had been perfectly chaste, but Judy had a way of going from teacher to succubus in the time it took to slam a car door, and as the dinner hour approached he wondered which one would drive him home.

Before he could consider the matter too deeply, the door burst open and Scott walked in, his coat open and his backpack over one shoulder. "Hey, Mom," he said as he entered the kitchen; a moment later, to Zach, "Hey, dude." He glanced at the toys lined up on the towel and added, "Nice balls."

The expected response jumped to mind immediately: *That's what your mom said.* But this time, Zach thought better of it.

"Would you like to help out?" Judy asked Scott.

"I'm coming and going," he replied. He grabbed a plastic container from the refrigerator, grimaced at its contents, and took an apple instead.

Judy asked, "Going out with Tally?"

Scott grunted a reply and bit into the apple. He fished

around in a cabinet and, coming up empty, made a growling noise, swiped a pile of papers from a counter, and stalked out.

"Make yourself a sandwich," Judy shouted.

"That bread is disgusting," Scott yelled back. "There's seeds in it and shit."

Judy sighed and offered Zach an apologetic smile as the door slammed. "Welcome to our happy home."

"Does he always talk to you like that?"

"Oh, yes, when he talks at all. Most days after school Tally comes swinging into my driveway in her little BMW, lets herself in the door and off they go to his room or to the den to 'watch TV.'" With her fingers she gestured quotes around the phrase. "It astonishes me, the way he'll do things for no reason other than to upset me. There's no reason for him to be carrying on in that den with her. The last thing I want to be thinking about, while I'm watching TV, is what my son was doing on that sofa."

Zach snickered. "Temple said something about that. How he does things just because he knows they'll make you mad. I think it's weird. I argue with my folks sometimes, but I always feel like shit when I truly piss one of them off."

She tipped her head and looked him in the eye. "So why are you friends with him?"

"I dunno. Because he's friends with my friends."

"You don't seem very similar to him at all."

"I'm not. But I'm a lot like the other people he hangs out with, like Temple. And Fairen."

At the mention of Fairen's name her mouth pursed. She said, "Tell me about New Hampshire."

"About New Hampshire? What about it?"

"What it was like. What you miss. Your school, your friends. Tell me about them."

It was a question as large as his entire life—his life up until this past June, at least. Stepping outside in the mornings, he still felt his heart sink, often, to see the mountainless horizon and realize he wasn't there anymore. It was too warm here. The leaves were dull, the forests paltry, the highways too broad and lined with too many chain restaurants cranking out food products matched to an assembly chart. Nobody, in the months since he had moved here, had asked him about his hometown. The truth was he *ached* to talk about New Hampshire, but knew nothing was more tedious than a new kid who won't shut up about how much better the old place was. And in any case, nobody cared. He was here now.

He smiled and shook his head, ruminating. "I wouldn't know where to start."

She rose and opened the refrigerator, rummaged around, and found a can of Coke. She cracked it open and handed it to him. "We have all afternoon," she said. "Nobody's here."

He set down the last ball of wool and took the soda. She nodded to a chair, and he sat. The silence of the house felt expansive around him, but private and still. He realized, in the emptiness, that he craved a listening ear more than anything else right now. He wanted no other Judy more than the one seated at the kitchen table just now, patiently waiting to hear him talk about home.

"It was like the forest in a fairy tale," he began.

The endless tree canopy is what he remembered first, whenever he thought of home. The way the light came through the leaves in darts and dashes, the way the dark felt so absolute, so complete, in the heart of the woods. In his neighborhood the roots rumbled up from underground, crumbling the sidewalks, twisting across the lawns. Nature curved above and below him. Nature did not deign to be ruled.

The yoga studio rose on stilts beside a small road, its

shingled sides faded by snow upon snow. The stilts gave it a treehouse look, but were necessary: it was built on a flood-plain. Behind it ran a shallow stretch of the Saco River, stone-dotted and barely deep enough to twirl around his ankles, but in the snowmelt it could become a torrent. Slim silver fish, disoriented, would slip by his feet as he played. The glacial rocks that bordered it were feathered white and pale green with lichen.

Upstairs in the studio, visible through the sliding glass doors, his mother moved through the *asanas*. She was an exotic bird in their small town, lithe and small with her swinging black ponytail, managing at once to be outgoing and above it all. People were always surprised to discover her husband was the big blond carpenter, and that the little boy with the bare wet feet belonged to her. She looked like the type of woman who could drop everything in a moment and jump on a plane for a backpacking trip through some remote country. And she would, were it not for the blond carpenter and the small boy.

He wondered if her restlessness was what had caused the problem. If she felt the need for an adventure, which he could understand. He wished he knew when her affair had ended, although he tried not to think about it, really. Because the child's looks, somewhere along the sliding scale between Chinese and Caucasian, would keep the secret; and in any case he would love her, because he already did.

Despite his effort not to, he thought about this as he scraped the dishes and loaded them into the washer, wiped down the counters, and heated water for her cup of tea. While it steeped he took the fruit peels and coffee grounds out to the compost heap and picked the last few late tomatoes from the garden. When he brought her the mug he found her sitting up in bed reading *Loving Hands: The Traditional Art of Baby Massage*.

"How old is that book?" he asked.

She gave him a sly smile and wrapped her hands around the mug. "Oh, about sixteen years, give or take."

"You never got rid of it?"

"I couldn't bear to. The pictures are so pretty." She looked wistfully at the cover and took a sip of tea. "I guess I always hoped I'd have another one, deep down."

"You got your wish."

She drank deeply and handed him the mug. With a sigh, she lay back against the pillows, her hand on her belly. Her tank top hiked up above her navel, exposing a wide band of skin. He watched as something beneath the surface, a foot perhaps, drew a path across her abdomen. Laying his palm against the opposite side, he waited until the bony little nub bumped against his hand.

"Gotcha," he said.

She laughed. They sat in silence for a few moments, Zach poking at the baby's foot, studiously ignoring his mother's loving gaze. Finally she asked, "How's Fairen?"

He chuckled with embarrassment at the question. "She's fine, I guess."

"I haven't asked you much about your life lately."

"It's cool."

"Are you involved with her?"

Involved with her. So that was how mothers asked the question. He tried to get the baby to move again and said, "No."

"*Were* you?"

He felt his face start to burn. Letting his hand retreat, he stared down at the quilt and answered, "Yeah."

Her smile was spontaneous. "Well," she said. "I'm sorry I missed asking about all that while it was going on."

"There wasn't much to tell."

"Are you brokenhearted?"

He shook his head.

"Am I embarrassing you?"

"Kinda."

She patted his cheek. "Do you remember, when you were little, how I used to carry you around on my back like a little spider monkey?"

"Not really."

"They have some nice slings now for that," she said vaguely. "But back then you just climbed up and I put my arms under your little tush and I carried you everywhere. You were the most affectionate child ever there was. I hope this baby will be like that."

"I just hope it *sleeps*."

"Well, then, she'd be *nothing* like you," she said, and he laughed. She asked, "Where are you off to tonight?"

"Scott's having some people over."

A shadow of worry crossed her face. "Will his mother be there?"

"I guess. I dunno."

"Zach…you know how I feel about unsupervised parties."

"It's not a party. It's just some people at his house. But I'll double-check, okay?"

She looked satisfied with the answer. "Will Fairen be there?"

"*Mom*. I don't know."

"Tell me just one thing," she coaxed. "Did it end badly?"

He gave a small laugh that sounded more like a sigh. "I don't know where any of that stuff starts or where it ends."

She nodded, her expression serious, thoughtful. "That's very wise of you to see it that way."

"I didn't handle it all that wise." He bent forward and rested his forehead against her knee. Her soft hands stroked his hair.

Closing his eyes, he emptied his mind of everything but the way her hands felt, how gentle, how warm.

"There is nothing lost or wasted in this life," she quoted in a whisper. "What is real always was and cannot be destroyed."

He breathed a sigh against her calf and felt the warmth of his breath double back to him. Hearing the words of the *Bhagavad Gita* calmed him. All his life she had doled out its wisdom to her students for meditation, and word by word he had absorbed it. Now it knitted together, ever so little, the edges of the wound Fairen had opened in him.

She said, "You'll learn, Zachary Xiang."

14

Russ left for Iceland at the beginning of November, carrying with him the large black suitcase that had caused so much trouble not long before. Two other professors from his department went with him, and so there was no ceremonial send-off at the airport; instead, I came home from work and found his bags gone from the foyer. In the past I would have felt slighted at the lack of a proper goodbye, but now I only felt numb. Later in the week, as I tidied up from dinner and prepared to head out to the open house Dan had scheduled, Scott casually mentioned he would be spending the night at Zach's. As soon as the words left his mouth I knew he was lying. Zach had been in my classroom only hours before. It was the sort of thing he would have mentioned.

At the open house I spotted Zach sitting on the stage with Temple, his colorful eurythmy robe still on, biding time after the evening's performance. It amused me that his teachers had recruited him for the demonstration of the technique—the "art of expressive movement" he had been learning, like all of his classmates, since grade school. Most likely they had singled him out because he was a new student and thus an easy target for what most of his classmates would avoid at all costs. But, too, he was probably good at the dancelike movements it required. His body moved with a leonine grace, that I knew well; it was one of the most attractive qualities he possessed.

I beckoned to him from my place near the entrance, and he hopped off the stage. When he was near enough not to be overheard, I asked, "Would you like a ride home?"

"Sure."

"Well, isn't that a little strange," I teased. "I was told Scott is spending the night at your house."

His eyes darkened with confusion. "No, he isn't."

"I know." The corner of my mouth twitched upward. "I assume he'll be at Tally's, or in a motel, or something. Who knows. He's eighteen now, and don't you forget it. But what he told me was that he would be at your place."

Zach shook his head, not catching on. As if speaking to a child I enunciated, "He won't be home."

"What about Russ?"

"In Iceland until Tuesday. I told you that yesterday."

"No, you didn't."

I tipped my head, feeling the hunger in my eyes barely contained. "You can call your folks from my place," I whispered. "Tell them you're spending the night at Scott's."

He winced. "I hate to lie to them, Judy. You know that."

"It's not a lie at all."

A sigh grumbled deep in his throat. *"Judy."*

"I can just take you home if you prefer. It's entirely up to you. I only thought, it's not every day that Scott enables this sort of thing. Usually you consider him something of a— what's the word you use? Buzzkill?"

He managed to snicker and roll his eyes at the same time.

"I need to finish talking to these parents in the hallway," I said. "Meet me at my car in twenty minutes and let me know the plan."

Zach wadded his filmy eurythmy robe into a ball and leaned over to grab the slippers he'd stashed away at the edge of the stage curtain. Temple had wandered off to speak with a teacher, leaving Zach alone on the stage. He felt deeply irritated at Scott using him, of all people, as a cover story. Without Zach's knowledge or consent Scott had involved him in a lie. It was especially galling in light of the way Scott constantly razzed him in public about his supposedly pathetic sex life, then depended on Zach to facilitate his own. He had half a mind to take Judy up on her offer just for spite. Not that Judy would care what his reason was, so long as he was in her bed.

He watched the few remaining little kids play with the picturesque toys the teachers had set out—a basket of knitted dolls, a set of nesting arches in rainbow colors, wooden figurines in the shape of characters from nursery rhymes. Dr. Beckett's kid lay on his stomach stacking the animals from "The Musicians of Bremen," seemingly oblivious to the wilder boys around him. Atop his corduroys and simple red T-shirt he wore a golden Michaelmas cape. The sight of it tugged at Zach a little bit, evoking a memory of being six and happy, standing before his teacher in a cape just like that one as his teacher presented him with his rough-cut Michaelmas sword. *Zachary, you have polished your sword so strong, so bright. Use it only for the right.* The Waldorf rhymes came back to him easily, carrying all his childhood memories on their words. *Enjoy it while it lasts, kid,* he thought to himself. Not very long ago that had been him, stretched out on the floor with a fistful of animals, and the land of make-believe was the only place he needed for a boost of courage, strength and might.

He caved at the last minute, jogging across the parking lot to catch up with Judy just as she climbed into her Volvo. She reached across to pop open the passenger door and started the car. He glanced at the gas gauge and noticed it was nearly at the empty mark. Briefly he considered pointing this out to her, then thought better of it.

"So where are we going?" she asked, and didn't seem surprised by his answer.

Without Scott present at the house, Zach decided to be nosy. He had always enjoyed exploring other people's houses, sometimes overstepping the bounds of good guest behavior. Judy, somewhat to his surprise, did not jump on him as soon as they walked in the door, and as she cleaned up the kitchen he felt free to roam. He had been in her bedroom several times before but always under the gun for time, in an elevated state of arousal before he even arrived, in a rush to leave as soon as they were finished. But tonight there would be no such restrictions, and the long stretch of time felt luxurious.

In the bathroom he found the drawer where Scott stored a selection of hair products that would make any girl proud. He flipped through the oldest photo albums, tuning out Russ's face and analyzing the looks of a much more youthful Judy. She had been cute back then, although no more his type then than she was now. He preferred blond and elegant to dark-haired and elfin, but, of course, Judy's looks had little to do with why he felt drawn to her. Her foot on his erection when he'd thought he was the one running the show: that's why he was with her. Because he could swim down into her desire as long as his breath would hold, and never find the bottom. And yet, at the top, the pool shimmered glassy and still. It was sexy as hell.

Avoiding Scott's room and Russ's office, he made his way around the top floor to the bedroom, where he crouched down and viewed the tattered cardboard boxes and dust bunnies under the bed. The night table drawer held a plastic comb, a few hair elastics and a copy of Anaïs Nin's *Little Birds*.

"Look at you, getting all up in my business," she teased from the doorway. A wineglass, nearly empty, dangled in her hand.

He turned around and grinned, only slightly embarrassed. "You've hardly got anything interesting in here."

"You just haven't been looking in the right places."

"And none of the normal stuff."

"Normal stuf?" Her brows knitted. "Like what?"

He stood up and hiked himself onto the bed. "Birth control. Candles. Those strips that go on your nose to stop you from snoring."

She laughed. "Neither Russ nor I snore. I keep my birth control pills in my purse so Russ doesn't find out about them. And I'm not a candle girl."

"Why not? I thought every girl was."

"Not me." She sat beside him on the duvet. "When I was little I had to read a book about a girl who plays with a match and sets herself on fire. *The Dreadful Story of Pauline and the Matches,* it was called. I can still remember nearly the whole thing." Her gaze shifted to the wine swirling in her glass. In a singsong voice she chanted, "'It's very, very wrong, you know. You will be burnt if you do so.'"

"That's a children's book?" He grinned. "Nice."

"Oh, yes. It's from the one I told you about in the woods that day." She swallowed the last of her wine. "At the end there's nothing left of her but a pile of ashes and her little red shoes, and only the cats mourn her. It gave me nightmares for weeks. It seemed like the most horrible thing in the world,

the worst death. Because of it I've never been much a fan of
fire."

"That's weird. They use candles at school all the time."

"Sure, and I'm okay with it as long as it's contained. I do
think fire can be beautiful in a terrifying sort of way. I just
wouldn't choose to put it around my house when I'm trying
to relax." She threw him a tight smile. "Or where it might
get knocked over. I'd find that inhibiting, wouldn't you?"

"Yeah, I suppose so."

She nodded and looked thoughtful. "I imagine it's where
people got the idea of God. Something beautiful and warm
that you feel drawn to, but powerful enough to devour you.
It's human nature to identify the natural world with ourselves,
and vice versa. We imagine that if a human could channel
the powers of nature, then there's someone to whom we can
plead our case, who could contain a disaster. But I've never
seen that work very well." She hopped down from the bed.
"I'm going to take a shower. There's plenty of food in the
kitchen if you're hungry. All the additives and high-fructose
corn syrup you could ever want."

He grinned. "I'll be all right."

He stepped out the back door, killing time as he waited for
her, into the yard bordered by a wooden privacy fence and
plenty of trees. A few wrought-iron armchairs were scattered
near a table that had once held an umbrella; he sat, polishing
off a Coke from her refrigerator. Nothing was stopping him
from getting into her wine, but he had considered and discarded the idea quickly. He still felt paranoid that Scott would
turn up, and that fight stood a better chance of being fair if
Zach was sober.

At one end of the yard stood a little playhouse, dilapidated
and festooned with chipped paint and a few scraggly vines.

He supposed it had once been the property of Scott's sister.
The one he had built was far more elaborate and better con-
structed. He thought back to the challenges of the joinery,
the pain-in-the-ass of replacing all the gingerbread after he'd
put it on backwards. He thought back to the kiss. The instant
before she moved, he knew she would, and then it happened
all at once: her body rising, her hands on his face, and then her
mouth astonishingly on his own: this teacher, this mother, this
minor flirtation like a tavern puzzle he'd been toying with at
a party. Weeks later, in the woods, there had been no way to
decipher who was seducing whom; but in the playhouse, he
knew perfectly well.

Not that it mattered now. He put a foot up on another
chair and slouched down to look at the sky: Orion hanging
above the treetops, Ursa Major, Venus' pale blue glow. The
absence of mountains still bothered him. Without their buffer
the Earth seemed too close to the sky, arching toward it like a
slavering dog on a leash, nudging impolitely into the territory
of God.

From inside the house he heard the squeal of pipes. He
glanced up at the second story, the light in the bathroom
window broken by her intermittent shadow as she walked
back and forth. By the time she got to him her combed wet
hair would be curling slowly as it dried; her skin would smell
of strawberry lotion, her mouth of wine. It was a mystery to
him why Russ left her alone. His best guess was that Russ was
having an affair of his own, which helped Zach assuage the
guilt that nudged at him. Lying to his parents, on the other
hand: try as he might, he couldn't quite stop feeling like shit
about that. But as he rose up through the deep of childhood
and into the shallows of adulthood, it seemed that on the
surface these shiny lies swirled like gasoline and, sooner or
later, stuck to everyone. He pictured his younger self barefoot

in his rolled-up jeans, hopping from rock to rock across the slow Saco River in the shadow of his mother's studio. The trees drooped an extravagance of green summer leaves high above his small dark head, the silver water swirled past stones rounded as toys, and somewhere not far past the singing insects and waving grass she was lying and lying, lying to his father, to him, lying with another man on a mat beneath her chalk-written quote from the *Bhagavad Gita* that read, *Observe your discipline, and arise.*

Even her.

He twisted off the tab of his Coke can and plunked it into the opening. Inwardly, he reprimanded himself for the melodrama of his thoughts. In truth, by the time his mother started screwing around with Booger, he was at least fourteen and spending his time on less innocent pursuits than catching minnows in the Saco. The problem with vague knowledge such as his own was that it caused her affair to stretch back infinitely far and infinitely forward, allowing every memory of being booted from the studio to take on a sinister sheen, forcing him to wonder whether she still kept her heart divided for that jack-off in the Lennon shirt. But now, of course, he was hardly in a position to criticize her.

He stood up and stretched, feeling the shock of cold air against his stomach, the pleasing shiver along his spine as his muscles relaxed. He could use a shower himself, and would probably get around to it before the night was over, but he knew Judy wouldn't care one way or the other. If anything she seemed to prefer him like this: nostrils flaring, tongue tracing his collarbone, it had some kind of feral draw for her. Inevitably she would press her face against his belly and, shoulders curling as she inhaled, proceed to tell him that he smelled amazing before promptly demonstrating that she wasn't just saying it to be polite.

Through the kitchen wall behind him, he heard the whistle of the sink turning on and off: Judy rinsing out her wineglass. He pressed each fist against the opposite hand, cracking his knuckles, and then headed in through the back door, where the decorous click of the latch was lost in her warm *hello*.

15

The chirping of birds outside the window told Zach it was nearly morning. He lay beneath Judy's duvet with his hands folded beneath his head, eyes focused on the slant of light from the streetlight that played against the ceiling. Beside him Judy breathed the slow rhythm of deep sleep, but Zach had lain awake every moment of the long night, occasionally drifting into a state of uneasy exhaustion that was not the least bit restful.

Someone could come home. He couldn't shake the feeling. Scott and Tally could have a fight; Russ, who never seemed to communicate with Judy anyway, could return early from Sweden or wherever he was. Whenever he managed to talk himself down from such concerns, other thoughts, some even more insidious than getting caught, crept into his mind.

Booger, for example. He pictured the guy's skinny pale legs, the way his arrogant gaze rested on Zach when he entered his mother's classroom, his narrow cyclist's hips in his snug black exercise pants. Everything about him—his manner, his looks, his simpering New-Age-i-ness—was repellent. Had

Zach hated all of those things before Booger made his appearance, or did he hate them all because they were aspects of Booger? Whichever it was, he couldn't help but imagine all the things Scott would despise about him, for the same reason, if he knew. Zach would become the measure of repulsiveness, fitted into the same category of Scott's mind where Booger now resided in Zach's.

He listened to the twitter of the birds and sighed quietly. The dawn chorus—a poetic name for a truly obnoxious phenomenon. He gave up on sleep and softly pushed back the duvet, moving slowly so as not to wake Judy.

She rolled over anyway, regarding him with eyes that were large and suddenly bright in the dark room. "You're getting up already?"

"I can't sleep." He pulled on his jeans and immediately felt a measure of relief. He was dressed now, more or less. That in itself was absolving.

"There are muffins in the kitchen."

"I'm all right. I'll eat when I get home."

"Are you leaving already?" Her voice was skeptical. "I'll drive you home if you give me a few minutes to wake up."

His laugh was short and abrupt. "I don't think I want my folks looking out the window and seeing that."

"They won't be up at this hour, will they?"

"I'll walk. It's cool."

She sat up, leaning on one arm. In the darkness she looked incredibly young. The shadowy light smoothed the fine lines of her face, catching in the whites of her eyes and the rounded edges of her teeth, giving her a doe-eyed, vulnerable look; her disheveled hair looked thoroughly black, unlaced with silver. Perhaps it was her nightclothes that sealed the effect: she wore an old T-shirt and, beneath the duvet, flannel-print pajama pants, like any girl his age. She was so damned *small*.

She asked, "Will you do something for me before you go?"

He lifted his shirt from the floor and looked at her with nervous impatience. His mouth felt cottony, his stomach empty, and, lacking new contacts or anything with which to clean the old ones, his eyes stung with dryness and fatigue. Most of all, he needed space. He felt a little ill with the gluttony of the previous night, a little dizzy and overindulged. It was not unlike gorging yourself on a giant ice cream sundae: past a certain point, you sort of felt like you wanted to puke.

But before he could utter a curt response she asked, "Would you fill up the Volvo for me?"

He smiled in confusion. "Your car?"

"Yeah. It's nearly out of gas, and Russ won't be back for days yet. I could ask Scott, but you know how he is."

"Is there some reason you don't do it yourself?"

She shrugged. "The smell bothers me, that's all."

"No problem," he replied, and he meant it. He stuffed his feet into his sneakers, fished her car keys and a twenty-dollar bill from her purse, and slipped out of the dark house into the damp morning air.

It felt good to be behind the wheel, with the cool wind rushing through the open windows and the radio, for once, set to a station he actually liked. At the gas station he filled the tank and browsed the mini-mart for necessities: a cold bottle of green tea, eye drops, and a breakfast of an apple and a bag of almonds, the only non-objectionable snack foods available. With most of Judy's twenty gone, he climbed back into the car and signaled his turn onto Crescent Road.

The town was still sleeping. Rising up along the road were the whitewashed cinder-block apartment buildings, the small postwar town houses, that marked off the hamlet of Sylvania from the sprawling prefab buildings of the larger suburbs. A banner hung above the road announced a community art

contest. Past the low-slung Catholic church—in whose shadowed lot he often met Judy in the evenings—lay Hauschen
Lake, glittering darkly beyond the pines. He followed the
uphill curve until he saw the sign for Judy's street, and then,
on impulse, turned his gaze toward the top of the hill and hit
the gas.

The road crested, then expanded toward a highway whizzing with cars. Even at this early hour the delivery trucks
raced along, the poor suckers with inflexible jobs tolerated
their commute, and Zach joined them. He drove without any
particular idea of where he was headed, following the curve of
the road as it roared past office buildings and storage facilities,
broken-down ranch houses and an electrical substation. After
a while he took an exit and the road grew narrower, flanked
by forest. The sky, glowing a deep hazy blue but streaked with
rose and yellow, looked like the painting on Judy's classroom
wall blurred by distance. On an impulse as immediate as the
one which had led him on the journey, he pulled onto the
shoulder and shut off the car.

His brain was tired, but the drive had turned the nause-
ated gloomy feeling into one of shallow exuberance, and he
gamely wished to follow that thread wherever it took him.
With his bag of almonds in hand, he crunched through the
russet leaves into the woods. The mild hill was slick with
pine needles, but he dug his toes in deeper, touching the trees
for balance, and made the climb. Farther in, a tall chain-link
fence marked some border that seemed to make no sense at
all; the woods continued beyond it, and no sign announced an
owner or reason. He clasped the bag of almonds in his teeth
and clambered over the fence, taking the eight-foot drop in
easy stride.

The forest. It felt good to be here. He breathed in the
piney air and hiked up the crest of the hill, where it leveled

off and stretched into a few acres of sweetgum and fir before flattening into farmland. Upon sight of the yellow fields he understood where he was. He had driven past this place with his friends before; it was an agricultural facility of some sort, a practice farm where they tried out new plant hybrids and fertilizers. Still, he had trees and space and he was blessedly alone. He sat down beside a spruce and ate his almonds, then lay on his back to watch the last of the darkness slip from the sky.

The November trees, their contorted branches nearly bare, made it easy to catch the subtle shifts that marked the sunrise. In his home state it would be far too cold to lie in the woods in nothing but street clothes and a down vest, but here he felt barely a chill. The leaves crackled beneath his back and, above, the last remaining ones shuffled softly to the earth, a sound best heard with his eyes closed.

Beautiful, he thought.

He breathed in the clear air and felt the living woods surround him, the ground buoying him on a litter of leaves, the sunlight a pale, narrow beam that promised warmth yet to come.

When he awoke, a county sheriff was glaring down at him, hands on his belt.

Zach's mind, most recently settled into the depth of the word *beautiful,* rose to the state of *oh shit.*

"You damn runaways always gotta show up here," the officer said. "You kids ever hear of the mall?"

Already pushing himself up on his arms, Zach mumbled, "I'm not a runaway."

"Get up. You got ID?"

Zach fumbled for his wallet, handed over his driver's

license, and rubbed the sleep from one eye with his palm. "I didn't know I wasn't allowed to be here."

"Of course you're not allowed. This is a federal facility."

"I thought it was a farm."

"It is—USDA. Licensed personnel only." The officer held up Zach's driver's license. "New Hampshire. Not a runaway, huh?"

After drifting off following nearly twenty-four hours without sleep, his body begged to be allowed to return to the forest floor. Even the presence of a police officer could not stop him from nearly falling asleep on his feet. Shaking his head groggily, he said, "I moved to Sylvania last summer."

"So what are you doing all the way up here?"

"Visiting my girlfriend."

The side of the officer's mouth lifted in a peevish smile. "Don't see her around here, do you?"

"No. I stopped here just to—see the woods. I like the woods."

"You walked from Sylvania."

He shook his head again and wavered on his feet. God, he needed to sleep. He couldn't even figure out how to put the words together to explain how he had arrived here. When he thought about Judy's car on the shoulder at the bottom of the hill, his thoughts melted into a puddle. He blinked several times in an attempt to clear his head, and the man asked, "How much have you had to drink?"

"Drink? Nothing. Just some tea." Coffee would have been a good idea, he realized now. He still wasn't used to choosing it, with one of his parents normally around.

"You expect me to believe that? Your eyes are bloodshot from here to hell and back."

"It's my contacts, that's all. Look at my license. I'm sixteen. I can't drink."

"Like that's ever stopped you kids before." The sheriff took him by the upper arm and led him toward a sand-colored car between the forest and the field. "You got a parent at home?"

The momentary prickle of fear that seized him quickly gave way as his mind finally kicked into gear. "Yeah," he muttered. "My stepmom."

By the time Judy appeared at the door of the security station, Zach felt considerably less agitated than he had in the first moments after being escorted into the officer's car. First, he gradually realized the man was not, in fact, a county sheriff, just some rent-a-cop who worked for the agricultural center and wore a brown uniform. Second, Judy's shrieking in his ear included a rant about how she *hated* driving Russ's car, which reassured Zach that he could count on her to bail him out, however grouchily. As the minutes ticked by and he scratched at a mark on the officer's desk with his fingernail, he grew to feel almost cocky. What was she going to do—report him to his parents? Ditch him? Refuse to let him tank up her car again? No—the power was all his. He had spent the past ten hours pleasing the living hell out of her. She was just fortunate that when he found himself being dragged along by a guy in a uniform, he had the good sense to keep his version of their relationship G-rated.

She caught his eye as the officer came toward her. She wore one of her baggy kindergarten-teacher jumpers over the T-shirt she had slept in, but her coat disguised the strange look. Her hair was back in a loose, messy ponytail. He shot her a smile and was rewarded with a venomous glare.

"Said he was visiting his girlfriend," the officer told her. "Staggering around like he's three sheets to the wind."

Judy responded with a few short shakes of her head directed at Zach. "I told you to stay away from that girl."

"I told him we could charge him with trespassing on federal property, but so long as there's an adult going to set him straight, we won't pursue it. I'll let you two work that out."

"Oh, we will," she muttered as she signed the clipboard.

Once enclosed in Russ's red sport-utility vehicle, Judy turned toward him with a look that made her earlier glare seem angelic. "What the *hell*, Zach."

"I felt like driving."

"You felt like driving. *My car.* And practically getting arrested. God, are you ever lucky I knew how to play along when he called."

Zach shrugged.

"And now here we are in *Russ's* car," she continued, "you in your T-shirt with cat hair all over it, forcing me to *sign off* on a document that says I picked you up at seven in the morning. How is *that* going to look? Are you *trying* to get me arrested? Or to find yourself in court giving a blow-by-blow of all this in front of your mother?"

He shrugged again. He recognized the melodrama. It was a mom thing. The best course of action was to shut up and let her vent it until she was done.

"You have nothing to say for yourself," she prompted.

He considered that, then said, "I've got to pee pretty bad."

She banged the steering wheel with both hands. "*Damn* you, Zach. You've got some serious nerve. You've got *chutzpah.*"

"*Chutzpah?*" He laughed. "Is that like *R-R-R-Rudi?*"

Her open palm collided with his face in a burning slap. Hand flying to his cheek, he sneered at her. "*Ow.* What the *fuck.*"

"Don't you mock me," she ordered, but her tone had a nervous waver.

"Don't you *hit* me, goddamn it. What the hell was that?"

She turned the key in the ignition. "That was me snapping you out of it."

"Snapping me out of *what?*"

"Your attitude problem is what."

"My *attitude problem?*" He felt his face growing hotter by the moment. "Who the fuck do you think you are, my mother? Even *she* doesn't hit me."

"Don't start with me, Zach," Judy warned. "It's not like you've never taken your aggressions out on me."

"When have I *ever* done anything like that to you?" he said. All the muscles in his body seemed to shiver with fury. "When have I *ever* laid a hand on you because I was angry."

"Why *would* you be angry?" she yelled, her voice filling the car. "You call all the shots. You're the one who walks away happy no matter what. You take advantage of me and scare the shit out of me and then you have the nerve to sit there with that smug look on your face mocking me for being upset. How *dare* you."

He set his jaw and met her angry stare. "You owe me an apology. It's one thing if you're pissed, but you don't *hit* me. Nobody hits me."

"I *am* pissed."

"That's fine. If that's how you want to be about it, I'm gone."

"Maybe that's not a bad idea," she countered. "Go. And rub it in my face while you're at it, so I won't be tempted next time you try to seduce me while I'm babysitting you. Go get in Fairen's bed, since she's obviously the one you really want. See if she puts up with your shit."

That hit a nerve. He remembered Fairen's cold eyes and angry words at the rest stop, the way his heart had lurched when she pulled her wrist from his grasp. He said, "Don't be a bitch."

She barked a laugh. "*I'm* a bitch. Imagine if that officer had done his job a little better. Found my car and ran the tags. Called your mother. I'd go to *jail*. My kids would never speak to me again, and my husband would divorce me. In twenty years I'd be living in some roachy little rented room and putting on a hairnet to go to work. All because I gave you a blow job."

He cast a narrowed glance in her direction. After a moment he said, "You've done a hell of a lot more than give me a blow job."

"Yeah, you seem to be suffering for it. *That* punishment fits the crime, don't you think?"

She threw the car into gear and turned the corner toward where her Volvo sat on the shoulder, not very distant at all. He rolled down the window and turned his face toward the wind, allowing his silence to be its own reply. When she pulled up behind the Volvo and cut the engine, he didn't budge. He stared out at the trees and let the stillness gather.

"You still owe me an apology," he said.

"Fine," she replied. Her voice was breezy and hard at the same time. "I'm sorry I hit you. All right?"

He said nothing. Her tone made it clear she felt no remorse. He felt a sting at the corners of his eyes and thought glumly back to the previous night, when he had found himself toying with the idea that he and Judy were a sort of dirty Bonnie and Clyde and that it bonded them somehow, made them not just two mismatched people who hooked up when it was convenient, but a pair. Now he felt foolish in his delusion.

"Do you accept my apology?" she pressed.

He sighed. "Sure."

Leaning back in her seat, she reached over and massaged him, the gesture conciliatory but her fingers pliant, confident.

He looked out the window carelessly and did not stop her. And that was the worst part: his desire for her, still intact. After all the fear and guilt and bullshit, he still wanted her.

16

The day of the Martinmas lantern walk had arrived, and after my last student left that afternoon I set out a sheet of poster board on the art table and spread around it every photo of Bobbie I had managed to hoard. The distraction, grim though it might be, was a welcome one. The momentary *pop* of my palm against Zach's cheek had grown into a thunderclap that echoed across the days. *Nobody hits me.* Afterward he had no choice but to return to my house to drop off the car, but he had also come inside, set his back against the closed front door, and accepted my makeshift apology in grouchy silence. It was enough to assure me his silent treatment wouldn't last long, but in the meantime I missed his company, in all its manifestations.

Since Dan's request that I put together a little tribute for Bobbie, my colleagues had come to me with whatever pictures they could find of her. I had waited until the last minute in order to be sure no one's photos were excluded from the display. Now came the difficult work of actually looking at them. Already I had painted the board in swirling pastels,

using the wet-on-wet watercolor technique that was a fixture
of our trade, and written her name at the top in the noble
and calligraphic Waldorf hand. Along the bottom now I attached one photo after another of Bobbie posing with her fel-
low teachers. In many, she was young and round-faced, with
her smooth brown hair in the bob she had always worn; in
the later pictures she was thinner, with a lavender bandanna
tied around her head. As I set to work arranging the earliest
photos toward the top, the task grew much harder. She had
done her training a couple of years after me, having grown
discontented with her experiences in other private schools
and envious of my enthusiasm and sense of purpose. But as
undergraduates our lives had been so intertwined almost to
the point of codependency, and as I looked at those pictures
I felt anxiety taxiing inside me like a plane down a runway,
filling my mind with the shrilling thought of *the loss, the loss,
the loss.*

There we were: two twenty-year-olds in brief white running shorts and emerald-green knee socks, standing in the
field of the inter-dormitory softball game and smiling as
though this were something we truly enjoyed. Her arm rested
over my shoulders; she balanced her weight on one foot in a
jaunty way, while I, short in stature and bird-boned, stood
with my hands folded beneath my sternum as though caught
in the act of prayer. Her smile was openhearted. Mine was
nervous, and with good reason. The semester before, I had
lost nearly everything in a fire at our previous dorm building. Bobbie had, too, of course—she was my roommate—but
unlike me, Bobbie didn't carry her whole life off to college
with her out of fear that her family would dissolve in her
absence and scatter her possessions to the four winds. And
also unlike me, Bobbie had not been dating the man who
had caused the fire by getting drunk and falling asleep while

smoking in bed. I felt responsible, in a way, because I had known of Marty's bad habits but did nothing to report or repair them. He drank when he was angry, which was often. On the night of the fire he and I had slept together; afterward, as I lay with my head on his chest watching the smoke from his cigarette curl toward the ceiling, a girl called. He had asked me to step out of the room so he could talk to her, and we argued. I had gone back to my own room feeling put out, and even months later my sense lingered that if I hadn't been quite so sensitive, several dozen people would have been spared the heartache and difficulty of losing all their things. And of course, Marty would still be alive.

You can't blame yourself, Bobbie had told me, and set to work making our new room as cheerful as possible to distract me from my gloominess. It was she who bought me a new *Last Tango in Paris* poster, pointing out that Marlon Brando could take anyone's mind off anything at all, and gave me a glass ball swirled with purple that hung in the window and captured the light, sending it off in little rays around our room. Even now it hung in my kitchen window, and like everything that bore the stamp of Bobbie's love, I treasured it as though it were the relic of a saint.

I taped the photo near the top center of the board, running a hand over it to smooth it down. As I did, my door thumped open and Sandy came in, carrying a rattling box of lanterns made of tall Mason jars covered in tissue-paper stars slicked down with white glue.

"I found these in my supply closet," she said. "Thought you might be able to use them for the younger siblings who show up without one. Will they do for that?"

I nodded.

"If you'd just put them back in my closet afterward, that would be great. I have to leave early… Hey, are you okay?"

"Yeah." My voice quavered. "I'm just…trying to pull this together."

She set down the box and looked over my shoulder at the poster. I felt her hand against my upper arm, brisk comforting strokes. Sandy was touchy that way, and although people like that tended to make me uneasy, I knew she meant well. It was her way of showing love, like Bobbie's way of giving out little presents. It helped if I thought about it in those terms.

"You knew her a long time," she observed.

I nodded again and wiped beneath my eye with the heel of my hand.

"You can talk to me about her, you know. You can't hold that kind of grief in. It'll gnaw and gnaw at you."

"It's easier if I don't talk about it. I'd be a basket case if I did."

"Not true. If you keep it inside, you'll really be a basket case. Talking is cathartic. Keeping quiet will slowly drive you crazy. As the song says, 'silence like a cancer grows.'"

"What song is that?"

"'The Sounds of Silence.'"

I gave an abrupt little laugh. "Simon and Garfunkel. Of course. Great stuff."

"For those of us old enough to remember them."

I laughed again, this time more sincerely, and also more hopelessly. I thought about my debate with Zach on the way home from Ohio and wondered which Mrs. Robinson I was to him right now: the temptress, or the lunatic. Certainly, they weren't mutually exclusive.

She pulled up a child's chair and sat beside me. She put her arm around my back, and her hand cupped my far shoulder with a firm pressure. I knew she wanted me to lay my head on her shoulder, to speak, to cry, but I just couldn't. It was as if the place that held my grief was so deep that no sign of it could make it to the surface. To cry on Sandy would be to usurp Bobbie's role and hand it to her replacement. My loyalty to Bobbie was too great to let me properly mourn her, because mourning is the beginning of moving on.

"Martinmas was her favorite festival here," I said. "She loved the fall, and watching the little kids go on their nature walks, and the way the air smelled. She loved the excuse to pull out all those big crazy sweaters she used to make. I want to honor her tonight. Not to cry or even talk. Just to make this evening a recognition of what she means to us, and to the school. What she *meant* to us, I mean."

"That sounds wonderful," said Sandy, and as she tightened her hug around my shoulders, I tried to pretend she wasn't patronizing me.

At dusk the children gathered in the school parking lot with homemade lanterns aglow, bundled up in thick wool sweaters and handknit mittens that reminded me, immediately, of Bobbie. My class had made their lanterns a few days before, gluing colored tissue to glass jelly jars and wrapping wire around the tops for a handle. With a tea light inside, the tissue—orange and yellow and red—glowed beautifully. The entire school community turned out each November to walk the few neighborhood blocks near the school, stopping at a few homes to offer a loaf of banana bread or a few cookies, before returning to the parking lot for cider and popcorn.

I loved it with all my heart. It was peaceful and cozy and blessedly free of any commercial attachment whatsoever. Some years—not every year, but often enough—I would look over the gathering of happy faces and feel as though I were reaching back through time, thousands and thousands of years back, to connect with the most ancient meaning of the word *tribe*. I needed that this year more than ever, and not only because of Bobbie. I needed to forget all about the stupidity that was Russ and my own roiling heart and my fears for the future of the school. Martinmas was simple: fire, happy children, shared food. I would place myself fearlessly in the present moment and think nothing of the dark surrounding world.

I held a lantern left over from when Scott was a child, and I walked. Neighbors, who had watched this procession for many years, came out on their porches to wave. The youngest children held their lanterns with gravely serious expressions, taking the adults at their word when they warned of the responsibility that came with carrying fire. The older children tried to make the light dance on the pavement in interesting ways. They looped around the block and made their way back to the parking lot, where a few of the teachers had set up an enormous kettle of cider on top of a charcoal grill. The scent of its embers rose wildly into the night air.

I set my lantern on the ground beside the building and stood, my hands folded respectfully, as Dan moved to the center of the crowd and began his little speech about Bobbie. He had known her for less than a year, and his words had a generic ring to them, like a pastor speaking at the funeral of someone whose name he had memorized on the way in. I knew so much more about her than he could ever say, and as he spoke, my mind, and gaze, began to wander. As it did I caught a movement at the corner of my eye and knew immediately, without even fully seeing him, that it was Zach. I turned just enough to view him. He wore a black sweatshirt with its hood up and black jeans, and he was easing himself down to sit on a concrete barrier at the end of a parking space. In his hand was a paper cup of cider. Fairen stood nearby, talking to another girl, but at the moment he was alone.

He nodded a greeting. In return, I waved hesitantly. I wondered whether his nod was meant to be curt or only covert.

There was a sudden rush of arms rising into the air as Dan began to offer a toast to Bobbie, and Zach disappeared behind the waving limbs; I drank, then cut my gaze sideways again. Zach drained his cup, glanced around, then rose and walked toward me.

"Hi, Teach," he said.

I laughed. I couldn't help it. But his smile was free of irony, and I said, "You seem to be in a good mood."

"So do you."

"I'm always glad to see you happy. You know that."

His smile broadened. "Speaking of which, what's the difference between the president and the *Titanic?*"

I raised an eyebrow. "What?"

"They know how many people went down on the *Titanic.*"

I grinned. "You're awful."

He stuffed his hands into the front pocket of his sweatshirt. "Sorry. I'll work on it."

Dan circled around a group and came toward me. I reined in my smile, and Zach moved past me, walking over to the curb where a group of his friends were playing Medieval Judo. He ducked an airborne kick and retaliated by lunging forward to grab his friend around the waist. I crouched down to meet Aidan, who approached me with his lantern held high and glowing with yellow candlelight, his father's large hand firmly wrapped around his free one.

"Did you show your father the beautiful job you did?" I asked.

He nodded and twirled the lantern to show me the way the orange tissue transformed the simple fire into a warm inward glow. I admired his work before letting my gaze drift over his shoulder to Zach, still good-naturedly play-fighting with the other young men, all grace and lean muscle and hidden sexuality. And as I looked I felt the victorious joy, the intoxication of pure possession. For here was this beautiful creature whom others would look at and desire, and I was one of the few who knew him secretly, whom he had allowed to be intimate with him. Never had I felt so much power in a secret, and never had I guarded one so jealously.

I rose to stand, lifting my lantern, and I thought: *as surely as one of these lanterns can light the next, so has the fire in him rekindled the fire in me.* Where once I had died down to nothing, I was alive again, and all was his doing. I was afire with him, and for once the thought was not terrible.

When the gathering was over, I collected the lanterns into a box and carried it back to Sandy's classroom, navigating down the hallway with my chin lifted above the height of the box. I joggled the doorknob with two fingers and, after the door swung open, carefully plunked the box onto the counter beside the craft closet. The room was dim; the gaps between the window blinds showed a few small lights distantly flickering, as children walked away from the school clutching a lantern in one fist, a parent's hand in the other. To my right, above the blackboard, the legend unfurled: *Man is both a fallen God and a God in the becoming.*

I swung open the doors of the supply cabinet and, quite unexpectedly, pulled in my breath. There on the top shelf were all of Bobbie's things from her classroom, crammed in together without care or curation of any sort. At the front stood her coffee mug with the rainbow on the side, perched on a smiling cloud; wadded beside it, the lilac-colored cardigan that had often hung beneath the middle monkey. There was a ball of yarn with a crochet hook jammed into it, a few rows of work hanging loosely from its pink stalk, and her soft-edged copy of Steiner's *The Kingdom of Childhood,* its bottom edge so well-thumbed that it rose like the edge of a wing.

I pulled each item toward the front, handling them, peering at them, in dreadful wonder at how Bobbie's things had been so unceremoniously shoved into a closet and forgotten. Sandy had done this, perhaps, or Dan; and it made me angry, this evidence that for all of his clownish frowning, all of his somber words about *our loss,* he and others had so little regard for what was left of her. I held the ball of silver-flecked blue wool in my hands and stretched out the rows of crochet work, trying to figure out what she had been making, and for whom. That person should have this, so they could hold it and know that even as she was dying, Bobbie had been working this little web borne of her thoughts for them.

And then I felt a hand sweeping my hair over my shoulder, followed, without hesitation, by lips touching my neck. I let out a small shriek and spun around, dropping the wool. Zach stood there grinning, his expression a little confused. "Sorry. I figured you heard me come in."

"No. What are you *doing* here? Go, before Ms. Valera comes in."

"She left. Nobody's coming in."

I picked up the ball of yarn from the floor and, as I straightened up, caught him undoing his pants. My face contorted with anger. "Jesus, Zach. *No.* Of all the places to come up with that idea. Not *now.*"

"Oh, c'mon. It'll take, like, a minute. I'll lock the door."

"No." I turned my back on him and grabbed the box of lanterns, wedging it onto the empty shelf. In the act of pushing its edge into place, the crochet hook slipped out of the ball in my hand and fell against the tile with a clatter. I tugged the string to bring it back up, and all at once, Bobbie's last few rows of crocheting came undone like a zipper pulling apart. This time my shriek was not small at all, but one of raw and ragged anguish.

"What's the matter?" asked Zach.

I dropped to my knees and picked up the raveled pile of yarn. The long string was kinked at regular intervals, like an undone braid. I looked up at Zach and in a furious voice asked, "Why did you do that?"

"I didn't do anything."

"Well, if you hadn't come in here and scared the life out of me—"

"I just thought you wanted to see me." His voice was hard, curt; as were his eyes. He pulled up his zipper and reclasped his belt. "Chill the hell out. It's *yarn*. Jesus."

He turned and left the room. The tile floor was cold even through my tights, and the slam of the door jarred me. And then I was alone in the familiar classroom, in its spacious silence, the shadows broken only by the hallway light that came through the small rectangular window on the door. I looked down at the loose pile of wool in my hands and, for the first time since the drive home after her funeral, cried in my grief for her.

17

The day after the Martinmas celebration, school was out for Veterans Day. Zach, having agreed to work for his dad for the day, awoke while it was still dark outside and groggily pulled on his clothes. As he nursed a commuter mug of green tea he stared out the window of the pickup truck at the abandoned Beltway, the white streetlights whizzing by in the darkness, the trees like thin, hard shadows behind them. His father, silent and nearly as tired as Zach, let the radio do the talking. Although he was the same age as Judy, his taste in music was better; he listened to the same stuff Zach liked, and Zach felt a fresh appreciation for it after weeks of tolerating Judy's dentist's-office radio station.

They arrived at the embassy, where his father was installing a new library, and carried in the tools. The buzz and whir of the saws brought Zach out of his drowsy haze, and soon enough he was hard at work. This job, like most of his father's, required precision, care and neatness; the entrance was draped in sheeting that locked them into a plastic cocoon, and Zach found himself doing as much vacuuming as carpentry.

Crouched on the floor and waiting for instructions, Zach watched his father work. Like Zach, he wore safety goggles, a dust mask and a hard hat; only a few chunks of his Viking-blond hair peeked around the edges. His blond-lashed blue eyes were serious and sharp as he measured, making rapid calculations in pencil on the two-by-fours. When Zach was a child his father had seemed so *big*, and even now, at his adult height or nearly so, the man dwarfed him.

His father glanced up, catching Zach looking at him. "I appreciate your help, son."

"Not a problem."

"It's good to have some time with you before the baby gets here."

"Uh-huh."

The older man stood and crossed the room, reaching into a bucket for a hammer. Zach pulled his mask down and took a deep breath, then coughed at the dust. His father grinned and passed him a water bottle.

"You're quiet today," he observed. "Something on your mind?"

Zach shook his head, but as was usual these days, he was lying. Alone with his dad, in the privacy of the shuttered room, he felt the uneasy urge to start a conversation he knew would lead to much more than he was prepared to discuss. If Judy were an ordinary girl, he would have a dozen questions for his father about relationships that moved too fast, and how to say no when it was what you meant deep down, and whether it was common for all the shimmer to burn off a relationship and leave only the sex. But he had grown to identify so strongly, and so uncomfortably, with his mother and Booger, that he was afraid anything he disclosed to his father would lead to him disclosing *that*. At one point he had wondered if he was wrong about his mother, if he was perhaps making too much of a simple flirtation; but now, older and wiser, he knew hiding an affair was so brutally simple that what he had witnessed was, at best, a poorly concealed one. He was glad he had not realized this while they were still in New Hampshire, or he doubted he could have restrained the urge to corner Booger on the path to the yoga studio and smash him into the pavement.

What a shit that guy was, Zach thought with a flare of anger. Walking right past Zach, and sometimes his dad as well, with his rolled-up mat under his arm, all serious about his advanced *asanas*. Zach suspected the furnace closet, with its collection of spare mats and the jutting towel-folding table of peeling linoleum. What kind of person had it in himself to do that—to politely ignore the kid and the husband while getting off with the wife-and-mother in between yoga sessions? What kind of guy would do that to someone as decent as his dad?

He hugged his knees to his chest and rocked on his feet, and his father said, "Sheesh, kiddo, are you ever flexible."

Zach stood up and vacuumed the floor, again.

That night he lay in bed with his hands behind his head, exhausted from the day's work, listening to the murmuring on the other side of the wall. His mother's voice was nearly inaudible; only his father's baritone vibrated noticeably through the drywall. He closed his eyes and tried to take advantage of the sound. When he was a child he had found it easier to fall asleep when he could listen to the meandering drone of his father's voice. But shortly he heard his mother laugh; the bed creaked, and before long the sounds grew different, more rhythmic in some ways, more random in others.

He turned over on his stomach and pulled the pillow over his head.

It had never bothered him before, but tonight it did. It was too easy to visualize now. Like learning a new language, the sounds didn't all run together like they used to—what each represented, he immediately recognized. It was *gross,* all of a sudden; but also, it gave him a feeling of dread. His mom was on bed rest. Rhianne had a long list of things she wasn't supposed to be doing, and this was one of them. He hated the thought that she was giving in to it anyway, driven by the same monster that he couldn't control, the same weakness that had driven her to Booger. She was pregnant. She was a mother. She needed to be better than that.

He pressed the pillow against his ears with his fists and waited until it was over.

At the funeral, back in July, Bobbie's grave had been a neat rectangle sliced into the turf. Its edges were so sudden and stark against the healthy grass that it might have been drawn by a child, Harold and his purple crayon, sketching an incongruous shape right *here;* because goodness knows none of us was quite sure how it came to be there. The rich gardening smell that rose up from it, good loamy soil, seemed like an affront to her, something to be ignored. Now, in the chill November air, everything was more correct. The yellow grass crunched harshly beneath my thin-soled shoes; the wind carried the smell of drying leaves, and where there had once been a gaping wound in the earth, there was now only a hard ridge, barely visible, like a scab.

I approached her headstone in my pea coat, flowerless and empty-handed. Prayers were not on my agenda; she and God could hash out her needs between themselves, and I knew I wouldn't be doing her any favors by offering myself as a reference. I stuffed my hands into the sleeves of my coat and spoke aloud to her, haltingly.

"Bobbie," I began, "I'm sorry about what happened in your classroom the other day. I know you would think I'm horrible for what I've been doing. Believe me, I think about that often. You aren't the kind of teacher who would ever have—done anything wrong with a student. I didn't intend to make you the host of anything like that." I took a long, shuddering breath. "I'm very sorry."

A small plastic nosegay had been wedged into the flower holder. Its lurid green stems shivered stiffly in the wind. I thought about how Bobbie had looked in the hospital that last week, lying in her bed under a jumble of clear tubing, her hair soft and short and growing back finally, her droll gaze gone flat and perturbed as she stared at the television. At one point her sister-in-law came in and told her she was putting up a great fight. *I'm not fighting anything,* she snapped. *I'm not winning. I'm not losing. I just lie here and it fucks me up. It's cancer, not a football game.* I felt terribly sorry for her then. I didn't pretend to know how she suffered, but I knew what it meant to feel helpless that way, invisibly taken over by a force that confounded you.

I crossed my arms over my chest, letting my coat bunch up against my chin. "I just don't know where to go from here. I can't stop, Bobbie. I crave him worse than I've ever craved anything. I just have to let it run its course until he gets tired of me. And I know he will. I know it, and I can't stand it. I'd do anything to keep that from happening."

I clutched my arms more tightly around my coat and snuffled noisily. Tears overflowed onto my cheeks and immediately chilled. I wiped my gloved hand beneath my nose and felt my neck tense with an unreleased sob. And that was the worst thing: knowing that I was speaking into the void, into the endless empty space before me. Because only Bobbie knew what the word *anything* meant coming from me, and if she wasn't here to stop me, who would?

★ ★ ★

On Tuesday the students returned to school punchy and disobedient, as though having one day off made them feel entitled to two and they would punish us for not granting it. As the day wound down, the low roar of teenagers being let out of Madrigals practice was audible from the opposite side of the school. I found Scott playing Medieval Judo with his friends in the hallway outside the multipurpose room. Zach was spread-eagled on the tile, apparently recovering from a mortal injury.

"Ready to leave?" I asked Scott. I looked down at Zach. "Are we taking you home?"

"Uh-huh." He raised his knees and then, with acrobatic quickness, leaped to a crouch and then straightened up.

As I had done before, I dropped off Scott at home with an excuse that I needed to stop at the grocery store across town. Once we pulled away from the house, Zach said, "I don't think he's going to buy that one much longer."

"He doesn't care. He isn't paying attention."

The side of Zach's mouth twisted with doubt. "I wouldn't be too sure. That's probably what my mother thought, too."

My heart palpitated. "Your mother found something out?"

"No, I mean, when she was getting with the yoga guy. She probably thought I wasn't paying attention."

"Oh." A cold light rain had begun to fall. The windshield wipers squeaked across the glass. "Okay, I'll try to be more innovative."

I turned into the school parking lot, but it was still full of cars from extracurriculars. "I forgot about that," I said. "Damn."

"It's not a good night for it anyway," Zach said. "I've got a lot of homework tonight, seriously. And I'm out of condoms."

"Your teachers know you had Madrigals tonight. They'll

let you slide on the homework. And we can go without the condoms."

"No, we can't."

"Yes, we can. I've been on the Pill for weeks now, and neither of us is sleeping with anybody else, so far as I know."

"Yeah, but it's still safer if you use them."

"Safer for what? I don't have any diseases. Do you?"

In a scornful voice he said, "No. But they say you ought to act like everybody does, anyhow."

I gave a deprecating laugh. "Oh, the things they teach you teenagers."

Zach sighed and looked out the window. I asked, "Do you want me just to take you home?"

"You may as well. There's really no place else to go."

"Oh, be creative," I suggested. "It's suburbia. Parking lots are a dime a dozen."

"We'll get caught."

"Not if we're careful." I turned onto the road toward the lake.

"I won't last."

I shot him a furtive glance. He sat with his knee against the dashboard, chewing the side of his thumbnail. "What?"

"I won't last. It'll be over in ten seconds. There's nothing in it for you anyway."

"Zach." I laughed. "Is that the real reason? Is that why you're so uptight about covering up? Because I swear you're like Linus and his blanket with those things."

"No," he said, the disparagement thick in his voice. He cut a glance toward me. "It's because I don't want you to get *pregnant,* for God's sake. If that happened my life would be over."

"I don't want that any more than you do," I told him coolly. "That's why I went on the Pill."

I turned the car into the deserted lot next to the lake and parked toward the back, near the woods. I laid a hand on his thigh and said, "Hey."

He turned his face toward me.

"Why are you so moody?"

"Because thinking about cops and babies doesn't turn me on."

"Is something else the matter?"

"No. I'm just tense. I'm *tired*."

I slid my hand beneath his hair and massaged the back of his neck. His skin felt warm, warmer to the touch than my own. For a moment he did not respond; then, not drowsily but deliberately, he closed his eyes. The tension in his neck dissipated beneath my fingers, but his body, even slouched low as it was, looked ready to spring. I rubbed my flat palm in small circles down his back. He curled forward in response, little by little, until his forearms rested against his thighs. His jeans puckered at the back of his slim waist, the bumps of his spine disappearing into the gathered elastic of his boxers.

"Do you remember," I asked, "when I took you out for coffee, back before, and you rubbed my feet, and you asked me—"

"Yeah."

"Why did you do that?"

"Because I wanted to see what you would do."

I grinned. "After I apologized a dozen times for that episode in the playhouse? That's not very nice."

He shrugged. His hair swung freely at the side of his face. "The apology felt a little phony. I was curious what would happen if I pushed it."

"Except I called your bluff."

"It wasn't a bluff. If it was, we wouldn't be here right now."

I stroked the small of his back, the skin so smooth it felt sculptural. "You're right about that."

He leaned his forehead against the dashboard and sighed. Then, extracting himself from my hands, he climbed over the center console into the backseat. The car rocked lightly on its shocks.

Twisting around to face him, I asked, "What are you doing?"

He loosened his belt and regarded me with an impatient gaze.

"You changed your mind?" I asked.

"You didn't change yours."

"I was just buying some time."

He beat an edgy rhythm with his palms against the leather. "You want it or not? Because I really do have a ton of homework, and it's getting late."

I cringed. "Don't say it like that. It sounds awful that way."

"Is that a no?"

I should have affirmed that it was. I knew the full litany of what he did not want to do, and this was where it began. If there had remained any possibility that life could throw a cup of cold water in my face and reverse the course of things, it would have been that moment, that question.

Instead, I climbed into the back of the car.

And it was at that moment that I stopped being a woman who had made a series of exceedingly bad judgment calls, and became a child molester.

PART II:
ZXP

18

When he finally got home, he clomped straight up the stairs and took a shower. As the water heated up he stared hard at himself in the mirror, his image growing ever-fuzzier in the steam, and took inventory of his flaws. His skin looked like crap. He needed a haircut. Without judo or yoga his muscles were going soft, and on top of all of that, he was still short.

He wasn't likely to grow much more at this point. Clearly he was, for all intents and purposes, a man. He didn't feel at all like an adult, and normally took pleasure in that fact. He had the rest of his life, after all, to muse darkly over the tedious matters of the world. As long as he had the freedom to dwell on the entertaining and the trivial, he would do just that. And so he hated it when adult concerns crept in.

He was pissed at himself for ejaculating.

He had felt sure he wouldn't. For that matter, he had been determined not to. He felt tired and crappy, and annoyed at her—no, *angry*—for driving him out to the geographic center of nowhere and leaning on him to have sex with her. She hadn't asked, hadn't felt him out—she simply took for granted that he was available for that purpose, as if, because he was sixteen and in her car, he was a captive audience with a permanent erection. It made him feel less like the irresistibly charming Zach Patterson and more like the sum of his parts.

Of course, he could have flat-out turned her down, but it felt like more trouble than it was worth. She would have come away with a bruised ego that could, in the long run, make his life extremely miserable. It was easier just to give her what she wanted and go home.

Still, he had thought there was no way he would finish. He wasn't in the mood, wasn't happy with her personally, and was terrified—despite her careless assurances—of getting her pregnant. It should have been a supernova of a buzzkill, but in the end, he couldn't help it. His body, which he loved, had betrayed him.

He scowled at himself in the mirror and got into the shower, leaning his forehead against the cool tiled wall. The hot water felt good on his back, but he seemed to be growing more tired by the moment, rather than more refreshed. When he got out he toweled off and pulled on a clean pair of boxers, combed his hair, and started down the stairs. He made it halfway, then stopped and sat, cradling his head in his hands.

"Zach, is that you?"

His mother came around the corridor and, one hand on her hip and the other on her belly, stopped to look at him in surprise. "Are you all right?"

"I don't feel so great."

She waved him down and he followed obediently, moving with what seemed like an enormous effort. She reached up—for he was taller than *her*, at least—and laid her palm, deliciously cool, against his forehead.

"Oh my goodness my," she said. "How hot was that water?"

"Normal. I feel chilly, though."

He walked past her and lay down on the sofa. She covered him with two afghans and returned from the kitchen with the basketful of lozenges and supplements and homeopathic tablets. And for the second time that day, he resigned himself to the fact that his body was, by an act of nature, about to let him down.

The next day, when I picked up Scott from Madrigals practice, I noticed Zach was missing from the group. Wednesday morning, I contrived an excuse to visit the Upper School and, peeking into the eleventh-grade class, saw his seat empty. That afternoon I worked up the nerve to call his mother.

"Does he need a ride to the choir concert Saturday evening?" I asked. Even to my own ears, the innocence in my voice felt forced.

"Thank you, but he won't be needing it," said Vivienne. "We'll drive him if he goes."

"Is he all right?"

"He's just got some sort of bug. Fever, cough, sore throat. I suppose he's all right."

I remembered massaging my way down his spine, taking note of the heat of his skin. The radiant warmth of him had felt sensual to me. It had never crossed my mind that it was abnormal, that he might be sick. How could I not have noticed? Had he been my own child, I would have. And he was *somebody's* own child. Vivienne's.

The groveling shame I had felt when he glared at me in the car returned, but a deeper part of my mind rushed to suppress it. I said, "Well, we'll miss him at the concert. I hope he feels better soon."

"That's kind of you. I'll pass the word on to him."

It was not until after I hung up the phone that the thought occurred to me: *measles*. I felt a rush of fear. Had I overlooked an illness *that* serious? But, no—it was most likely just a cold. Of the fifteen children who had contracted the virus, none were Upper School students. There was little mingling between the two sides of the school, and most of the unvaccinated students were in the Lower School.

Then I thought of Zach in my kindergarten classroom. Not once. Many times.

I thought of everything he had told me about his family. Everything I knew about his body. I thought, *these people are true believers.*

And then I thought, *it can't be.*

Before school began I slipped into the main office in pursuit of Zach's student file. My surreptitious search turned it up quickly, the only P in the bunch, marked with a yellow tape flag that indicated it was one of the files missing either a vaccination record or a signed exemption. The only health-related paperwork it contained was the birth history survey filled out by his mother, describing in lyrical prose his home birth in rural New Hampshire. If I wanted to know whether Zach was our latest case of measles, I would have to ask him myself.

As soon as my last morning student left with his mother I tore out of the parking lot at a speed unbecoming of a kindergarten teacher. Once on Zach's street I slowed to a crawl, scanning his driveway and the curb in front of his house for cars. Both his mother's sporty little Volvo convertible and his father's green pickup truck were gone. I parked one house down to be on the safe side and crunched through the dry leaves that covered his lawn. When I knocked on the door I felt a moment of wild fear that his mother was home after all, but just as I backed away from the door it opened, and there he stood in the living room's muted light, wearing a gray

T-shirt and baggy pajama pants. His jaw and upper lip were stubbly with the beginnings of a beard that matched his hair, and he wore glasses with thin, black-wire frames. The effect was jarring. He looked ten years older.

"Hey," he said, opening the screen door. His voice sounded lower and raspier than usual. "What's up?"

"Your mother said you were sick. I wanted to, you know, check in."

"Kind of dangerous for you to just show up like this, isn't it?"

I folded my arms over my chest. "I can't check in on Scott's friend?"

His laugh, accompanied by a curled lip and half-rolled eyes, frightened me. "You're lucky my mom's not here," he said. "She went to see the midwife because she's worried the baby's not kicking enough. Kinda ironic, huh? She's paranoid about the baby, and then *you* show up."

I winced a little, and he sighed. "C'mon, it's cold out. You'd better come in."

I stepped into the foyer. Newspapers lay strewn on the dining room table, and a basket of laundry overflowed on the sofa. A cat meowed at me from atop the pile, but didn't come over to investigate.

"Doesn't look like Luna likes you," Zach said as he walked toward the kitchen. I took a few tentative steps in the same direction, watching as he picked up a blue-glazed mug and drank from it.

"Are you feeling better?" I asked politely.

He nodded, still drinking. "I'll be back on Monday."

I followed the rest of the way into the kitchen. "I was afraid you had the measles."

This time he shook his head. "No way. I've had my shots."

"Have you really? I wasn't sure. I checked your file," I said, then immediately regretted the confession. "It was flagged for missing an immunization record," I added, as if my nosing around had been merely a clerical matter.

"Really? My mom must not have gotten around to turning it in yet." He nodded to a blue homeopathic-remedy tube on the counter. "She's got me on phosphorous. She tried three others and none of them worked. I've also been ordered to drink a truckload of Yogi Tea."

"Is the phosphorous helping?"

"I guess." He downed the rest of the tea and turned toward the sink. On the counter was a cutting board with a half-sliced lemon on it, and a teddy bear-shaped bottle of honey. As he rinsed the mug, he said, "If you want anything out of me, now's not a great time. I haven't taken a shower in two days."

I balked at his assumption. "I wasn't thinking that. You're sick."

He shrugged, his back to me. His shoulders, thinly covered by the ancient T-shirt, looked slight. "I was sick on Friday, too. Didn't seem to bother you."

"I had no idea you were sick. You never said a word."

He set the mug on the drainer and turned to face me. "I had a fever of a hundred and one. You were in my *lap*."

"*Zach,*" I hissed, horrified to hear him say it aloud. "I'm *sorry*. But I just came to check on you because I was concerned. Don't make it sound like I only care about one thing. That's simply not true."

He leaned back against the counter, and suddenly the vague swagger of his posture, the way the window framed his strong, lean body, conspired to make me feel as if I were ten years old. "Name a second thing," he suggested.

I replied with a nervous laugh. "What do you mean?"

"What I said. Name a second thing."

He looked at me, his hands braced against the counter

behind him, and waited on my answer. I hesitated, and not because I didn't have a second thing to name. Since the weekend of the marathon playhouse construction, I had turned the puzzle of my attraction to him over and over in my hand, held it to the light, examined its every facet. He was good-looking, but Scott had plenty of friends who were more conventionally attractive than Zach, and none had ever tunneled into my mind the way Zach had. As a lover he had proved himself more competent than I would have expected from one so young, but that alone would never lead me to take the risks I took for him. No, the reason was something else entirely—that his very being tugged at my mind as though anchored somewhere in its darkest depths, and that the act of seducing him, regardless of whether he reciprocated the pleasure, calmed a place inside me that had never been calm. But I could put none of that into words. I only knew the power of the way my mind stirred at the thought of him, recoiled at the notion of losing him, and loved him with the hollow, groveling love a hostage has for her captor.

So I said, "I can't answer that. I don't know why I'm doing this at all. I don't get a thrill out of the risk, that's for sure. And I've certainly never felt attracted to a teenager. Not as an adult."

His laugh was quick and harsh. "You're doing a good job faking it."

"So are you."

"I'm just taking what's available."

"Then maybe *you* only care about one thing," I suggested. "Or perhaps we both have reasons we're not owning up to. I could take a stab at what mine might be. And maybe for you it's about all the time you spent imagining that yoga student going to bed with your mother. But regardless, I'm not thinking about anything else when I'm with you. Are you thinking about your mother when you're with me?"

"No," he said curtly.

"Then we're on the same page. You call the shots here, Zach. You decide when enough is enough. I made a mistake last week, and I'm sorry. But if I was any good at thinking straight when I'm with you, then we wouldn't be in this situation, would we? If you're fed up with it, fine. Tell me to my face, and then stop asking me for rides home. You can't come looking for me after school and then get angry with me when I feel the same way. You have to just say, 'No, Judy, I'm not doing this anymore.'"

He took a deep breath. "No, Judy, I'm not doing this anymore."

My heart lurched, but I said, "Fine. Then I'm not offering anymore, and you're not asking."

He looked at a point over my shoulder. "What if I slip up?"

"I'm not a prostitute, Zach. Make up your mind and let me know what you decide."

The cat wandered into the kitchen and curled around his legs. Sighing, he slipped his fingers up under his glasses and rubbed the bridge of his nose.

"I'm glad you're feeling a little better," I told him. "That's all I came to ask."

He squeezed his eyes shut tight and gave them a final rub. When he looked at me, his eyes were tired. In an edgy voice, one I couldn't read at all, he said, "Thanks for stopping by."

19

By Friday morning Zach felt better, his mother's mystery teas and phosphorous tablets having worked their magic. He shaved off his week's worth of beard, blinked his contacts back into his eyes, worked some goop into his hair, and almost looked normal again.

Almost. Something didn't seem the same. He shook his hair from his eyes and peered closely at himself in the mirror, just as he had a week ago, after the crappy night with Judy. For once his skin was clear, but the difference was more than that; the angles in his face looked sharper. He pulled up his shirt and examined his midsection. His stomach and chest looked the same, but his face suggested he had lost a few pounds. Not surprising, given the fever that had sapped his appetite as well as the fact that, under stress, his stomach had a tendency to return anything delivered to it. He fixed himself a cup of chai and a bowl of granola with milk, and, when it all stayed down, he figured it was time to get back to the grind.

Back at school, his friends were glad to see him. A few girls in his class even hugged him. As he settled into the morning's

Main Lesson he tried to focus on the teacher to gather in all the information he had missed, but as usual, *Dante's Inferno* failed to hold his attention. His gaze wandered toward the windows, to the trees shedding the last of their crackling brown leaves into the chilly wind. Distantly, at the end of the building which housed the Lower School, the voices of children echoed from the playground. He watched the little kids chasing each other and digging in the sand with their red metal shovels, the teachers in barn jackets walking among them, their heads all covered.

None of the teachers was Judy. These children were older, second- and third-graders probably, but still his mind meandered to the kindergarten classroom: its miniature town of wooden buildings scattered on the floor, the beeswax gnomes pressed against the window glass, the protective inward curve of the rose-colored walls where the corners would be. Its windows overlooked the playground on one side, and on the other, the garden. The first time he had come to her, after the day in the woods, she had not drawn the shades. Anyone could have seen them. So blinded had he been by what he wanted, so surprised by the ease of acquiring it, that he had not considered the danger. Neither had she; they had never discussed it, but he had read a lot into her foolhardiness that day. Since then, she had made a habit of drawing her shades at dismissal time.

He bided his time through Spanish, and then, as lunchtime arrived, gathered his books and hustled past the multipurpose room. By now Judy would be outside with her morning class. She caught his eye as he approached, a small figure dwarfed by her canvas jacket, her face half-hidden beneath her kerchief. Sexless creatures these teachers were, bland to the point of invisibility. He knew better, of course, but in some sense he enjoyed the illusion of it: that she was a blank canvas onto which he could scribble everything he had ever wanted to do to any woman, that she set out the raw material of story or craft but his imagination gave the spark that brought it to life.

"You're better now," she observed. "All shipshape."

"All shipshape," he agreed. Her face was impassive. He added, "My voice is still a little rough, so I'm skipping Madrigals tonight, but I feel fine."

She nodded. Then she asked, "Where are we?"

"The Lower School playground."

"Come on, Zach, you're a more abstract thinker than *that*." Her gaze burned into him, but, unsure of what she meant, he gave no reply. She asked, "Are you still upset with me?"

He shook his head. *Upset* was the wrong word. He didn't offer up any that felt more accurate. *Numb. Hard. Resentful.* He felt duped by a bait-and-switch maneuver: led in by the illusion that their affair was based on primal, mutual need, only to discover, when he felt none, that she would take from him anyway. Her apology had taken the edge off his anger, but it also proved a point that made him feel gloomy and helpless: he could have her the way she was, a dark star of desire for him, or he could have her not at all. If his time with her had taught him one thing, it was that he had been keeping his own set of desires on one hell of a choke chain, and he had little motivation to try to order the animal back into the cage. But he didn't have to be nice about it.

"Come by my classroom when everyone else is at Madrigals," she said, her voice a low monotone. "I'll give you a better apology then."

"I don't want that." At the moment it held no appeal to him. To be vulnerable to her, needy of her willingness, in her debt. He wanted to establish to her how he felt about her now, and that wasn't the way.

She shot him a nervous glance. "What do you want, then?"

"Russ is teaching tonight, right? I'll meet you at your house. I'll tell my folks I'm going to the library or something."

She frowned. "During Madrigals? That's not very convenient as far as timing goes."

"I don't care."

Her lips tightened in disapproval, deepening the lines at the corners of her mouth. The edges of her Russian-grandma headwrap fluttered in the wind. "You're still angry. This is your way of getting me back."

"No. This is my way of getting *laid*. It's been over a week. I don't want a BJ. I want a *bed*."

She sighed. "Well, I guess I ought to be grateful you're still coming to me for that."

"Yeah," he agreed. "You should."

She shot him a sideways look, her gaze lingering on his face for a beat, seeming to take in his grim expression. He shoved his hands deeper in his vest pockets and hunched his shoulders against the wind, then turned and headed back into the school.

His anger left me anxious all afternoon. I poured myself what apple juice was left in the bottle from the children's snacktime and dosed it up with Bach's Rescue Remedy to calm my nerves. My students engaged themselves in a game of tying on a golden silk cape from Michaelmas Day, back in September, and chanting its rhyme for each other in turn. *Aidan wears a cape of light. It gives him courage, strength and might.* As soon as the cape went on, the child's expression would change, grow prouder and more noble; occasionally a beaming smile would cross his or her face. If it was a girl, she might spin in a circle; a boy would plant his fists against his hips. I sat in a tiny chair, my knees hiked up beneath my jumper, and wished Steiner had thought up an equivalent item for adults. What I needed was a sweeping velvet cloak with a hood, panther-black, to make me feel aloof and mysterious instead of groveling and desperate. But I would have to shed it anyway to give Zach what he wanted, so I was fresh out of luck.

As the school day ended I sent each of my students, one at a time, off with their parent or caregiver. Easing them through these transitions was an important part of my job, and one I valued, but today I felt impatient to get these rituals over with and move on to the business of smoothing things over with Zach. But after the last child left, as I moved around my classroom tucking in chairs and straightening baskets, Sandy stepped in.

"Judy?" she began. "Do you have a moment?"

I turned to face her, and she perched on the edge of the shelving unit beneath the window. "I saw you speaking with Zach Patterson on the playground earlier. He's one of my students."

"Is he?"

"Yes, and something's off about him. He doesn't even make a passing effort to pay attention in class. You should see his notebooks. I've seen fifth-graders turn in better work. Clearly he's not *stupid*. I mean, I don't think he'll be discovering the cure for cancer, but I'm sure he's not as...*boneheaded* as he comes across in my classroom."

I nodded, then shrugged. "Kids that age. They can be pretty disengaged. Scott's the same way."

"I know you've spent a lot of time with him lately. Helping him get in his service hours, and all that."

"Yes."

Her hands moved in a searching gesture, slowly stirring

the air. "Has he—said anything to you? Indicated if there's a problem at home? Does he seem distressed to you?"

I offered her a small smile. My heart was beginning to settle down from the panic that had trickled into me when Sandy began asking her questions. Now I understood the situation was simple: Sandy wanted me to tell a story. In the Waldorf teaching college we had learned the right way to tell a story, and that way is quite different from the common wisdom. It calls for the teacher to speak in a near monotone, absent of animation, never varying from the script. A story told this way is almost hypnotic, sending the child's focus to the words rather than the storyteller, allowing her to memorize the tale and grow familiar with it until it is drawn into the heart. This is a very good way to tell a fairy tale, and also an excellent way to explain a complicated lie. I was a master at Waldorf-style storytelling, because I had been using these techniques all my life.

"Yes," I admitted. "He's had problems with that girl. Fairen Ambrose."

"Ah." Her face rearranged itself instantly into a look of total comprehension. "He told you this?"

"Oh, yes. She plays games with him. Strings him along. I saw it myself on the choir trip to Ohio. Playing footsie, back massages, and then when he pursues it she turns him down. He's a bit stymied by it. Embarrassed. He covers it up by acting like he doesn't care."

"That makes sense. I'm trying to get to know all these kids, but it's a process. You've known most of them since kindergarten, I've been told."

I nodded. "It's interesting how little they change. Fairen, for example. She's very bright, but she uses terrible language and doesn't have much respect for adults. She was the same at five. And of course, since she spends a lot of time at my house

and I have a son, there are other things I don't love about her.
To put it politely, she's very liberated."

Sandy laughed. "No wonder Zach likes her."

"Yes, I'd say that's an ill-advised match for a kid who seems
pretty naïve."

She nodded, then leaned in and said in a stage whisper, "I'll
change my seating arrangements at the end of the term."

I chuckled. "Good idea."

"God, isn't it hell?" she said. "Being that age and dealing
with all the romantic drama? There's no amount of money
you could pay me to go back and experience all that again.
Remember what it was like?"

I smiled again, the muscles in my face going taut with the
effort. I remembered.

"Lift."

I followed Zach's command and raised up my end of a
folding table, taking a few mincing steps forward as he strode
backward. His biceps bulged forward; the tendons in his forearms shifted beneath his skin.

"This weighs about twenty pounds more than it ought to,"
he observed.

"Well, it's pretty old."

His voice was derisive. "*Everything* in this school is pretty
old."

"I beg your pardon."

He caught my smirk and returned a patient half smile.
"Present company excluded, Mrs. McFarland."

"*Zach*. Please."

He eased the table down into its spot and I gratefully followed suit. Banners were already strung high above our heads,
the distinctive Waldorf script lettered in a dusky rainbow of
colors by hardworking eleventh-graders. Baskets full of crafts

were stacked three high along the walls. Zach's beautiful playhouse sat at one end of the room as the crown jewel between
the two silent-auction tables, its leafy top fluttering slightly
beneath the whisper of the heating duct. I thought about my
conversation with Sandy the day before, the questions I had
answered for her about Zach's distraction and Fairen's negligible morals. The devil, it is said, will draw you in with nine
truths and one lie.

"Still got a pile of these left to put in place," he said. "You
want me to get one of my friends to help instead?"

"I'll be fine. I'm stronger than I look."

He circled around the table and walked a diagonal line
across the room to the storage closet. Leaning across a table
stored on its side, he shifted his balance forward to remove
some obstacle from the floor, revealing beneath his hiked-up
shirt a band of skin on his lower back. In the small room,
with the door blocking any curious eyes peering in from the
hallway, I felt the urge to run my hand affectionately over the
bumps of his spine, but restrained it. Since he had gotten well
and returned to me, Zach was all business. He was still willing, but no longer warm. It made me anxious, but I consoled
myself that it was probably meaningless in the long term.
Despite his youth he was a man like any other: he would get
over whatever made him petulant, so long as I kept it coming.

Footsteps behind me forced my thoughts back in line.
I rested my hands appropriately on the table and turned only
when my name was called.

"Phone for you in the office."

Even over the phone line, the tension in Russ's voice
sounded thick enough to close off his windpipe. "I got a call
from Maggie," he told me. "We need to go up there and bail
her out."

I turned my back to the secretary. "I'm sorry. Did you say 'bail her out'?"

"They picked her up at a protest. She crossed a line or yelled at a cop or something, beats the hell out of me. I can't even tell for sure whether they actually set bail or they're just being pains in the ass and won't let her go unless we show up to claim her. She wasn't exactly forthcoming with the information."

I grunted an exasperated sigh. "What sort of protest?"

"Something about the impeachment. Some campus group protesting against it, and she was in the group on the other side in favor of it. They clashed, and now we've got a two-hour drive ahead of us. I vote we leave her there overnight, to tell you the truth. You want to play, you gotta pay."

"That's impossible. The bazaar is tomorrow. I have to be here." I pushed my hair back with stiff fingers and heard the squeak of tables being dragged around in the multipurpose room. "Russ, can't you just go get her yourself? They need me here to set all this stuff up."

"I can't."

"Why not?"

"Because I'll kill her."

I closed my eyes and considered it was probably a poor idea to let him loose on distant roads with his system full of pharmaceuticals. The last thing I needed was two family members in separate jails around various parts of Maryland. "Fine," I said. "I'll be home in a few minutes. Just—gas up the car before I get there, all right?"

20

We drove north. Along the way, Russ played his Ken Burns Jazz Collection CDs until I felt tempted to kick the player through the dash and into the engine. At one point, when he changed discs, a snippet of radio blasted through. I recognized the tune, a song Zach frequently sang along to, headphones on, as he worked on the playhouse. *She comes 'round and she goes down on me.* Filthy lyrics, all sex and hard drugs, a capella in Zach's angelic pitch-perfect tenor. I tuned out the jazz and let myself drift on the memories of Zach as he moved around the workshop, in those last hours when I accepted that he was completely beautiful and completely untouchable. I longed to turn the car around and go home.

"Ironic, isn't it?" Russ asked conversationally. "We got arrested twice for protesting the Vietnam War, and now here our daughter is getting arrested for being a right-wing nut job. Where did we go wrong?"

I took my eyes off the road long enough to glance at him. He sat back easily in the passenger seat, the corner of his mouth upturned in an ironic smirk. He had voiced no objection when I asked for the keys, although the car was his. Perhaps he had loaded up on downers, because he seemed nothing like his usual self.

"She's determined to do things her own way," I replied. "Come hell or high water."

"Ah, the folly of youth. Maybe we pushed it all too hard. Crammed our views down their little throats. But Scott doesn't seem to be any worse for wear. Just Maggie."

I didn't answer right away. After a minute I said, "Scott doesn't care one whit about anybody."

"It's just his age. They're all self-centered at that age. Give him a few years and he'll probably become a civil-rights lawyer."

I grunted in reply.

He offered a mild scowl I could see only at the edge of my vision. "You take everything too personally, Judy. If somebody gives you a negative answer, for whatever reason, it's like from your gut you react as if it must be about *you*. If Scott's unfriendly, it doesn't mean he hates you and everything you stand for. It probably just means all the room in his brain is taken up with cars and boobs. To look at it any other way, it's narcissistic."

I snorted a laugh at that one. "I'm a narcissist," I said in a mocking tone. "*I'm* a narcissist."

"And there you go, right there," he continued. "A little constructive criticism, and you're giving me that slit-eyed glare like you're going to set me on fire."

"That's not funny."

He shifted in his seat. "It wasn't intended to be."

When we arrived at the police station, I hung back and allowed Russ to do the dirty work. Maggie, sullen and uninterested in communicating either explanation or apology, stepped out from the cell when the guard unlocked it but said little to

either of us. On the drive back to her dorm Russ regaled her
with stories of his own jail stints for civil disobedience, but
she only stared out the window and toyed with the necklace
she wore, a gold cross smaller than a pinky nail.

After a while I cut him off. "You're not exactly encourag-
ing her to avoid this situation in the future," I chided. "How
about telling her what a criminal record will do for her job
prospects?"

"At least she's standing up for what she believes in," he
replied. "And no employer's going to turn her down because
she got arrested for protesting. That's a rock-solid American
tradition right there. Thomas Jefferson would heartily approve."

I heard Maggie shift in her seat. Turning to Russ, I asked,
"Are you planning to ask Thomas Jefferson for a loan to pay
for her lawyers?"

"You don't need lawyers if you can sweet-talk the cops
into not charging you in the first place. Why don't you offer
a little of your motherly wisdom on that one?"

I offered him an icy glare before I turned away. Behind
me Maggie asked, "Mom, did you get arrested for protesting,
too?"

"Yes," I told her. "Several times."

Once Maggie had been safely returned to her dormitory,
Russ and I drove down the main strip until we found a motel
that catered mainly to alumni who were rabid college-sports
fans. Team paraphernalia decorated the lobby, along with a
display of brochures for caves, natural bridges, old-fashioned
train rides and outlet shopping centers. I thought of Zach
and his friends back home in Sylvania setting up the bazaar
without me, the darkened and nearly-empty school thicken-
ing the camaraderie between them, the temptation to exploit

the school's shadowy corners with the adults in short supply. I thought of the way Fairen Ambrose, my wry little kinder-gartner grown up into a fair-haired and foul-mouthed swan, seemed always to have her gaze turned the same way mine did. Eventually she would quit holding back, and that worried me. Zach was neither particularly discerning nor difficult to please.

Russ accepted the key cards, and I followed him down the sidewalk to a room with a dull green door. Inside I set my overnight bag on the luggage rack and locked myself in the bathroom to take a shower. We would need to set off early the next day to make it back to Sylvania in time for the bazaar, which began at eleven. Already it was past midnight, and af-ter only a few hours of sleep the driving would probably fall again to me, because Russ would likely still be conked out on Nembutal. Not that he had told me this—I had picked up a prescription drug guide to figure out what exactly my husband was doing to himself. Whether the dosages applied to drugs purchased over the internet from Mexico, I had no idea.

I undressed and leaned into the mirror to evaluate the depth of the dark circles beneath my eyes. That was when I noticed a fan of fingertip-shaped bruises a little above my left breast. I looked at the right and saw an identical set of marks. Reflex-ively my hands lifted to touch them. They were unmistakable: eight purplish prints and, nestled in my cleavage, a lighter, smaller one for each thumb.

The memory rushed back to me in a jumble of images: myself lolling in euphoria, and Zach above me, freed from the constraints of patience, allowing all his subdued frenetic energy to surge into his muscles at once. Anger, still linger-ing, gave his passion an edge that was a little selfish, a little sadistic; I didn't mind. Once he had dutifully attended to me he seemed to disappear into himself, black bangs swinging, breathing heavily through his mouth. His bottom teeth were exposed by his grimacing lower lip. At the time, the grip of his fingers hadn't hurt at all. The endorphins pumping through my veins were to thank for that.

I checked the lock on the door and got into the shower. When I came out of the bathroom, I expected to find Russ knocked out in one of the full-size beds. He was in his pajamas and on the bed, all right, but with his glasses on, watching the news on the small TV.

"Poor Bill," he said. "They caught you red-handed, sucker."

I took a container of hand lotion from my overnight bag and smoothed a dollop onto my hands. When I folded down the coverlet on the other bed, Russ asked, "What are you doing over there?"

"Going to sleep."

"In *that* bed?"

"Why wouldn't I?"

He held out his arms to indicate the breadth of the bed in which he sat. He had already removed the bedspread, of course; hotel bedspreads, to Russ, were flower-print petri dishes. "You never sleep in a different bed at home."

"We have a king. These are full-size."

"Ah, so what? Don't be a stranger."

Unintentionally, I snorted a laugh. "Russ, really."

He pushed himself down the bed on the heels of his hands, then spun sideways to face me. He rubbed a knuckle against my knee and said, "In college we used to make do with a twin."

"I'd never want to do *that* again."

"By that measurement, a full is luxurious."

I peeled down the blanket and top sheet. "What's luxurious

is a full night of sleep, which I'm not going to get anyway. And I have a full day tomorrow, with the bazaar."

"Hell, I'll come by and give you a hand. You make the sacrifice, I will, too. Call it teamwork. How does that sound?"

"Fantastic," I said dryly. "What a way to recruit volunteers. Mind getting the light?"

"Not at all."

He got up to hit the switch, and I climbed under the stiff covers and rolled onto my side. Light from the security lamps in the parking lot glowed around the curtain, but I felt so exhausted it would hardly bother me. I rearranged the pillow and closed my eyes. Then Russ climbed in beside me.

I didn't move. I felt too surprised to react. When was the last time he had tried to have sex—had it been this year, or the previous one? Despite the conversation, I had assumed he was making a nominal attempt to come on to his wife so he could tell himself it was her fault he wasn't getting laid, in service to his ego. Never mind his complete disinterest in the act itself.

But he didn't seem disinterested now. He tried to roll me onto my back, but I wadded the blanket into my hands and refused to budge. In response, he nuzzled my neck and pulled up the back of my nightgown.

"*No,* Russ," I said, and elbowed him away.

"Why not?"

"Because I need sleep."

"But we've got a hotel room all to ourselves."

"Russ—we always have a whole bedroom all to ourselves."

"Yeah, but at home I'm always wrapped up in the dissertation." He rubbed my arm. "I'll be quick if you want me to be. Or slow if you prefer."

"No. Leave me alone."

I writhed away from him, but he grabbed my elbow and

pulled me back. As I tried to jerk my arm away, I wriggled onto my stomach, but he held on and moved as I did. His weight on my back, with my face against the scratchy sheet, made me feel half-suffocated. He must have heard my struggled breathing, because he rose up on one arm to make room for me to stretch my neck.

"Now, Judy," he said, his voice placating but his fingers still tight above my elbow, "you know I'd never *make you* do anything."

I took several deep breaths and swallowed.

"So I'm *asking* you to be nice to me. Because I work my ass off, and you're my wife, and it would be awfully damn considerate if you'd allow me the privilege of having sex with you on the rare occasion my schedule permits."

I relaxed a little, and in turn, he eased his grip. When I turned onto my side he curled up behind me, and after that I didn't protest any further. I stared at the band of light around the window and tried to ignore Russ, who didn't seem to notice, or care.

The streetlights still shone halos of yellow against the charcoal sky when we climbed into the car the next morning, groggy and unsettled, as if the previous night's events had embarrassingly revealed just how far gone our marriage was. Perhaps it was only my own perception; Russ, loaded up on medications, could no longer be depended on to display a reaction that meant anything. This time he took the driver's seat, and I did not complain. My exhaustion was probably as debilitating as whatever state he was in, and he could throw back his black coffee much faster than I could.

Neither of us spoke for the first thirty minutes or so, allowing National Public Radio to hold up its end of the conversation unassisted. Two Congressmen, one Democrat and one Republican, argued over the impeachment proceedings, and for once I thought Russ's jazz CDs might be welcome. I thought back to Zach's opinion of the whole thing—that the president had been betrayed, his private business hung out so his enemies could make an example of him, that it was frivolous and absurd. Zach's interpretation was simplistic, but naturally I appreciated his take that privacy trumps all else. I slowly sipped my coffee and gazed out the window at the low blue hills, hazily beautiful against the yellowing grass of autumn.

"So when are you going to stage an intervention?" asked Russ.

I turned in surprise to look at him, and then, finding his small smile unreadable, stared back out at the road. "Your business is none of mine," I said.

He chuckled. "Sure it is. I pay the bills. I stay at this damn job so our kids can get tuition remission." He let go of the wheel long enough to hold up his left hand. "I keep the ring on."

"How kind of you."

For a moment he met my eye and scowled. "I've never known you not to have an opinion about something. I keep waiting to come home and find you and Scott and my boss and whoever else sitting around in a circle ready to haul me off to rehab."

"Do you want me to?" I asked, cool-voiced. "Because to this point I was under the impression that Scott and your boss were the last people you would want me to tell."

"They are. I'm just surprised you haven't done it anyway."

"You sell me short," I told him. "You always have."

His mouth pulled into a slow, thin line. "I married you," he reminded me. "In spite of everything."

"In spite of *nothing*. I rest my case."

"Bull*shit*," he countered. "Marty didn't fare so well. Did I hold that against you? No. And damn well I should have."

"What happened to Marty was an accident."

"Like hell it was. And it damn near took out the entire dormitory. People who pass out drunk don't spill vodka over their entire bed. They also don't light cigarettes after they've passed out. I gave you benefit of the doubt then, because I knew you wouldn't stage something that evil. But I wonder now and then."

"You *wish* now and then," I corrected. "I was innocent when I had what you wanted, and twenty years later, when I'm entitled to half your retirement, I'm guilty. Drunks do things like that all the time, and Marty was one of them. It was terrible what happened to him, but I can't say I'm sorry. He was abusive."

"You think everyone is abusive. You think *I'm* abusive."

"I beg your pardon. You strong-armed me into bed last night and nothing burned down. I wouldn't consent to you abusing me. I'm above that."

"Lucky me. Did you enjoy it?"

"No."

He snickered. "I would have stuck around for you if you'd asked."

"I'm fine, thanks."

His expression, focused distantly on the road, was placid. "You're probably having an affair. Even when you're pissed as hell, it's not like you to turn down an orgasm."

"Maybe I'm done with both opinions and orgasms."

He grinned. "Not you. You're certainly hitting the wine these days, though. Maybe that has something to do with it."

"With which part?"

"Either. I'm willing to bet it's either chilling you out or warming you up. Our recycling bin looks like the day after a faculty party every night of the week. Maybe we *both* need rehab."

"I don't. If you do, feel free to go. I'll hold down the fort."

He glanced at me. "I bet. I think the difference between you and me is that you're still in the denial stage, and I'm starting to move past it."

"Oh, not at all," I said. "I didn't deny a thing."

For a long moment he considered that in silence. Finally he said, "Judy...it could be better than this. I think they're going to clear me to graduate in the spring. After that I'll take the summer off, we'll clean up, get the last kid out of the house, take a vacation. Maybe you can get some counseling, deal with how low you've been since Bobbie died. We'll both get better. Put all this crap behind us and get on with the rest of our lives."

His words sounded sincere, but I knew Russ better than this. His first loyalty was to his ambition, and if at the moment he was turning it back toward me, it was only because he didn't yet know to whom he would need to pay obeisance in order to resume the climb. In the vacuum of authority he could let his eyes rest for a moment on his small wife, and make me feel cruel to harden myself against the gentleness I knew from experience would not last long. Regardless of his sincerity, our dreams had diverged so completely that I could not imagine how we could share a life much longer. Russ wanted to move forward into an accomplished and respected advanced adulthood, while I yearned to fall back and back, recapturing all I had lost along the way to this place. Because I have learned that all anyone ever wants is to feel at peace with the sadness and love they have cobbled together into a life, with opportunities missed and those misguidedly taken, and for Russ that peace stretched like a ribbon between two posts lodged at a point in the future. My peace, that paltry ball of tangled wool, lay abandoned on a straw bale somewhere in a past that shifted each time I reached for it; and of all I remembered from that room full of shit and salvation, nothing had lasted except a love that was almost pure.

"I've already put this crap behind me," I told Russ. "I'm already getting on with my life."

He sighed deeply. The corner of his mouth tugged toward his ear. "Let's not say it for now, all right?"

"Say what?"

"The D word." I frowned, and in an exasperated voice he added, "The one that means a marriage is over."

"That's two D words," I corrected. "Doctoral dissertation."

He laughed loudly and raised a hand from the steering wheel to rub his weary eyes. "Oh, Judy," he said. "God, how I've fucked it up."

I turned and gazed out the window at the spare rural landscape, the red barns that dotted the dying fields, like chambered hearts in the midst of nothing.

21

Through the window, the barn looked little different from the houses around it: plastered white and half-timbered, with a sloping tangerine roof set with metal brackets to hold the snow. Past the dust of the barnyard, green hayfields waved all around it. She leaned her forehead against the glass and sighed. Two weeks had passed since she had last tried to visit. She passed the long days in her bedroom for the most part, lying on the floor in front of the whirring fan her father had bought for her at the PX, reading her worn copies of *The Blue Fairy Book* and *The Secret Garden* and two *Bobbsey Twins* mysteries. Now and then she took out *Struwwelpeter* and turned its pages slowly, translating in her mind as she mouthed the German words, mulling over its subtitle: *Merry Rhymes and Funny Pictures*. And then, when her father was home, Kirsten would knock on her door and send her out to the garden to play. Except for today, when he had decided they would all go on one of his cultural excursions together, with Kirsten joining them to provide "context."

"Off we go, sport," said her father. "Ready for an adventure?"

She let the curtain drop and followed him and Kirsten out to the Mercedes. Judy climbed into the back; Kirsten took the front passenger seat. Judy scowled and curled against the opposite door, keeping her gaze on the landscape as the car rumbled off toward the village of Aichach.

They were visiting Burg Wittelsbach, a site outside the main village which Judy understood, from its name, to be a castle. Along the way her father rolled down the windows, letting in the rush of the wind, which battered Judy's face with the scents of grass and fertilizer. The town rose up alongside the road, the staggered medieval buildings at its center flanked by modern ones. And then the land opened again into its summer splendor: ragged and stretching stalks of feed corn, lacy columns of hops climbing their trellises, combed fallow fields the color of coffee grounds. In the very middle of one of these stood a wooden crucifix as tall as a man. Its Christ suffered beneath a small peaked roof that protected him from the elements. The base of the cross stuck deep in the rich, crumbling soil, amidst the long mounds ready for the planting of cabbages. She would miss this place. All of it: the mountains and the snow, the smells of field pollens and manure, the windows thrown wide open to the air, the imposition of nature. The imposition of God.

They turned onto a smaller road and came to a very old church. Her father parked not far from it and opened the trunk to retrieve his walking stick—a shining length of knotty wood covered in the small souvenir medallions collected by German hiking enthusiasts. They set out in the direction of the church and then hiked into the woods, where the thin trees grew straight and dense toward the sun, some burdened with lush bands of clinging ivy. Ahead of her Kirsten walked in her boxy, methodical way, skirt swinging like a cowbell. The fabric, white and sprigged with flowers in Easter-egg colors, was the same as the dress her friend had been wearing in the barn. Kirsten wore an apron over hers, knotted demurely on the left side, to indicate she was single.

"Here we are," her father said, as they arrived at a large block of granite covered in moss. "This marks where the castle used to be."

Judy screwed up her face. "You mean there's no castle?"

"Hasn't been since the year 1209. But this is where the foundation was. Don't pick at the moss, Judy."

"Why'd they take it down?"

"Because Count Otto murdered King Philip of Swabia," he told her, and Kirsten nodded. "Then Count Otto tore it apart and used the stone for other things. Probably to build his own castle someplace else. Or to throw over the walls at people who liked King Philip better."

She ran her fingers over the German script carved into the stone. Behind the rock sprouted a crowded assortment of trees, their trunks fanning out at angles, all vying for the light. Other than the marker, there was no sign that this place had ever been anything but woods. In a way it was a gravestone, no different from the ones she and Rudi had played among the past winter, but for a place instead of a person. A gravestone for a home.

"Well, I guess we ought to go take a look at the church," he said. His walking stick thumped against the dirt. "Another day, another plaster Virgin Mary. Lead the way, kiddo."

"We can skip it. I don't care about it."

Her father shot her a disbelieving look. "Are you kidding? You love that stuff."

She shook her head. She would never be able to explain
it in a way that made sense. Lately, during meals, her father
had begun to make optimistic small talk about her mother's
condition, how much better she would likely do once she was
moved to a civilian hospital back in the States, how glad she
would be to know Judy was being well taken care of. *Kirsten,
now, she has been invaluable,* he would say then. And thus would
begin a long segue into Kirsten's virtues, his voice enthused,
verb tenses muddied enough that Judy understood he had no
intention of leaving the girl behind. At one point she might
have confided her fears to Rudi, but now to approach the barn
was as daunting as her own home. She had muttered a shy,
stammering *Ave Maria,* and the universe had only twisted the
blade.

"Well, *I* want to see it," he said. "How can you choose to
skip a four-hundred-year-old church? You know you've been
in Europe too long when *those* have gotten routine."

He started toward the church, with Kirsten falling in line
behind him and Judy, in turn, behind her. As they walked
Judy picked red currants from the bushes along the path, and
Kirsten gazed up at the trees, pointing out birds and nam-
ing them for Judy. *Rotkehlchen. Spatz. Krähe.* Her wandering
reminded Judy of the story in her schoolbook about the little
boy who walked around with his nose in the air, never paying
attention to where he was going until he fell into the river.
Das ist ein schlechter Spaß, warned the book. *That is a bad game.*
The illustration showed the half-drowned child being dragged
from the water with poles, mocked by a trio of fish. *Merry
Rhymes and Funny Pictures.*

"You'd better pay attention to what you're doing," Judy
warned her in rudimentary German. "If you don't, you might
have an accident."

The girl cast a nervous glance at her and hurried ahead

to where Judy's father strode onward, walking stick pressing him steadily forward through the forest. The word for *accident* was so simple in German: *Unglück*. The opposite of luck, the kind that nobody wished for you in pink icing. It could mean *accident*, but it could also mean *curse*. Or *catastrophe*.

"Come on, kiddo," called Judy's father. "Pick up the pace."

Kirsten looked over her shoulder at Judy, and Judy smiled. Three at a time she popped the red currants into her mouth. She was the cavechild, eating the food the primeval garden offered her, following the tribal king. Speaking the language that winnowed words down to their simplest terms, forcing them into meanings that were foggy yet dense, like the morning.

The girl Rudi liked so much couldn't stay there forever. The following week Judy returned to the barn, because she harbored a dogged hope that things might return to normal, but also because time was getting away from her and she wanted to cherish what remained with Rudi. At the gate that marked the edge of his yard she turned and caught a glimpse of her own home. It stood in the near distance at the rise of the hill, cheerful and half-timbered with geraniums in the window boxes, the lovely cottage which Kirsten had turned into a jack-in-the-box of primal fear. It was Judy's mother's tidy domain, but while she sat by the window in a sanitary room and waited for her senses to come back to her, the natives back home were throwing a party. To her father, the topography of Germany was a thin surface of charming, sportsmanlike, well-organized modern life laid over the deep crackling roots of a barbarian land. The hardy knots of the old ways still broke through, and must be negotiated: the peasant good cheer of their festivals, the pagan earthiness of their Christianity, the temptation to cradle the cheek of a subservient virgin and see whether she would dare say no.

The old green station wagon belonging to Rudi's family was missing from their gravel driveway; they all appeared to be gone except for Kirsten, who was at the Chandlers', but Judy checked the barn anyway. Rudi's black rubber boots rested beside the pile of hay bales. The cow, large-eyed and full-uddered, swished her tail at Judy. The barn was dim in the late-afternoon light, smelling more strongly than usual of manure. She looked up at the crucifix on the back wall, witness to numerous sins. She thought about the puffs of crinoline on either side of Rudi's hips, how he must have pulled the girl against him to make them flare wide open like flowers in a time-lapse filmstrip. The barn had that effect on people. *They stay warm by their own body heat,* he had told her, his back to the counter and his rough hands resting against it on either side. In embarrassment her gaze had fallen to his suspenders loose at his waist, his navel that seemed an odd reminder of infancy on his grown male body. *You can eat it for a cookie, and there is no sin.*

She walked through their yard to the shed, as she still occasionally did, to look in on the family of hedgehogs. The gasoline fumes gave her a mild headache, but it was worth it to play with these little animals Rudi agreed were precious. Yet now they were gone; where they had been there was only a fluff of dry grass interspersed with brittle brown leaves. She crouched on the hard-packed soil beside it and poked with the end of a trowel, but it was useless. The family had disappeared, and she could not guess where they might have gone.

She stood and set her hands on her hips, digging the toe of her saddle shoe into the ground. The shed was small and close. The tractor fit into it but left little space for anything else. Along the far wall rested a cluster of tools, hoes and

spades and a rake with rusted tines; beside it sat a pile of rotting baskets and a stack of milk pans. A sack of fertilizer sat
near the door, its top gaping open. She turned a basket upside-
down and sat on it, then took from her skirt pocket the little
stack of matches she had been hoarding from the box in the
kitchen. They were so much larger than the small ones people
used to light cigarettes, and the strike-anywhere feature still
amazed her. When she moved too skittishly, either the match
snapped in half or nothing happened at all. But when she
snapped it decisively, nearly every surface became a runway
for the most forbidden thrill she had yet encountered. *Snap:*
the split-willow side of the basket became a co-conspirator.
Snap: the sole of her saddle shoe brought a second flame roar-
ing to life. *Snap. Snap.* She let each burn down almost to her
fingers, then dropped it on the dirt floor. The humid ground
offered no fuel to the fire, and every match burned itself out.
A little pile of wood ash formed beside her, and she thought
of the illustrations in the story about the girl who played with
matches, the cats' tears pouring like an open spigot beside the
little volcano of ash that had once been Pauline.

But there was no concern for that. Pauline *jumped for joy and
ran about,* while Judy sat still. When she dropped her last match
onto the ground, she fed the small flame with a leaf from the
hedgehogs' nest. It fluttered and rose to a high peak, and the
effect pleased her enough that she sprinkled it with a bit of
grass from the nest; next, a broken bit of twig from a basket.
Now she had a very small campfire, a doll-sized one, suitable
for her imaginary journeys into the land of the cavechildren.
Onto it she dropped another tuft of grass, then looked around
for steadier fuel. The bag of fertilizer gaped beside the door;
she took a handful of the gray granules and fed one to the little
campfire. *Snap:* but instead of a flame, it popped and gave off
a flash of light. She fed it a second one, then a third.

The shed door creaked open, and Judy swung her head around in alarm. She quickly dropped the fertilizer onto the ground and stood, setting the basket like a cap over both the fuel and the small fire. Standing at the door was Kirsten, her blond braids crossed demurely over the part in her hair, her green flowered apron neat at her waist and Rudi's big boots on her feet. She took a step inside and said, *"Oh. Hallo, Judy. Was machst du?"*

"Playing," she replied in English. She saw the incomprehension in Kirsten's eyes, and she stood taller and straightened her skirt. The girl looked nervous, as though she meant to inquire further but lacked both the nerve and the English skills to do so. Judy moved toward the door, and Kirsten's gaze followed her. There was that look again: the one of a girl with her pockets turned inside out. The mute plea. When Judy reached the doorway, Kirsten squeezed past her and headed toward the milk pans at the back of the shed. She stopped halfway and looked around, raising her face as though detecting, now, that whatever she had suspected was wrong was indeed very wrong. Observing this, Judy felt a twist of fear. She did not want to be caught and reported, banned from Rudi's property. And she did not want to see her father and Kirsten taking sides together against her. That could not be borne.

And so she did a simple thing. She banged down the latch, and she backed slowly away.

A chicken behind her heel squawked and fluttered. She turned, then hurried back toward her house. Closing her eyes, she tucked her hands into the small pockets of her skirt and walked into the burgeoning wind, to where the house awaited, calm and empty, to where the thistles were beginning to bloom.

22

Zach caught up with Scott at the side door to the multipurpose room. The bazaar was in full swing, with kids running
rampant on the playground and drivers with "Visualize World
Peace" bumper stickers flipping each other off in the parking lot.

"Dude, it is *crammed* in there," said Scott. "And about four
hundred degrees."

"Is anybody else here?" asked Zach. Scott, he knew, would
understand this to mean any of their friends, since otherwise
the question was profoundly stupid.

"Everyone. Even Tally'll be here in a while." They made
their way into the hallway, where Zach got jabbed with the
stick end of a little girl's ribbon wand. To the left, a teacher's
demonstration of wool felting was attracting a huge crowd.

"Do you know who won the auctions yet?" Zach shouted
over the noise.

"No. They don't start until four."

They squeezed into the multipurpose room. The fifth-
grade teacher was guiding a group of enthralled children in

making beeswax gnomes. Zach guessed they were kids from the larger community and not the school, since by the time he was seven he had made enough beeswax gnomes to populate Middle-earth. At another table, the first-grade teacher was selling handmade soap. The smell of calendula oil drifted out gently from her stand, and Zach felt a wave of nostalgia. His mother's remedy for nearly every scraped knee or boo-boo: calendula cream and a Band-Aid. It was the scent of a mother's healing.

Across the room, Fairen and Kaitlyn jumped up and down and waved. They were directly behind the bake sale booth, working with Judy. Temple grinned beside them and held up a hand in greeting. Zach restrained the urge to roll his eyes. There was nothing more singularly uncomfortable than being in the company of both Fairen and Judy at the same time. At the moment he didn't feel like dealing with Judy at all, but it looked like Fairen would be there for a while, and he wanted even less to make her feel slighted. Scott had walked ahead and was already beside the table speaking to Temple. As Zach approached the group from the side he made his entry by executing a judo hold on Scott, who, with his pathetic green-belt karate skills, disengaged himself and whipped around into a fighting stance.

"No karate in the bazaar," called a teacher.

"Busted," said Temple.

Fairen held both her arms high in the air and beamed at Zach. "You're finally here. We've been waiting all day for you."

He stepped into her hug, and she wrapped her arms around his neck and let him lift her. Over her shoulder, Judy caught his eye with a glance that held a shimmer of reprimand. He scowled at her.

Fairen handed Zach a chocolate chip cookie. "Try these. Mrs. McFarland baked them."

He held up a hand. "I'm good."

"Eat." She prodded the cookie toward him, and when he took it, poked him in the stomach with her index finger. "You don't need to be turning down cookies, trust me."

Judy lifted a metal tray and tapped it against Fairen's arm. "Fairen and Scott, could you run to the kitchen and get the other two trays?"

Son of a bitch, thought Zach. As his friends walked off he narrowed his eyes at Judy and tried to wander away, but Judy grabbed the hem of his T-shirt.

"What are you doing tonight?" she whispered.

"I need to work on my history project. What the hell was that about? Don't act so goddamn jealous. She's just being friendly."

Her laugh scoffed at him. "Oh, please. I'm not being jealous, not of *that* girl. I'm just making her do the job she signed up for."

"Yeah, bullshit. Hands off the merchandise, that's what that was about."

"Don't be silly." She accepted a dollar bill for a brownie. "The house will be empty between seven and nine, if you want to take a break from your project."

"I think I'll pass."

She cut a sidelong glance at him, her mouth set in a light-hearted mom-is-warning-you way. "Don't *you* sound indifferent," she said. "Better watch out. You're going to need a college recommendation one of these days."

"That's not funny," he said. He glowered at her.

"It's a joke, Zach."

"It's not funny. Don't you pull rank on me like that."

"I'm not pulling rank."

"You just did. That's real shitty of you."

"Zach." She put her palm out to accept a handful of change, but looked at him urgently. "I'm sorry. Don't get into it with me right now. There's too many people around. If you're mad, we can talk about it later."

"I'm going to be busy later. Why do you do this shit to me? Talking to me like you're my goddamn guidance counselor. I was gonna say, 'where do you get off?' But oh, wait. I know the answer to that question."

She turned to him with an icy glare. *"Knock it off."*

"Can I go now, then? Mrs. McFarland?"

She turned her back to him to pass a child a cookie, and he wandered off toward the exit doors, passing Scott and Fairen with their trays of cookies along the way. He burned with indignation at her guile. He ought to be the last person on Earth she wanted to piss off, especially after the things he'd let her get away with in the recent past. The slapping incident still loomed large in his mind; he had dropped it with her only because he understood he had hit a nerve with his crack about the German guy. If she couldn't take a joke about some guy she knew thirty years ago, she ought to be more cautious about the impulses she *could* control.

He headed back out the door and sat on the asphalt, leaning his back against the brick. He watched his chemistry teacher lead a group of children in a cooperative ball game, and tried not to think about Judy.

"Zach. Hey."

He turned his head at the sound of his name and saw Scott, standing with one hand on the doorjamb. Behind him stood a tall, middle-aged guy with glasses. Zach knew instinctively who the man was. His stomach seemed to twist inside him.

Scott gestured with his thumb to the older man. "Have you met my dad?"

Zach nodded a greeting. "Nice to meet you."

"He's going to be helping out with the ring toss."

Here of all places, thought Zach. The man had never shown his face at a Madrigals concert, turned up at a school function, or given Zach a ride home. The way Judy described it, he only climbed out of his laptop long enough to eat, take a piss, and yell at her before vanishing back into the ether. Since when did the guy volunteer at school fundraisers? How did that figure into his life-or-death reasons for parting from his dissertation?

Scott was shooting him a strange look. Zach understood that Scott expected him to shake his father's hand. There was no way around it without being obviously rude. Zach got to his feet and extended his hand.

"So you're in the chorus with Scott," said Russ.

"Yeah."

"It's very selective. You must have a lot of talent."

"Thank you, sir."

"What do you sing? Tenor?"

"Yeah." The man seemed perfectly friendly. He didn't come off like a fire-breathing demon the way Judy had characterized him. Zach was becoming familiar with the differences between an adult's public face and their private one; doing puppet shows among the five-year-olds, Judy didn't seem like a nymphomaniac, either. But even so, holding the eye contact unnerved him deeply. He shook his bangs into his eyes and stuffed his hands down into his pockets.

Russ smiled broadly. "That's great," he said. "Wish I could hear you boys sing more often. Music's gotten away from me over the years. My wife and I used to go to rock concerts all the time when we were younger. Of course, that was back in the '70s. Nothing that would be your speed."

Zach shook his head. "Not really."

Russ nodded and grinned again. "Good to meet you, Zach. Hope I'll be seeing more of you once I get work under control."

"Thank you, sir."

Scott and his father walked off toward the outdoor games area, and Zach took off in the opposite direction. He made it as far as the trash Dumpster, then ducked behind the tattered enclosure and wrapped both arms around his stomach. It didn't help. He leaned over into the corner, braced his hand against the wall, and puked up the contents of his stomach. One Dr Pepper and Judy's chocolate chip cookie.

He spat onto the concrete. The saliva dangled from his lip and refused to completely fall. He wiped his mouth with the back of his hand and steeled himself for another round of cramps. At the same moment he heard a quiet voice call, "Zach?"

He knew it was Judy. He didn't turn around when she stepped into the enclosure. She asked, "Are you all right?"

"I just met your husband."

"Oh. So he actually showed up, huh? What did you think?"

Fear of embarrassment overrode psychic distress, and his stomach settled down. He moved away from the puke and sat on the ground beside the Dumpster. The cement felt nice and cool, and he fought the impulse to lie down on it. He cradled his head in his hands and felt the sweat beading his temples. "He didn't seem so bad."

She laughed ruefully. "Don't be fooled. Normally he's a royal pain in the ass. He's just in a good mood because he got laid last night."

Zach felt his stomach lurch again. "Thanks for telling me that. Really, that's the vision I needed to keep going just now."

"I'm sorry." She crossed her arms over her chest. "I was trying to find you so I could apologize."

"You found me."

"I see. I think my husband makes you sick to your stomach. That's okay. He has the same effect on me."

Zach managed a small laugh.

She squatted down beside him. "I'm very sorry about what I said," she told him quietly. "It was stupid of me. Are you angry?"

"I don't know." He felt weary, not angry, but he knew he might feel angry again later.

"Tell me what it will take to make it up to you."

He looked into her eyes, struggling for clarity, but only felt dizzy. He pulled his knees up against his stomach and wrapped his arms around them.

"I don't want you to be angry," she whispered. "I care about you. I love being with you. And you can move on, but everything is at stake for me. My career, my marriage, everything. You know that."

She waited for him to respond. He maintained eye contact, but said nothing.

She unbuttoned her blouse halfway and pulled it open. Her bra, black and lacy, stood out against her pale skin. Beneath her collarbones, like tattoos, lay the twin arches of bruises shaped by his fingertips. He thought back to their two trysts the previous week, the state of his mind and body: still ragged out by illness, constrained by the clock, afraid he wouldn't finish in time—and angry. As desire bloomed in him, so rose his anger at her; he couldn't differentiate the two, and hadn't cared enough to try. But had he really used enough force to *bruise* her? The evidence bewildered him. He wondered, but dared not ask, if she had taken pictures. Sex Ed lesson number three hundred and eighty-six: it's dangerous to sleep with people you don't fully trust.

"If Russ saw these," she told him, "I would be screwed. And not by you."

"It was an accident."

"I'm not blaming you. I'm saying, this is how much I don't want to mess things up with you. I can live with this. You could do this to me every single day and I'd just hide it and hide it and hide it."

He dropped his head to rest between his knees.

"Tell me what it will take to make it up to you," she repeated.

He stared down at the gritty concrete. All he wanted to do was take a few deep breaths and Zen out and forget about all the shitty complications that kept creeping into his life. He didn't even want to ditch Judy, because then he'd have the ditching of Judy to deal with on top of everything else. He just wanted to take a mental break from all of it—not only Judy but also school and Fairen and his homesickness for New Hampshire.

He looked up at Judy and, in the nicest possible voice, asked, "Can I have a blow job?"

She smiled. "Of course you can. Come with me. I think I left some extra cookies in my kitchen."

"What I want the American people to know, what I want the Congress to know, is that I am profoundly sorry for all I have done wrong in words and deeds."

The rising volume of the television caught my attention as I took a tray of cookies from the oven. I turned off the heat, then walked into the den, where Zach sat on the sofa with the remote in his hand. A white-haired and pallid-looking Bill Clinton stared back at him from the screen, speaking from the Rose Garden. It didn't sound like a Rose Garden sort of speech.

"What's going on?" I asked.

"They impeached him."

"What? No."

Zach gestured to the TV. "This is from yesterday. CNN's running it again because they just approved another item of impeachment or something."

I frowned. "I don't think that means he's impeached quite yet. But it doesn't sound good." I listened for another minute and asked, "Did you know about this?"

"Sort of. My dad said something last night."

"This is what I get for going out of town," I murmured. With a subtle shift of my gaze, I peered down at Zach. He seemed to be trying to watch intently, but his eyelids drooped as though he were fighting sleep. His gray shirt was bunched onto his stomach, his belt notched tightly but his fly still undone.

The voice from the television filled the silence between us. *So nothing, not piety, nor tears, nor wit, nor torment, can alter what I have done. I must make my peace with that.*

I looked at Zach again and asked, "What do you think about all this?"

He rested back against the sofa with a tired half smile. "I think he should have turned down the BJ," he replied. "Just say no to head."

"They're not impeaching him for the impropriety," I explained. "They're impeaching him for lying about it under oath."

Zach shrugged. "He wouldn't have had to lie about it under oath if he hadn't gotten blown."

"True. He knew they would hang him for it. This wouldn't have happened in Europe. I think they're slinging mud at him just for the sake of it."

"Oh, I didn't say that," he replied. "I think it serves him

right. He ought to have had the self-discipline not to take it when it was offered, even if he *is* a politician. 'Without being attached to the fruits of activities, one should act as a matter of duty.'"

I stared at him in dismay. "Where did *that* come from?"

"The *Bhagavad Gita*," he mumbled. He chewed the side of his thumbnail. "It's a yoga thing."

"So you think it's karma."

"That's exactly what I think it is."

"That's not what you used to think about this situation," I reminded him. "Back in the fall you thought he was getting a crappy deal."

"Yeah, I changed my mind. I think he's getting what he deserves for lying to everybody. Cheats and liars need to be brought down."

"You think so." I took a few steps forward so he could see me more clearly. "And where does that leave us?"

He removed his thumbnail from his mouth just long enough to answer. "Fucked."

Back at the school, Zach lingered in the parking lot for a few extra minutes as Judy carried the cookies inside, in a sort of halfhearted nod to her paranoia. Russ was over in a sandy section of the play area, stationed at the ring toss, shouting in a friendly way to the little kids as they set their tongues between their teeth and gave the game their best shot. Whether they did well or poorly, he congratulated each with a high-five. Zach stood at the edge of the lot with his thumbs in his pockets, watching him plainly, making no effort to be covert. He was taller than Zach by several inches, lean for a guy of his age; his face, fair-skinned and spectacled, carried a kind of arrogance that evoked in Zach feelings of both respect and scorn. Regardless of the present state of his marriage, he was

Judy's real lover—the one who found it no trouble to handle her, who was even bored of going to bed with her, who would no doubt laugh if he knew the boy watching him at the edge of the grass was also the object of her attentions, because was that the best she could do?

He ground a patch of gravel beneath his shoe and considered that he ought to admit defeat—to go to Judy and say, *I'd like to be excused now,* then return to his day job of currying the favor of a girl his own age. In the months since Ohio, Fairen had gradually warmed to him again. When they met with Temple to discuss their history project, she often sat beside him at the table now, rather than across. At Madrigals practice the week before, after the third run-through of a song none of them particularly liked, she had dropped her head back—he was standing just behind her, on the risers—and rested the crown of it against his chest, sighing and meeting his eye to express her aggravation. For a long time after Ohio, resentment still shadowed every interaction he had with her, and his enthusiasm for Judy left him unmotivated to set aside his anger. But now, not much older but a whole lot wiser, he felt ready to lay down his sword where Fairen was concerned. If she wasn't holding a grudge, then neither would he, for he hated the sense of waste that welled up in him when he mused that in his greed to have her he had lost her entirely.

He wandered back into the gymnasium and caught up with his friends. The whole group of them, Scott included, was now gathered at the bake-sale booth, but Judy was absent, and so Zach happily joined them. By the time the bazaar began to wind down, he was in high spirits; Fairen had flirted with him, Russ stayed out of sight, and for a precious couple of hours life felt entirely normal.

Temple offered him and Fairen a ride home, and Zach was glad to accept. He sat in the back with her until Temple pulled up in front of her house—an odd route for him to take, given that hers was midway between his and Zach's—then climbed into the front passenger seat for the ride back toward Sylvania. "You forget where I live?" Zach asked him as he pulled on his seat belt.

"Nope. Just wanted to talk without Fairen here."

"What about?"

"Tacitus."

Zach laughed and set his foot against the dash. "You picked the wrong person to talk to about that. Fairen's the one who's doing all the reading."

"This is all stuff we went over in class," Temple said. "Remember the part about how they used to hang traitors from trees, and stake down the prostitutes in the swamps, and drag women—"

"Through the streets naked. Yeah, I was listening for that part. What about it?"

"She talked about how certain crimes were punished out in the open, so they could make an example of the people, and for the ones where they considered the people *polluted,* they had to, like, destroy them and all the evidence. I was thinking about that—"

Zach squinted at him. "Man, that's got nothing to do with our report. Does it? It's supposed to be about Maryland, right? I think we can sneak in the Bunny Man thing, but not anything about them staking down hookers in Hauschen Lake."

"Stop interrupting me for a minute and just *listen.* I've got a point to make." His voice had grown tighter; Zach glanced at him. "I was thinking about how what it gets at is that, anywhere you go, the tribe doesn't want people breaking with the code. The individual threatens the group, so the group threatens the individual. You know what I'm saying? In a small, tight society, they had to be real brutal with the violators to

make sure the code gets followed. People still broke it sometimes, even though they knew what was coming. Maybe they
thought they could get away with it, who knows. Maybe they
just got sidetracked by whatever they were after and it made
them stupid."

Zach nodded absently and turned the hot-air vent to blow
toward him.

"Dude," Temple said, and Zach looked up. Temple's eyes
looked wincing, and his voice held a hard edge of regret.
"You're sleeping with Mrs. McFarland."

For a brief moment nothing on him, in him, attached to
him moved. His blood seemed to pause in his veins, the food
balled in his stomach, the air stung his unblinking eyes. Then
he swallowed against his dry tongue and asked, "What are
you *talking* about?"

"I don't *care* that you are," Temple hastened to add. "I guess.
I mean, it's none of my business—"

"Man, I am *not*. That is so not true. Where did *that* come
from? I thought you were talking about Tacitus and all that
Germania crap."

"I am," said Temple. "I'm talking about how you're being
an example of the sort of shit that really pisses off the tribe.
It's obvious, and it's not cool, my friend. If I were you I'd
get straight with that before Scott figures it out, if he hasn't
already. Because he will, and when he does, he'll spread it all
over the school."

"Name an example," Zach challenged. His voice quivered
but rose. "I want to know where you came up with an idea as
fucked-up as that one. Because you've got some serious nerve
to accuse me of *that* shit."

Temple didn't shift his gaze from the road, but his eyebrows
rose, and his face took on a smug assurance that filled Zach

with fearful rage. "Three hours ago. You went home with her."

"She left stuff at her house. I had service hours. Nice try."

Temple's laugh was musical with sarcasm. "Hell of a way to earn them. It's not just one day or one thing, man. It's a lot of stuff all the time. You vanish with her every time she snaps her fingers. You guys look at each other all wrong. When she gives people rides home, she *always* drops you off last. Just now you noticed I dropped Fairen off first even though that didn't make any sense. How do you think it looks to the rest of us when *she* does it?"

"So that means I must be sleeping with her," Zach retorted. "Because it's not like I have any other reason to be around her, like my *mother* arm-twisting me into volunteering for this damn bazaar. No, it's gotta be for sex, right? It's gotta be for sex with *Scott's mom*." He had worked himself into an indignation so profound, he almost believed it himself.

Temple shook his head again. "Dude, I'm being a friend to you."

"The hell you are," Zach half-shouted. "Telling me Scott's going to come after me for some crap you all are inventing. What do I care what Scott says? Everybody knows he's an ass. Nobody would believe something that stupid out of him."

"They will if they think there's a kernel of truth to it," warned Temple. "You know, far be it for me to tell you who you can lay. But dude, that's some nasty, dirty gossip. I don't know if you think it's cool or if she's sexing you up so good you can't think straight, but if that gets out, nobody's going to see it in whatever way you do. And you better believe *Scott* won't. He'll fucking humiliate you. You'd be better off getting caught in the bathroom with a guy."

Zach snorted a sigh and slumped in his seat. "I don't even know what to say to something that retarded."

"I won't tell Scott. You've got my word," he promised. "I've got no idea why you'd do something like this, but I think it's dangerous as hell. Scott's dumb, but he's not half as dumb as the way you two are handling it. Have some goddamn *discretion*."

Zach cast a gloomy gaze out the window, at the trees rushing by at the side of the road, the endless loop of the telephone wires. He stared at the scrubby grass and felt the hollow burden of all he was carrying, all he needed to keep secret, all that stood to go awry if he confided in anyone at all.

"Why would you do that, Zach?" asked Temple, and although the fatigue in his voice made the question rhetorical, Zach knew his friend would welcome an answer. For a moment Zach's silence hung between them. And then, as if all the possible reasons proved too inexplicable or too ugly to consider, Temple sighed, "I don't know," and fell silent as well.

23

He lay awake on Sunday night, staring at his ceiling, his mind racing over all the things Temple had said. He worried certain phrases like a palm full of stones, but they grew no smoother for the handling. *Nasty, dirty gossip. He'll fucking humiliate you. It's not cool, my friend.* He had hoped to wear away the sting of the words, but instead only rubbed his conscience raw.

At one in the morning he lifted the receiver of his bedroom phone and listened to its monotonous hum, wrestling inwardly over whether to call Temple. The urge to confess, to simply purge himself of every dirty secret, was almost physical. Temple would keep his confidence; of that he was sure. But as long as Zach denied it, maintained the pretense that his friend accused him wrongly, he could resist seeing himself through Temple's eyes. As long as the two of them agreed the very idea was wrong and repugnant, they could still be friends in spite of the lie.

He drifted into a few hours of uneasy sleep and got up when the alarm woke him, dressing for school with the reluctance of the small boy he was no longer. Outside the sky was still the blue dark of a winter morning. He felt tempted to claim sick and crawl back into bed, but already he had missed a week of school with the flu, he couldn't afford to miss any more work, and staying housebound all day was likely to drive him insane. What he needed was to distract himself through the day and then gather the *cojones* to talk to Judy. He needed to tell her they'd been caught, they needed to stop hooking up, stop riding in cars together, stop *looking* at each other for God's sake because they couldn't even do *that* right; and above all he needed to pass on this information to her without taking advantage of the privacy to get in one last adrenaline rush. To that end, as he filled the pockets of his jeans, he deliberately skipped over the stash of condoms at the back of his underwear drawer. Weeks ago he had resorted to buying his own when he grew embarrassed at how many he was taking from Rhianne, and, as hard as it was for him to believe, he had actually developed *preferences*. If he could go back in time and tell his September self that in a few months he'd be a prima donna about condom brands, he never would have believed it. Even Rhianne's assurances had seemed fantastical then.

Rhianne. Maybe he ought to run his problems past *her*. She had told him over and over that she was there for any question he might have. He was sure she wouldn't approve, but no doubt she'd heard worse, and if she judged him for it, well, she'd be out of his life soon enough. The thought of confiding in her raised his spirits just slightly, and he headed off to school with the small hope that he might, after all, find a solution.

His optimism lasted just long enough to get him to the door of his classroom. There his Main Lesson teacher greeted him with his usual handshake and a warm "Good morning, Zach." Then he handed him a hall pass and said, "Ms. Valera wants to see you this morning."

"What? Why?"

"She just wants to speak with you. It's between you and her."

"I can just talk to her after school or something, can't I? I don't want to miss class. I've got my *Inferno* summary in my Main Lesson book to show you. I know it's late and all, but—"

"Zach," said his teacher. He looked at Zach over his glasses. *"Go."*

As he walked down the hall, Zach felt his anxiety level spiraling upward by the second. Temple had ratted him out. *I won't tell Scott,* he had said. *You've got my word.* But he had never promised not to tell an adult, and now here Zach was, on his way to the classroom Temple must have visited first thing that morning. He could almost hear Temple's end of the conversation, his SAT-genius, teacher's-pet explanation: *I tried to explain it to him by what you taught us about crime in* Germania, *but he just denied it and denied it. And I'm really worried about him. He's not keeping up with his end of our project because of his relationship with the kindergarten teacher.* Left foot, right foot; fear and fury throbbed in him, each in turn, with the pounding of every step. Temple had forgotten: traitors hung from trees.

He walked past classroom after classroom. From each came the chorus of the other students chanting the morning verse:

> *I do behold the world*
> *Wherein there shines the sun*
> *Wherein there gleam the stars*
> *Wherein there lie the stones.*

Normally he slogged through it, by rote. At the moment, though, he would have enjoyed nothing more than droning out a scripted introspection about his soul if it meant he could circumvent a conversation about it.

He stepped into Ms. Valera's classroom, which was empty of students—her planning period, he supposed. Straight ahead was the supply closet at which, not very long ago, he had attempted to get a little attention out of Judy and she had freaked out like the entire concept astonished her. The history classroom was a Bermuda triangle in which Judy was chaste, Temple was a rat, and Zach wished to be in the presence of anyone but the hottest teacher in the school. It was no wonder the previous teacher had died. The place was cursed.

"Have a seat, Zach," Ms. Valera said. "I'm glad you're here."

She sat at its far end at her desk, scribbling onto a stack of papers, her long hair brushing her arm as she wrote. Objectively speaking, she was probably still hot, but at the moment she looked simply terrifying. He sat in the chair nearest her, which was not on the opposite side of her desk but rather very near her own seat, to diminish any sense of her as an authoritarian figure. He would have preferred the desk in the way, as a sort of emotional shield.

She turned to face him and crossed her legs, resting an elbow on her knee. "Do you know why I asked you to come see me?"

Oh yeah, he thought, but there was zero chance he would offer that answer. He decided to plead the Fifth. "No idea."

"Sure you do. I can tell by your answers that you're not doing the readings. Your papers are hastily done, and in class, you always have this look." She waved a hand up and down in front of her face slowly. "Glazed as a donut. Do I bore you?"

"No. Of course not."

"I try to keep it interesting. I spoke to some of your other teachers and they report you seem distracted, but to some extent they write it off because you're new here and still getting acclimated. But I'm in the same boat, and I think it's something else. What do you think?"

The back of his nose began to burn, near his throat. He looked away and replied, "I've just been real busy in the evenings and not getting enough sleep."

"So you feel you're under a lot of stress."

"*No.* I'm just *busy.* It's not necessarily stress-busy. I like to hang out with people after school and I don't want to have to give that up to read fucking Dante." She cocked an eyebrow, and he muttered, "Sorry. But I don't."

"How's the Tacitus project coming along?"

"It's done, mostly." This was true, and he felt a little defensive at the question. "Me and Temple and Fairen knocked it out pretty quick after you assigned it. Ask Fairen, she'll tell you."

"I believe you. I spoke to Temple about it yesterday, actually. He filled me in on everything you've been doing."

It was involuntary, but Zach dropped his head down and cradled his forehead in his hand. He rubbed his eyes, and Ms. Valera asked, "Are you all right?"

"Yeah," he said, grimly. "Listen, anything Temple's telling you is stuff he's just coming up with on his own. I know he's really smart and all, but that doesn't make him a mind reader. I don't tell him anything, so I don't know where he gets this stuff from."

Ms. Valera folded her hands on her lap and absorbed this information with a blank stare. "So are you telling me he has no idea where you're at on the project? Because he told me everyone had their part finished except for the illustrations."

Zach looked at her unblinking, his mouth partly open. He couldn't figure out whether she really didn't know, or was trying to get him to own up to it without having to drag it out of him. Why else would she have called him down here, on today of all days? To discuss his *grades?* In his mind he heard Temple's voice again: *it's obvious, my friend.* Or was it?

"Something's off about you, Zach," she said. "I wish you'd air it with me so we can work through it. It's very clear that you're capable of much more than you've given lately."

He pushed his hair out of his eyes. "Yeah, you know, I worked all term on that playhouse for the auction. Did anybody mention how great that turned out? The school got over five hundred dollars for it. So the stuff I care about, I *am* working hard at. And the stuff I don't care about can just take a number."

She nodded again, more slowly this time. After a pause she said, "I'll be a little more direct. Is there a particular person who's distracting your attention at school?"

He met her gaze with a look of pure, undiluted fear. "No."

"Because I think that's the root of the problem. If you'll open up to me about it, I can rearrange things for you so it's less of a concern. But there's nothing I can do if you won't talk to me."

He shook his head, but it seemed to take a monumental effort to do so. His stomach started to ache with the acid burn that had sidelined him at the Christmas bazaar. He tightened his folded arms and girded himself to get through this meeting without either confessing or vomiting.

She watched him for a long moment. Finally she sat taller and said, "I'm sorry. I didn't mean to make you so uncomfortable."

"Can I go?"

"Just bear in mind what I've said, please, Zach. You can confide in me, and I'll help you."

He nodded and, without word or smile, hurried out the door.

Judy smiled when she opened the door to find him there, pushing the storm door latch to invite him inside. "What a nice surprise," she said, as if he were there to drop off a plate of holiday cookies. "I just got home half an hour ago."

"Is Russ here?"

"No. Neither is Scott. Aren't you supposed to be at Madrigals?"

"Yeah." He knew Temple would note his absence, and in his paranoia—because everything looped back to his paranoia now—guessed what he would suspect. But Zach felt virtuous for his real intentions. Temple could take his eagle-eyed observations and shove it.

"Listen," he said. "We need to talk."

"Sure." She smiled. She began walking up the stairs and, out of habit, he followed her. She had changed from her work clothes and, for once, was dressed like a normal person instead of a Waldorf teacher, in jeans and a pink button-down shirt. Once her bedroom door was locked, she rubbed his arms and said, "You look cold. Why didn't you stop by my classroom? I would have given you a ride home."

"Yeah, I know. So does everybody else." She creased her forehead quizzically, and he continued, "Temple confronted me about you."

"Confronted you?" Her voice nearly mocked him.

"He told me he knows I'm sleeping with you. That it's obvious, and we'd better get it back under wraps before Scott figures it out."

She folded her arms, her face set in a look of only mild concern. "And on what does he base this crazy story of his?"

He rattled off a list of Temple's observations. "He says it's obvious. That we look at each other wrong. I don't know what the hell to say to that one. 'No, we don't'? How do I know how I *look* at anyone?"

She nodded and seemed to consider her reply. "So how did you respond?"

"I told him he was smoking crack. What was I supposed to say? That he's right? Because I'm telling you, Judy, he had it *down*. It's like he's been watching us for months. He had no doubt at *all*. And then Ms. Valera called me in today, telling me she knows someone's distracting me at school and she can help me avoid that person if I'll just come clean about it. I almost puked on her desk when she said that. She let me go without saying anything, but between her and Temple, it's like dry fucking timber for the next person who notices something's up."

She eased her arms out of their crossed position and tucked her hands into her back pockets. For a moment she regarded him with weary concern. Then she said, "Stand still."

He did as she asked. She circled behind him and helped him out of his down vest, then lifted his T-shirt and thermal off his body in a single piece. Once the clothes lay in a pile on the floor she embraced him from behind and, her fingers splayed against his pectorals, kissed him between his shoulder blades. Then she sat on the bed and smiled.

"Sorry about that," she said. "Please continue."

"What was *that* for?"

"I thought you might be wearing a wire."

He stared at her in disbelief. "You thought I was trying to *turn you in?*"

"It's happened to women in my position before. I just wanted to be sure. Your line of conversation was sort of painting me into a corner there."

"God *damn,* Judy. How can you not fucking trust me *now?* After all this."

The corner of her mouth twisted. "It's not you I don't trust. It's all the adults around you. If they wanted to hang me, they wouldn't give you a choice. They'd slap a wire on you and send you in here saying, 'Go do your thing.'"

She had a point. He leaned back against the dresser and closed his eyes in exhaustion.

"First of all," she began, "Temple doesn't know anything. Not unless you said something to him. He's jumping to conclusions and that's his own problem. If you deny it and I deny it, there's no issue. As long as we don't get caught *in flagrante delicto.*"

"What does that mean?"

"It's Latin for 'fucking in the car.'"

In spite of himself, he laughed. He rubbed a hand down his face and said, "We're not doing cars anymore, remember?"

"I remember. And as for Ms. Valera, I think you're just reading too much into whatever she said to you. She thinks you're bent out of shape because Fairen is toying with you. I told her myself."

He felt the ghost of a smile rise to his face. "Seriously?"

"Yes. A while back she asked me if I knew why you're having those issues in class. She figured since you and I spend so much time together, I might know. So I told her. You want Fairen, but she's a tease. It eats you alive."

This time the grin broke through, small but genuine. "Good call. That explains it, yeah."

"Thank you. I specialize in fairy tales, remember."

He looked off toward the window. The lacy curtains let in just enough light to show the dark-blue twilight sky of winter. Soon he would need to be home for dinner. In his panicked state he had expected he and Judy would agree to an urgent lockdown of their relationship, an easy out, brought on not by rejection but by necessity. The thought had been soothing, in its way. The affair, however guilty or forgivable, however abhorrent or deliciously forbidden, had burned through its fuel and needed to fall, empty, to earth. Yet in this room with her he had not expected to be reminded of all the things he genuinely liked about her: her quick wit, her ability to listen and be calm, the sensuality that thrummed just beneath the surface of her small uptight form. He liked her better, wanted her more, when she kept her grace—a shell of *no* enclosing a liquid center of *yes.*

"You need to *relax,*" she said. "Stop sweating the small stuff. Could I offer you a foot rub? Because it seems like something's blocking your *chi.*"

He rubbed his palms against the edge of the dresser and acknowledged the comment with the wicked grin it deserved. She waited for his response, and finally he said, "I came here to say I think we ought to take a break for a while, until people stop sniffing around."

"I thought we already were taking a break," she parried. "I haven't seen hide or hair of you for a week."

He considered that. "Has it been that long?"

"It has. Since the bazaar. When I found you tossing your cookies, very literally, next to the trash cans, and you begged me to go down on you to cure your tummy trouble."

"Yeah. Temple noticed we slipped away."

"What do you mean, 'slipped away'? We were back inside of half an hour. And *that* raises Temple's suspicions? I would think a progressive boy like him would have higher standards than that."

He drummed his knuckles against the dresser and stared at the carpet. She slid off the bed and came to him, cupping his face in her hands. He met her eyes and let her kiss him softly on the mouth.

"But we can take a break whenever you want to," she whispered. "You call the shots, remember. Are you leaving right away? Or are you staying a few minutes longer?"

"I didn't bring anything with me."

She nodded. "It's your call, then."

"We'd better not."

She nodded again, but as she took a step back he reached for her upper arms and kissed her again. Then again; and of course she did not stop him, and of course he did not want to stop. A tumult of conflicting thoughts rushed forward in his mind, then fell like lemmings off the edge of the cliff past which he knew, good or bad, right or wrong, he was going to do this.

What is it about her? he wondered hopelessly. What did she offer him that he couldn't find elsewhere? Why did he persist in seeking her out, thinking of her, *wanting* her, when she was exactly wrong for him in nearly every way? Why was he willing to be this adversary to Scott, to Russ, to his own father—to scatter principle to the four winds and scuttle off to hunt what was forbidden?

But that question was its own answer. *Because* it was forbidden. Because fucking a woman in a crashing plane is a thousand times more exciting than in the bedroom of a nice home.

It occurred to him, as he crawled onto the bed and nestled himself into the welcome of Judy's body, that he suddenly understood all he needed to know about his mother's affair. That it had nothing to do with him. Nothing to do with his father. Nothing connected to it but the drumbeat inside her that called her to the atrocity. It was comforting to understand, at last, his own irrelevance. In the moment of this realization he felt a momentary spark of sympathy for her, before other feelings overwhelmed him and snuffed it out.

24

Maggie called while I was untangling a knotted thread with my teeth, working on a dream pillow that had gone all wrong. Right away I knew this was not going to be a pleasant phone call. Maggie never called to chat.

"You can use my room for storage or whatever," she said. "I'm not coming home for Christmas."

"What? Why?"

"Because I'm going home with my friend Elise. I'll be in Hagerstown. I'll give you the number so you can call me or whatever."

"Maggie." I sat on the edge of the bed and rested my forehead against my hand. "We've got the tree up already and everything. I'm counting on you coming home. It won't feel like Christmas if you're not here, and it's hard enough already this year." I did not attempt to go into detail as to why.

"I want a real Christmas," she replied, her voice attempting a breezy note but leaking venom nonetheless. "One with Jesus in it. Elise's family goes to church and all that stuff. I need to experience this for myself."

"You know perfectly well there's Jesus in our Christmas," I said, feeling my blood pressure rising with each word. "God only knows they've been hammering Jesus into your brain at school since kindergarten. I make those damn salt-dough nativity scenes with my kids every year. I *know*."

"That's that Waldorf phony crap. The 'Cosmic Christ.' Puh-*leeze*. And that stupid story about how there used to be two baby Jesuses and one died and was reincarnated as Buddha or something—"

"'The Two Jesus Children.'"

"God, what *crap!* How can you teach that stuff to kids? Do you have any idea how ridiculous it sounds?"

"I *don't* teach that stuff," I reminded her. "I don't believe in anything at all."

"You think you don't, but you would if you pulled your head out of the Steiner sandbox long enough to consider the possibility. You would have handled it a lot better when your best friend died if you'd had some kind of context to put it in, but instead you fell apart like wet toilet paper."

"Thank you."

"My point is, Christmas is about a miracle. And I want to spend it celebrating that miracle. I hope you can honor that."

My lips pressed into a brittle smile. "I understand better than you might think."

"Good." Her voice sounded assertive but a little confused. "Merry Christmas, then."

"To you, too." A pregnant silence hung across the low static of the phone line. "And when the trap snaps closed, I'll understand that, too. You can cry on my shoulder then."

"What are you talking about?"

"Your ideas. Your miracles. They're just peanut butter on some fucked-up cosmic mousetrap. I've been there. I've wanted that, too. And what I've learned is, seek out what's beautiful and love it before it rots. Because there's not a damn thing in this world that doesn't."

For a long moment she said nothing. Then she said, "I hope you're not teaching *that* to the kids, either."

"No need," I told her. "They'll learn it on their own."

He felt ashamed after the afternoon with Judy, displeased with himself for his lack of self-discipline. After the day of the holiday bazaar, when he had puked by the Dumpster and she consoled him with her version of chicken soup for his morally conflicted soul, he had told himself they needed to break things off. The dreadful conversation with Temple only steeled his resolve, not just to end it but to erase it, to bend his eleventh-grade year into an arc that, as far as it mattered, had never included Judy in the first place. It helped to focus on the negative: the time he was feverish, the slap to his face, the sickening guilt, and, of course, the times he'd turned in a lousy performance and felt himself revealed as a hopeless amateur.

And then—every once in a while—there was a rip in the fabric. Monday afternoon, for example: when his desire did not feel like a backburn to her wildfire, when everything flowed, and at the end he rubbed his eyes and felt restored. He could almost convince himself they were two normal people doing what normal people do, until he peeked between the blinds before she opened the door and he was reminded that everything he took he was stealing.

When the temperature reached sixty-seven degrees one December day, Fairen cornered him after Main Lesson and suggested they cut out early. She had twenty dollars from babysitting. She wanted to get a pizza.

They slipped out as if going to the workshop, then hustled into the woods. The trees were bare gray skeletons against the sky, but the air had a springtime headiness to it, fragrant and brisk. Once on the sidewalk, Fairen reached for his hand. It was a friendly, tentative sort of hand-holding, fingertips loosely intertwined, but it gave Zach hope. She had invited him, after all.

The pizza place was not far away, in a minimall with a barbershop and variety store. Signs plastered to the brick advertised an upcoming festival at the lake. Fairen ordered a mushroom-and-green-pepper, size large, and two giant Cokes.

"Because I know you eat like there's no tomorrow," she said.

"There isn't."

She gave him a strange look and he said, "Carpe diem."

She smiled approvingly. As they waited on the bench, she played footsie with him. There were no tables or chairs, so when their pizza was ready, they carried the box to a small underpass beneath the street, built like a stone bridge to shelter a sidewalk. It was cozy and relatively private, and Zach felt a little saddened to realize that he enjoyed her chaste company as much as the non-chaste. Had he realized that months ago, he might have saved himself a lot of trouble.

"We need to go on another choir trip when the weather's like this," she said as she wiped her hands on a napkin. "So I can have another excuse to corrupt you."

"Who needs an excuse?" he asked. She smiled, and he ventured, "I thought you were done with me since I tried to scalp you."

"I wasn't in love with that. But the rest was really great."

"You thought so, seriously?"

She nodded. "*Really* great."

"I'm sorry I pulled your hair," he admitted. "I just got carried away, but I didn't mean to hurt you. I really had no idea what I was doing."

She looked uneasy at his apology. "I think I blew that out of proportion. I just felt uncomfortable that it happened at all, because I hadn't planned it. I got caught up in the moment and…" She shrugged.

"Yeah, me too."

"But I felt even worse after, when you lost interest so fast. I figured you'd moved on to somebody else, and that made me feel pretty awful."

He tipped his head. "Why did you think that?"

She smirked. "Because you lost that desperate vibe. There's only one explanation when a straight guy starts acting like he doesn't care if girls like him or not. He must be getting laid on a regular basis. It made me jealous."

Zach laughed. "That's goofy."

"It's true. And I couldn't figure out who, and it was driving me crazy. I know every girl at Sylvania. It's not any of them. So who is it?"

He grinned. "It's Ms. Valera."

She broke into laughter. "Oh, *no!* That's why she called you out of class last week, huh? So she could molest you in her supply closet?"

"Yep."

Her laugh carried the music of her lovely soprano. She rested her elbows against her knees, leaning toward him. He looked at her: at her silver-trimmed ears with her pale blond hair tucked behind them, at her broad beautiful smile, at the way her crystal necklace dangled above the dark shadow of her cleavage. He didn't want her jealousy; he didn't want her to know at all. The way she leaned toward him, he suspected she would welcome it if he kissed her. But he couldn't do it. He would be cheating on her before they even got started.

She was too beautiful to be led into the muck he had made out of his sex life in the short time since she had introduced him to that pleasure. And so he tossed a piece of ice into her cleavage and made her scream.

"Any day now," said Rhianne, patting Zach's mother on the stomach and slinging her stethoscope around her neck. She helped her to sit up, and Zach had to smile at his mother's cumbersome movements. All his life she had been lithe and graceful, but now she was in full waddle mode, swaybacked half the time from her burgeoning stomach.

"Pregnancy is a beautiful thing," said his mother, "but I can't wait for it to be over."

"You're not the first woman I've heard say that. Take it easy, all right? Make this one treat you like a queen." She gestured to Zach and winked. "I'll see you in a week, or less if you're lucky."

He followed Rhianne to the foyer, opening the door immediately to let her out. She looked amused by his rudeness, but he rallied by trailing her out the door and closing it behind them. The porch light shone bright above their heads, a white moth beating against it in looping arcs.

He asked, "Are you in a hurry?"

"Of course not. What's up?" Over her coveralls she wore a thick down vest, forest green. Her breath came out in clouds.

With a deep exhale of his own he pointed toward the driveway, indicating they should walk. She took the cue, pulling her knit cap from her pocket and tugging it over her short low pigtails. They stuck out like the ends of paintbrushes when she turned to him again, hands crammed deep into the pockets of her vest.

"I'm in a relationship of sorts," he said carefully, "and it's a problem."

"How is that?"

"I don't want to be."

Rhianne nodded. "But you feel afraid to break it off. Is that it?"

"Yes and no." He sighed heavily, sending a whirl of condensation into the night air. "I've tried. But it's almost like I'm addicted to her body. About ninety-five percent of me doesn't enjoy it at all anymore, but the five percent that does won't give it up."

"And what about her? How does she feel about it?"

"Fine, as far as I can tell. I don't think she feels conflicted like I do. Not in the same way, at least."

She tipped her head in a musing way. "Do you feel maybe she loves you, and you're not so sure?"

"No. Love's not part of the equation at all. It's just sex. Which I also feel pretty shitty about, to tell you the truth. I don't think you need to be in love, necessarily, to have sex with somebody, but I don't think it's supposed to be this totally meaningless, either. You'd think that would make it easy to give it up, but if you did, you'd be wrong. Really, really wrong." His laugh sounded hollow even to him.

"Zach," said Rhianne, "I understand this is the first sexual relationship you've had—"

"It's not."

"Okay, well, the first that's felt like this. But you don't have to stay in any relationship that isn't rewarding. There will be others, and you'll enjoy them just as much."

He shook his head. "Not like this. Not like her. She's insane. She's always on, *way* on. And knowing I shouldn't be doing it makes it even better."

Rhianne frowned. "Why shouldn't you be doing it?"

He sighed again. "Because of who she is."

"Who is she?"

The curiosity in her eyes was so polite. Somehow he had assumed that as soon as he brought it up with her she would know the situation was skewed and abnormal, that she was being called in like a hostage negotiator or a bomb technician, because what else would explain how he had found his way into a woman's bed? Yet she seemed unsurprised, as though she saw nothing out of the ordinary in the fact that a girl had said yes to him. Well, she was about to be surprised now.

He squinted against her coming reaction and said, "She's a teacher at my school."

Rhianne sucked in her breath. Zach knew he could trust her, but still the force of her response made his stomach cramp up. She asked, "One of *your* teachers?"

"No, no. In the Lower School."

"Is she young?"

He shook his head. "She's in her forties someplace."

Her mouth twisted harshly to the side. Nostrils flaring, she stood silent in the cold, clearly weighing what he had told her. Watching her, Zach felt a sense of dread that he had told her as much as he had. He had expected her to share his sense of shame, but not to look so angry.

Finally she said, "Zach, you need to put a stop to it. What's going on is wrong."

"I know. That's why I'm talking to you about it. If I thought it was all hunky-dory I'd just keep banging her and stay quiet about it."

"Does anyone else know?"

He gave an ambiguous nod. "One of my friends thinks he does, but I swore up and down it wasn't true."

"I mean anyone who works at your school. Any other adult."

His laugh was scornful. "Hell, no. I'd be expelled for something like that."

She seemed to wince. "No one is going to blame you for being—for being victimized. You do realize it's statutory rape, don't you? That what she's doing to you is considered rape?"

He dismissed the idea with a shake of his head. "Believe me, I'm not having any trouble doing my end of the deal. No trouble at all."

"That's not the point. It's rape just because of your age."

He shook his head again firmly. "Technically, maybe, but that's bull if you ask me. Nobody's raping anybody. My problem is I don't know how to get myself to stop." He laughed humorlessly. "I don't know how to make myself stop wanting to be raped."

Rhianne regarded him with a hardened gaze, her lips pressed together. "Then you just have to resolve it to yourself, Zach. Tell yourself it's over and stay away from her. If you want, I can talk to her for you."

With a grimace, he turned down the offer. "Uh-uh. That would just be a bad idea."

"Promise me you won't see her again."

"I can't do that. If I could promise anyone that, I would have promised myself a month ago. I tell myself I won't and then out of nowhere I'll want her. It's like bloodlust. It just comes over me and then there's nothing but that. I can't control it."

Rhianne listened, eyes watchful. For a long moment his words hung in the chilled air. Then she said, "Well, don't fool yourself into thinking *she* can't control it. She's using you, Zach. I don't have to know who she is to know that. She's flattered you into thinking you're her unstoppable sex god, but really, she's got you by the balls."

Zach looked at her sharply. "No, she doesn't. Nobody does."

"Then break it off. You're not so hopped up on hormones

that you can't turn down a middle-aged woman. She'd like you to believe you are, but you've got your free will."

He sighed heavily, his breath clouding the air between them. "Well, it sure doesn't feel like it right now. I keep laying down rules for myself about lines I just won't cross, and then I run right over them. Before this, I thought I was a pretty nice guy. Now I look at myself in the mirror and think, 'what a scumbag.'"

Rhianne reached for his hand and held it between her two gloved ones. He felt his teeth begin to chatter, but it didn't seem to be from the cold so much as from his hammering heart. When he dared to look at her, she gazed out at him with hard eyes beneath the rim of her wool cap.

"You are a good person, Zach," she said quietly. "Too young to know how ordinary these things are. Everybody struggles. Everybody loses sometimes. Even the people we love and look up to. I think you know that."

He gritted his teeth and searched her eyes for meaning.

"If you want to solve your problem nice and quickly," she continued, "turn her in to the police. Or if you don't want to, I will. It's the right thing to do. A *teacher,* for God's sake."

He shook his head and let his hand drop from hers. "No way. If I did that, everybody would know. It'd be in the newspapers, and—no." With a grimace and a shudder along his shoulders, he wiped the thought from his mind. "I just want to make it go away. Break it off, like people do all the time. I'm not out for blood or anything. I just want to stop *wanting* her."

A shadow of irritation moved across Rhianne's face. "Get your head away from the idea that she's somehow your lover. She's manipulating you. Coercing you. This is what abusers do, Zach. They make the victim feel like they deserve it."

He looked away. Now he wished he had never confided

in her. She meant well, but she heard him only as a mother would, without comprehension of the roiling dark inside him. He could leave bruises. He could delight in seeing her on her knees.

"If one of your friends was in your shoes," asserted Rhianne, "what would you tell him?"

Zach considered the question for only a moment. "That it's stupid. That there's no reason to be all hung up about some old chick when you could hook up with somebody hotter."

"So why don't you follow your own advice?"

He bent his head and rubbed his eyes with the heels of his hands, weary with the fruitlessness of the conversation. "I'll think about it."

"Tell me her name."

He looked up. "What?"

"Her name. Tell it to me."

She looked calm and even-tempered, but he shook his head, for the first time ever feeling frightened of her. "I'll deal with it on my own."

25

It began to enter my mind that I should see a doctor.

The reason was Bobbie. I had managed to stay composed for so long, but now my grief over her loss came in thundering waves. All day long tears welled up at unexpected moments; the cuffs of my sweater were constantly damp. The more perceptive of my students gazed at me with serious faces, their brows tightened by worry. I found that intolerable. My job was to shelter them from the fraught world of adulthood, not to wander among them trailing it like noxious fumes. I took to drinking glasses of apricot juice dribbled with Bach's Rescue Remedy. The five homeopathic flower essences didn't seem to be enough for whatever ailed me, and I envied Russ his stash of meds.

You can talk to me about her, Sandy had said. She had offered herself up as a new friend, one who could be the rock for me that Bobbie had been. But what would I tell her? That I was afraid my sixteen-year-old lover was growing tired of me? Haunted by the characters in children's tales? Anxious that I often looked at the silvery-eared blonde who, at five, had been nicknamed Fairygirl by her mother, and pondered how much more pleasant my life would be without her?

It could be worse. I knew, because it was getting there.

Inexplicably, Russ canceled his Friday night class the week before finals. He stayed home, and instead of locking himself in his office upstairs, he sat in front of the television and watched old episodes of *Three's Company*.

From the kitchen, I stared at the back of his head. I drummed my fingertips on the counter. Earlier I had snagged Zach in the parking lot and told him I would meet him in the church lot at seven; when Russ changed his plans, I'd been forced to make a dangerous phone call which fortunately Zach, and not either of his parents, had picked up. The longer Russ sat in front of *Three's Company*, the more I seethed. What right did he have to cancel the class they paid him to teach, for no reason at all, and throw all my plans for a loop? And so what if those plans weren't exactly kosher? It wasn't as though *he* planned to spend time with me, ever, or consider that I might deserve a husband who did more than take up space. Were it not for the fact that my lover was sixteen years old, I might rub the fact of him in Russ's face just to make the point that my life as a woman hadn't ended the day he fell in love with his thesis.

I headed upstairs to the master bathroom and began drawing myself a nice hot bath. If I couldn't have Zach, I could at least have that. Then I noticed the pill bottles cluttering the sink: the Nembutal, the Xanax. These days he took them by the handful, right in front of me. The quantities were appalling. I was sure he was in imminent danger of an overdose, but nothing ever happened.

I picked up the bottle of Nembutal. This was the one he took in the evening, to counteract whatever the Dexedrine had been doing all day. I shook three capsules into my hand, then four. Then six.

The water had filled the tub halfway. I shut it off, let it drain and returned to the kitchen. Russ was still watching television. The laugh track rose and fell in waves, although Russ sat mute, his stocking feet perched on the coffee table. I poured myself a cup of coffee and sat at the kitchen table with the newspaper. When the first cup was finished, I poured myself another.

Eventually the sound of a commercial came on: an arthritis remedy, targeted depressingly at people our age. Russ got up and went to the bathroom. Very quickly I slipped into the living room and, one two three, dumped out all six caplets into his soda can. By the time the toilet flushed, I was back at the kitchen table reading the articles of impeachment against President Clinton.

Six might have been too many. Or, it might have been too few. I didn't know. Also, I didn't particularly care. As long as he fell asleep long enough to serve my purposes, I couldn't bring myself to care when he woke up, or if.

When Zach picked up the phone, he heard Judy's voice on the line for the second time that evening.

"Can you come over?" she asked. "Right now, or very soon?"

He sighed hard against the phone. "You already told me we were off for tonight."

"I know, but the house is clear after all."

"Judy…" He gritted his teeth together hard enough to send a needle of pain through his jaw. "We talked about how we're taking a break, remember?"

She answered with a scoffing laugh. "Oh yes, I seem

to remember you told me that right before you got in bed with me."

He had been afraid she would point that out. "Well, I've got plans," he countered. "I'm meeting Scott and people in an hour."

"Oh?" asked Judy. "Where are you going?"

Zach bristled. "I dunno. Hang out. It's to finish up our history project."

"An hour is plenty of time," Judy said. Her voice turned husky. "There's a lot you and I can do with just fifteen minutes."

He slid his back down the kitchen wall and rested on his haunches. "I dunno," he said again. He craned his neck to look for his mother and then dropped his voice. "You know I feel weird hanging out with Scott right after we screw."

"Oh, you can work past it. You have before."

"I don't know if I'm in the right mood."

"Zach," said Judy, her voice starting to take on the wheedling note he hated, "*please* just come by. I promise I'll make it worth your while. I've been thinking about you since the minute I got up this morning. You wouldn't believe how much trouble I went to to get the house clear."

He rested his forehead against his hand and breathed out a slow sigh. This was the obstacle he had faced for weeks. As with any destructive habit, kicking sex with Judy was fraught with moments of almost evangelical determination, periods of refreshing apathy toward her, and then worming little slivers of weakness where he thought, *what's one more going to hurt?* It had almost gotten him that afternoon; after school she had grabbed his upper arm in the parking lot and all but ordered him to show up at nineteen-hundred hours. He had grunted a reply but not exactly agreed. Temple's warning had forced him to view his actions through a new lens, and the wider angle showed a Zach who made dumb mistakes, failed to see around corners, planned for the hypothetical but not the obvious. Even so, the temptation stalked him. He told himself he would stand her up, but his inner voice didn't sound as convinced as he wished it did.

And so after she called to cancel that evening, he had told himself it was an opportunity and he was done with her, really done this time. He did round after round of crunches, push-ups, and chin-ups in the basement, drank a liter of spring water, practiced judo on the heavy boxing bag, and stripped down to his underwear to admire himself in the full-length mirror. It was a good body, it worked well, and he was proud of it. Fairen had complimented it many times. Judy couldn't leave it alone. He wasn't going to be especially tall and his babyish face still didn't match his build, but he felt happy with what he had. He took a shower to wash off the exercise sweat, jerked off while he was in there, and collapsed into bed for an hour-long nap, feeling physically and sexually sated independent of Judy McFarland.

And now here she was again, pleading with him across the phone line. She shifted to stroking his ego, throwing a little dirty-mouthed phone-sex talk in there for good measure, then moved in with a side assault of guilt. She had moved continents to make the house available. She hadn't denied him, had she, when he showed up unannounced the previous Monday? And she would do anything he asked, which she knew, with him, could mean quite a lot.

"Okay, okay," he finally told her. This was the part Rhianne didn't understand, the part that had less to do with his hormones than with his patience. "I'll walk over. Give me twenty minutes."

When he arrived at the house she opened the door slowly, lifting a silencing finger to her lips. As he stepped into the foyer, she gestured toward the ceiling and mouthed, *he's up-stairs.*

Who? he mouthed back.

Russ.

Without really meaning to, he rolled his eyes. In a low voice he said, "You told me nobody was home."

Judy waved her hand to dismiss his concern. He followed her to the den, where she closed the door and turned the lock. He looked at Scott's math book on the table with papers shoved in it and remembered what Judy had said about Scott's preference for hooking up with Tally on that very sofa. Beside it sat the Christmas tree, bright rainbow lights shining.

"He's sleeping," she whispered. "He'll be up there all night."

Zach leveled an irritated gaze. "What if he comes down to get a snack or something?"

"He won't. Trust me."

And then she unbuttoned her shirt and put her arms around his neck. He felt her teeth on his earlobe, the warmth of her breath. She eased his vest from his shoulders and let it fall to the floor. As she ran a finger beneath the neckline of his shirt to kiss his collarbone, he stared at the twinkling lights and the jumble of ornaments made of construction paper and curling ribbon. An awkwardly woven straw Star of Bethlehem. A ceramic ballet slipper. Zach had no particular attachment to Christianity—when his mother discussed the subject, she always quoted the Dalai Lama saying *my religion is kindness*—but he was enough of a child of his culture to think there was something deeply screwed up about having illicit sex in front of a Christmas tree.

"Let's go down to the basement," he said.

"It's a mess. All the Christmas stuff is pulled out of storage." She nuzzled his neck, her hands slipping to his waist, the small of his back. "Boxes. Furniture moved around. God, you feel good."

She undid the top button of his jeans, and as if by reflex he pushed her away. He didn't feel the least bit aroused by her. He looked toward the closed door and said, "Listen, I'm just not in the mood."

Her laugh was uneasy. "You came over, didn't you?"

"Yeah, but I changed my mind. I think we ought to stick to what we decided. Take a break."

"You don't mean that."

He bristled. "No, seriously, I really do. And it sort of pisses me off that you think you can bring me in here when your husband's sleeping upstairs and I'm not going to mind. Maybe it's honor among thieves or whatever, but that's some scummy shit."

She lifted her brows in a placating way and hooked a finger in his belt loop. "It didn't even enter my mind," she explained. "Russ and I live separate lives. He doesn't care what I do. And right now he's too drugged up to notice."

Zach met her eyes. "Drugged up?"

"Nembutal. He goes through it like candy. It amazes me that he keeps breathing." She took advantage of his surprise to sidle up to him again, her warm hand sliding up into his hair, her mouth dipping to kiss his neck. He felt the edges of her teeth, gentle for a moment, then unexpectedly—yet not unpleasantly—painful. He grimaced and pulled in a slow breath. Judy never bit. She was afraid of marking him. Yet this time she did and wouldn't let go, and finally he clawed a hand into her hair and pulled her back.

She winced, and he kissed her on the mouth. Under normal circumstances the bite would have won him over, but not here or now. He said, "Seeya."

Disbelief edged her voice. "You're not really leaving."

He lifted his vest from its place on the carpet and shrugged it back on. "I gotta meet up with Scott and people."

She shifted a few steps to the left. Now she was standing in front of the door, complicating his exit route. He was certain it wasn't accidental, and that pissed him off.

"Just spend a few minutes with me, since you're already here," she implored. Her hazel eyes, so placid when he had first met her, stared back at him full of determination. The softness of her voice and the appeasing set of her mouth did nothing to fool him into believing she would leave the decision to his good judgment. He remembered the night she had stroked his feverish back before taking advantage of him, and he knew she had no intention of letting him leave until she got what she wanted. As he glowered at her, Rhianne's face, framed by night and white with cold, flashed into his mind. *She's manipulating you,* Rhianne had said. *Coercing you.* The anger that had already kindled in his gut now flared fully to life.

"Are you gonna hold me hostage?" he demanded. "Is that what that's about?"

She shook her head. "I just want to be with you. That's all."

He moved toward the door, and she backed against the doorknob, reaching to loop her fingers into the waistband of his jeans as though that were the reason for his approach. She tugged loose his thermal from his pants and slid her hands up his chest.

"I know you don't have much time," she whispered.

He leveled his condescending glare on her and felt all his tumultuous thoughts reduce to a single sentence: *just get out the fucking door.* She broke away her gaze and nuzzled his neck, softly this time, her hands roaming everywhere despite his utter lack of response. He closed his eyes and fantasized about Fairen. Of her body, her face, the way she sneered at people who perturbed her, her dirty mouth. Then his eyes snapped open and, abruptly, he spun Judy to face the wall, shoved her skirt up, and did what he needed to do.

A handful of her hair fell from his fingers, once he was done.

He opened the door immediately and zipped up as he walked through the kitchen. His down vest was still on, and heat spiked on the back of his neck. He heard her footsteps behind him, the slight pat echoing each thump of his sneakers.

"Zach," she said.

He turned at the front door and looked at her. With one hand she rubbed the back of her head. Her shirt still hung open, revealing the strip of black satin at the center of her bra that reminded him of a semibreve rest on a musical score. *Pause and breathe,* the universe seemed to be telling him, and the wisdom resonated just now.

She smiled with an affection than looked almost pained. "Thanks for coming over," she said. "It's always good to see you."

Without a word he headed out the door.

26

He jogged through the dark neighborhood to the main road. Once on the sidewalk, its ancient cement crumbled by giant tree roots, he faced the remaining half mile like an obstacle course. Goal: to get to the McDonald's parking lot as quickly as possible. Action hero Zach Patterson, third-degree black belt, able to leap orange construction netting in a single bound. He jumped over a Jersey wall, scrambled up the chain-link fence behind the Planned Parenthood clinic, dropped onto the lawn of a rehabilitation center and, with an elegance that he felt in his bones, vaulted with one hand over the ranch-style fence on the lawn's opposite side. He ducked through some brush, and voilà, emerged on the far end of the parking lot of the McDonald's. Temple stood outside the van, leaning against it with his ankles crossed, waiting for him.

"Where the hell were you?" he shouted across the lot.

"Yardwork."

"At night?"

Zach shrugged. *My stupid parents.* He knew Temple wouldn't buy the excuse for a second, and with a hard glance he dared his friend to pose a theory. But Temple only threw an arm in the air in a gesture of frustration, then said, "Get in the car."

Zach climbed in the side door. Kaitlyn was in the front, munching on a cheeseburger; Fairen sat on the bench seat beside him, while Scott and Tally were thigh-to-thigh in the back. Scott had his arm around her shoulders. He did not acknowledge Zach's wave of greeting. Being around Tally always made Scott so self-consciously cool that Zach felt clownish in contrast; he always felt the impulse to make an ass of himself in a way Scott couldn't help but acknowledge, to throw him off-base. He grinned and faced the front of the van, trying to ignore the slightly nauseating smell of mass-produced cheeseburger.

The engine rumbled and turned over. "So about this hospital thing," Tally said. "Are you sure this place is safe?"

"Actually it's extremely unsafe," Zach told her.

"And illegal," Temple added.

"Then why are we going?"

"Because it'll be fun," said Scott. "It's trespassing. Therefore, it's fun."

Fairen reached over and rubbed Zach's forearm. For a moment she laced her fingers into his, then let her hand wander onto his thigh. He looked down at his leg in surprise.

Tally asked, "Have you ever actually seen this Bunny Man person Scott was telling me about?"

"Nope," said Temple. "And we won't tonight, either. But Fairen'll get some good photos for our report."

Kaitlyn began to sing, "'One night in my ramble I chanced to see, a thing like a spirit, it frightened me—'"

Scott threw a balled-up receipt at her head. Fairen snickered, but Temple said, "Hey. Don't throw shit while I'm driving."

Fairen let her hand come to rest on the inside of his thigh, her fingers tucked between his leg and the upholstery. She wasn't particularly high up, only a bit above his knee, but it didn't matter. He put his arm across the seat back, slid his hand under her hair, and stroked the nape of her neck.

Temple pulled into the parking lot of the town house complex, and Zach regretfully disentangled himself from Fairen. He would rather have sat with her in the van all night than gone looking for some guy in a rabbit costume, as entertaining as that search could be. Something about her touch felt restorative just now, when he still felt dirty from his tryst with Judy. Why had he even shown up? When the hell had he started feeling so *obligated* to her, as though she were some sort of girlfriend he couldn't shake loose? And in the end it had been so pointless, so remote from the allure that had once felt infinite to him. He itched to take a shower.

Fairen slung her camera around her neck and hopped out of the van. They hurried through the forest, past the swamp that gleamed like obsidian and smelled like rot, and emerged in the shadow of the hospital's towering main building, all the while peering around for cops. Scott—Indiana Jones all of a sudden, now that they had his girlfriend in tow—led the way toward the black gap that formed the building's front door. Tally hesitated at the entrance, her slim fingers on the moulding, and peered cautiously around inside.

"I'm not so sure about this," she said.

Temple jostled her from behind. "Get in, quick, before the cops see us."

They gathered in the broad center hall, each switching on a flashlight. Pale green paint peeled off the walls in sheets; Zach's narrow light fell on a constellation of spotty black mold growing along the plaster. A smell of wet rot permeated the air, hanging heavy as moss. Jagged rings of water stains dotted the ceiling, and a jumble of iron water pipes lay on the floor near the crippled staircase. The white light from Tally's flashlight lit up Fairen's face with a ghostly pallor. She shifted her place in the circle to stand beside Zach, and clutched for his hand.

"I feel weird about this," she said under her breath. "There's broken glass all over the place. We should have brought gloves."

"Don't pick anything up and you'll be fine."

"What if I catch tuberculosis?"

"You won't. That was fifty years ago."

Scott turned his back to the group and shone his flashlight up to the balcony of the second story. Zach couldn't resist the opportunity to mess with him. He handed his light to Tally, then rushed up behind Scott and twisted his arm behind his back, uttering a loud "Yah!"

Scott's light clattered to the ground, spinning the beam into a twist of brightness and shadow that, for a moment, disoriented Zach. In that time Scott gained the advantage, releasing himself from Zach's grip and forcing Zach into a headlock. Zach, calling upon ten solid years of judo experience, immediately realized Scott wasn't playing.

Zach jabbed an elbow into Scott's side and grasped his wrist. But Scott—in a blatantly illegal move—jerked Zach's head back and threw him to the ground. Zach broke his fall with his hands and coughed reflexively. Before he could gather himself Scott was on his back, holding him down with his body weight. He locked his arm around Zach's neck again and jerked his arm behind his back, sending a lightning bolt of pain from Zach's wrist to his shoulder. Scott was taller, heavier, and—Zach understood—angrier. He held on.

"Get him off the damn floor, Scott," Temple yelled.

"Let him up," urged Fairen. "That's disgusting. There's glass."

In the darkness, the others couldn't tell that Zach could barely breathe. He felt Scott twisting him against the gritty floor and desperately coached his own mind. Scott's fighting skills were shit. His own were superb. He wasn't being overcome; he was being psyched out.

"Stop playing, you idiots," said Fairen.

Zach gathered what little oxygen he could and surged up from the floor, throwing Scott to the ground and, at long last, rising to his feet. He took two steps back as Scott got up and squinted when Temple shone a flashlight on them. Scott walked back to Tally, leveling a cool-eyed gaze on Zach. This time Zach understood that what he felt was not paranoia. Scott knew.

He returned to Fairen's side, recoiling as she reached for his hand. His wrist felt as though it had been crushed beneath a school bus. She touched his shoulder and asked, "Are you okay?"

"I'm fine."

They followed the others around the staircase and entered a long hallway. The light from their Maglites was entirely ineffective. Circles of brightness swirled on the walls, bringing out hanging black wires and inkblots of mold, crumbled plaster and more loosened flaps of sickening green paint. When Temple's light turned onto a broad doorway, they passed through it into a cavernous room.

"Is anyone keeping track of the way we came in?" asked Kaitlyn.

Fairen said, "I've been dropping bread crumbs all along."

"That's not funny," Kaitlyn replied. Her voice wavered.

"There's something stuck in the bottom of my shoe," whined Tally. "Can we stop for a minute?"

Scott shook his head. "Don't pull it out. It could be glass and cut you. Or a nail with tetanus."

"Tetanus?" asked Tally. Her voice had risen by an octave.

They shone their lights on the walls. Graffiti was everywhere: trios of meaningless letters, curse words, the occasional swastika. The room was empty of furniture except for a desk that sat askew beside the farthest wall. But the floor was littered with napkins and fast-food containers, a filthy blanket, two garbage bags and a snow boot.

Scott focused his light on a wall. "That looks like gang graffiti."

In a disparaging voice Fairen asked, "Scott, what would *you* know about gangs?"

"He grew up on the mean streets of Sylvania," Zach said. His wrist pounded as though his heart had been relocated there. "The Waldorf thug life."

"Shut the fuck up," said Scott.

"Damn, Scott, chill out," said Temple.

"I don't like this," Tally informed them, her voice wavering. "I'm going back out to the hallway."

"Hang on a sec," said Scott, looking over the graffiti.

Tally turned. "I'll meet you out there."

"That's not the way," Fairen called. She shone her flashlight on Tally's retreating back. Suddenly Tally vanished, and screamed.

"What the *hell!*" yelled Temple.

Scott ran across the room to where she had disappeared. He stopped at the doorway and leaned into the blackness. She was still screaming.

"It's an elevator shaft," he said. His voice was hard but framed by panic.

"Oh, Christ," said Zach.

"Get me out of here!" shouted Tally. "Get me OUT!"

Temple began tearing around the room, presumably looking for some sort of rope. Zach dared not approach Scott.

"We're getting you out," said Fairen. She sounded confident and comforting, like a nurse. "Don't freak out. Just take a deep breath and hang on."

"There are needles down here!" Tally cried. Then she screamed again. *"Get me OUT!"*

Temple returned to the group. "I don't see anything around here. I'm afraid to go into those bags."

"Just tear them open, man," Scott ordered.

Temple raised his eyebrows. "You want 'em open, *you* do it. I'm not coming out of here with six kinds of hepatitis. Have at it."

"Then go downstairs," Scott told him. "Take Kaitlyn with you. See if there's an opening down there."

Tally began to sob. "I don't want to die here," she cried. "I don't want to die."

"Calm down, Tally," said Fairen, her voice echoing in the shaft. "Nobody's going to let you die."

Scott squatted down and leaned into the hole. "I'm here, baby," he called. "Temple and Kaitlyn are coming down to let you out."

Fairen looked over her shoulder nervously at Zach. Scott caught the look and twisted on the balls of his feet to face Zach. "Go find help," he said. "Just in case."

"You mean leave the hospital?"

"Yeah. The place is crawling with cops. It shouldn't take you long."

"Temple ought to go," said Zach. "He's got the car."

"That's why he needs to stay. If we get her out of there and she's injured, how else are we going to transport her?"

Zach stalled. He looked around the room and said, "Why don't we give Temple time to find her a way out of there? He only just left, and if I bring the cops back, we'll probably all get arrested."

Scott sneered at him. "Quit being such a pussy and find a goddamn cop."

"I'm not being a pussy," Zach argued, his voice rising. "I'm being logical."

"Oh, is that right?" Scott retorted. "I guess you get real smart when you hang out with teachers in your free time. You ought to be Albert fucking Einstein by now. Who do you think's smarter, you or Fairen? Let's ask her."

Zach felt his stomach go cold. He glanced at Fairen, but she was leaning into the shaft again, cooing to Tally.

He took off.

The beam from Zach's flashlight shivered against the floor as he ran down the hallway and into the center hall. Glass crunched beneath his feet. He paused just outside the main doorway and shone his light around, looking for police. Seeing none, he considered his path—back through the woods toward the town houses, or deeper into the hospital complex where the police likely were? He swerved his light toward the woods and recalled the journey through them: two blocks' worth of underbrush and deadfall, with only the narrowest of paths marking the travels of derelicts like him.

He turned and ran along the access road toward the children's hospital. The weather had turned cold, and his down vest, unzipped, provided only thin protection from the chill. His right hand grew slippery with sweat and he tried to switch the flashlight to his left, then immediately regretted the attempt. Even the small weight of the cheap plastic light sent hammering pain through his wrist. He stopped at a sharp turn and peered into the darkness, then looked down and shone the light onto his wrist. It was beginning to swell. The back of his hand looked pink and puffy beneath the glare. He stepped off the shoulder into the road, shone his light in both directions, and saw nothing but the low mist they had seen on their first visit. That, and black looming darkness.

A terrible thought occurred to him: what if the police presence was an urban legend, and the Bunny Man was real?

You're losing it, Zach, he thought.

He looked in the direction from which he had come. The hospital was a fair distance away now. Somewhere in there was Tally, present state unknown, and Fairen, unprotected, and Scott, who might at any moment get fed up with Zach's failure and start running his mouth about—about what? How in the hell had he found out?

Zach blocked it all—the pain, the fear—and began running again, up the road and past the children's building. Beyond that were a series of decrepit outbuildings—staff quarters, laundry, a heating plant. No cruisers anywhere to be found. An access road looped past the heating plant and toward another large structure; maybe the cops congregated over there, where they would be less visible between the buildings. He held his left arm against his stomach and ran up the access road. Trying to hold his wrist motionless didn't help much, and the darkness still offered no sign of help of any kind. Between the buildings he stopped again and set the flashlight between his neck and shoulder, cradling his wrist in his right hand. His nails were filthy from scrabbling around on the floor with Scott, and for a moment he thought of that creepy guy Judy had described. *Der Struwwelpeter, here he stands, with his dirty hair and hands.* And Zach was a monster indeed, in Scott's eyes at least. That much was certain.

Around the side of the furnace building, he heard the snuffling and footsteps of an animal. The shock of it jarred him, and when he snapped his head to look toward the sound, the flashlight clattered to the ground and rolled away. He scrambled after it. Sweat stung at the corners of his eyes. The footsteps came closer, and as Zach groped for the light and pointed it in the direction of the noise he saw a tall grayish-white figure, much larger than a human, with a glinting blackness perched behind it. He screamed, pure fear pumping into his veins, heart accelerating so rapidly it thudded in his ears. His feet at first refused to obey his mind's frantic command to move, but as he collected himself enough to take two steps back, the light shifted, and staring back at him were a mounted police officer and his very unimpressed horse.

"Son," said the officer in a low drawl, "what in the hell do you think you're doing?"

Zach exhaled, all at once, all the air left from his screaming. "Jesus Christ. I thought you were the Bunny Man."

The officer smirked. "You wish."

"You are such an idiot," said Fairen. "I can't believe you mistook a horse for the Bunny Man."

She was sitting on the molded plastic chair beside him in the orthopedics unit of Holy Cross Hospital. The slow-ticking clock said it was two in the morning. His left arm lay swaddled in a black splint. They sat waiting for his discharge papers, and Fairen had just now dared to ask him for the details.

"I was freaked," Zach replied. "Sometimes when you're looking for something, you know, you just see what you're expecting to see instead of what's really there."

"But you were *trying* to find a cop."

"Yeah, but I was pretty disoriented."

"I'll say." She traced a finger along his good arm. "We're damn lucky they're not charging us with trespassing, especially with you coming on like such a goober."

"Hey, I got help for Tally. Cut me some slack."

"I *am* cutting you slack. You have no idea how hard I'd be razzing you if you *hadn't* helped Tally."

Someone from the nurse's station called his name, and he was handed a packet of papers. Fairen had called his father, and he was on his way. In the meantime there was nothing to do but wait, with Fairen to keep him company. He could think of worse ways to spend an evening.

"Your shoe's untied," she observed as he sat down.

He held up his splinted wrist helplessly.

"Oh, yeah." She bent to tie it for him. "Does it still hurt pretty bad?"

"Not as bad as before. The Percocet helped."

"What's Scott's beef with you, anyway? The way he went off on you was completely mental."

"Beats the hell out of me."

"I swear, he and Tally are made for each other. Between him coming after you like a pro wrestler and Tally hallucinating she saw needles in that shaft, they're like the king and queen of overreactions. This was just supposed to be a simple tour of a historical site, for research purposes. It's not even their project, and they had to go muck it up."

She traced the Velcro bands of his splint, lightly, where it rested on his leg. He said, "Thanks for everything. For taking me to the hospital and calling my folks and all that. And for doing three-quarters of the project. I guess I should mention that part, too."

"It's no problem."

"Well, I won't forget it. I've had better nights than this one, that's for sure."

She ran her hand along his inner thigh. "Me, too."

For what seemed like the first time in hours, he smiled.

"What are you doing Monday night?" she asked. He

glanced at her, and she added, "The school's doing Advent Spiral tomorrow, but I thought maybe you and I could do something over break. Not with the whole crew. Just us."

"I don't even now if my folks will let me go to the Spiral, after this. I'll probably be grounded."

"I doubt that. I already covered for you. Told your folks it was all Tally's fault. She called Scott in a panic from the elevator shaft and he dragged us all there to rescue her. You're a hero."

He laughed. "That's awesome. I hope they bought that."

"They did. Monday I'm supposed to be going to the Wicker Man Festival at the lake, with my cousin. Celebrate the start of vacation. We already have tickets, but I can get you an extra one. I have connections."

"That sounds cool."

She smiled. "Awesome. It'll be good to spend time with you again. On a regular date. Act our age this time."

He nodded and examined his wrist. "I can't even tell you how good that sounds."

27

When I came to bed late that night I sat on the edge of the mattress cautiously, as though Russ might flop over like a corpse in a movie, arms splayed, eyes fixed. But beneath the covers it was warm. I leaned over him and tipped my ear toward his face. He snored faintly, the same as always.

I turned my back to him and bunched the covers beneath my chin. My scalp still felt sore where Zach had pulled my hair. My skin burned from the friction that had lasted just long enough to rub me raw. He was often rough, but normally a little apologetic about it, and when he took it too far I found subtle ways to turn it around. This time I didn't dare, suspecting he was doing what he needed to do to make it work. I could bite my lip through an encounter that felt more than a little like rape, or I could have nothing.

I took the rape.

I thought of him out somewhere in the night with Scott, free-spirited and cheerful, the way he had been when I had first met him. I pictured him with his foot up on a chair in some fast-food restaurant, the razor-trimmed edges of his black hair framing his smiling face, purged for the night of all his tension. He was with them, but in some secret place in his mind he was remembering the moments with me. I felt perversely grateful for that.

With Russ dozing peacefully behind me, I drifted off to sleep.

And then the phone rang.

"Why are you at the hospital?" I asked Scott groggily.

He rattled off some story I could only understand in pieces: an elevator accident, Tally was a little bit hurt but hardly so, a police escort, Temple was in trouble.

"What kind of trouble?"

"For bringing us to Pinerest Hospital."

"I thought you said you were at Holy Cross."

Scott growled into the receiver. "Damn it, Mom, I don't think you listened to a freakin' thing I said. *I need you to pick me up.* Do you get that part?"

"Scott, there's no reason to be surly about it. I can barely understand you."

"Yeah, story of my life."

At the hospital I found Scott easily, sitting in a molded plastic chair near the exit, alone. He didn't look to be in any way injured, which relieved me, considering how little I'd managed to put together from his phone call. I asked, "Where's Tally?"

"Her folks picked her up."

"And they didn't offer you a ride?"

"They're not exactly happy with me right now."

I sighed. "What about the rest of your friends? Was anybody else hurt? Does anyone need a ride home?"

"No."

In the car I pieced the story together slowly, using

yes-and-no questions that forced Scott to produce answers. Finally I asked, "So how did you manage to get help?"

"We sent Zach out."

"Oh, so Zach was there."

"Yes, Zach was there," he said peevishly. "Zach is always around when you need him."

I slowed for a red light. "Well, even if the police aren't charging you with trespassing, I think we'll need to have some consequence. You should have had better sense than to go to a place that dangerous."

"A *consequence*. Gosh, I didn't realize you were still playing that game."

"What game is that?"

"The mom game. You haven't even asked for my grade report from last month. I got my SAT scores in October, and my boot is still sitting by the fireplace."

"Is it my job to put your boots away now?"

"I put it there for St. Nicholas Day. It was over a week ago. I put out my boot for you to put candy in like you always do, and it's still sitting there with nothing in it."

I chuckled, but an immediate wave of remorse seized me. Scott was right. Every year of his life I had filled his boot with candy and little toys, or, in recent years, a gift card or two. Always the candy was special and unusual: barley lollipops made in antique molds, hand-pulled candy canes, marzipan animals from Germany. It was the joyful, noncommercial version of Christmas that I delighted in more than the shock and awe of Christmas morning. This year it had not even entered my mind.

But I turned to look at the tall boy beside me, with his five o'clock shadow and his broad shoulders, and I said, "I thought you'd gotten a little old for that sort of thing. You spend nearly all your time these days holed up in the den with Tally, and don't think I don't know what you're doing in there. I don't think that girl has ever bothered to say hello, but I'm hearing plenty from her, believe you me."

"At least Tally likes guys her own age," he muttered.

I took my eyes off the road to glare at him. "I beg your pardon?"

"You heard me."

"What's *that* supposed to mean?"

He shook his head, his eyes squinting in disdain. "Come on, Mom. You aren't fooling anybody."

"I have no idea what you're talking about."

Silence iced over the car. After a minute I said, "Go on. If you've got some nonsense you want to throw at me, throw it."

In my peripheral vision I could see him staring at me, the tightness around his eyes still prominent. When he spoke, disgust tinged his voice. "Mom," he said, "I don't use condoms."

It took me a moment to put together what he was telling me.

"Well," I replied, turning onto the exit toward our house, "you should."

Scott went straight to his room, without a good-night or a thank-you to break the silence that had descended after our abbreviated conversation. It was three in the morning. Wide awake now, I turned on the gas beneath the teakettle and glanced into the living room. There was his blue-and-white ski boot, tongue pulled forward, askew by the fireplace. I had no idea how I had managed not to notice it. But then, maybe I should not have underestimated the lapse in my attention. Fallout from it seemed to be everywhere.

The truth was, I realized gradually, I didn't really care if Scott knew. If he wanted to heap resentment upon me for it, then he could just add it to the pile he'd been shoveling since he was about thirteen. I felt relatively certain he would not tell anyone, because I could imagine no embarrassment greater to a teenager than for his friends to discover his mother is sleeping with one among them. I cared if he told his father, but mainly because Russ would destroy me in the divorce—and that was a genuine concern. Russ would not be likely to keep his mouth shut. He specialized in preemptive criticism, delivered by deadly accurate, laser-guided verbal missiles loaded with contempt. He would wedge as much distance as possible between himself and my dalliance, and he would do it by digging up all the dirt he could find and broadcasting it like seeds by the handful. And of it there was plenty.

Off went the stove. I picked up Scott's boot and put it away in the closet. Poured a cup of tea with my shivering hands.

Then I turned on the coffeemaker and sat down with a bag of Russ's pills, hoarded in a corner of my purse and a meat mallet.

Zach slept most of the day and awoke when Fairen called late that afternoon, her bright, energetic voice breaking through the wall of his fatigue. She wanted to know if he needed a ride to the Advent Spiral, and he was happy to take her up on the offer. By the time she arrived he had managed to work in a shower and an enormous bowl of lentil dhal, and felt almost human again.

The multipurpose room had been emptied of all its chairs and tables, leaving a wide parquet floor on which pine boughs had been arranged to form a great spiral. The room was deeply dark. Only a few candles in the corners provided a small light, their white flames flickering under the invisible draft from the heating ducts. Zach followed Fairen to the section of the floor where his classmates sat. Temple was there, but Scott did not appear to be present; Judy, too, was blessedly absent, so far as he could tell. He guessed the open flames were not her thing. The Advent Spiral was the school festival most likely to end in third-degree burns, which, to Zach's thinking, also made it the most interesting.

A teacher struck up a few notes on a harp, and a young teenage girl stood and walked forth into the spiral, carrying in her hands a crimson apple fitted with a glowing white candle. At the center of the spiral she stopped and set down the candle beside a bough before slowly walking back out. One after another, the younger children, and a few of the older ones, followed her lead, each leaving their candle and its apple at a point along the path. Now and then a child's toe struck an apple, and a flame wobbled. Other times, the hem of a dress breezed just above a candle. A bucket of water sat next to the stage, but if it came to that, things already would be quite fascinating.

"I'm going to go up," Fairen whispered. "Are you?"

He shook his head.

"Oh, come on," she encouraged. "What kind of Waldork are you?"

"Not as big of one as you are, apparently."

She stuck her tongue out at him and rose, collecting her candle-fitted apple from a teacher who stood at the spiral's opening. Her hair was up in braids that crossed at the top of her head, like a Swiss peasant girl. He supposed this was in deference to the St. Lucia theme of the celebration, and since she was too old to crown her head with a wreath bearing four candles, she carried on the childhood tradition with an approximation of it. She lit her candle and progressed slowly up the spiral, and he watched her reverent face, her sly eyes gone childlike beneath the gossamer crown of her braids.

To wonder at beauty, he thought automatically. The first line of the Bell Ringing Verse from his grade-school years. All the compromises he had made, moral and otherwise, to be with Judy, had not corrupted his ability to observe beauty when it happened upon him. He sent his thanks out to the universe for that reprieve. The other imperatives tumbled forth in his mind: *stand guard over truth. Look up to the noble. Decide for the good.*

He had lost sight of these things. He had been a bad Steiner student, not for the narrow reason of sleeping with the kindergarten teacher, but for allowing his life to tumble into an amoral and disorganized mess. In all the hand-wrought and color-blended loveliness of the Waldorf environment, what outsiders often failed to see was the rigid order that lay beneath it all. What seemed to others to be hypocrisy made perfect sense to him. Freedom can only exist where there is structure. Without it there can be no understanding of how to be beautiful, how to be good.

At the center of the spiral, Fairen turned and began walking the opposite way, still holding her candle. She caught his eye and almost smiled. He smiled warmly back at her, then clasped his hands around his knees and resolved two things to himself.

One, he would not sleep with Judy again. Really and surely this time around, regardless of what happened with Fairen, but especially because of her, too.

Two, he would stop eating meat. It was time.

The second would be easy—well, easy enough, in any case. The first would be more problematic. He could control his own impulses, but when Judy came toward him with all guns blazing, as she had the night of the trip to the abandoned hospital, he had no idea how to defuse her without just nailing her and getting it over with. In his mind he pictured two comets racing toward each other, immolating each other in the explosion.

Then, in a burst of awareness, he realized he had it all wrong. What he had learned in judo flashed into his mind: *when you are confronted with force, give way to it. When you are pushed, pull. Apply your opponent's force against him.*

It was so obvious he couldn't understand why it had not occurred to him weeks ago. Rather than meet her lust with a stronger, angrier lust of his own, he needed only to get out of the way and let her energy consume itself. It would not be easy to watch, but it was the only route to a takedown.

It was what he needed to do. To produce *peace in his feeling,* as they said at school. *Light in his thought.*

Beside him, Temple recrossed his legs and leaned back on his palms. Zach stared out at the floor dotted with candles, a nameless constellation being formed one star at a time.

"I'm sorry I lied to you," Zach said quietly.

Temple glanced at him in mild surprise, then looked back at the spiral. "No prob," Temple replied. "I didn't blame you."

28

I managed to stay out of the house all day on Sunday, coming home late to find Russ's office door closed and the light glowing dimly beneath it. More and more these days he ended his late nights with a nap on his office sofa. When I awoke Monday morning and found him at the breakfast table reading the *Post* over a bowl of Familia, I felt my hands clench into a spasm so hard that my fingernails left eight red crescents in my palms. He was like Rasputin, the mad monk of Russia. A fairy-tale foe who would not die.

I took a large mug of coffee and a blueberry muffin, and left for school.

I arrived late. Sandy Valera was working in my classroom, directing the early arrivals to the coatrack, the bathroom, the play table. She shot me a searching look when I dropped my scarf on my chair and plunked the coffee on a windowsill, so I said, "Car trouble."

She nodded. I had not noticed the other woman in the classroom, kneeling beside a child and unraveling an absurdly long hand-knitted scarf from around his neck. When the woman rose Sandy said, "Judy, this is Rhianne Volker. She is considering Sylvania Waldorf for her children."

Rhianne's smile popped out immediately, then stayed stiffly in place. "Oh, Judy and I know each other," she said.

I nodded.

"Well, now that you're here, I'll get back to my office," said Sandy. As she brushed past me, Rhianne tucked her hands in the side pockets of her overalls and regarded me with a look even more searching than Sandy's.

"Judy, I had no idea you taught here," she said.

"Since Maggie was little."

"Amazing. Small world. Small *community,* I suppose I should say, but surely you know that." Her brows knitted beneath the close-fitting winter cap she still wore. "Surely."

"It's one of the things parents love about Sylvania," I replied automatically.

"I'm sure. I've seen several familiar faces this morning." She looked me up and down. "How is that prescription working out for you?"

"Fine," I said. "So how old are your children?"

"Nine, six and four." She turned to look over my romping students, then back toward me. "I have met all the other Lower School teachers but you this morning. A nice bunch."

"Yes," I agreed, "and very skilled." But I remembered quite well that she had no children. She had told me herself. I felt a chill of fear, like a pearl of ice behind my ribs. It grew larger by the moment.

"One of my clients recommended this school to me," she continued. "Vivienne Heath. Perhaps you know her."

"I don't think so," I hedged. "How old is her son?"

She grinned. Her full mouth of teeth seemed to ooze poison. I realized my error as she took a step closer. With a curious tip of her head, she said, "He is only sixteen."

I responded with a twitching shrug. "I only work with the young children."

She replied, "That's not what I've heard."

Despite the blasting heat of the forge, Zach's bare arms felt a chill as he moved around the workshop, gathering materials to work on his first blacksmithing project. The bottom of the long black apron flapped against his legs. Making a fireplace poker didn't hold a lot of interest for him, but the opportunity to play with fire and red-hot metal cheered him. So did the fact that school would be over in an hour, heralding the beginning of Christmas break, and he'd be saying goodbye to this place until January. His classmates were all talking about the Wicker Man Festival that evening, and he felt glad to have been invited by Fairen; finally, it seemed, he was beginning to feel like part of the tribe. He missed New Hampshire less today than at any point since the move.

Putting on the gloves and mask, he turned toward the crackling forge and felt a tingle of anticipation. The instructor, his watchful gaze cast on a handful of students in various stages of metalwork, was being nice to allow them to fire up the forge so close to the end of school. Zach set the rod of metal with the tongs and thrust it into the fire, which spit and crackled, blindingly orange. With one hand still in the brace it was an awkward process, but the tools felt secure in his hands, and the fire was mesmerizing. An echo of Judy's voice spoke in his mind: *I do think fire can be beautiful in a terrifying sort of way.*

"Sure you got it?" his teacher asked, hands hovering around his as Zach removed the rod from the flame.

"I'm sure."

He placed it on the anvil and, with another student holding it in place, used his good hand to give the rod four strong whacks with the hammer. It was coming along respectably enough, for a one-handed first try. He geared up again for a second chance at the fire.

A draft blew toward him, and he looked up just in time to see Judy entering the room, a small figure in the cavernous space, her movements deliberate among the narrowly organized chaos. She made her way between the worktables, her arms crossed, rubbing her forearms as though cold. Her khaki jumper dress was like a lunch sack, but her long dark hair looked unnaturally smooth, combed precisely. She blinked at the heat of the forge and asked in a low voice, "Can I talk to you a minute?"

"Sure," he said, his voice muffled by the mask. There was no point in play-acting as though he expected the conversation to take place right here. He lifted the mask and set it on the table, slipped off the gloves beside it. His instructor met his eye, but only by way of accounting for his safety; nice to see someone at this school paying attention to that, for once.

She stood beside the door that led outside, her hand on the push bar. It was brazen of her to corner him like this, long after the bazaar was over, with no conceivable excuse for pulling him out of class. He hadn't spoken to her since their ill-conceived rendezvous the week before; and earlier that day he had, in the courtyard, succumbed to the urge to kiss Fairen, to the approving whoops of the few present to see it. It would not surprise him to learn that Judy had been spying on him. It had to be the most tedious part of sleeping with somebody's mother: no matter what you did with her, she was still a mom, and the eyes on the back of her head seemed to have twice the range when she was creepily obsessed with your body.

He dropped the apron on a stool and followed her out the door, bracing himself against the rush of frigid air and a flurry of small icy snowflakes. She made her way toward the corner of the parking lot that bordered woods, but he stopped where the asphalt did and refused to step into the brush. Something felt off about her. He knew she felt hurt and possibly angry and, undoubtedly, full of anxiety, but he sensed a harder edge that made him cautious. Not that Judy posed a danger to him—she was barely over five feet tall, for Pete's sake—but there was a bobcat energy to her that he didn't care to incite.

She turned at the tree line, giving up on luring him further, and tucked her hands in her sleeves. She had looked relatively normal when she came into the workshop, but already her face was blotchy with tears. He felt taken aback by how foolhardy she was, out here where anyone could see them. He wasn't going to entertain this very long. She could take a hit for it, but he had no intention of doing so.

"You're *done*," she accused.

He shrugged. "Yeah, I am."

"You've taken up with Fairen."

"Is there something wrong with that?"

"I can't say I'm surprised," she spat. "You wanted her all along."

He felt his lip curl. "Who cares whether I did or not? And since when do *you* give a shit about what I want? I say no, and what do you do? You blockade the goddamn door."

She pushed the heels of her hands across her cheeks. Shaking her head, blinking down at the ground, she said in a hopeless voice, "I ought to turn you in for what you did to me that day. I never…*invited* you to do anything that…*violent*."

He bristled and felt something inside him turn. "You go ahead and do that," he retorted. "You're going to do—what? Accuse me of rape?"

"Maybe I will."

Snorting a laugh, he recoiled, taking a step backward. "Go

for it. Get right on it. Bet you they'll find evidence for it all over the fucking place. Bet Russ is sleeping in some of it right now." He shook his head. "Maybe I'll turn *myself* in. Would that simplify it for you?"

She lifted her face in a delighted smile, as if he'd just told a great joke, her eyes bright. "I wouldn't do that if I were you."

"Damn, you're big with the threats all of a sudden. Why can't you just let it frickin' lie? It ran its course. Get over it, move on."

Her shoulders heaved with an enormous sigh, and she took two steps forward to lean against a tree. She looked exhausted. He almost felt sorry for her.

"Couldn't we just be together one more time," she proposed in an even voice, "so the time in the den doesn't have to be the last memory?"

When pushed, pull. He shook his head. "No."

She shifted her gaze sideways, toward the line of cars. "Maybe we can drive someplace after school, just discuss it?"

"No." She wanted to blow him, anybody could have guessed that. He wasn't even the smallest bit tempted. It wasn't out of the question that he'd find his orgasm interrupted by an icepick in his chest, like in the movies. Not a turn-on.

She nodded, resigned. "Can I hug you goodbye, at least?"

"No," he said a third time, but she was already coming toward him, arms outstretched, and there hadn't been a great distance between them to begin with. Stiffly he allowed himself to be hugged, and with a quick economy of movement she slipped her retreating hand into the front of his pants. He grabbed her by the wrist.

"I said *no*," he told her.

Her smile was brittle. She'd only managed to get her hand between his jeans and boxers, and with his hand clenching the tendons in her wrist, her cold fingers flailed like a mouse caught by the tail.

"I hope she enjoys it," she said. "It's wonderful."

She retreated and walked past him into the school, her body small beside the hulking frame of the workshop. Zach turned toward the building, looking around guardedly for faces in the windows; finding none, he ran a hand through his hair, the snowflakes melting at his touch into pinpoint cold. With a low grumble in his throat he made his way back toward the workshop, hiking his jeans higher on his hips, to face the forge.

Rhianne had said nothing further before she left me that morning. She didn't need to. She had said enough.

After she left my classroom to tend to her three imaginary children I retreated to the bathroom, where I threw up three times. Coffee splattered on the rim of the toilet bowl, on the tile, on my jumper. I rested my forehead against the cool tile wall until I heard a knock and a small voice saying, "Mrs. McFarland, I have to go pee."

I called in the music teacher to watch my children for the day. Then, except for a detour to the workshop, I went home, where I retired to the floor of a bathroom reserved for my own use. And there I stayed, my hands sweaty on the porcelain, staring into the water.

The water in the sink floated with my mother's underwear, broad polyester panels that undulated like jellyfish between the dollops of Fels-Naptha foam. Next to it, shucked aside at a careless angle, sat the box of matches. The old wooden radio, elegant and well-dusted, blared out a melody at high volume: *baby don't leave me ooh please don't leave me all by myself.* The matches smelled of sulfur. The flame, in its small way, held the whole spectrum of color. *It's very, very wrong, you know,* said the rhyme in my schoolbook, and even at ten my nerves tingled at the thought of it, perhaps because I was my father's daughter.

Each doorknob was cold bronze. Turn, turn; and then again, turn. The irony: I knew before I opened it what I would see, and instead I saw nothing. But it burned into my mind anyway, skipping right over the part I could reach and embedding itself in the deepest recess, a stone falling into a pool so fast and so smoothly that the surface records barely a ripple. And now, having dived much too deep into that part of the water lately, I could brush against it without meaning to. There it was: two adults nude and sweating, Kirsten's head hanging off the edge of the bed, her braids loosened and flopping against the mattress, a sloppy metronome. My mother's pillow wedged beneath her back, my father's face snarled like that of a barbarian from a warlike tribe, hideous and rude and dismal to behold. The smell of it was thick in the air, her arousal and his, entirely foreign to my senses. And if the language of that nation sounded to me like the original speech of humanity, then here was that which came before language—the voice at the core of every human in the world, when the breath moves in concert with the drive to continue the species.

Forget about it. Banish it. God help you that you should look upon such a scene and realize that someday you will want it, too.

I thought the horror was in what I saw, but I was wrong. The horror came as I realized that, for what he had done, the child in me was right to blame him entirely, and the adult in me blamed him not at all.

Russ stayed in his upstairs office the entire evening, and for once I did not resent his absence.

Once my stomach ran out of things to throw up I sat down at the table with a cup of weak chamomile tea dribbled with honey and Rescue Remedy. I thought about the day Zach and I had felted balls for the craft sale, standing at this same table, apart in body but our desires, no doubt, the same. I had felt powerful then, exalted by him, an object of mystery. I had the power to grant any wish he might dare to utter. Now I was garbage to him. The kind that smelled.

There was a hard knock on the door, and I rose to answer. I felt relatively sure of who it would be, and was not surprised.

She said, "I'm not done talking to you."

I stepped aside to let her in.

She entered my kitchen and stood beside the stove, her arms crossed over the front of her overalls. Her russet hair was ponytailed back. I looked past her to the teakettle on the back burner and checked to see if the gas was on.

In an indignant voice she demanded, "What the hell is wrong with you?"

I said nothing.

"How could you?" she snapped. "*You*. Princess Fairy Pixie-dust. Miss Wear Your Woolens So You Don't Catch a Chill. *Explain* yourself."

I wondered if Russ would hear her and come down to see what the commotion was, if it became a commotion, which seemed likely. I dearly hoped he would not. I felt competent to handle an angry midwife, especially in the kitchen, but less sure of how to manage Russ. Most likely he would turn up the Ken Burns Jazz Collection and think harder about fish.

Her face darkened with frustration at my silence. More loudly, she asked, "How could you *fuck* a sixteen-year-old boy?"

I replied, "How does anyone fuck anyone?"

The answer didn't appear to satisfy her. "Do you know

who's been supplying him with condoms all these months?"
she asked. "*Me*. Because it's the job of *adults* to teach teenagers
to be responsible. That's what grown-ups do."

"You've done an admirable job."

She picked up the jar of comb honey beside the stove and
flung it at me. It missed my arm and hit the refrigerator, sending an amber trail trickling down the white. The jar rolled
across the floor with an undulating glassy sound, dispensing
with bits of comb that flecked the tile.

"I ought to turn you in," she yelled, and now I felt real fear,
more of Russ than of her. "I told him I wouldn't, but I'm *very*
tempted. Someone needs to hold you accountable, even if he
won't."

"I don't believe he told you anything," I said quietly.

"Oh, he sure did."

"I don't believe you. I think you're just guessing in the
dark."

She leaned forward from the waist, her eyes large, face jeer-
ing. "You're wrong. I was *shocked*. I would never have guessed
a Sylvania teacher would do such a thing. To a *boy*."

At that moment the chain inside me broke. "He's not six
years old," I shouted, my hands in fists at my sides, my neck
arching toward her. "He's not a child. He knew what he was
doing and he came after it like he had a free pass to fucking
Disneyland. He wouldn't be taking all your precious condoms
if he wasn't dying to use every last one of them. And who
are you to him? Nobody at all. Just another adult he likes to
talk to about sex. And you're jealous. You wish *you'd* had the
nerve."

Her lip curled like a dog's. "That's bullshit. How dare you.
You're so twisted you don't even know what it is to feel protective of somebody who's young."

"Oh, I know what that's like. But my *kindergartners* aren't barging in and dropping their pants in my classroom two minutes after dismissal. Which is what your little angel has been doing for *months*. He doesn't want to be protected. He wants to be blown."

She rested her hands low on her hips and came toward me. "You need to turn yourself in."

"I'm not turning myself in for anything. I'll turn him in first for ripping half my hair out the last time I *victimized* him."

Her face was inches from mine. I could see every puckered pore along her cheekbones, every haphazard eyelash. "Turn yourself in or I will."

I cuffed her ear with my open hand and shoved her as hard as I could, sending her stumbling backward into the stove. As she winced, I grabbed the glass sphere Bobbie had given me, delicately streaked with color and hanging in the window by a thread, and flung it at her. She ducked, and it shattered against a cabinet in a spray of shards.

"You're insane," she shouted. "You need to be evaluated. There's something wrong with you, Judy. I mean it. I'm calling a psychiatric transport on you."

"Go ahead," I yelled back. "Be my guest. Make sure they've got a rape kit."

She stared into my eyes for a long moment, then brushed past me and out the door.

29

On the night of the Wicker Man Festival, Fairen came by to pick up Zach, her small white car turning sharply into the driveway with a grace he had to admire. They stopped to get sandwiches, then sat in the car for a long time, heater blasting, making out. For once he didn't mind the setting one bit. It wasn't half bad, this business of hooking up in cars, if one respected the limitations of the space. The frustration of wishing he could take her elsewhere had its own peculiar excitement.

Once at the lake they ducked through the trees and entered the park, where the party was already in full swing. To the right a band played in an amphitheater; straight ahead, in the lake itself, scaffolding supported a high platform on which the wicker man was suspended. It looked less like wicker than like blocks of straw held together with metal bands, and, Zach guessed, the burn would be fast and messy; chunks would probably fall off, necessitating the midlake location. The pyrotechnics guys, two shadowy figures moving around a control box, looked like they were making the final preparations.

Fairen set down her backpack and unfurled a quilt onto

the cold ground, a little distance from the amphitheater. She waved to a couple in the crowd, dancing to the modern-Celtic music coming from the stage, heavy on the drums. "Want to dance?"

"Not yet. Maybe when the burn starts."

"Oh, c'mon. Don't be inhibited."

To distract her, he chose to deliberately misinterpret her meaning, and leaned in to kiss her. She laughed and kissed him back, and after a little more of that he playfully wrestled her down onto the quilt. A pine bough sheltered them somewhat, but people were everywhere, and so he contented himself with the sort of kissing that didn't quite qualify as public indecency.

A whoop went up from the crowd, and Zach looked up to make sure it wasn't a reaction to him and Fairen. Instead he saw a tongue of flame lapping at the leg of the wicker man. He rolled himself back up to a sitting position, and watched as the legs, and then the torso, gradually caught fire. Fairen moved across him, sitting backwards on his lap briefly and taking a moment to kiss him again before standing up and reaching out her hand.

"It's started," she said. Her smile was almost persuasive. "Come join me."

"I liked what we *were* doing."

"There'll be more of that later. C'mon."

He grinned and hesitated, trying to think up a new way to lure her back. But then, behind her, he saw a woman walking swiftly toward them, wearing a down vest much like his own. As she came closer he realized it was Rhianne.

"There you are," she said, clearly exasperated. "Zach, can I have a word with you privately?"

He immediately stood up, and Fairen shot him an odd smile and a small wave. "Catch up with me in a minute, okay?"

"Sure thing." She walked off, and he asked Rhianne, "Is my mom in labor?"

"No. She's fine. I'm glad I found you. Seems like every kid from Sylvania is here." She took a deep breath. "Zach, listen to me. You have to break things off with Judy McFarland right away."

His eyes widened at hearing her name from Rhianne. Immediately he felt the gut-level panic he had feared for months at being found out. He said, "I already did. There's nothing going on anymore."

"You're sure she understands that. Because that woman's not stable, Zach. She's dangerous, and she might try to say you raped her."

He shook his head. "She won't really do that. She's just upset and got her feelings hurt. I didn't do anything to her that she didn't want me to do."

"Well, you need to be prepared for what she might accuse you of, if she's crazy enough to try. Which she might be. She hit me and shoved me into her stove."

"Really?" He half laughed, and Rhianne gave him a look of alarm. "Glad it's not just me. She gets pissy when you tick her off."

"I'd get a restraining order if I were you."

Now his laugh was outright. He felt impatient to get back to Fairen. "You've seen her, right? She's about the size of a twelve-year-old. I'm not worried about it."

"I think you're underestimating her."

He shrugged and let his gaze wander over her shoulder. "People mouth off when they're mad. Word getting out about what happened is the last thing she wants, trust me. It'll blow over."

Fairen was wandering back toward him, her gaze curious, her purple ski vest swinging stiffly in the cold air. Her flaxen hair was backlit by the wicker man in a halo of yellow. The drummers in the circle stepped up the rhythm into a near frenzy, hands striking drumskin with a force he could feel in the ground.

"Come on," she yelled, gesturing with a broad arc of her arm. "You said you'd dance with me!"

He offered Rhianne an apologetic nod and walked over to where Fairen stood, smiling and dancing, her hair aglow in the light of the burning.

I needed to get my head together, as Scott said. To sit and think.

I drove out to the lake, where I imagined I could park in the shadowy little spot where Zach and I had often stopped, and look out at the water, and talk myself back into a clearer frame of mind. Beneath those trees I could consider the full arc of our relationship. There I could follow the trail of memories from our first covert, intoxicating visit to that space to the last, when I climbed onto his lap and felt his skin blazing hot around me, delighting in it for the last precious moments before the just universe would begin to confront me with every sorry truth about who I was. Before it dismantled the playhouse my mind had built, hoping it would serve as a fortress.

But the parking lot was jammed full of cars. I had never seen it so full. I heard music not far away and realized there was a festival going on. Gradually I remembered seeing the posters around town, a straw effigy burning in some sort of Celtic winter ritual. I parked my car illegally on the painted stripes beside a handicapped spot, and left my motor running.

In spite of the crowd, I stared out at the water and called up my memories. In my mind I could still see the urgency in Zach's movements the first time we stopped here, hear the ragged sound of his breathing that seemed magnified by the deep silence around us, like a voice calling across a field on a snowy day. I remembered the bone-deep comfort of wrapping my arms around his body and pressing my face against his belly, and knowing there was no chance he would send me away, because the car was mine, and the keys were in my pocket, and I had something he very much wanted.

I sighed brokenly and pushed my hair back from my forehead. Through the windshield I watched a couple making out, and envied them their passion, their indifference to the crowd around them. The young man turned the girl onto her back and climbed over her, and quite suddenly, from the shape of his arms and shoulders and the angle at which his bangs fell, I realized it was Zach. I exhaled hard in surprise, and then, as he kissed her from above, cupping her breast with his free hand, I felt a tightness gathering around my heart. How easy it must be to be done with me when he had the willing blonde. The lawyers' daughter, the one forever kissing boys on the playground, the girl with her bent knees now on either side of Zach's hips.

I pushed in the cigarette lighter.

A breeze blew at the stand of pine trees in front of me, and through their wavering branches I caught sight of the straw man beginning to burn above the water. The man was unrealistically silent, but the crowd screamed for him. The flames spun around the body like a swarm of bees. I pulled a Martinmas lantern out from the box on the floor behind the driver's seat, wadded in the cleaning cloth for my sunglasses, and dug into my purse for the vial of Bach's Rescue Remedy. Its maker purported the flower essences were blended specifically to help in traumatic situations, and whether or not they worked as claimed, I was certain the alcohol tincture would function reliably.

I doused the cloth in Rescue Remedy and stepped out of the car. When I dropped in the cigarette lighter, the instant blaze shifted the lighting such that I could see my reflection in the car window: hair long and wild, expression blank, eyes dark hollows that disappeared into my face. The image was strangely soothing. I had become nobody, only a caricature, a cautionary tale of the body gone terribly awry. I was a book of moral lessons, and children had reason to fear me.

The wind had calmed. I stepped toward the trees, but to my dismay Fairen was gone. Now Zach stood speaking to a woman who, as I drew closer, appeared to be Rhianne. She gestured to him with broad, adamant strokes of her hand, and although he kept his distance and shook his head, I felt a chill that countered my burning hands. Then Zach stepped around her and walked toward the dancing group, hands in his pockets, leaving her standing beside the blanket in a disgruntled posture.

I sighed and set the lantern on the asphalt. The flames leaped well above its rim, but I doused it with my leftover cup of coffee, and it sputtered out.

Then I jammed my keys in the ignition and headed back home.

When I returned to the house there was an ambulance sitting in the driveway, all its red lights whirling. The front door stood open. I gathered my purse and walked up to the door, where a medical technician in a blue uniform greeted me and told me Russ was dead. I felt anxious and a bit surprised. Scott had found him, they told me; and only then did I realize this explained why Russ had not come downstairs during my disagreement with the midwife. The two medics told me the police would arrive soon, as a matter of routine, so I sat in the rocking chair and waited for them. While I waited I wound balls of yarn, as I often asked my students to do during quiet time.

When they arrived they appeared surprised to see me there. The one policeman said, it doesn't seem to come as much of a shock to you that your husband is dead in his office. So I said, Officer, my husband has had a drug problem for a long time now, and I warned him that eventually he would probably die without treatment. So I suppose you could say I feel a bit resigned.

What sort of a drug problem, said the other officer, and I said, prescription drugs of all kinds, I can show you the bottles if you like. And so I did. They said, do you have the original prescription for these, and I said, what do you think?

There's no reason to get snotty, he said. And that's when I saw Scott standing in the doorway, with a look on his face of absolute shock and dismay. I could see his heart was breaking. So easily had I come to take the addiction for granted that I had forgotten Scott didn't know. And I felt very relieved that when it finally happened—almost exactly as I had anticipated, facedown on his laptop with vomit in the keys—it had been none of my doing. Because of course it could have gone very differently.

Life can be ironic that way. They took his body for toxicology tests and then sent him to the funeral home to be cremated. And when I sorted through his desk and found the letters and underpants from the graduate student he'd had an affair with two years ago that I never knew about, I thought, well, we're even then. You maintained the illusion that you wanted us to stay married, and I maintained the illusion that I wanted you to stay alive.

It all seemed fair enough, in the scheme of things.

On Christmas Eve, three things happened.

I picked up Russ's ashes from the crematorium. In the morning, because of their reduced holiday work hours.

On the way home, I stopped at the automatic teller machine and discovered my paycheck had bounced. That was when I knew I did not have a job anymore. That my son did not have a school anymore. It still stood in the shadow of trees, set back from the road on its wooded lot, but it was a relic now of a vanished past. No money, no school. Even a fairy-tale kingdom can't run without gold.

And then there was the note from Scott, saying he had gone to stay with Russ's family in Virginia, his aunt and uncle. Staying in the house freaked him out now, he wrote. But I knew the house was just a ruse. It was me he didn't want to be near.

I suppose four things happened on Christmas Eve, really. But the fourth happened because of the three.

30

My car had no trouble finding the town house development and the woods behind it, driving there as if of its own volition. When I arrived, two rotting wooden posts flanked a newer metal gate, secured by a chain, which blocked my entry. So I put the Volvo in Reverse, rammed down one of the posts, and drove right up to the edge of the trees.

As I made my way into the woods I saw nothing of the lush landscape that had welcomed us barely months before. The trees jutted from the ground like dead sticks, not expansive and multicolored as they had been the day Zach brought me here. Where the crackling leaves had lain there was only a dry, dusty mulch, and the glint of sun through the trees was obscured by the mottled gray sky. Here was the tree he had leaned against, his hands weary as they rubbed his face, worn down by the immensity of his desire. Here was the patch of ground where I knelt above him, offering him a last chance to deny me before the jagged teeth of his zipper bit into the flesh of my inner thigh, before his indulgent grin tricked me into believing he could offer consent as competently as he offered pleasure.

I leaned back against that same tree and squinted up at the tangle of branches. The bark felt rough through my thin cotton shirt, but the panorama of the forest, in all its rotting loveliness, was still enchanting in its way. I dug into my purse for a small bottle I kept there, opened it, and swallowed a few of Russ's Nembutal pills. The police had seized all the large bottles I had pointed out to them, but I still carried quite a lot in my purse, for reasons that were now irrelevant. I shook a few more into my hand and looked into the middle distance. Not far away there lay a swamp I had never noticed before. The sight of it made my heart lift a little. A body of water would be a good place to be when I fell asleep. I could vanish utterly, pulled back into the earth without a sound or a sign, and with no chance at all of waking.

I walked ahead a little ways and stepped into the swamp. The cold water squelched into my shoes. I bit my lip, but pressed on. Ankles, shins. The mud sucked my shoes from my feet, so I let them go. My toes, already adjusted to the temperature, shocked to the smooth, enveloping grasp of the mud. At the center of the mire I fell to my knees, steeling myself against the shock of the cold. I swallowed the pills that remained in my palm, then lowered my hand into the water to steady my balance against the shifting ground. My fingers came up covered in green and gray, like a swamp creature.

A flash of colored light in the distance caught my eye. It was a police car—no, two—investigating my car at the edge of the forest. I sighed deeply and sat back on my heels. Very soon, they would come into the woods and find me. I had no time to die. They would take me home, or more likely to a psychiatric ward, where I would play sane and soon be sent home with a bottle of Prozac. It would buy me just enough time for the gloom to pass and anger to set in, and I would decide it was better to stay alive. And alive, I was a menace. I had done bad things, and they weren't nearly as bad as the things I had left to do.

The officers shone their flashlights into the woods: two discs of pale yellow light, like the centers of daffodils bobbing under a child's hand. From the very bottom of my spirit I wished for only one thing—to speak to Bobbie now, to hear her speak the sorry truths about my dirty heart, to coax me into doing the right thing. But I knew Bobbie was not here to speak with, and if she had been she would have told me to use my liar's talents for the good of all: to tell the story without embellishment and animation, so the listener's mind can hear through the make-believe the sound of resonating truth.

Man is both a fallen god, and a god in the becoming.

With difficulty I rose from the dark water and trekked across the forest, my bare feet gathering leaf litter in their coat of mud. At the tree line the two officers looked up at me, their hands instinctively rising to their holsters.

I said, "I would like to confess to the murder of my husband."

In the dark bedroom Zach's mother appeared a bent black shape on the sheet, her body curved in a Z around the quilt. Rhianne's inclined head was a shadow, hair sticking from her ponytail like raveled black threads, her whispers ghostlike.

Zach sat on a chair in the far corner, his usual place when Rhianne was present, a silent watcher. His father, on his knees beside the bed, clutched his mother's hand and whispered earnestly in a reassuring baritone. If Zach slipped out, no one would have blamed him. The normally cool room was downright hot, the thermostat kicked up to eighty-six degrees, and his mother wore a black athletic bra and nothing else, although at the moment her body lay entwined in the straining sheet. Rhianne's usually warm and easygoing manner toward Zach was gone, replaced with an edgy impatience that made Zach suspect she was angry at him, or secretly expecting something to go wrong.

But he was determined to be present. This was his sister, yes, but for some other, less explainable reason he felt obligated. It seemed a reckoning, to sit and observe helplessly this other side of passion, to watch how nature accounted for the pleasure. After all his indulgences, he owed himself that much.

Despite the whispering, nothing in that room was quiet; specifically, nothing about his mother. Fighting through what Rhianne called *transition,* she groaned and sobbed, took great gulps of air, then clutched the corner of the pillow to her face and sobbed even more. Her ankles strained, pulling the sheet tight between them. The white of her face and dark of her hair flashed strobelike as she twisted against the pillow.

Zach observed, not for the first time, that it looked disconcertingly like orgasm, this business of labor. The momentum of moans, the forgetting of breath, the pinpoints of sweat—at the crux he could not help calling forth images of Judy and of Fairen, their open mouths, the tendons in their necks, the wild hair. It was as though pleasure and pain were not a spectrum but a wheel, and when a woman pushed past one end or fell back through the other side, she would find herself in the state of his mother. Into his mind flashed a quote from her studio chalkboard: *The end of birth is death; the end of death is birth. Therefore grieve not for what is inevitable.*

She screamed—a long, impossibly deep, animal sound—and swelled in a curl around the balled quilt. Rhianne waved a hand urgently, and Zach's father climbed onto the bed and wound himself behind his wife. As he turned himself into a sort of seatback for her, Rhianne moved to the front of things, and Zach knew it was almost over. He unfolded himself from the chair and came forward, touching the tall bedpost, peering over Rhianne's shoulder.

"Can you see from there?" Rhianne asked him, and as he nodded, his mother grimaced and groaned and arched back against his father. Rhianne laid a hand intimately on the inside of her thigh and said, "Shhh, there, you're close now, so close." His mother gritted her teeth, the muscles in her legs tensing and jumping, and Zach recalled Judy telling him Scott had been born at home, doubtless in a scene much like this one. Spontaneously he wondered how he could ever have presumed to know her, this woman who had traveled through time and pain in ways that seemed impossibly distant to him. She had borne Scott in her own bed, her darkly polished sleigh bed, and with him the chain of time that would bring Zach to that same place eighteen years later, his knees planted where her hips had been.

With that, his sister's fuzzy head burst forth into the world in a gush of water, mouth agape, fat limbs flailing, streaked in blood and greeted with their mother's sudden turnabout laughter. And this, Zach thought, was the natural order, indeed: love everywhere, and also, a terrible mess.

31

When his body wrapped around mine, I felt safe. Behind me, chest to back, leg to leg, he became the opposite of a shadow: a stronger, larger, taller me who could not be bullied or broken. His hands cupping mine made a nest out of my palms, a promise that nothing would bite me, nor would I be allowed to crush what I held.

Once, I had imagined that in a jail cell I would curl on the bed and think of nothing but the beauty of Zach's body. But as I fell asleep in the back of the police car my mind sought only those hours with Rudi, in the barn or shed, in the snow. Where the world was the fairy tale, and hard nightmares were the stuff of books and outposts where Jesus did not tread. As I drifted off, in my mind's eye I sat on a straw bale and rested my cheek against Rudi's arm while he paged through my book of moral tales, laughing at the absurdity of horror. The bare wooden walls marked the edges of my world just then. I was a good little girl, not a bad one, and I had never considered that a teacher might be wrong.

Seek out what's beautiful, I had instructed Maggie, *and love it before it rots*. But I had been wrong. Beautiful men stay beautiful forever. That which is lovely remains so, preserved behind glass in one's mind.

And so I carried it all with me, the beautiful and the terrible alike, to keep me company, and left the ordinary world.

ACKNOWLEGMENTS

With deep appreciation, I would like to acknowledge the individuals who walked with me along the path of writing this novel.

Stephany Evans, my wonderful agent, who had faith in my idea and my ability to bring it to light. Thank you.

Susan Swinwood and the team at MIRA Books, for believing in the manuscript, and for doing a stellar job in editing and taking it to market.

My first readers and tiny fan club: Amanda Skjeveland, Kathy Gaertner, Jassy Mackenzie, Sara Roseman, Randi Anderson (also known as Mom), Laura Wilcott, Hillary Myers, Elizabeth Gardner, Stephanie Cebula, Gary Presley—and a special thanks to Erica Hayes. I am also thankful to the judges and reviewers at the Amazon Breakthrough Novel Award who gave the book an approving nod.

D.S. and S., whose candid insights brought Zach and
Judy to life in my mind.

I would like to express gratitude, amorphous though
it may be, to the cities of Greenbelt, Maryland, and
North Conway, New Hampshire, as well as to a
certain little Waldorf school that welcomed my family
when we were young and broke. I hope my fondness
for each of you is visible in this text.

And finally, my husband, Mike, and all four of my
children—for your sacrifices, for your patience and
for the steady supply of caffeine, I thank you from the
bottom of my heart.

We hope you enjoyed The Kingdom of Childhood,
*and that the following Questions for Discussion
help to enhance your book club discussions.*

1. The story is set in 1998 amidst the release of the Starr Report and President Clinton's impeachment, and as the novel opens, there is intense discussion in the media about these subjects. Do you feel the "national conversation" about the Lewinsky affair opened avenues of discussion that would have been inappropriate for Zach and Judy otherwise?

2. The first few chapters of the novel show an increasingly skewed set of boundaries between Judy and Zach that allow the affair to occur. Did this seem realistic to you? Was the process of dissolving their boundaries similar to what happens in affairs between consenting adults?

3. The Waldorf school movement is an educational approach that is widely practiced around the world and yet little known outside those communities.

Its philosophy extends beyond the classroom to the entire lifestyle of the families involved. How did you feel about the way of life Zach's family, and the others in the story, have adopted? Did it seem appealing or too intrusive? Were there any aspects that stood out to you? Judy's children, Scott and Maggie, both rebel from their upbringing in different ways. Did you blame them for rejecting the Waldorf way of life, or did it seem understandable?

4. Both Judy and Zach are influenced by experiences in which they are confronted with their parents' sexual misdeeds. Each struggles to reconcile their idealized sense of their parent with their parent's human failings. In what ways did you feel those experiences affected their choices with each other? In the case of Zach, did you feel that his mother's affair made an affair with a middle-aged woman seem more natural to him, or only increased his level of guilt about his role in it?

5. In the flashback scenes, Judy's mother is institutionalized due to mental illness, which leads to Judy's father's affair with Kirsten and her own isolation and dependence on Rudi. All of these factors set the stage for her later affair with Zach, which in turn leads to her own unraveling mental state toward the end of the story. Did you sense she was mentally ill throughout the novel, or did the stress of the affair cause her to "crack"? How did her family history of mental illness factor in to your impressions of or sympathy for Judy?

6. On the way back from Ohio, Zach and Judy discuss the song "Mrs. Robinson" and the idea of older women who pursue younger men. While society considers it "creepy" when an older man pursues a young girl, in popular culture it's often held as funny or tantalizing when an older woman—a "cougar"—does the same with a young man. Do you agree that this double standard exists? Has your perspective changed after reading *The Kingdom of Childhood*?

7. During the scene in which Zach comes over to spend the night, he reflects on his first kiss with Judy. In the version he remembers, she was the aggressor, which is quite different from the earlier version told from Judy's point of view in which the kiss is instigated by Zach. Which version did you believe?

8. In Part II, after Zach feels Judy forced herself on him in the car when he was sick, his attitude toward her changes significantly. Still, he continues to be with her. Have you ever had the experience of being in a relationship you knew was toxic while finding it impossible to let the person go?

9. Throughout the story, numerous people—Sandy Valera, Temple, Rhianne—attempt to interfere with the affair (to the extent that they know about it). Yet none is truly successful in making a difference. Did you feel any of these characters pushed too hard, or not hard enough, in their attempts? How do you think they could have been more effective?

10. Although it isn't mentioned in the book, the story is set around the same time as the real-life conviction of teacher Mary Kay Letourneau for her relationship with a twelve-year-old student. Such cases are not uncommon in the news, and often the perpetrator is a devoted teacher who has a spouse and children. The question always asked is, "Why would she risk everything for an affair with a boy?" Did the story leave you with a different perspective on how these events occur? Do you believe that such relationships are criminal?

11. At the end of the book, did Judy redeem herself to you in any way? Did you feel pity for her? Also at the end of the book, Zach is experiencing the birth of his sister. Did you have the sense that his life would get back on track after this, or that the story's events would continue to complicate things for him?